First published 2015 by

This is a work of fiction. All the characters and events portrayed are either products of the author's imagination or are used fictitiously.

This book is licensed for the personal enjoyment of the reader.
It is the copyrighted property of the author and may not be
reproduced, copied, or distributed for commercial or non-commercial purposes without prior written permission.

Copyright © Thomas Wymark

INHERITANCE

By Thomas Wymark

CHAPTER ONE

I had never been a violent woman.
I never swore (too much).
I never really wanted to hurt anyone — much less kill them.
And doctors never really used to be weird.
But things can change.

'The good news, Mrs Marsden, is that you were only unconscious for six or seven minutes.'
He didn't smile. He wasn't joking.
But I couldn't see how being unconscious for *any* amount of time constituted "good news". Unless the *bad* news was *really* bad.
The doctor clicked the end of his ballpoint pen. Was he emphasising a point, or just trying to annoy me?
'And we're pretty sure —' *click, click, click* '— there will be no lasting damage. In fact —' *click, click, click* '— everything appears to be more or less normal.'
I was not without imagination or humour, but *normal* seemed to be stretching it.
'And the bad news?' I said.
He frowned. 'Bad news?'
'You said that being unconscious was the good news.'
'There is no bad news. The fact that you were unconscious for only a relatively short period of time is good news.'
Definitely weird.

I had been admitted to hospital two days earlier.
As they wheeled me onto the ward I spotted my details written on a white-board: *Christine Marsden - concussion - skateboard injury.*

I smiled, in spite of the pain. The truth was, I had never been on a skateboard. The throbbing wounds on my face and head didn't tell the whole story.

I was a teacher at a primary school in Bath. Parents' evening was just around the corner and we had all been working late. Teachers do that. Work late. And long. And at the weekend. But that's our choice.

Parents' evening always caused mild panic throughout the school. Two days before the actual night, would see the wrong teachers going into the wrong classrooms "by mistake" or under some pretence or other, just to see how the other teachers had made their classrooms stand out. Desks were scrubbed clean, dustpan brushes (never the dustpans) appeared from nowhere and all the bins overflowed with screwed up paper and dried out paint pots.

Where I could find good reason I'd make sure the kids' work was marked as positively as possible.

As tempers frayed we all watched each other in the staffroom, from behind our coffee cups.

It would all be fine, the morning after. But until then, I was working late.

My self imposed deadline was 7pm. Get it all done by then and then get out. My stomach had already started to moan by 5pm. In all the panic I'd forgotten to eat lunch (again). At five to seven I'd had enough. I was ready to kill for food. And ready to kill any teachers or parents who didn't appreciate the work I'd put into making the classroom look as good as it was ever going to look.

Neil would have already made tea for himself and the kids. I was going through another vegetarian phase, so I knew he wouldn't have made anything for me. Which was fine.

The journey home was a struggle right from the start. My seatbelt wouldn't pull across properly and when it eventually did, it was twisted. OK. I could live with that.

Within minutes of leaving the school car park my eyes started drooping. Too many late nights backed up by too many early mornings. There was no way I was going to be bothered to faff about with any vegetables when I got home. Something "ready made" from the supermarket felt like the right move.

I steered the car with one hand and checked the contents of my purse with the other. Several coins fell out, one dropped between the seat and the handbrake — no doubt the highest denomination I had. The car juddered as I tried to adjust my eyes to the darkness, and to counting the money as I drove. There wasn't enough. Even if the missing coin was worth the most, I still didn't have enough cash for a cheap vegetarian ready-meal. And I wasn't even being fussy.

Of course I had my bank card. But that was a whole other matter.

At the best of times I found the 'chip and pin' scenario in supermarkets awkward. I knew how to stick my card in the machine. Sometimes I got it the right way round first time. Often I didn't. I had enough brain capacity to remember four digits. Sometimes I remembered the correct four digits for the card I was using. Often I didn't. And even if I remembered the correct four digits and the correct card the right way round, I didn't always get the digits in the right order.

It wasn't because I was stupid. It was because I was stressed.

As a teacher, I should have been used to stress. And in a class full of kids, I was. But at the head of an ever growing queue at the supermarket checkout the stress hit me. That was my weak point. The checkout. I'd overheat. I'd have to take my coat off, if I was wearing a coat. My cardigan, if I was wearing a cardigan. My face would flush red, which would make me even more stressed.

And if by some miracle I managed to get the whole thing working perfectly — card in, four digits, correct order — I would forget to cover what I was doing as I did it. It was as though I was showing the world — *look, I can do this*.

'Someone will see your number,' Neil would say. 'You need to cover it up. They'll steal your card. Then what will you do?'

Maybe it was Neil's fault that I got so stressed.

At a cash machine I was fine. No problem with cards the wrong way around. No problem with remembering a four digit sequence in the correct order. No problem covering the whole thing with my other hand.

So my usual method to buy things consisted of: go to cash machine; get cash; buy stuff.

So simple even a primary school teacher could master it.

I left my purse open on the passenger seat and concentrated more fully on the road. Darkness, tired eyes and hunger did not make for a comfortable journey. After ten minutes I saw the lights of the supermarket on the high street. The cash machine was built into the side of the supermarket.

Perfect.

Except that the easiest way to get to the cash machine was to park (illegally) at the bus stop opposite, run across the pavement and get the money out, run back to the car and then drive around the end of the road to the entrance to the supermarket car park. Clever to have a cash machine attached, stupid to position it on the wrong side of the supermarket entrance. Great for pedestrians, or people wanting to catch a bus.

I checked in my rearview mirror. No buses as far as I could tell. I'd only be a few seconds. A minute or two at the most. Just get the cash and straight back to the car. Where was the harm in that?

I pulled up at the bus stop, grabbed my purse, shoved it in my handbag and opened the door. Then stuck the hazard lights on. Then turned the engine off and put the keys in my handbag. A quick last check, no buses, and then a sort of semi-running movement to the cash machine. Although the cash machine was a shining beacon, the surrounding street lights seemed to be down a bulb or two. That was good. I didn't want any of the kids, or their parents, spotting me parking illegally to get money from the cash machine. Little things can turn into massive stories in a school environment.

I checked over my shoulder a few times, covered my digit-pushing fingers and requested £50. Enough for a slightly better meal and a half tank of petrol for the car in the morning.

I slipped the money into my purse, slipped my purse into my handbag and headed back, semi-running movement, to the car.

Halfway between the cash machine and the bus stop I heard a noise. Almost felt the noise. Like a train ratcheting over the tracks, with a gust of wind running before and after the carriage. That was what it was like.

The reality was a boy on a skateboard shooting out from the darkness, skimming along the pavement, heading towards me.

He wore a hoodie. And a smile.

I halted my semi-running movement and stepped backwards, away from him. As he drew level he reached out an arm and grabbed hold of my handbag. I gripped it tight and brought him to a stop. I yanked the bag, trying to pull it away from him. But instead I pulled him nearer. He breathed alcohol and sweat.

He still had the bag, and he was much closer to me than I was happy with. I opened my mouth to scream. But in the time it took for the sound waves to fulfil their side of the bargain he flicked his skateboard up, caught it with his free hand and brought it crashing down on my forehead. The pain was instant and piercing, unlike my scream which turned out to be a forced grunt. Briefly my world became a blazing bright white.

CHAPTER TWO

When I woke up, the pavement was cold beneath my body, but my head and neck felt warm. My eyes were open, but everything looked smudged, like a swirling mist had come along and messed with the surroundings. There was someone at my side. A man, I thought. He was very short.

No. He was kneeling. His smudgy mouth moved but I couldn't hear anything. Then voices came. But they were a long way off.

I tried to speak. 'Tell Neil. Tell Michael and Rose I'm OK. Tell them not to worry. I won't need any tea. I'm not hungry anymore.'

The distant voices didn't say anything recognisable. They probably hadn't heard me.

My forehead started climbing the temperature scale. Warm to hot. Hot to burning. Was I on fire? I didn't want anyone to see me with my hair burned off. What about Neil? What about Michael and Rose? How would they recognise me with no hair? The fire must have burned me to sleep.

The next time I opened my eyes I was still lying on my back, but now I was rocking from side to side. The world wasn't nearly as smudged as I remembered it. I was in an ambulance. Something cold and sharp bothered the back of my hand. I turned my head to find out what it was. A clear tube ran from the back of my hand up to a clear bag of liquid hanging above my body. Everything swung in time with the moving ambulance. But I couldn't hear a siren. That was a good sign. A man wearing green was sitting beside me, but he wasn't looking at me.

A smell hit me. Alcohol again. The boy on the skateboard? No this was different. I choked.

He looked then.

'Don't worry,' he said. 'You're OK. You've had a nasty fall. A bang to the head. We're taking you to hospital now. But you're OK.'

I tried to say *he hit me* but nothing came out. My throat was too dry, too raspy. I tried again.

'Water?' I said.

A better effort.

The man at my side smiled. And shook his head. 'I can't give you anything to drink until they've had a look at you. I'm sorry. The drip should help. It should ease the pain a little, and keep you hydrated until we can get you something proper to drink.'

If they wanted me to get better, why not let me have water? I knew what I needed. I tried say *water* again, but my voice turned to gravel. I fell asleep again.

By the time they wheeled me onto the ward I'd received twelve stitches at the back of my head and four on my forehead. They had cleaned me up a little, but dried blood cracked and itched the back of my neck, and I could feel lumps of it in my hair. The drip tube still swayed from the back of my hand. The back of my hand throbbed.

'My car?' I said to the man pushing my trolley bed, 'what happened to my car?'

Of course he had no idea.

'Don't worry. They'll sort all of that out for you. You just concentrate on getting better. Is anyone coming to see you?'

Of course I had no idea.

I had no idea whether Neil knew what had happened. I had no idea what the time was. Had everything happened just minutes ago? Or had I been unconscious for days?

A nurse directed my trolley to the corner of a small ward. I counted four beds, all empty. I was wheeled to one nearest the window. Three or four nurses appeared and I was moved onto the bed. Although the other beds were empty, curtains were pulled around my bed, enclosing me in a light green world of polyester. The wheels of my trolley squeaked as it was pushed away. I followed the sound along the corridor until I could no longer hear it.

My head thumped. The wounds at the back and front seared into my skin and penetrated deep inside. I lifted the hand without the tube dangling from it and touched under my right eye. It felt puffy. I touched a little harder and regretted it. From nowhere my stomach cramped, and churned and I put my hand to my mouth.

'I think I'm going to be —'

One of the nurses grabbed a cardboard bowl from a cabinet next to my bed. But she was too slow. I threw up all over her arm and the bed. I tried to apologise but just gargled with the vomit still stuck in my throat. My puffy eyes stung even more and I started crying. The smell was awful.

A clean cardboard bowl was dumped onto my chest and I spat into it several times. Was that blood?

'Don't worry,' one of the nurses said. 'We'll get you cleaned up. It's the medicine making you sick. And the shock of everything. The doctor will be along shortly to have a look at you.' She looked at one of the other nurses, who nodded. 'And I think the police are waiting to have a word — when you're up to it.'

At that moment I wasn't up to anything. I wanted to sleep; to be sick; to be home; to see Neil and Michael and Rose. I wanted to be almost anywhere other than where I was.

'Does my husband know I'm here?' I asked the nurse with vomit still on her arm.

'I think someone's trying to contact him now. I'm sure he'll be along soon. Have you got kids?'

'Michael and Rose. He's eleven, she's eight.'

The nurse nodded. She seemed oblivious to the sick on her arm as she worked away at changing my bedsheets. I wanted to tell her to wash her arm. To not get any sick on my clean sheets. She bundled the dirty ones together and swished through the green curtains. One of the other nurses followed.

'What time is it?' I asked the one left behind.

She looked at the watch on her uniform then stuck her head out of the curtain, presumably to check with a larger clock on the wall somewhere.

'It's twenty to nine.'

'Morning or night?'

'In the evening.'

'What day?'

'Wednesday. Wednesday the ninth of February.'

So there I had it. A little under an hour and a half had passed since I had parked illegally at the bus stop to withdraw money from the cash machine. Since then I had been attacked; knocked unconscious; brought to hospital; had stitches put into my head and thrown up on a nurse. Inside and out my life had changed forever. Of course I didn't know that then. But I knew the pain I was feeling. I threw up again.

This time into the bowl.

CHAPTER THREE

Half an hour after being sick for the second time I was speaking with two police officers. I had thought that police officers were supposed to be young and tall. The one asking the questions looked fairly short, not much taller than me, and was quite round with a light covering of grey hair on his head. His female colleague was petite and very pretty, her dark hair pulled back tight against her head. I wondered why she was in the police force when she looked like she could have been a model.

They were both sitting on plastic chairs next to my bed and they both smelled of damp. I guessed that maybe it was raining outside. Grey hair asked me another question.

'So what time would you say the person on the skateboard came past you?'

'He didn't go *past* me. He stopped and attacked me.'

'And what time would you say that was?'

If I'd had to bet on it, I would have said that his tone was condescending. I felt like telling him to "fuck off and find the bastard".

'I think it was about 7:15.'

'And why do you think that?'

'Because I left the school at 7:00 and it takes about ten minutes to get to the cash machine from the school. I was only at the cash machine for a minute or so, so it must have been around 7:15.'

He wrote something in his notebook, tapped his pen against the page and glanced at petite beauty. She nodded back at him. I wished I hadn't been sick on the nurse and instead saved it for these two.

My throat felt dry and bloody. My teeth tasted like metal

when I ran my tongue over them. A drink would have helped. Something strong. Something with bite. Perhaps Neil might turn up with a bottle of something. Where the hell was Neil?

'Is my husband coming?'

Grey hair looked at petite again. And, despite my weakened state, I wanted to punch him.

'We have sent someone to speak to him,' he said. 'I would imagine he'll sort something out.'

What the hell kind of answer was that? *I'd imagine* — ? I wanted to *know* — not imagine.

'Is he on his way or not? And what's happened to my car? Did the mugger get away with my handbag?'

I told myself that if he looked at petite again I would rip the needle out of the back of my hand and stick it in his eye.

He looked at her.

For the first time, she spoke. 'I can chase it up for you and find out what's happening. I understand you have children. He might be trying to sort something out for them. I don't think it would be a good idea for them to see you like this. Not so soon after the … you know.'

How bad did I look? And why couldn't she say the word *attack* or *mugging*? I was still reeling, literally, from being assaulted and she couldn't even find the right word to use. Or any word.

The green polyester swished and a nurse poked her head through.

'Your husband is here, Mrs Marsden. Would you like to see him?'

I felt the tears welling up before she had even finished speaking. My chest heaved and huge sobs poured out of me. The tube in the back of my hand swung all over the place as I cried. I couldn't stop it — the tube or the tears. For a moment, in front of two police officers, my whole life had turned to tears and was flooding out of my stinging, puffy eyes. Neil moved through the curtains and reached for my hand. I wanted him to hug me, to hold me so tight it hurt. But he sat down in an empty plastic chair, held my hand and spoke softly to me.

'Don't worry. You're going to be OK. What an experience you've had. Michael and Rose are fine. They're with Oliver and Abi.'

Through my bleary eyes I could see grey hair looking at petite. I turned to Neil.

'I'm so glad you're here. I'm so sorry.'

Grey hair stood up, petite followed suit.

'We'll leave you alone for a while,' he said. 'But we will need to come back and finish asking you questions later.'

Neil stood up and nodded a *thank you* to them. I turned my head away and shut my eyes. They swished through the curtains and disappeared. Neil sat down again.

'I need a hug,' I said.

He hesitated and looked at the tube hanging from my hand. He looked at the scar on my forehead. And I know that he looked at my mouth. I had forgotten that I'd been sick. Nevertheless, he hesitated a little too long in my mind.

'Poor you,' he said as he leaned forward and, rather awkwardly, put his hands on my shoulders.

He tried, but failed to get his arms all the way round me. I was wrapped in a hospital blanket, on a bed, with a tube hanging from me. His failure was understandable. But inside I still scolded him for it.

'Poor you,' he said, again.

I had been expecting *I love you, are you OK?*.

My eyes hurt like hell as I closed them. I kept them shut and swallowed. A rush of cold flowed into the back of my hand from the tube and, for a moment, I saw a grey space. Empty, cool and soft.

It was in that brief moment that I realised something was not quite right. The clarity that came with the empty space enabled my mind to catch up with reality.

I was not myself.

Something within me was different. I opened my eyes again. Neil stared down at me, his face creased and concerned. I stared back up at him and thought about how I had wanted to stab the police officer in the eye. I was a primary school teacher. A wife. A mother. I had never in my life wanted to stab anyone in the eye. Or anywhere else.

Neil had come as quickly as he could. He had dealt with the police coming to see him. Dealt with Michael and Rose. Oliver and Abi. And I was angry as hell because he hadn't cuddled me straight away. Because he'd said "poor you" instead of "I love you". Because he had hesitated for half a second before getting close to me.

I had wanted to be sick on the police officers. In my mind I'd told grey hair to "fuck off".

From nowhere, an anger had appeared in me like I'd never felt before. I knew it was because of what had happened. Knocked down by a skateboard smashing against my skull. Almost killed when I hit the pavement with the back of my head. Deep wounds front and back. I must have lost a fair amount of blood. My teeth must have split my lip or the inside of my mouth from the impact.

No wonder I was moody.

It made sense to be angry. All these feelings, powerful and physical, would pass, I was sure. Once I had slept, drunk something, eaten something. Once the pain had subsided and the scars healed — then I'd be fine. Then I'd be the same Christine I always was.

I wondered how long these things took. How long before I would be back to normal? How long before the anger was gone? The hate gone? There was no room for these things in my life. Primary school teacher, mother, wife. No room for anger or hatred. No room for physical violence. I taught little children.

'Neil, I'm scared. I don't like feeling like this.'

'I know. The pain will pass. They'll get you better before you know it. You'll be fine.'

I wanted to tell him that wasn't what I'd meant. It wasn't the feeling of pain I didn't like, although that was bad enough, it was all the other feelings. All the *not me* feelings of aggression and anger. I was scared of those feelings. Of what they might mean.

And what if they didn't pass?

But they would. I pushed the fear down inside me. Forced it down with my mind and all the strength I had.

But that was when the madness started.

CHAPTER FOUR

When they first saw me, Michael and Rose were shocked.

They didn't want to touch me in case they hurt me. They thought the whole of my body must be in pain. And to a certain extent it was.

But a little over a week after Neil had helped me through the front door, they were over it. Rose even ran her finger gently over the train-track stitched scar on my forehead.

'Does it hurt?' she said.

'A little.'

She said sorry, and smiled. It was the smile that gave her away. It excited her that her finger could cause tiny spasms of pain to shoot into my head. She touched the scar again.

The police had finished asking all the questions they wanted to ask. The doctor had told me that I had suffered only "an insignificant amount of damage" and my intense rage had subsided. A little.

Curiously, my sense of smell had heightened. The slightest whiff of anything had me looking around, hawk-like, trying to find the source of it.

Some smells I couldn't identify. They were strange to me, and not easy to pinpoint. I became temporarily consumed with some of them. I couldn't even make a guess. One in particular stuck with me. A sweet smell, sometimes sickly and stifling. I'd have to open the windows around the house and try to snort it from my nose.

I received endless emails, texts and calls from the school. Every day I opened another "Get Well Soon" card made by a fellow teacher's class. I sniffed each card, ran my fingers over the paint and glue, some of it still damp.

Margaret, the head-teacher, told me to take it easy.

'We can cope, Chris. We do not expect to see you again until you are one hundred percent better. *Totally* recovered.

At first, well-meaning comments like that seemed to make me feel worse. What if I was never one hundred percent better? What if I never totally recovered?

To get over my insecurities I gave myself a recovery deadline. Two weeks and no more. That would surely be enough. Certainly enough to go back to school.

Every day I made progress. Every day I felt a little better than the day before. I still had aches and pains. Still had scars and wounds. Still had a bizarre sense of smell. But as my two week deadline approached I felt pretty confident about making it.

Coincidentally (and I thought, significantly) my first day back at school was due to be Tuesday 29th February — the extra day of the leap-year. That was the plan.

At least it was, until I had the dream.

On the morning of the 29th I woke up, shaking. My pyjama top was damp, not only from sweat, but also from tears. I had been crying in my sleep. I ran the back of my hand along my hairline, and my ring caught the scar on my forehead. I squeezed my teeth together to stop from making a noise. The back of my legs felt wet. Wet and cold.

And I could still see her.

Not her face. Not her features. But her terror. Her weakness. I could still see everything about her that was possible to destroy. My heart rate picked up and the scar at the back of my head throbbed in time. I suddenly felt as though I'd just taken a run around the neighbourhood. A run where I had been pursued, almost to exhaustion. Sweat or tears trickled past my ear and dropped onto the pillow.

I had obviously shifted about a lot because Neil had woken

up. He usually slept through everything, including the "extra loud" alarm we'd had to buy for him. So I must have been practically punching him in my sleep.

'Are you OK?' he said.

I opened my mouth to speak, but stopped myself. I knew if I started, I would cry. And I felt like I was done with crying. I had cried almost every day since the attack. Sometimes in pain, sometimes feeling sorry for myself. Sometimes because of rage.

When I first came out of hospital I had still been experiencing the dark feelings I'd had directly after the attack. For the first time I had understood what people meant by the phrase "pure hatred". I had felt that. Not just for my attacker, but for people in general. For the world. And it really had felt "pure". Not a dirty or evil thing, but a natural, free-flowing hatred of everything mankind. For a few days I felt addicted to it. I sunk myself into the feeling. Thought about people, some I knew, some I didn't, no matter. I hated them all. Not Neil, or Michael or Rose. Not really. But everyone else.

If I ventured out of the house, I felt as though I could hurt people simply by looking at them. *If looks could kill.*

Christine Marsden — Primary school teacher, wife, mother. That had been me before some little shit had come along and messed up my life, and now I killed people by looking at them. Christine Marsden — eye-stare killer.

So I didn't want to cry again. I nodded in response to Neil's question.

He persisted. 'What is it, Chris? Are you in pain? Are you hurting?'

I moved my hand across the bed and scrabbled about for his. He found mine and stopped it scrabbling. From somewhere in the house, the sweet, sickly smell hit my nostrils.

'I had a nightmare,' I said, and waited for the floodgates to open.

My eyes stayed dry. Neil said nothing.

'It was *like* a nightmare,' I said.

'What do you mean?'

'It felt like a nightmare — it *was* a nightmare — but somehow more intense. More real.'

'The doctor said you might experience some problems for a while afterwards. "Post-traumatic-stress symptoms".' Neil squeezed my hand. 'He did say you might even have nightmares.'

My eyebrow prickled with sweat and I let go of Neil's hand so I could scratch it.

'I know that's what he said. But this was different. I don't think this had anything to do with what happened. I don't think this was related to the attack at all.'

Neil smiled a *poor Christine* type of smile. Condescending fucker.

'Even if it wasn't *about* the attack,' he said, 'it was almost certainly brought on by it. The doctor said —'

'Shut up about the doctor!'

Neil shut up. Another condescending look.

'I know what the fucking doctor said. But listen to what *I'm* saying. This was not related to the attack. N-O-T.'

I slammed my arm down on the bed and accidentally caught Neil's arm. I opened my mouth to say sorry, but managed to snap it shut before anything came out.

'This was a nightmare,' I said, 'but it was most definitely not related to the attack.'

Neil managed to keep his face expressionless. He didn't look at me, or away. He tried not to nod or shake his head. He did everything within his power to remain neutral.

I started crying again.

He opened his mouth to say something but I waved him away. He shrugged, climbed out of bed and walked into the en-suite. To stop my tears I focused on what he was doing.

The shower door creaked as he opened it; he turned the shower on; the door creaked shut again; the water hit the shower floor, then the sound changed as Neil stepped under the water.

I shut my eyes but the vision of the nightmare was still there. Like a negative on my eyelids, waiting for me every time I chose to come back to it.

Neil started humming.

My stomach cramped up and the last few deep-set sobs bubbled up from beneath my ribcage. I could feel my nose running.

I rolled out of bed, grabbed my bathrobe and took the few short steps from our bedroom, across the landing to the main bathroom. "The Kids Bathroom" we called it. It was a mess in avocado-green. The sink was caked in dried toothpaste spit, the ragged, blue bathmat was screwed up and damp on the floor. The toilet seat was up and there was something in the toilet that probably should have been flushed away. How the hell did the kids get ready in this? They must surely come out more filthy than when they went in.

I should have checked it. I had been so wrapped up in myself since the attack. I wished I had checked it.

Why the hell couldn't Neil have checked it?

CHAPTER FIVE

The last time I'd showered in the main bathroom had been after dinner one night when Neil and I had argued over how much petrol I was putting in the car. I ended up not talking to him, quite rightly, and we'd both stormed out of the kitchen — evidently with the same thought in mind — have a shower to give ourselves and each other space to calm down.

We'd both stomped up the stairs. But Neil had been ahead of me. Naturally he turned left, to our room, which meant I had to turn right, to the main bathroom. I'd vented my frustration then by scrubbing at all the dirty footprints and ingrained muck on the inside of the bath — not stopping until the shower water started running cold and goosebumps sent shivers over my back. Avocado-green never looked clean.

But now, with the nightmare still fresh in my mind, the footprints and toothpaste stains could stay where they were. I just wanted to get clean. The tears had made my neck feel dirty and my upper lip was sticky from my running nose. I wanted to wash the tension out; wash away the nightmare; clean my eyelids of the image imprinted on them; wash away the endless tears; wash away what had happened to me. The smiling hoodie. Stinking of booze and sweat; the heavy skateboard gashing my head; the hospital, with its clear tubes, polyester green curtains and my vomit.

And I wanted to wash away the police officers who had come to see me; wash away Neil — humming in the shower, not saying the right things at the right time.

He used to know me so well. We always knew what the other one was thinking. We didn't finish each other's sentences, but we both knew we could. And now he was in the en-suite and I was in the bathroom. When I needed him most, we were separated. He couldn't understand me. I felt alone.

My hair hung in straggly wet coils down my back, touching my spine and sending tingles through my upper body. I let my head fall forward and the warm water hit the back of my neck. I stretched my head down toward my chest, extended the tendons in my neck, mentally released the pressure. I pushed my shoulders back and let the water flow over my breasts. The water was warm, but still goosebumps covered my body.

Slowly I leaned my head back. The scar on the back of my head stung, but the one on my forehead wasn't so bad. I imagined I was having a massage. Warm hands pressing over my body, manipulating the knots of pain and tension, smoothing them away. Just like Neil used to make me feel — whether he touched me or not.

I shut my eyes and waited. No image. My eyelids seemed clear. I took a deep breath, held it, and imagined it escaping out the top of my head, taking all the dirt inside with it, cleansing my mind. For the briefest moment I forgot. I forgot everything. All that had happened to me. Not just from the last two weeks, but everything. I forgot who I was; forgot that I was married; forgot Michael and Rose. In that passing moment everything else ceased to exist. Every person ceased to exist. I ceased to exist.

'Mum!'

It made me jump. Michael, pounding at the door.

'Are you nearly done?' he said. 'I need a wee.'

How the hell had he known it was me in the shower and not his father? Michael always seemed to know. Whenever he was in bed, he always knew which one of us was coming up the stairs to say goodnight or to go and have a shower. It was as though he sensed us.

'I won't be long, Michael. Can't you use the loo downstairs?'

'Rose is using it. I'm desperate.'

The shower suddenly burned hot on my skin and I stepped

out from under it. Rose must have flushed.

'It's OK, Michael. Rose has finished now.'

I stretched out my arms and examined them. There was still a small lump on the back of my hand where the needle and tube had been inserted. A cannula. It still felt a little sore, even after two weeks.

I thought about getting ready for school, and my breathing changed instantly. The air felt thinner and my lungs felt as though they had contracted. Butterflies kicked off in my stomach and I felt so light headed I had to lean against the bathroom wall. The cold tiles made me jump back straight away.

I crouched down and held onto the stainless steel handles embedded in the sides of the bath. I lowered myself all the way to sitting and let the shower water sprinkle over me. I was a child again, sat in a puddle, enjoying the warm summer rain pattering against my head. No worries, when you're a child. Everything can be fun, when you're a child.

Except I was pretty sure that the person in my nightmare had been a child. And not everything is fun. Some things are most definitely not fun, when you're a child.

I stood up, turned the shower off and realised that my towel was still hanging over the radiator in the en-suite. *Shit.*

'Michael? Are you still there?'

Of course he wasn't. He had been desperate.

For a second or two it crossed my mind that I might actually be going mad. Neil was getting ready for work; the kids were getting ready for school, and I had been sat in a puddle in a mucky bath letting the shower water pour down on me like rain.

Why had I dreamed about a child? Why the nightmare with the child? Perhaps I had been more nervous than I'd realised about going back to school. Anxious about being back in class, teaching little children again. That must be the connection.

Kids at school — the child in the nightmare. But I was certain the child in my dream had been older than the kids I taught at school. I looked back into the dreamscape, watched it swirling around my mind. She was definitely older. I didn't like it. I tried to push the vision away. I didn't want to see it or think about it anymore. But there it was. It had happened and there wasn't any way to undo it. I couldn't make it *not* have happened.

I shook my arms and kicked my legs out to try to dislodge water droplets from my body. I had dropped my bathrobe on the floor on the way in, too far away to reach it from the bath. I tried anyway and my foot slipped backwards against the inside of the bath. I steadied myself on the side of the bath and decided it would be safer to simply climb out, add my own wet footprints to the general mess on the floor, and climb into my bathrobe.

My arms and shoulders, my back and my bum, the tops of my legs all immediately stuck to the material, making it difficult and uncomfortable to put on properly. I ran across the landing and back into our bedroom. Neil was out of the shower and almost completely dressed for work. I nipped into the en-suite and dried off properly. When I came out he was pretty much done.

'Are you OK?'

I wasn't, but I had calmed down. 'I'm fine.'

That was obviously the answer he'd wanted to hear. He smiled and checked his tie in one of the ceiling-to-floor door mirrors in our bedroom. He fiddled with the knot and tilted his head on one side, as if he was getting a second opinion.

Perhaps I hadn't calmed down after all. I wanted to punch him in the stomach for looking at his tie.

And he still hadn't asked me what my dream had been about. The *"doctor prescribed"* nightmare that it was perfectly normal to have.

Downstairs Michael and Rose had started arguing. Outside of me, everything was normal.

Barely above a whisper I spoke to Neil.

'I hurt someone.'

CHAPTER SIX

Neil's shoulders dropped a fraction. He didn't need this.

'What do you mean?' he said, more irritated than questioning.

'In the dream. I hurt someone.'

Neil looked around for his suit jacket, checked himself in the mirror again.

'What do you mean?' he said again. 'Who did you hurt?'

I turned my back to him and looked into the mirror as well. Looked at us both. I spoke to myself in the mirror.

'It was a child, I think. Maybe a teenager, maybe younger. I think it was a girl. Everything was so hazy and unclear. There was a fight between us, but I don't know why. I heard a sort of screaming noise — a screech or something. It was frightening. I think that's what woke me — that noise.'

'It was just a bad dream, Chris. God knows I've had some nasty dreams in the past. Ones where you feel you just can't shake them off once you're awake. They seem so real.'

His hand moved to his tie again, and he looked like he was smirking. Perhaps it was the mirror.

'It is horrible,' he said, 'when you get dreams like that. And after what you've been through it's hardly any wonder.'

I watched him in the mirror still. His eyes flicked left and I knew he was checking the time on the bedroom clock. When he spoke again he sounded distracted.

'You should mention it when you see the doctor for your checkup tomorrow. The dream I mean.'

I knew what he meant.

'The checkup is the day after,' I said.

'Yes, of course.'

He wasn't interested. He wanted to get off to work. Deal with the "wife crisis", come up with a solution and move on.

I turned to face him.

'Neil?'

His eyes met mine.

'I don't think it was just a fight between me and this girl.'

He frowned.

I struggled with what to say. Searched for the right words. It was only a dream, perhaps, but the monster had been me. The girl had been my victim.

'I think … I raped her.'

The frown vanished from his forehead and I could see that "getting off to work" had been temporarily overshadowed. He smiled. A sort of crooked kind of smile. Was I joking? Was I being serious? He was on dangerous ground. Say the wrong thing and he could start me off crying again. Or get me angry. Again. He had to handle this just right.

'Raped?'

Good move. Put it back to me. Perhaps he did still know me after all.

'I can't be sure,' I said. 'But I think I raped her. Or at least smothered her with my body and forced myself down on her. Pinned her to the ground. It was all so grey. Swirling and grey. And the screeching screaming thing.' I swallowed hard. I wasn't going to blub anymore. My eyebrow itched again, probably something to do with the nerves running down from the wound on my forehead.

Neil wanted to say something. I could see that. He felt like he should say something. Probably something profound. Something to make everything better.

'Chris, I don't know what to say.'

In truth, I didn't know what I wanted him to say either. Even in a dream it was inconceivable that I could have raped a young girl. It was too horrific, too unreal. It wasn't possible, physically or mentally.

'I don't know what to say either.'

I felt a rumble in my stomach, and a gathering of bile or liquid, burning inside me.

'I think I'm going to be sick.'

I made a dash for the loo in the en-suite and sat down in front of it. I was burning hot and sweat prickled the back of my neck. My stomach went into spasms and I threw up into the toilet. Something splashed back onto my face and I tried to wipe it away with my hand. My eyes started to water and I thought I wasn't going to be able to breathe again. Whenever I was sick, I always thought I was going to die, that I would suffocate, or choke and not be able to breathe back in.

I gripped the rim of the toilet and realised that the seat had already been up when I had come in. I swore at Neil under my breath.

I sensed him behind me, keeping his distance. I hated being touched when I was being sick, I didn't want anyone rubbing my back or stroking me, trying to make me feel better. I waved my hand behind me, shooing him away.

Every breath brought more sick. My stomach felt as though it had been torn inside. I was happy to die. Happy to choke and to not breathe again. Bring it on.

Below the en-suite, in the kitchen, something smashed. It would be Michael. Although he was eleven years old, he was outclassed in the kitchen by Rose. I hoped it wasn't one of the plates Neil's mother had given us.

But it took my mind away from retching. I started breathing again. I relaxed my grip on the toilet rim and sat back on my haunches. I was exhausted. Not even an hour had passed since I'd woken from the dream and already it felt like a week.

The school would have to do without me for an extra day. Neil would be at work, the kids at school. I would be fine tomorrow. All I really needed was sleep. And maybe a small drink, just to relax me, help numb some of the residual pain. It had certainly helped during the previous two weeks.

Neil's voice drifted up from downstairs. He had obviously heard the smash too. His voice was muffled and I couldn't work out what he was saying. I wondered if he'd bother coming back up again, or just head off to work. The school minibus would be arriving any minute, and he always liked to have left before then.

I stood up and filled the sink with cold water, splashed it onto my face with cupped hands. I dried off using the back of my arm and stepped out of the en-suite just as the bedroom door squeaked open.

'Chris, are you OK? I'm really sorry, but I have to go. I'm running late as it is. I don't think you should go back today,' he looked at his watch, 'and they wouldn't expect you to anyway. Just give them a call and go back to bed. You're not ready yet.'

He kissed me on the cheek and I went to put my arms around him, but was just too late. He practically ran down the stairs and out of the front door.

The young girl floated back into my mind. Me, smothering her with my body; bearing down on her with more than my weight; her screaming. Was it the screaming that had woken me?

I tried to think of something different. Tried to drag my mind away from where it was going.

I knew what was happening. My mind wasn't *just* replaying what had happened in the nightmare — it was clarifying it.

And then recording it.

CHAPTER SEVEN

When I rang the school I noticed the telephone receiver was shaking in my hand. I tried to stop it.

'Christine, we weren't expecting you back so soon anyway,' Margaret said. 'You have to get better!'

I could see her, sitting behind her desk, "Head Teacher" written on a white sticky label, still stuck to the back of her chair from when we'd had a big change-around of offices and classrooms. She was probably wearing her woollen suit with a skirt, her hair tied up and her glasses crystal clear. Good old Margaret. Good, old, predictable Margaret. I wondered whether Matthew was in the room with her, fawning around her every word and deed. He'd been creeping around all over the place ever since he'd heard Margaret mention the possibility of a "Deputy Head" position. She had asked me if I would be interested in putting myself forward but I'd said no straight away. I loved teaching, not being in charge of teachers. In fact being anyone's boss didn't really appeal to me. But I was flattered she'd asked me.

'I thought I was better,' I said. 'But then I was really ill this morning. I'm sorry, Margaret.'

I didn't tell her about the dream.

'Don't be so silly,' she said.

'How are the children?' I said.

'Missing you, of course. But they all want you to get better?'

She paused and I wondered if I had mis-heard her. Wondered if I should be saying something. Then she spoke again.

'Chris,' she'd lowered her voice. 'Have they found him — the person that did this to you?'

I had heard nothing from the police for nearly a week.

'I don't think so, Margaret. You know, it's funny — I couldn't help wondering if it was someone I taught once, when they were younger. Had he come through my class? It's funny what you think isn't it?'

'Well whoever it is, I hope they catch him soon. He's a menace and needs putting away!'

She didn't mean it. Margaret was one of those people who thought that learning was the key to everything. Punishment was always surpassed by coaching. Give someone responsibility and they won't let you down. If they ever did catch him, Margaret would want him going through some sort of reconciliation programme or community service, rather than going to prison.

'Let's hope so,' I said. 'I'll keep you posted on how I am. I want to come back as soon as I can, get back to normality.'

After the call I made straight for the kitchen. I had worked my way through several bottles of wine since the attack, mostly to numb the pain and help me sleep. But the previous night I had only had one glass, knowing that I had my first day back at work the next day. So I still had a bottle to finish.

I poured half a glass and mixed it with lemonade. It smelled so intense to me I had to hold my breath as I drunk it. I wondered how soon my sense of smell would recover, how soon I would be rid of the unknown smells. That sweet, sickly smell. Sweet alcohol.

The phone rang. It was Neil. Much easier for him to talk on the phone than it was face to face. His voice sounded like it used to. It sounded fun and exciting. I'd always thought he had a hint of menace in his voice. I loved that.

'Don't worry,' I said. 'I'm fine. I'm not going in - they said they didn't want to see me again until I'm completely better. The kids got off OK. Both still arguing of course.'

I managed another three glasses of wine and lemonade after

Neil called. And I had a couple of paracetamol. I desperately wanted to go to bed, but the thought of dreaming scared me too much.

I considered curling up on the sofa, using daytime telly to purge my mind and help me to slip into an empty space as I dropped off.

I had been watching quite a bit of that sort of TV during the days I had been recovering. At first it had been entertaining, but by day three I found myself getting so wound up I wanted to throw something at the telly.

The wine helped with the anger. Helped to dampen it down a little. I had no idea why I was feeling so enraged with people. I had always been a "people person". Loved socialising. But now I felt as though I could kill people. Actually, really kill them. I had never felt so angry before.

It was during these rages, often silent, that I became aware of a sensation in my thigh. My left thigh, a few inches below the hip. It was very specific in position, but dull in feeling. But it was something. And it only seemed to happen when the anger boiled up inside of me. It must have been from the attack. I must have hit it when I fell down. But there was no mark. I wondered if I'd bruised the bone or jangled some nerves or something and it made it worse if I became angry. But I hadn't felt the pain in the hospital and I had been pretty angry then.

The wine started to work and I decided I could cope with bed.

After the attack I had asked Neil if we could move. Not too far, I still wanted to teach at the school, just a different house. He told me we couldn't afford it. And, besides, he liked it where we were. I think really I had just wanted an escape. And after three glasses of wine I was viewing bed as my escape. But it was an imperfect one. As of that morning it came with flaws.

I slept fine. That day and the next. And the next. No dreams, no nightmares and no disturbances. In fact, just one week into March, I was back at school, teaching my old class.

I pretty much felt OK. I was a bit self-conscious. I asked Margaret if I could wear a floppy hat in class, just until the scars healed over a little. I knew how cruel kids could be. But within a couple of days I had got over that and just covered the scar on my forehead with a little foundation. The stitches were out, but the train-track look persisted. At first I let my hair fall over the ridges to hide them a little more, but after a while there seemed to be no point.

'Does that hurt, miss?'

'Why did someone hit you with a skateboard, miss?'

'Will it make you die, miss?'

Children have a way of getting right to the heart of things. It seemed pointless trying to cover it up after that.

Being back at school gave me the focus I needed. The pain from the wounds to my head subsided and I was able to control my anger more. I still felt it though. The anger. And the pain in my thigh. And smelled the strange smells.

The doctor said that I was recovering well. He said that people who experienced head trauma, car crashes and the like, often had their sense of smell affected, although normally it was deadened rather than heightened. He said he would arrange to have an x-ray carried out on my thigh, just to make sure there was nothing serious happening in there. But he thought it was more likely just to be internal bruising of the bone. It would heal in a few weeks.

The anger, he suggested, might be a delayed fighting-back phenomena. Or might simply be the fact that I was angry for being attacked in the first place.

I wondered how much doctors earned.

The hair on the back of my head started to grow back where they'd had to remove some of it to stitch me up, and I started to feel better about life.

Neil and I had a tense few weeks at home. Every morning, after the dream, he was afraid to look me in the eye in case I had had it again. I had to reassure him just to make him look at me straight on.

I cleaned the whole house. Tried to get rid of the smells. I got ratty with Michael and Rose. Got ratty with Neil. And got ratty with the police — still nothing. I suppose I should really have got ratty with the smiling skateboarder. But I didn't know him.

Then I had the dream again.

CHAPTER EIGHT

The same one. Only this time it was more clear. Even more real.

It was late and I had fallen asleep on the sofa. My intention had been to go up to bed with Neil, but I'd needed a quick drink first. One led to two, and two led to more. And I fell asleep.

I can see her walking along the path. Coming in my direction. Mist everywhere; hard to make her out exactly, but I know it's her. I recognise her. Can she see me yet? I am hiding, I think. Prickly bushes in front of me, but I can still see her. I think she is smiling. I think her hair is blowing. I wish this mist would clear. I want to see her. See her face. I am waiting for her. What's that smell? My arms flex, my legs bulge. Such strength. Enormous power. I stand up and smile. Does she smile too?

Prickles from the bush scratch my arms as I lunge forward. I am on her. I force my hand to her face. She falls backward and I am on top of her. She struggles underneath me. Writhing around. There is something else moving about beside her. What is that? I lash out and it disappears. But her mouth is free. There is a scream. I think it's a scream. Is it coming from her? Is it coming from above? Such a noise. I must make it stop.

I woke up on the sofa, perspiration dripping from me. I wanted to shout out. Call for Neil. But the children were asleep. I didn't want to wake them. The wine glass was tipped on the carpet, red wine had trickled out. For a moment I thought it was blood and I stifled a scream.

I shivered. My whole body rippled with goosebumps and the back of my neck felt cold, as though a window was open somewhere. I needed to get upstairs to bed, quickly. I really needed Neil. I rubbed my left thigh. Tried to rub away the dull ache deep inside.

What if the attacker had come to the house? Our address would have been in my purse somewhere, or my handbag. What if he had got in while I'd been sleeping. Maybe that's why I'd had the dream, maybe I had sensed the danger. Maybe it was some sort of warning. A warning that he was already in the house. A warning that he'd got in through the window. That chill on my neck.

I opened my mouth to shout for Neil, but stopped. If the attacker was in the house, he'd hear me shout, he'd know there were others there too. He might find Rose or Michael. I scrabbled about for the empty wine bottle. Any weapon would do, but the wine bottle was nearer than the knives in the kitchen.

I heard a bump upstairs and sat bolt upright on the sofa.

'Neil!'

Nothing. I shouted again. And again. I climbed to my feet, gripped the neck of the bottle hard and crept to the bottom of the stairs. More bumping from upstairs, and footsteps coming along the landing. I pushed myself against the wall, tried to make myself as flat as possible and raised the bottle ready.

The light from the little table lamp next to the sofa cast a huge shadow behind me, so that I was as obvious against the wall as I would have been anywhere else in the room. I wasn't thinking straight.

'Chris?'

It was Neil.

'Don't worry Mikey,' he said. 'You go back to bed now.'

Michael must have woken him up. Perhaps I'd woken Michael. I felt like shit.

Neil strode down the stairs. I reached out and pulled him against the wall.

'I think someone's in the house,' I hissed. My eyes must have looked like they were on stalks. I looked in all directions, all around the room, up to the ceiling. Everywhere but at Neil. 'I think he's got in!'

'Who has got in?'

'The guy who attacked me. I think he's here.'

Neil took hold of my arms and pushed me away slightly. I tried to claw my way back again.

'Chris, calm down. Look at me. Where do you think he is? I didn't hear anything.'

Neil looked around too. I could see he was thinking maybe I was right.

'I had the dream again,' I said. 'I think it is a warning. I woke up and felt a draft. I think there's a window open somewhere. I think he's here.'

'Stay here,' Neil said. 'Let me look around.'

'Stay here with me! Don't leave me alone.'

'Chris, I need to look. Just stay here. You'll still be able to see me.'

Neil took the empty wine bottle from my hand and held it, by the neck, down by his side. Although nearly six feet tall, he looked like a little boy in his dressing gown. He looked so vulnerable. I felt sick.

He moved slowly around the living room, his feet soft on the floor. I could hear his breathing. Relaxed and deep, through his nose. Once he had checked the room he looked over at me. His smile was grim. I wasn't reassured. He indicated the kitchen and moved toward it. Everywhere was so shadowy from the little table lamp. I wished I had left some main lights on instead.

My heart beat faster and I fought to keep the sick feeling down. I was certain I could see the dark shape of a crouched intruder everywhere I looked.

Neil disappeared into the kitchen. I didn't realise I was

holding my breath, until I heard the loud crash and clatter from the kitchen. I screamed.

'Neil!'

Nothing.

'Neil!'

Then from the kitchen.

'Shit,' Neil said. 'It's OK, I dropped the bottle. It's all OK in here.'

I ran to the kitchen door. Switched the light on and held onto Neil's arm. He was warm and still smelled of bed. I wished we were there.

'Neil, look at the microwave!'

He looked.

'And the cooker!'

He looked there too.

Both sets of digital clocks were flashing. Their times had been reset to zero. Exactly what happened if the electricity was switched off and then on again.

'Neil, I know he's here.'

Even I recognised the panic in my voice. 'He's here, somewhere.'

Neil didn't bother picking up the dropped bottle but made straight for the knife rack. He took the biggest one. And the next biggest.

Why had the intruder turned the electricity off? And why had he switched it back on again now?

I picked up the phone. The click and dial tone sounded so loud. I cupped the receiver with my hand, thumbed the number nine, three times.

'Police please, I think there's someone in our house.'

We both heard the noise in the living room. Neil moved toward the doorway, raising the knife. I could see his knuckles white as he gripped the handle. He moved his other hand behind his back, hiding the other knife.

I clung onto the phone.

'Hurry up please,' I whispered. 'He's here right now!'

Another noise from the living room. A shadow moved across the wall. Someone had just walked by the table lamp. Neil clicked off the kitchen light. I froze.

CHAPTER NINE

In a sudden movement Neil was out of the kitchen and into the living room. A scream I recognised, and a grunt from Neil.

'Michael!' he said. 'What are you doing out of bed? Where's Rose?'

'She's in bed. I heard a noise. I wondered what you were doing down here. My clock has broken. The time is flashing.'

'Michael,' Neil said. 'Go into the kitchen and wait with Mum for a minute. I need to go and make sure Rose is OK. I'll check your clock for you. Just go into the kitchen.'

Michael appeared at the kitchen door. I didn't need to ask if he was OK. His face said it all. He was reluctant to come straight to me, despite me holding out my free hand to him.

Of course, just minutes earlier, I had been a perspiring wreck on the sofa, having dreamt of attacking a child. I was still probably slightly drunk, and definitely on the edge. Now I was holding on for the police with one hand and holding out for my son with the other. My hand was shaking and there was broken glass on the floor. Michael looked at me, then the flashing digits on the microwave and cooker. He was pale and had dark rings under his eyes. I had no idea what the time was.

He took the last few steps to me, but didn't get close. I didn't blame him. I didn't need my extreme sense of smell to tell me that I was not pleasant to be near at the moment. Sweat, booze and fear. And I probably looked as bad as I smelt.

I gave the police our address and they told me to stay on the line. To wait on the phone until they got to the door. I worried about Rose.

'Michael, was there anyone upstairs?' I said.

I know it's not right to worry your children unnecessarily,

but I wasn't thinking straight. Michael hesitated.

'Was there anyone upstairs!' I pulled his hand, yanking his arm. He pulled it away from me and stepped back.

'Rose is up there,' he said. 'No one else. Just Rose!'

I put my forefinger to my lips, told him not to shout. He looked angry.

'What's going on?' he said. 'Why are you and Dad acting so weird? Is there someone in the house?'

I had successfully freaked him out. Woken him in the middle of the night and then scared him half to death with my rantings.

'Michael, everything is going to be OK. The police are on the way. I thought I heard a noise, that was all. I'm sure everything will be fine.'

Where the hell was Neil? Why wasn't he back down yet? I listened out for footsteps above us, but I didn't want to move the phone away from my ear. I wasn't sure if my heart could cope with everything. It actually felt as though it might just stop.

The stairs creaked. The third step up, it always creaked. It sounded like Neil — but surely it could be anyone, making the stair creak.

'Neil,' I whispered as loudly as I dared. 'Is that you?'

Neil came to the kitchen door.

'Everything is OK,' he said. He was pale too. 'Rose is fine. She's fast asleep, surprisingly. I checked all the rooms upstairs. And it's all clear downstairs. There's no one here.'

'What about the cupboards? The airing-cupboard? What about the downstairs loo?'

'Chris, I've checked everywhere. There is no one here.'

He walked to the knife-rack, replaced the knives. He tried to shield what he was doing from Michael. I guess he didn't want to encourage Michael to go for the knife-rack at the first sign of trouble. He was probably right.

I had let the phone receiver move away from my ear. So I didn't hear the person on the other end telling me that the police were at our door. So when the knock came, I almost died. That was also the point that I realised I really needed the loo.

'Who is that?' I said to Neil.

'Probably the police?'

I brought the phone up to my ear so fast that it slammed against the side of my head. I just managed to stop myself from swearing in front of Michael.

'There's someone at the door!'

The person at the other end of the phone told me not to worry, that it was the police, that we were OK to let them in.

'We need to let them in.' I said and looked at Neil.

The police officers (two, again) followed Neil into the living room. Neil waved a hand at the sofa and invited the officers to sit down. Neither accepted the invitation.

Their skin looked grey.

I checked the clock over the fireplace. Because it was powered by battery it was one of the few clocks in the house showing the correct time. Twenty-five minutes past two. Shit.

They looked at me, then Neil. They glanced at Michael and then spotted the fallen glass of wine on the carpet. The tallest one spoke.

'I understand that one of you reported an intruder,' he said.

Neil nodded at me.

'My wife thought there was someone in the house,' he said.

He made it sound like he was having doubts. Like he was blaming me.

'I woke up and felt a draught,' I said, touching the back of my neck. 'As though a window was open, or a door. And then I thought I sensed someone in the house.'

'Sensed someone?' the tall one said.

I burned inside. I wasn't going to be made to look stupid in my own house.

'And heard someone,' I said.

'What did you hear?' he said.

'Just a noise, I think. I don't know what it was. Just a noise, like a bump or a footstep or something.'

He turned to Neil.

'Were you and your wife upstairs when this happened?'

Neil hesitated.

'I fell asleep on the sofa,' I said. 'I called for Neil to come down. And then Michael woke up too.' I looked over at Michael. He was so tired. So little all of a sudden.

'We all went into the kitchen and that's when we noticed the flashing clocks. All of the digital clocks in the house are flashing. Someone has turned the electricity off and on again. Now why would someone do that?'

'We have had a few reports of a power-cut in this area tonight. It caused one or two problems for some of the elderly residents. Did you notice any lights going out for a while?'

I hadn't considered a power-cut. None of us had.

The policeman studied my face then looked again at the fallen glass.

'I've been through a lot recently,' I said. 'I was attacked a few weeks ago. Ended up in hospital. I just wanted to relax on the sofa with a glass of wine before going to bed. But I fell asleep. When I woke up — that's when all this happened. I must have knocked the glass over. Unless the intruder did.'

I moved across the room to pick up the glass then stopped. 'Should I leave this? In case you need to check it for evidence or fingerprints or something?'

The smaller officer smirked.

'I think it will be alright to pick that up,' he said. He turned to Neil.

'Have you had a chance to check the house, sir. Have a look

around?'

'I've checked the whole house, upstairs and down,' Neil said. 'And all the windows and doors.' Neil looked at me, eyes slightly downcast. 'It's all clear. There's no one here at the moment, as far as I can tell.'

Small nodded. Tall spoke.

'Do you mind if we take a quick look around, just to be sure.'

It wasn't a question. They would do it whether we wanted them to or not.

'No problem,' Neil said. 'I'll show you around. Our daughter is upstairs asleep at the moment.'

'It might be better if you stay down here with your wife,' tall said. 'Perhaps you could go and get your daughter, bring her down here. At least then you'll all be together.'

I didn't understand what was going on. Why would we want to bring Rose downstairs? Why wake her when she was sleeping? I started to panic. Started to worry that these two men weren't actually policemen at all. Started thinking that they might be in on it. One of them might be the intruder.

'Neil, I'm worried,' I said. 'I don't want these men in our house anymore. I'm scared.'

'We only want to have a quick look around,' tall said. 'Just for your, and our, peace-of-mind.'

'I want you to leave,' I said. The fear was starting to rise up inside of me. I felt prickles on the back of my neck. Felt like I was being chased by someone. I practically screamed at them. 'I want you to leave my house. Straight away!'

Michael ran over to Neil. Neil held him close. Told him to run up to bed and try to get some sleep. Michael did as he was told.

'Chris, they're only trying to help. They need to check the house to make sure it's safe.'

He turned to the tall one.

'Maybe I could check the house with you,' he said. 'I think

we might both be happier with that.'

He glanced at me to check whether I approved. Reluctantly I nodded.

It took them less than ten minutes to check the entire house. They reassured us that everything was secure and that they would pass by the door periodically for the rest of the night.

'It's probable that some of our colleagues may come by tomorrow in the daylight. Just to check the outside. Make sure there's nothing we've missed on the windows or doors.'

I thought about school the next day. I didn't think I could deal with it, not if the police were coming round. I worried how Margaret would be with that. Worried what she might think.

Neil walked with the two police officers to the front door, I stayed by the sofa, staring at the fallen wine glass.

I heard their muffled voices. It was hard to make out what they were saying, but I was pretty sure I heard Neil say: "hit on the head" and "drinking".

CHAPTER TEN

The police searched our garden the next day, and found nothing.

I calmed down a little, although I still hadn't slept much. Neil took the day off. We kept Michael at home too. I watched the police through a window, hunting around outside, and determined to get control of myself.

Despite being only a fraction over five and a half feet tall, I had always been quite a strong person. When we first got together Neil used to call me "the mighty atom". Even at school I had been feisty.

The skateboarding incident had knocked it all out of me. I had allowed myself to become a different person. One who jumped at the slightest sound. One who expected the worst around every corner. But that really wasn't me

I decided to buy a diary.

When I was ten years-old our family cat died. I was heartbroken. Dad told me "write your thoughts down in a diary — it helps you to make sense of things". So that's what I did. I wrote and wrote. About boring, every-day things, about arguments with Mum and Dad, about schoolgirl crushes. Tears and fun. When the diary ran out of pages I bought a notebook and wrote in that too.

I wrote diaries and journals almost every day until I was about fifteen years old.

It had been a good idea then, and I reckoned it would be a good idea now. I wanted to make sense of what was happening to me. Of what I had been allowing myself to become.

Neil offered to come into town with me but I wanted to go alone. I could see he was tired. The last few weeks had taken their toll on him as well as me. He'd been snappy with the kids about silly little things. More grumpy with me. I knew he wanted me to move on from what had happened. I could see he was struggling to cope with it at times. It made me realise how strong I had been before. Perhaps even strong for Neil. He wasn't falling apart, not like I felt I was, but he was struggling. I wondered whether I might have been his strength too.

'Neil, we should do something nice,' I said.

His face had an "are you serious" look about it.

'I think we need it,' I said. 'The weather has been getting warmer lately, why don't we have a barbecue — get Abi and Oliver over. It could be for my birthday?'

'It's not your birthday for another five weeks,' Neil said. 'Is it really a good idea to have people round, you know, at the moment?'

'It's exactly the right time, Neil. I think I need it. I think we need it. Take our minds off all of this.'

He wasn't convinced. I tried a different tack.

'And I think it would be just what Michael and Rose need, having Jessica and Josie here. It would let them know that everything is normal. That Mum and Dad are just as they always have been.'

Neil gazed up at the ceiling. I wasn't sure if he was thinking, or looking at where the kids' rooms were.

'I'll let you do the cooking?' I said.

When I arrived back home with my diary Neil was in a happier frame of mind.

'I've spoken to Abi,' he said. 'She's going to check with Oli and come back to us,' he smiled.

I realised it was the first time I'd seen him smile for quite a while.

'I suggested this coming weekend,' he said. 'The weather

forecast looks good.'

'I'll write it in my diary,' I said.

The night before the barbecue I had a little more to drink than usual, just to calm me down. Abi and Oli were old friends, the best, but I still needed an extra glass or so. Apart from day to day stuff at the school, this was the first social occasion since the attack.

I dropped off to sleep thinking that maybe we should get in another couple of bottles, just for the barbecue.

It's very windy. I can hear a rushing sound, like waves or a gale. It's not cold though. Will that smell give me away? Will it stay on the ground after I've gone? On the bushes? Like a dog who sprays his territory? This is my territory.

I can hear her now. And I can also hear... what? Panting? Heavy panting. Is that her? These damned bushes are in the way. She is coming fast now. She doesn't know I am here. She isn't expecting me.

I step out from behind the bushes, look behind me and all around. Only us. I brush my sleeves, make it look like I was just looking for something. Just out for a walk. Are my sleeves brown?

She sees me. Hesitates for a moment — then a smile. Does she recognise me? I think she does. I think she knows who I am. I smile too.

I woke up in a sweat, heart thumping. My head felt crushed, probably from the wine, and my left thigh hurt.

My first thought was to wake Neil, but I stopped myself, lay there for a few minutes and tried to bring my breathing under control. Consciously tried to slow my heart rate, gently stretched my neck a little. The smell buds (if that's what they are called) in my nose were working overtime. I had always thought that the only thing to smell in the morning, in the bedroom, was stuffiness and stale air. How wrong I was.

Sweet floral scents came to me, then thick, sugary smells. Chemical odours too. I was sure I could smell the paste holding the wallpaper to the walls.

I rolled out of bed, trying not to wake Neil, and pulled on my bath-robe. My diary was downstairs, so that's where I headed. The third step from the bottom creaked and a cold shiver hit my neck. *Come on, Christine. Pull yourself together!*

I had left the diary on the small glass table next to the sofa. I was sure there had been a pen resting on it when I'd gone up to bed. Now the pen was on the floor. Had Neil come up after me or before? I couldn't remember. Had he read my diary? He had sworn that he wouldn't, that he knew it was my space for trying to get back on track. Perhaps it had been Michael.

I hadn't written much anyway, yet. But it was the principle. I eventually supposed that the pen might simply have rolled off the diary in the night.

I wrote down everything that I could remember about the dream. About the wind and the rushing noise. I tried not to assume things or jump to any conclusions. I just tried to write about it as objectively as possible. As though I was just an observer.

Technically, of course, I was just an observer *of* the dream. I was most definitely not just an observer *in* the dream. I wrote what I could about the girl. Her face was more abstract than anything, but I had sensed that she knew me — or at least, wasn't too scared of me to make her want to run. I remembered my brown sleeves and how I came out from the bushes brushing them off. I couldn't remember what the smell was that I thought I had been scenting the area with. Also, it felt significant that I hadn't attacked her. That I had woken up before anything like that. So I made a note of that too.

As my pen moved across the page I could feel the tension lifting from my shoulders. I felt as though I was doing something proactive, rather than just being a victim of something. It had been the right thing to do, to come down and write about it, rather than wake Neil. I would maybe try to not even mention the dream to him.

I wrote about how worried I was feeling. I just couldn't understand why I was dreaming about hurting people. Hurting girls. I worried, still, that it might somehow spill out into my school life. That I would have to stop working with children.

I wrote in large letters, taking up half of one page, the words: BE STRONG. Underneath that I wrote: IT MUST STOP!

I read them back and thought about the girl in the dream. Wondered whether I should have written: *I* MUST STOP!

The stair creaked.

'Neil! You scared me.'

'Sorry,' he said. 'What are you doing down here? It's six o'clock.'

'I had the dream again.' Inside I kicked myself for mentioning it so quickly. 'I didn't want to disturb you. I'm just writing a few notes. I'll probably be up again soon.'

He shrugged and rubbed the side of his nose with his fist, then pushed his head back and yawned loudly.

'You go back to bed,' I said. 'I'll be up soon.'

He nodded and plomped back up the stairs. His footsteps sounded heavier than normal. I hoped he was OK. The bedroom door squeaked and I heard the door of the en-suite slide open. The toilet flushed — and then all was quiet.

I sat still for a few minutes, listening to the silence. Then I closed my diary and wandered through to the kitchen. I was far too awake to go back to bed. It was way too early to start preparing things for the barbecue that evening.

I thought about opening a bottle of wine.

And decided to start on the barbecue after all.

CHAPTER ELEVEN

Oliver and Abi had been our closest friends for more than ten years, both physically and emotionally. I once suspected Neil of having a fling with Abi. They had worked together some years earlier and became very close. Too close, I thought. He always denied that anything had happened between them. For a while I tried to catch Abi out. Asking subtle questions about Neil; checking dates and so on. I never found anything out, and shortly afterwards Abi left the company to have Jessica. I never asked Abi straight out whether anything had happened. Maybe I should have.

I thought about getting too close with Oli, but it wasn't in me. He was a nice guy, but not like that. In the end I just had to let it go and assume that Neil had told me the truth.

The front doorbell rang at four o'clock.

Neil was already outside in the back garden, with firelighters and briquettes, trying to start the barbecue with some very old matches. Michael and Rose had been like demented pixies all day, running around everywhere, shouting and laughing. I made them tidy their rooms but hadn't bothered checking them. Some battles were just not worth fighting, especially with how I was feeling. And I knew how messy Oli's and Abi's kids' rooms were.

Jessica was almost eight years old and Josie was the same age as Michael. They never seemed to tire of playing with each other, despite being at school together all day.

I went to the front door, demented pixies following at my heels.

'Happy birthday!' Abi said, thrusting a wrapped present at me.

I had forgotten that I'd suggested to Neil that this could be an early birthday treat. They had obviously taken him at his word.

'But it's not for weeks yet!' I said.

'It's never too soon for birthday presents,' Oliver said. 'Happy birthday.'

They both kissed me. Josie and Jessica rushed in like water bursting through a dam. The floors thumped as the kids all charged upstairs. The rest of us made for the kitchen.

Outside Neil had his back to us. Small drifts of smoke circled up around him. I tapped on the kitchen window. He turned around, red faced and stressed. His face changed once he saw Oliver and Abi. He waved. Oliver made his way through the back door. A loud bump came through the ceiling.

'That'll be Michael,' I said. 'God only knows what he's doing.'

'Can I help?' Abi said.

'Yes, you can get yourself a drink. And fill me up while you're there please.' I drunk what was left in my wine glass and passed it to her. 'Red, with a little lemonade please.' I tapped on the window and made a drinking motion with my hand. Neil pointed at his glass and shook his head. Oli nodded and gave a thumbs up. 'And whatever Oli wants,' I said.

Abi poured the drinks. Her eyes flickered briefly over the scar on my forehead.

'So, how are you, Chris? You look great.'

She took a long sip of her drink and looked out of the kitchen window.

'I'm OK,' I said. 'You know.'

Obviously Abi didn't know. It was a stupid thing to say.

'I'm not always sleeping great,' I said. 'This helps,' I held up my wine glass, 'just at the moment.'

Abi smiled. 'I'm so sorry, Chris. That all this has happened to you. It's all so horrible.'

I wondered if she knew about the dreams. Surely Neil hadn't told them? I felt the heat in my cheeks. I would die if he had told them.

'I'm getting over it,' I said. 'Getting back to normal. You and Oli being here is so wonderful. It really helps.'

The back door opened and Oliver stepped in, a huge grin splitting his face.

'I've been sent in for some oil,' he said. 'To coat the ribs, apparently.'

I passed him the oil.

'How's it going out there?' I said. 'Has he set fire to the house yet?'

'Only the shed so far,' Oliver said. 'That's why he needs the oil, the house is more difficult to get going.'

Abi held out a drink for him.

'Come on Abi,' I said. 'Let's go and watch two grown men struggle with the cooking.'

We followed Oliver outside. It was very smoky. Neil looked up as we came closer. His eyes were red and streaming, and perspiration had formed on his forehead. He forced a smile, but his face told the whole story.

'Everything is going according to plan,' he said.

We smiled. It was clear that any plan had gone up in smoke long ago.

'All I need is the oil to coat the ribs and the cooking surface and we'll be away.'

Oliver passed the oil to Neil and hung around, while we retreated to the relative calm of the garden furniture to watch the entertainment. Neil poured some oil into a small bowl and produced a long handled brush from a small plastic case containing what looked like newly purchased cooking utensils. I had not seen them before. He dipped the brush into the oil and started brushing the metal grill of the barbecue. Instantly the brush sizzled as the synthetic hairs melted. Smoke billowed upward and the odour of burning nylon hit my nostrils.

Neil held the brush up in front of him, like a child whose ice-lolly had fallen from the stick halfway through licking it. The brush ends were frizzled and black. Neil and Oli surveyed the scene with the utmost seriousness. Abi and I cracked up laughing. We laughed so loud, even the kids tramped down to see what was going on.

'Dad's giving us a lesson on how to melt plastic on a barbecue just before putting food on it,' I said.

All four children inspected Neil's work. It held their interest for almost ten seconds before the call of electronic gadgets and games called them back upstairs.

'We'll be eating soon,' I shouted after them. 'Hopefully.'

Neil got to work with a wire brush and metal scraper. I prayed he would get all of the burned brush hairs off before cooking anything on it.

Ten minutes later he forked the first of several very dark sausages onto a plate.

'Who's first?' he said.

None of us answered his question. The sausages looked as though they had been through the worst of the flames. He resorted to putting everything on a large plate and told us to all help ourselves.

I nipped into the kitchen to get the salad and warm rolls. I also checked on the chicken drumsticks I had put in the oven just in case. I had bought a trifle for pudding and some chocolate mousses for the children.

This was all good for me. Allowing me to escape from myself for a while. Concentrate on something else. And it was nice spending time with Abi and Oli. Nice to see Neil in a more relaxed state. Apart from when he was burning the food.

Halfway through the evening I watched Abi watching Neil. I

spent some time watching Oli. He smiled at me.

I had quite a bit to drink during the meal. I probably didn't need it, but I had got into the habit of always having a drink, either in my hand or nearby, when I was at home.

I'd be fine soon. Once I'd got over it all. I wouldn't need a drink.

I would be fine.

Neil ate most of the burned food — I think so that the rest of us wouldn't have to. We ate all of the chicken drumsticks from the oven.

After we finished eating, the children were banished indoors so we could talk and drink some more. The smoke cleared and the afternoon warmth turned to an evening chill. It was almost dark when Oli looked at his watch.

'It's getting a bit late, guys,' he said. 'I hate to be a killjoy, but I need to be up reasonably early in the morning. I've got a match.'

Abi was a golf-widow. I was sure I wouldn't let Neil play as much golf as Oliver did.

'I suppose it is getting on a bit,' Neil said. 'I think I've had a bit more to drink than I intended, too. We don't want you having a sore head when you tee-off tomorrow.'

I hadn't had anywhere near enough to drink. I could quite happily have sat there for several more hours.

For the first time in weeks I felt happy. I enjoyed being with my friends. I enjoyed seeing Neil more himself. And I enjoyed the kids being occupied.

'Do you really have to go?' I said, holding my glass up. 'Is it really that late?'

Neil looked at me. A dark look. Maybe I had slurred my words. I didn't really care. I was having too much fun.

'It is the weekend,' I said.

'Sorry, birthday-girl,' Abi said. 'But we really should get going.'

I was going to remind her that it wasn't really my birthday — but it sounded sulky, even in my head. Oli opened the back door and shouted to Jessica and Josie to come down and get ready to go.

'I've had a lovely time,' I said. 'Thank you so much for coming,' I waved in the direction of the still smoldering barbecue, 'and for putting up with our burnt offerings.'

Oli came back to the table and grabbed his almost empty glass.

'A toast,' he said. 'To Christine: Happy birthday and a speedy journey on this road to full recovery.'

They all shouted "Happy Birthday" and then started singing the song to me.

They were almost at the final "happy birthday to you" — when all four children tumbled out of the back door. I saw them first, I think. It took a moment before the image registered. But when it did — that was when my heart stopped.

The sweet, sickly smell of chemicals smacked into me. A grey fog drifted in and a swirling torrent rushed around my ears. My hair blew wild and my arms were buffeted by the wind. The sound was deafening. Instantly I knew where I was. The only thing that was missing were the bushes in front of my eyes.

I tried to stand up but faltered. My eyes felt as though they had doubled in size, my heart felt like it was constricting inside me. I had the sensation that all the blood in my body was rushing toward my feet, and my head was suddenly so light I thought I was going to fall over. I dropped my wine-glass.

As it splintered on the patio, shards of glass and droplets of wine hit my ankles. I forced the scream down, but the gurgling noise that came from my throat must have sounded worse. The singing stopped and all eyes turned, first to me, and then to what I was staring at — Josie.

Neil quickly came to me, put his hands on my shoulders. I was shaking, I had no control over it. Josie looked as though she was about to cry.

'We're grown ups,' Josie said, pulling a jacket, taken from my wardrobe, tightly around her body. 'We've put make-up on too.'

It was obvious that they had raided our bedroom cupboards. Michael wore one of Neil's ties, even Jessica and Rose had make-up on.

But it was Josie. She was the one that had caused the reaction deep inside me. Caused me to feel like my whole body was shutting down.

Josie had taken me into my dream.

CHAPTER TWELVE

In the background I heard Neil's voice.

'What's wrong, Chris? What's the matter?'

I fell back onto the chair, almost tipped it over. It sounded as though hundreds of trees were blowing in a gale, but I could still hear Neil's voice over the noise. I looked about to see if the trees nearby were bending against the wind.

'She knows me,' I said. 'She's coming to me. She knows me.'

I gripped the table to steady myself. It started shaking too. Josie started crying. Oli went to her, Abi reached out for my arm.

'Chris,' she said. 'What's happening. Are you OK?'

The horrendous noise calmed a little. Oli stood in front of Josie. I could no longer see her. I started coughing and sneezing. It was as though my body was trying to rid itself of the overpowering smell of chemicals. The fog cleared and I became aware of being in the back-garden, sitting at the table — shaking.

'I'm so sorry,' I said. 'I am so, so sorry.'

'Should I call the doctor, Neil?' Abi said.

Neil shook his head. 'I don't think so. I think she's OK. Would you mind getting her a glass of water from the kitchen though?'

Did he think I was drunk? Was that what he thought was going on? Well, let him think that. It was better that than the truth.

My mind rushed through images. The girl in the dream. The fog. Josie. Had I dreamt of attacking Josie? My best friend's daughter? One of my son's closest friends?

Had I raped Josie? Was that what was happening in my mind?

Something inside was telling me I should go to her, to make sure she was OK, but I couldn't. I tried to push my body to move, but it wouldn't. My hand, clamped to the table, was as paralysed as the rest of me. Apart from the shaking.

My mind, though, was far from paralysed. It tore through everything that had happened. I had been happily sat outside in the safety of my own garden, when everything changed. Physically, everything changed. Surely Abi had seen the trees blowing. Surely Neil had heard the howling wind. Surely Oli had been as lost in the fog as I had.

My mind shifted beyond that. How would I move forward?

What would I say?

I didn't think I could tell Neil — or anyone — what was really going on inside my head. The school wouldn't want me to continue working there. Abi and Oli wouldn't want me as their friend, when in my head and in my sleep I had attacked their little girl.

The shaking turned to shivering, but I wasn't cold. I had goosebumps on my arms and up the back of my neck. I was petrified. I had never known fear like it. Even when I was being attacked I hadn't felt fear like this. Suddenly I realised I no longer had control of my body or my mind. If I couldn't stop these thoughts coming into my head and becoming reality to me, how would I live?

The fingers of my clamped hand sprung open and the table shuddered free. I forced my body to move, and stumbled to the back door. Broken glass crunched under my feet. Oli moved Josie out of the way and the other children scattered to let me through. I told my legs to run, but they would only stagger. I pulled myself up the stairs. The third step squeaked as I stepped on it, under my breath I told it to fuck off. I slammed the bedroom door shut behind me and collapsed on the floor, next to the bed.

Our bedroom window was slightly open and I heard the

commotion I had left behind outside. Josie was sniffling and Jessica asked Abi what was wrong with her sister. Then she asked her what was wrong with me. Neil's voice drifted up. I had forgotten how soothing his voice could be.

'Christine's not been feeling very well recently,' he said. 'Since... you know.'

Not feeling soothed, I half crawled, half walked to the en-suite and locked the door behind me.

I felt so sorry for Josie. But why on earth had she dressed up like that? What had made her do it? Why did she choose that jacket, why that make-up?

I heard Neil again.

'It wasn't you Josie,' Neil said. 'You haven't done anything wrong.'

I imagined Abi stroking Josie's head. Maybe Oli was making sure Jessi was OK. Neil trying to calm everyone down, reassure our friends, trying not to be embarrassed by his drunken wife.

'What a fuck up!' I whispered. 'What a total fuck up!'

I slumped to the floor and sat my elbows on my knees.

I knew I was a little drunk. Maybe even a lot. But I reckoned I was always able to function when I was pissed. I always knew what was happening and what I was doing. I reckoned.

My face felt tingly.

I buried my head in my hands and rubbed my cheeks and forehead. Ran my hands over the back of my neck. Tears dropped onto the floor between my legs.

That was the first time I wished I was dead. In my head I prayed to a god I didn't believe in. Prayed that He would take me. That I would die and it would all end.

I was to pray it again in the weeks and months that followed. Many times.

Eventually I heard the final goodbyes and apologies. The front door slammed. Muffled voices below told me that Neil was speaking to Michael and Rose. I heard Neil's footsteps on the stairs.

A knock at the bedroom door.

'Chris,' he said. 'Chris, are you OK?'

I started shaking. The bedroom door creaked open. I wished that every damn thing in the house didn't make such a bloody noise. Neil tapped on the door of the en-suite.

'Chris, are you OK? They've gone now. The kids are getting ready for bed. Are you alright?'

Neil's voice sounded soothing to me now. A tear dripped to the end of my nose and tickled it. I rubbed it away with the back of my hand.

'I'll be out in a minute,' I said. I tried to shake the feelings away. Stretched my neck and looked up toward the ceiling. I pulled a wodge of toilet paper from the roll and dabbed at my eyes. I didn't want to look in the mirror. My head was swimmy, and for once I regretted having had so much to drink.

'Chris, are you coming out? Are you OK?'

I wasn't sure if he was anxious or annoyed. Probably both.

'Just a minute.' I did my best to sound in control, but when I did look in the mirror I almost lost it again. I was a wreck. My cheeks were blotchy. Red and white with an unhealthy dose of black mascara thrown in. I wasn't big on lipstick, but what little I had was now crumbled, dry and sparse. My eyes were completely washed-out.

I needed Neil now. I flicked the lock on the door.

'Come in,' I said.

As Neil came in, I put my face in my hands. He put his hands on my shoulders, then put his arms around me. He didn't speak, just held me. I felt the warmth of his ear against mine. He held me for nearly a minute before speaking.

'Chris, what happened? What was it downstairs?'

He stepped back and tried to ease me out of the en-suite. I let him. We sat on the bed and I looked into his face. He smiled at me.

'I'm sorry,' I said. 'Were Abi and Oli OK? I'm so sorry.'

'They were fine. Oli said it was probably my cooking that made you feel ill. They were just worried about you, that's all. Abi wanted to call the doctor, but I said you were probably just a bit off colour. Do you want me to call a doctor?'

I shook my head.

'Neil, it was Josie. You know how she was all dressed up. She looked older, but also she looked — different. Something happened to me the moment I saw Josie.'

I shivered and looked behind me to see if the bedroom window was still open. It wasn't. Neil was always closing the damned windows.

'What happened?' Neil said.

'She triggered something in me. The dream. You know the horrible dream I keep having? Well Josie triggered it. But this time it was different.'

Neil shook his head and frowned.

'I don't understand,' he said.

'The dream I've been having, where I attack someone — the sight of Josie brought some of those things from the dream to me. It was as though I was transported somewhere. It was as though I was dreaming downstairs. I could hear similar noises from the dream, feel the blowing wind, smell the same smells. Didn't you hear the wind? Didn't you see the fog?' I wiped the back of my hand over my itchy eyebrows. 'And then a girl. I saw a girl and I saw her face.' I swallowed hard and looked away. I didn't feel like I could look into Neil's eyes anymore. Not while I was talking about this. He touched my hand and held my fingers. 'The face in the dream downstairs was like … was like Josie's.'

'But you were looking at Josie,' he said.

I shook my head. 'Josie was the trigger, I think. Then she was lost in the fog, like everything else. And that's when I saw this other girl. Saw her face. The face like Josie's.

Neither of us said anything for a moment. After about ten seconds Neil let my fingers slip from his.

'What do you mean "was like" Josie's?'

'Their faces were almost the same.'

'So are you saying that the dream you've been having, the one where you attack a girl, she looks like Josie?'

'Not exactly,'

'So she looks a bit like Josie?'

'That's not really what I'm saying either.'

'Chris, help me out here. What exactly are you saying?'

'Josie isn't like the girl I've been dreaming about. I've had the dream three times now, each time a little clearer than before. I still haven't properly seen the face of the girl in the dream, but I know it is nothing like Josie's.'

Neil shrugged his shoulders.

'Neil, Josie isn't like the girl I've been dreaming about. The dream I had just now, downstairs in our back garden. That was a different dream. Same place, same sounds, same smells — but not the same girl. This girl, the one who looked a bit like Josie, this girl was *another* one.'

The bedroom door burst open. Rose ran in, tears pouring down her cheeks.

'Michael says I've got to clean my teeth first,' she said. 'But I got washed first. He should clean his teeth before me.'

Neil took her hand and led her out of our bedroom.

'It doesn't matter who cleans their teeth first,' he said. 'As long as you both clean them.'

I watched him take hold of our little girl's hand — and I cried.

CHAPTER THIRTEEN

Abi rang me the next day to see how I was. I recognised the number and let it go to answerphone. I couldn't face speaking to her so soon. She left a lovely message.

I rang her the day after that.

'I'm so sorry, Abs. It must have been the booze and the painkillers, you know? Is Josie OK?'

'She's fine, Chris. We're all just so worried about you.'

She started crying, which surprised me. I started too, which didn't. I didn't mention the dreams. Or that Josie had been some kind of trigger.

Abi was a star. She made me feel better, made me laugh and made me think there was nothing to worry about. She made me feel good about Neil, and we both laughed about his culinary skills at the barbecue. She said how wonderful the evening had been and how sorry she was that I had been "unwell". Bless her.

The dreams and visions started coming every day. Sometimes several times a day. I spent my days twitching at every gust and breeze, and my nights awake in bed shifting from one position to another, and then back again. My eyes became dark holes with painted red rims.

I was a zombie around the house. Neil and the kids made every excuse they could not to be with me. The kid's homework must have been at an all time high. And if Neil went to bed any earlier I'd have had to wake him up for his dinner.

The dreams weren't always complete. Sometimes just brief snatches or sensations. A whiff of something on the air would make me turn my head to see who was there. No one, of course. Or I would just pick up a noise. Distant, but definite.

I was taking more and more days off work. I wanted desperately to go in, mostly because I missed the routine of real life. But also to make sure Matthew wasn't getting in with Margaret. From somewhere within me, a competitive streak had emerged and it now seemed vaguely important to beat Matthew to a job I had never really wanted in the first place.

When Neil and I did come together, his eyes would dart everywhere but straight at mine.

He was full of helpful comments though.

'Chris, I think you should maybe visit a doctor.'

I knew that he meant it for the best, but it pissed me off. Did he mean for my mind or for the pain in my leg? Or was he just exasperated? Maybe he meant it for my drinking.

'What for?' I said. I was in the mood for being moody.

At last he looked me square in the eye. No hesitation.

'Because of these dreams — and the sensations that come with them.' He folded his arms. 'You keep smelling things; you hear and feel things, things like the wind and the rustling of branches. You are having day dreams when you're not even asleep. Something is wrong Chris, from when you got attacked; where you hit your head. Something is wrong at the moment. I'm sure the doctor will know what it is, you know, a loose connection or whatever. But I think you should go and I think you should tell him everything that's happened.'

That pissed me off even more, mainly because I knew he was right.

But even the thought of going to the doctor made me have butterflies. I didn't want him to find anything badly wrong inside my head. And I couldn't face telling anyone else about the things I was dreaming about. I was a school teacher — at a Primary school. It wouldn't look good.

'I'll come with you,' Neil said. 'If you want me to?'

By now I was writing so often in my diary, my hand ached. But no matter how much I wrote, I still couldn't make sense of what was happening to me. I wanted to ring Dad and talk to him about it, but him and Mum had been so upset about the attack, and I didn't want to add to their worry.

Dad had always had a way of making things seem better than I thought they were. It was more than perspective. He somehow managed to make things softer. More cushioned.

Neil was more of a "let's get on with it" kind of man. Solid and reliable, but very little softness. When I needed a hard-man, Neil was there. But I didn't think I needed that, not yet.

Eventually I caved in and drove to their house to see them.

'I think maybe you should go to the doctor,' Dad said.

Inside I felt disappointed. The only outward sign was an involuntary expulsion of breath. It wasn't the cushioning I had been hoping for.

'If I go to see the doctor, it's like admitting that there's a problem.'

Dad looked at Mum. That was the only answer I needed. So much for "Dad always making things better". He didn't even point me in the direction of a diary.

Mum rubbed her eyes. If she started blubbing I knew it would set me off too.

'They're being great about it at school,' I said. 'Margaret says she's fine with me having days off here and there. They just want me to get better. We all just want it to get better.'

I hadn't mentioned the dreams to Mum and Dad. Mum was too close to the edge anyway. I didn't want to push her all the way over. I thought about getting Dad alone and just talking to him. He would be OK with that. I held the thought in reserve, just in case. I was sure that "cushion" was still in there somewhere.

'I'll come with you if you like?' Dad said. 'To the doc's.'

I shook my head, while my heart screamed out 'YES'.

'Don't worry, Dad.' I said. 'I'll sort out an appointment. I'll be fine.'

He looked at Mum again, and smiled. She forced one too.

CHAPTER FOURTEEN

The next day my doctor prescribed Citalopram.

'They're anti-depressants,' he said. 'They will make you feel better. They block the anxiety from getting through to your brain. And they're not addictive.'

'I'm not depressed.'

He smiled.

'And I'm not anxious.'

'These are often prescribed in situations like this,' he said.

'Situations like what?'

'Like yours.'

I had always trusted Doctor Jones. But now, I wasn't so sure. I'd read dozens of stories in the weekly magazines about people addicted to their anti-depressants. I wasn't sure I wanted that worry.

But I needed to do something. I had noticed my hands shaking when I lifted my coffee mug (or wine glass), and the furrows on my brow looked like they were in danger of becoming permanent. The kids needed a better mum, and Neil needed a better wife. And I still wanted that to be me. But anti-depressants? I opened my mouth to throw out my next objection, but the doctor saw it coming.

'Do you have internet access at home?' he said.

I shut my mouth and nodded.

'There are some websites I'd like you to visit. You might find them helpful.'

He pulled a pink post-it note from a multicoloured stack and scribbled on it. He stuck the post-it on the table in front of me.

'*Moodworkout.com*?' I said. 'And *victimstrength.org*?'

My tone of voice said it all.

'I think you should consider both of them. The Citalopram

may take a couple of weeks to kick in and these websites might help you get better quicker.'

He might as well have written down *you'reanangrybitch.com* and *stopkillingpeoplewithyourstares.org* as well.

'I don't feel like a victim,' I said, controlling just such a stare. I obviously wasn't in a position to disagree with the mood thing.

'That's really great,' he said. 'But you have been a "victim" of crime. There is a difference. This website will introduce you to others who have had a similar experience — which you may find helpful.'

I stopped controlling the stare.

'I don't want to "share my experience" with other people. I've moved on from it. The only reason I came here today was because my father and my husband suggested it.'

Odd that I put Dad before Neil.

'And I think they were right,' he said.

My killer stare obviously wasn't working. Either that or doctors were becoming stupid.

'It is important to recognise that others have gone through what you are going through. That you're not in this alone, so-to-speak,' he said.

Obviously stupid.

'No problem,' I said. 'I'll check them out when I get home.'

If I had said — "when I get home I'm going to run across the ceiling in flippers" — it would have sounded more believable. We both knew I was talking bollocks. He tried a different tack.

'These dreams you're getting may well be as a result of post-traumatic stress,' he said. 'If they continue or get worse you should consider going to see a counsellor — someone who is trained in helping people overcome these issues. I can recommend someone if you like?'

I shook my head. I couldn't speak because I felt dizzy. I knew he'd *said* "counsellor", but I'd *heard* "psychiatrist".

'OK,' he said. 'But I want you to come back to see me in about four weeks time, I can make the appointment for you now.'

'Why will you need to see me again?'

'I need to make sure the Citalopram are working OK, and that you aren't having any side effects.'

'I though you said they weren't addictive?' I said.

'They aren't. But they have some mild side effects. And a month will be about the right time to make sure your head is healing properly.'

I was about to punch him, when I realised he was talking about the scars.

'What side effects?'

'You might feel a touch nauseous and you may have increased sweating. There may even be some sleep problems.'

I didn't even go there.

I threw the pink post-it away within five paces of the health centre.

I took the first tablet as soon as I got home, before reading the notes in the box which said I should take them first thing in the morning. Off to a great start.

Neil's face changed when I told him I was now on anti-depressants. He seemed pleased. More relaxed somehow. That wasn't the Neil I knew. He wouldn't even take a paracetamol for a headache. He loathed medicines and drugs. Believed in self medication by exercise and positive thought. He was too strong for tablets.

'They aren't addictive,' I said, thinking that that would be uppermost in his healthy mind.

The look on his face told me that the thought hadn't even occurred to him.

'Do they work straight away?' he said. 'Or is there a delay?'

'A few weeks,' I said. 'I've got to go back to the doctor in a month.'

Neil nodded. His eyes glazed over and he suddenly wasn't there with me.

'Are you OK?' I said.

My question seemed to reach him slowly. Then he was back.

'I'm fine,' he said. 'I was just worried about you. I'm pleased you went. I think it was definitely the right thing to do.'

I winced as a thudding pain jumped inside my thigh. Neil missed it. It thumped again. I kicked myself for not mentioning it to the stupid doctor.

I had never been in this situation before.

I don't mean the situation of having been mugged, or hit with a skateboard or even being on anti-depressants (although I never had been in any of those situations).

I had never had the feelings that I was now regularly experiencing. Bizarre opposites of absolute power and strength coming from deep wells of anger, surging up from within me, contrasting with utter weakness arising from not knowing how to deal with the feelings, not knowing if the mugger was still after me, and not knowing when my night frights might end.

All my 'taking control' actions hadn't seemed to help much. Diaries and positive thought had struggled to keep up with my inner movements, over which I seemed to have less and less control.

Getting back to school seemed only to serve as a reminder that, somewhere within me, I had the ability to attack (and god only knew what else?) a child. A girl. More than one!

I knew they were only dreams. It seemed far fetched to consider that I could actually attack and injure a child. But with the anger inside me, coming from nowhere, and the episode with Josie at the barbecue when it seemed like all reality had changed, I had no real idea what I might be capable of at all.

I could smell the slightest changes on the air. My arms and legs felt more powerful than ever before. And I was left feeling more out of control than ever before.

After popping the tablet I decided I would do whatever it took to get my life back.

On a sheet of paper I wrote down everything I wanted to accomplish.

1. Get control of mind
2. Show Neil that I'm in control
3. Get back to school
4. Put skateboard twat out of my mind
5. Come off the tablets!

I didn't set myself a deadline, because I intended to start immediately.

1. Get control of my mind.

I started by trying to analyse what had happened to me when the "dream" at the barbecue had kicked in.

The trigger had been Josie. But had anything else happened before I saw her? I remembered drinking the wine, I remembered everyone singing "Happy Birthday", but was there anything else? We had all finished eating, all of the chicken had gone. There were still a few of Neil's cremated sausages left. The smells. Barbecue smoke, burned food.

I made a note on the back of the sheet of paper. "Smells".

And then Josie. There was something about her that had launched the full-scale onslaught of the "dream", complete with blowing gale and demented trees.

It was the fact that when I had looked at her — she hadn't been Josie. She'd looked older and different. Still a child, but an older child. She had looked like someone else.

I started to wonder if what I was experiencing was some kind of premonition. Not that I believed in any of that stuff. But maybe the trauma to my head from the skateboard and the pavement had caused some sort of lucid area of my brain to open up. Maybe my mind was seeing things that could happen. An overactive imagination of some sort. I wrote "imagination/premonition/lucid brain/future possibilities".

I immediately felt a lift in my heart. If all it was was just my imagination on overdrive, that was great. I could deal with that.

I let this possibility sink in, and instantly all the dreams and visions became less real. I saw them for what they were. A product of stress and trauma and a couple of large bashes on the bonce. They were nothing more than dreams and flashes of imagination — seemingly very real at the time — but with no foundation in reality at all.

I re-read the few words I had written and turned the sheet back over to my original five goals. I added one more.

1a. Stop drinking.

I leaned back against the soft sofa and shut my eyes. For the first time in a while I didn't hesitate before closing them. My cheeks felt warm and I smiled.

I'm not sure what happened next. I remember the sweet sickly smell like a punch, and I remember hearing the third stair creak. But I don't know which of those came first.

I spun round on the sofa and a whirlwind pulled my hair back from my face. The pain in my thigh screamed.

A girl stood on the third stair. A shroud of mist enveloped her making her features difficult to comprehend. I stumbled backwards off the sofa, my eyes fixed on her. For a moment she seemed to smile. A second later her head jolted back and I felt the scar on the back of my head throb. A second after that, nothing. She was gone.

I stayed on the floor, staring at the stairs. I felt damp on my face as though it had been sprayed with a fine mist. I felt relieved that I could feel my heart pounding away in my chest, letting me know it was still there and working — overtime. No smell, no wind, no pain. My mouth was open and I heard a scream I thought could have been mine. And then nothing.

When I woke up I was lying on my back on the floor. The sheet of paper with my goals lay beside me. The pen underneath me.

For a few moments I didn't move at all, apart from the involuntary up and down of my chest with each breath. I was surprised how deep and long my breaths were. Calm, almost.

Then the dull, constant pulse of pain in my thigh reminded me it was there. My forearms ached but felt tremendously powerful at the same time. It reminded me of the feeling I'd get after helping Dad prune the roses in the garden when I was little. The repetitive snipping of the tough twigs making my arms ache, but wanting to carry on to please Dad (and to watch all the dead-heads tumble to the ground).

The back of my neck ached too and a snapshot of the girl on the stair with her head thrust backwards zipped in and out of my mind. I lifted my head off the carpet a little. It felt like whiplash. My shoulders felt tender. And then the pain in my thigh shouted at me.

I reached over and grabbed the sheet of paper and held it up.

I lay my head back on the floor and looked up at my list of goals and I realised that I probably had more of a problem than I had thought.

The clock showed 11:30 am. I had been on the floor, either asleep or unconscious, for about 15 minutes.

It was possible that I had simply fallen asleep when I'd leaned back against the sofa and shut my eyes. Possible that I was so exhausted that I had fallen into unconsciousness in an instant. And then I had dreamt the smell and the creaking stair. I had dreamt the vision of the girl standing there. A dream like that would be sure to make me thrash about a bit. No wonder I had ended up on the floor. And that must have been what woke me, enough to realise I was on the floor and there was no girl and no whirlwind or sweet sickly smell.

But what if I hadn't fallen asleep?

I propped myself up on my elbows and scanned the room. Everything seemed OK. The sofa was between me and the stairs, so I couldn't see them. I would have to make more of an effort for that. I knew I wouldn't see anyone on the stairs. But still I hesitated a little before standing up.

Stairs clear, living room clear, head clear.

The sheet of paper in my hand felt like just that — a sheet of paper. I realised how insubstantial my attempt to repair that situation had been.

A few sentences on a single sheet of paper.

I needed to do more.

CHAPTER FIFTEEN

I was used to being in control of my own mind — mostly.

Of course, like everyone, I 'lost it' every now and then. Usually with Neil, or the kids. But generally I was pretty much in control.

As a teacher, control is important. I don't mean in a repressive way. When you're stood before thirty or so kids who are shouting at each other, shoving and laughing, passing notes and generally doing everything they can to put you off, it's important to be able to control a classroom appropriately. And it's even more important to be able to control yourself.

Apart from the obvious feelings I was experiencing from seeing visions in my living room, and from brutalising girls in my sleep, I was also trying to deal with the feeling of fear. Fear of losing control completely. I had been pushing the feelings down. But I knew that lurking somewhere within me was the real fear that I might actually not be able to combat or stop what was happening to me. I wasn't sure how to deal with this enemy, because the enemy seemed to be my own mind. And I had no idea how I could fight that.

'You need a "constant" to hold on to,' Neil had said to me once.

He'd said it during an argument. We were arguing about the guttering. During heavy rain, water poured over the gutter and slammed down onto our living-room window. I told him it needed sorting out and he said he'd look at it — which I naturally took to mean he'd fix it. Months later, and we still had Niagra pounding at our window when it rained.

'You were going to fix it!' I reminded him.

'I was going to look at it,' he reminded me.

And so the argument progressed.

I became more and more wound up and angry with him because he seemed to be totally relaxed and unconcerned — and I wanted him to be angry too!

'How can you be so calm?' I didn't scream it — but it was close.

'Because I always hold on to a "constant",' he said.

At the time I think I was ready to kick him really hard somewhere very soft. He smiled at me before I followed through.

'You need a "constant" to hold on to,' he said. 'So that you can pull yourself through shitty situations.'

I wasn't sure if he was talking about the argument, or something more serious (like us). I held onto the kick and threw instead a well placed 'what the fuck are you talking about?'

'Although we're having a shitty argument,' he said 'I know that you love me — and that I love you. That's my constant.' Another smile.

At the time it killed the argument dead and wrapped an emergency blanket around my angry heart.

Looking back, I'm surprised I didn't knock him out for being so arrogant.

I thought about my current situation and deemed it shitty enough to require a "constant".

But knowing that I was loved by my family and friends, although wonderful, wasn't enough to pull me through this. Because I was fighting something from within I felt I needed something from within to bring to the battle. But there didn't seem to be anything in me that was constant at the moment. Since the skateboard attack everything seemed chaotic. That was the whole point. There wasn't a "constant".

Except that there was.

My sense of smell.

The one thing that had happened right from the start of all this, and had remained with me throughout, was my heightened sense of smell. Every aroma and every scent on the wind had hit me with an intense rush, sometimes good, sometimes bad. I was convinced that I had even been able to smell things that wouldn't ordinarily be picked up by other people. Perhaps only animals.

And every time I dreamed, or had the visions or experienced whatever it was I was experiencing, the sweet, sickly smell was there too, pulling at my senses. It was even possible, I thought, that the smell was a precursor to the dreams — that maybe the smell was the thing that opened up the dark curtains of my mind to the horrors not so deep within.

If I could find a way to control my sense of smell — that would provide my "constant".

I certainly wasn't going to go back to the doctor. He had said that my sense of smell would return to normal over time.

'Just enjoy it while you've got it,' the doctor had said. 'Only don't get too close to anything unpleasant.'

Doctors and policemen... I had thought at the time ...what wankers. Unkind, I know, but I wasn't myself then.

And I obviously still wasn't.

I remembered reading about antique vinaigrettes (not the salad dressing). Little silver ornamented bottles for carrying around sweet smelling perfume, like potpourris or smelling-salts or something like that. People wore them around their neck in the days when sewage was a more common sight in the street. Just so they would always have something pleasant to smell. Obviously things like that were necessary back then.

I could surely make my own. A small bottle of perfume, or maybe a little bottle of whiskey with the lid off. That way I could really numb things if I needed to.

Garlic might do the trick. I had read in one of my magazines that *Roger Daltrey* would eat a clove of garlic to clear his sinuses if he had a cold. If garlic was strong enough to clear a cold it could be just the aroma I needed to clear my head.

I wondered what would happen if I had a cold. Surely my sense of smell would be wiped out by that. If only I had a permanent cold.

A cold…

I ran upstairs as quickly as I could. In the bathroom sunshine poured through the frosted glass windows. Twisted shards of sunlight mottled the tiled walls. In better times it would have looked beautiful. I couldn't have cared less. Instead I yanked open the bathroom cabinet, pushed aside the empty paracetamol boxes and found the little blue jar with the green screw-top lid. "Vicks VapoRub". Absolutely bizarre and extraordinarily effective for clearing the sinuses. And what a smell.

I remembered Mum gently dabbing it under my nose when I was little and had a cold, so I bought a jar for Michael when he came down with the sniffles.

I unscrewed the lid and immediately the smell surrounded me. I knew that, with my heightened sense of smell, I wouldn't need much of it. I dipped my forefinger in and scraped it over the surface, then under my nostrils. I breathed in deeply through my nose. A little too deeply. I felt my head spinning and I grabbed hold of the sink to stop myself from losing my balance. The giddiness passed and I took the jar downstairs.

I put it in my handbag. Maybe I would buy another jar as well. Just to be on the safe side.

Sense of smell sorted — "constant" found.

Now I needed to gain control of my mind.

That probably wasn't going to be as simple as rubbing "Vicks" under my nose. I needed something a little more drastic.

I wondered if it was possible to compartmentalise my mind.

Split it into sections and close parts of it off. If I could do that, I could shut off the part with the horrors in it and just use the "summer and light" bits.

I'd heard about a young woman who'd had a personality disorder (probably yet another story in yet another of those magazines I read). She'd had multiple personalities. Apparently she would unknowingly slip into any one of dozens of different personalities to deal with daily problems and issues. The problem was that she had so many, she wasn't in control of her life anymore.

I thought this through. By my reckoning, I already had a couple of personalities. I was a mild mannered teacher by day. And a murderous maniac by night (and obviously at any other time of the day not of my choosing).

The point was, I had no control over my life. And I had no control over when the murderous maniac would take over the mild mannered teacher. I needed someone else. Another me that the murderer knew nothing about.

I had no idea whether it was even possible to develop another personality. I was also aware that most people with multiple personalities regarded it as a problem — not a solution.

I decided that if I was going to actively develop another personality I might as well try to make it a good one.

I needed a name.

Agatha came to mind.

Not Agatha. I wanted it to be anonymous. Not strong, but not weak either. A name befitting a personality that was quiet and unassuming. I didn't want to stand out.

Anne.

I'd had an Auntie Anne. She was quiet and gentle and had a beautiful soft Scottish accent. She had always reminded me of The Queen. I loved my Auntie Anne.

My new personality had a name.

Anne was to be soft and strong. Determined but humble.

Small but sturdy. I would probably forgo the Scottish accent.

I wrote a list of all the things Anne would do — the way she would live her life. I filled three pages. I gave her a background, parents, brothers and sisters. I gave her a job. Wrote down all the things she liked to eat and drink. Her hobbies and interests.

I made her a widow. I wanted her to have the strength of someone living on their own. Someone who had seen sadness and trials, but had come out the other side. Still strong and still gentle.

Anne was older than me. I made her 52 years old. Wise and still vibrant. Anne loved life. And she loved the smell of "Vicks VapoRub".

My insides were fizzing. I felt like I was full of energy and spent thirty seconds skipping around the living room and kitchen, flapping my arms like a demented windmill. Shadows from the suns rays piercing through the blinds and hitting my whirling body made the whole room dance with me.

I could see no problem with multiple personalities.

I wondered if that was a problem in itself.

CHAPTER SIXTEEN

Later as I hunched over the kitchen sink, straining a boiling saucepan of spaghetti for tea, I heard Neil at the front door, back from work.

I glanced up at the kitchen clock. It was almost six.

Neil was normally back by half-five. Half an hour late.

Scalding steam plumed up from the colander and I moved my head to avoid it.

I heard Neil drop his briefcase in the living room and as I turned from the sink he appeared at the kitchen door. His face was blotchy red and his eyes looked a bit wide.

'Are you OK?' I said.

He seemed not to hear me. I wondered if it was because I was being Anne. Perhaps I was talking too quietly.

'Neil!' He heard that. 'Are you OK?'

'Sorry,' he said. 'Yes, I'm fine. Just a bit hectic at work, that's all.'

His eyes searched the kitchen.

'You're a bit late,' I said.

Eyes still scanning.

'I know, sorry. Had a ton of paperwork to do. Just had to get it done.'

'Just you?' I said.

'What do you mean?'

'I mean was it just you that had to work late. Or did you all have to?'

He started opening cupboards, then the fridge. Still looking for something.

'Just me really. I didn't have to I suppose. But I just needed to get it done.'

He stepped on the pedal bin and peered inside. He was

starting to piss me off.

'Have you lost something?'

He looked up, foot still resting on the pedal bin pedal.

'Neil, what are you looking for?'

'Have we got any wine open?' he said. 'I really need a drink.'

I must confess that the last few weeks had seen me open a bottle of wine daily. Perhaps more than one. So it was not uncommon for Neil to arrive home from work and find opened bottles of unfinished red, white or rose dotted about the place.

I wasn't trying to hide them. Not consciously anyway. But because my mind was so scatty, I did leave them in odd places.

He reached into the bin and pulled out two empty bottles. He looked at me.

'I've not had any today,' I said. I found those two opened and emptied them down the sink.'

His eyebrows raised a little. Pleasantly surprised? Or slightly suspicious?

'Seriously,' I said. 'I'm knocking it on the head. I don't think it's helping me very much at the moment.'

I didn't tell him about the one unopened bottle that I couldn't bring myself to throw. Just in case.

He stared back at me. I read nothing in his face. I could see why his eyes were so wide now. He was forcing them open.

His brow was furrowed and he hardly blinked. His eyes were watery and he had dark semicircles under them. He was tired. Exhausted.

His eyes flickered and dropped slightly, so that he was looking under my nose. "Vicks". I'd forgotten I had it on. And the fact that he was only just noticing it made me realise that we hadn't even kissed since he'd arrived home from the bank.

'I think your nose is running,' he said. 'A little.'

Instinctively I wiped the back of my hand under my nostrils, even though I knew it wasn't running.

'"Vicks",' I said.

'Have you got a cold?'

'Just a little,' I said. 'I'll be OK.'

I decided not to go into the real reasons for the "Vicks". And I certainly didn't want to tell him about Anne.

'Are you OK?' I said. 'You look tired.'

'I've not been sleeping too well,' he said. 'Not recently anyway.'

Was that a dig? I had been going to bed later than Neil. I had wanted to stay up and drink. And I think that subconsciously I was scared to shut my eyes and sleep in case of what it brought. Perhaps even consciously.

'Have I been waking you when I come to bed?' I asked. 'You haven't said anything.'

'No, it's fine. Maybe occasionally,' he said. 'But I've been waking in the night for some reason. And then not been able to get off again.' He closed his eyes and rubbed them with his knuckle. Rubbed them hard. One of his eyes squeaked. 'I think maybe I'm just a bit stressed,' he said. 'What with all this,' he waved his eye rubbing hand. 'And work and stuff. I'll be fine.'

And stuff?

I should have noticed. How long had he been like this? A week? Two?

I had been so wrapped up with my own issues — and drinking too much — that I hadn't noticed what was happening with Neil. What else had I missed? What about Michael and Rose? Were they struggling too?

I put the colander of spaghetti on the sink drainer and moved toward Neil. He seemed surprised. Maybe even flinched a little. I hugged him, tried to pull him close.

'I'm sorry,' I said. 'I've been so caught up with what was happening to me — I wasn't paying enough attention to you.'

His arms tensed around me, but not in a loving way. It was almost as though he was preventing me from getting any closer.

'I'm fine,' he said. 'Just overworking at the moment. That's all. It'll be fine.'

I thought I could smell alcohol on his breath as he spoke.

'Have you had a drink already today?' I asked.

He stepped back from me and wiped his mouth with the back of his hand.

'I had a quick one at lunchtime,' he said. His tone was defensive.

It smelled fresher than lunchtime to me. I wondered whether he had stopped on the way home. Perhaps that was why he was late. I decided not to push it.

'I don't blame you,' I said. 'That's what's been keeping me going since the attack.'

I smiled at him. He managed one back.

'I'll dish up the tea,' I said.

He nodded and mumbled something. I couldn't hear what.

It had been four weeks since the attack. I couldn't believe how rough Neil looked — I felt shocked that I hadn't spotted it until now. It had obviously been happening over a period of time.

And then I considered how rough I looked, how much I had changed over the last few weeks.

Over tea I studied Michael and Rose. Scanned every inch of their faces. Bloodshot eyes? — no. Pale skin? — no. Looking tired? — a little. Quieter than usual? — definitely.

Michael slurped the spaghetti into his mouth. Rose made a face. Neil looked distracted.

'Will you have to work late again tomorrow?' I said.

He looked up. 'Maybe. We're doing an audit at the moment. And I generally seem to be running a bit slower than usual. I might have to do a bit.'

'Can you let me know if it's going to be too late. Just a quick text will be fine.'

He nodded. Forced another smile.

'This is lovely,' he said, looking down at his plate.

The throbbing pain started in my thigh. I concentrated hard on being Anne, stretched my left leg out under the table, accidentally bumped Neil's foot. His chair scraped against the floor as he moved it back a couple of inches.

The pain intensified and I breathed deeply through my nose. Sucked up the vapours, made myself be Anne. *Speak softly*.

'I hope you manage to get it all sorted,' I said. 'At work. I hope it goes well.'

He must have noticed my tone. I was Anne, not Christine.

'Thank you,' he said. 'I think it will be fine.'

His shoulders moved a little. Less weight on them.

CHAPTER SEVENTEEN

When Neil put the children to bed I was surprised to hear him get straight in the shower. It was pretty early, even by his standards.

Twenty minutes later the third stair creaked and Neil appeared, bathrobe tied tightly around him.

'Rose is a bit quiet tonight,' he said. 'And Mikey too. He's not really himself.'

'Is he ill?'.

'I don't know. He asked me if I thought you were still beautiful.'

'Michael asked you?'

'If I thought you were still beautiful, even though you had scars on your head.'

'He must be ill. What did you say?'

'I told him that you and Rose are the prettiest girls in the world.'

'And what did he say?'

'He said you aren't a girl and that Rose isn't pretty, she is his sister.'

'I wonder why he asked you that?' I said.

Neil wandered through to the kitchen. 'You know what kids are like,' he said.

I heard the tap running and a glass clinking as he took it from the cupboard. His night-time routine. Down from the shower, glass of water, straight to bed. I was surprised he had stopped to talk to me about Michael.

Obviously Michael had noticed how "off" Neil had been, how "off" I'd been. Perhaps he was worried about us splitting up.

Although I was being "Anne", which I thought meant I was nicer to be around, and Neil had looked more relaxed after his shower — he still went straight to bed. Still without me.

It was probably just as well. I stank like a menthol and eucalyptus factory. By the time I finally climbed under the duvet next to him, he was in a deep sleep, snoring. I wondered if it was the exhaustion or the drink making him sleep.

I lay back in the darkness, eyes open. Although it was pitch black outside, I could still make out the edge of the curtains at the window. Patches of lighter darkness seemed to creep around them.

As I lay there I thought about being Anne. I had done pretty well, I thought, through dinner, and the kid's homework. While they were supposedly getting on with it, Neil and I had sat in the living room. I tried to work my way through a word-puzzle book, tried to keep my mind busy (not drinking, remember) and Neil had sat open-mouthed in front of the telly. He wasn't really watching it but was nevertheless absorbed. It was as though it had sucked all the stress and thoughts from his mind and left him just sitting there. Numb. Empty.

We barely spoke. And then at 8:30pm he'd announced that he was going to put the kids to bed.

I had coped well with that too, I thought. The silence. Especially as he had come home late AND smelled of drink. I thought about Abi. About when Neil and she worked together. He had worked late a lot then. Had something happened after all? Was something happening now? I blinked my eyes in the darkness of the bedroom. They felt tired and sore. I held them shut for ten seconds or so, tried to relax, tried not to think about Neil working late, about Abi.

My leg thumped. Brought me back on course. *Be Anne.*

I decided I would try to be Anne all the time now. If Neil called me Chris or Christine I would imagine that that was just a nickname, that everyone called me that — but my real name was Anne.

I felt goosebumps on my lower back. The tip of my nose felt cold, as though a breeze had swirled through the bedroom. I pulled the duvet further up the bed, covered the tip of my nose, and then pushed it away again. I didn't want "Vicks" on it.

I wondered what the skateboarder was doing now. Was he in bed? Was he alone? With someone? I wanted to hear the phone ringing, for the police to call and tell me they'd caught him. I wanted him to have had an accident on his skateboard. To have hurt himself. Badly.

I wanted the fucker here, in front of me. Not dead, but suffering. I wanted to make him suffer. Prolong his agony. But not let him die. Not let him off the hook.

Breathe deeply through your nose, Anne. Feel the vapour purifying your mind. Cool vapour. Speak softly. Think softly. Be gentle. Be Anne.

The first thing I noticed was the wind. Loud and ferocious. I wanted to cover my ears to protect them from the buffeting and the hideous noise. The wind was wet, as though it was full of rain. But it wasn't raining. It was daylight. Very bright. But that mist.

I was out in the open. Not hiding this time. I could see the girl walking up the hill toward me. I couldn't make out her features through the mist, but I knew it was her. She was dragging something along with her. What was that? As she grew closer I could feel myself smiling. A huge, broad smile. I sensed she smiled too.

And then I was walking up the hill with her. Talking to her. Asking her about someone. Then I asked her about the thing she was dragging. I still couldn't see her face clearly because it was dripping wet. The wind had soaked her, making her features distorted. But I knew she was still smiling.

I was pointing somewhere, over toward the gorse bushes. We

walked over together. It was important that I take her there. I had something to show her. A crashing, thunderous roar came to me. Louder than the wind, but carried on it. She was speaking, but I couldn't hear what she was saying. She was shaking her head, pulling back a little. I moved towards her and took her arm. Why wouldn't she let go of that thing she was pulling. It was as though it was tied to her.

Behind the gorse bushes now. There was the thing I had to show her. A container of something. Liquid. In a bottle.

Then I hit her. Forced her down to the ground. Kicked the thing she was dragging. Covered her mouth. She wasn't smiling anymore.

I smelled *Vicks*. Shifted around in my bed. *Vicks*.

And there was Neil. His eyes were so dark and wet. His breath felt hot and smelled of Christmas Pudding. He didn't know I was there. Didn't know I was watching him.

Vicks. More shifting.

And now a woman sitting at a table. What is she doing? Writing? She looks up at me. She is pretty but plain. She is my age. Perhaps a little younger. Dark hair, pulled back into a rough ponytail. Do I know you? She closes the book she was writing in. She looks scared. I move closer to her. She seems blurred to me. I can't see her too clearly now. I feel different. I feel like I want to hurt her.

Vicks. More shifting. *Wake up, Christine. Wake up.*

And then I'm awake.

The dark glow from outside was still creeping around the curtains. Neil had stopped snoring. The bedside clock flashed 4:15am at me.

I moved my head on the pillow and felt a damp patch on the back of my neck. Despite the cold weather outside I had been sweating. I didn't feel hot.

I rubbed my forefinger under my nose and breathed deeply,

longing for the *Vicks* to work its magic.

But all I could smell was garlic. I sniffed the back of my hand, then my arm. Just garlic, seemingly seeping out of my skin. Not unpleasant, to me, but not what I was expecting.

I realised I had been cooking a lot of meals with garlic.

I thought about what had just happened in my sleep. I remembered it all. The girl in the gorse, Neil looking tired. And a younger-than-me, pretty (ish) woman sitting at a table, writing.

Three dreams. I wondered if they were connected. Whether they were all one dream, albeit a little disjointed.

Again I thought about premonitions. Wondered if I had somehow gained access to the future. Wondered whether the doctors really had any idea what they were talking about at all.

But if I was seeing the future, then maybe Neil was with this other woman. Maybe I'd wanted to hurt her because of that. Perhaps I'd seen her writing to him. Perhaps the child in the gorse was their child.

I felt a rage surging up in my belly. I wanted to elbow Neil, sleeping beside me in silence. Wanted to "accidentally" kick him in my sleep. Wake him too, at 4:15am.

And then I heard a noise outside the bedroom window.

CHAPTER EIGHTEEN

Neil always insisted on having the bedroom window shut. I always liked it slightly open at night — even in the middle of winter. Otherwise I woke up with a headache. Neil had closed the window when he came to bed. I opened it when I came up later. Let him question me about it in the morning.

At first it sounded like leaves blowing in the wind. Scraping along the patio, whirling against the side of the house.

But then something heavier came to me. Like a shuffle. A footstep. Just below the bedroom window.

I fought against the urge to bury my head under the duvet. To hide from the noise. Instead I turned my head slightly. Turned my ear to the sound.

Another shuffle. And another. Definite footsteps. And then they stopped.

I wondered if it was a hedgehog snuffling around. Trying to find a morsel amongst the dead leaves.

And then I heard a rattle. A tinny sound. It wasn't a hedgehog.

I nudged Neil. Gently. He mumbled in his sleep. I whispered to him.

'Neil. Neil. Wake up. There's someone outside.'

I nudged him again and he turned to face me.

'What is it?' he said. 'Are you OK?'

I told him to shush and listen.

The tinny rattle came again. Then a sound like deodorant being sprayed.

Even in the darkness I could see Neil's expression change. This wasn't another imagining from my mind. This was real.

Neil swung his legs out from under the duvet and reached for his dressing gown on the floor.

'Don't go to the window,' I whispered. 'You don't know who

is out there. I'll just call the police.'

'Wait a minute,' Neil said. 'We need to see what it is first. It might just be nothing.'

We both knew it was *something*.

I picked up the phone from my bedside cabinet and Neil nodded.

I sniffed the air. Over the garlic, and remnants of *Vicks*, I could smell something. It wasn't deodorant. It was more chemical than perfume. A fire starter of some sort? I dialled 999.

Neil kept half a wooden broom handle by his side of the bed *"Just in case…"*. I saw him fumble for it now.

More rattling from outside, and more chemical spray.

Then very heavy footsteps. Running away. I heard the dustbin clatter. Whoever it was must have misjudged the path around the front of the house.

Neil ran out of the bedroom door, broom handle at the ready, just as someone came to the other end of the phone.

'999 emergency, which service please…'.

I couldn't believe how long it took for the police to get to us. It was almost 5:45am.

Whoever had been outside could have come back with his mates and had a party in our garden in the time it took for them to arrive.

No sirens and no flashing blue lights. They obviously hadn't been in a hurry.

As soon as they arrived, Neil shoved the broom handle he'd been gripping the whole time into the corner of the living room.

'Just in case,' he said to me.

We had already been outside and seen the results of our nocturnal visitor. I was still trembling. Michael and Rose were still in bed. Hopefully asleep.

I had rubbed copious amounts of menthol and eucalyptus under my nose. I was wondering whether to just give up trying to be Anne.

"BACK OFF CUNT".

Spray-painted in red letters against the back of the house. Letters about a foot high with drips, which looked like blood, coming down. The words went across the brickwork and the back windows of the living room.

There was a dead fox, horribly mutilated, spread out on the ground below the words.

'Do either of you have any idea what it means?' a police officer asked.

I had thought it was pretty much straight to the point. But I knew he didn't mean that.

We both shook our heads.

'Is it possible you might have upset anyone recently,' he said. 'Or had any disputes with any neighbours?'

'It's not really that sort of neighbourhood,' I said. 'And we've not fallen out with anyone.'

'You'd be surprised,' he said. 'Even the nicest areas have their share of nutters.'

'I was attacked four weeks ago,' I said. It sounded like a blurt — but it wasn't.

'So I understand, Mrs Marsden. Do you think this has anything to do with that?' He looked surprised that I had mentioned it.

'The person that attacked me got my handbag. It had all my stuff in it. My purse, with all my contact details, driver's licence and stuff. So he knows where I live.'

'That doesn't necessarily mean it was him,' he said.

'AND he has my house keys and car keys too,' I said. 'It has to be him.'

'I understand you were advised to change all the locks on the house after that,' he said.

Neil looked up at him. 'We did all that. Perhaps it's a message to the police?'

I looked at Neil — not really sure what he meant. The police officer looked at him too.

'If he thinks you're getting close to finding him, maybe he left this as a message to you.' Neil said.

'I don't think he would leave a message to us on your house,' the officer said. And then he smiled. 'And besides, the last word is singular, not plural.'

Neil stared at him. 'Is that a joke?'

The officer blushed.

But I wanted Neil to be right. I wanted it to be aimed at the police, not at me.

'I think we disturbed him,' Neil said. 'I think he ran off before he finished.' He looked at me and nodded. 'And he left it on our house so that the police would know it was to do with the attack. If he had written it on the police station wall, it could have been from anyone about any case. This way he knew you would get the message.'

I was convinced, even if the police officer wasn't. He still had a smirk on his face, either from his attempt at a joke or from his disbelief of the scenario Neil had just painted.

The officer nodded and turned back to join his colleagues.

The stench of the dead fox was horrible. Even the gunk under my nose didn't stop it from making me feel sick. It smelled like a butcher's shop where all the refrigeration had packed up several days ago. No on else seemed bothered by it.

As the light of dawn slowly reached us, the full impact of the words could be seen. We asked the police to be as quiet as they could so as not to disturb Michael and Rose, but they still made an unruly racket. In the light I recognised some of the faces. They had been here before.

Eventually they took photographs of the words, scraped some of the paint off the wall and window, and took away the fox.

'We probably won't get much from it,' one of them said to Neil. 'But if someone's gone to all the trouble of doing that to it, it's probably worth a look.'

What an inspiration of hope. I decided not to hold my breath.

'Can we get this washed off?' Neil asked.

'Go ahead,' said the officer. 'We're done with it.'

He hadn't meant that — but he didn't push it. At least if we did it ourselves we would know it was done properly. And the sooner the police were gone, the sooner it would feel like getting back to normal.

As soon as the last officer left, Neil's expression changed. I saw an anger in his eyes, more intense than it had been earlier. But I also saw something else. Fear, I think. He looked like he was ready for a fight, but it was as though he thought he might not win. I had never seen a look like that in him before. The Neil I knew was scared of nothing and confident about everything. A little too confident sometimes. I had no idea what it meant.

'Do you want to go and check on the kids,' he said. 'And I'll make a start on this.'

When I came back outside a few minutes later, Neil had already hosed away the residue from the fox. I felt my stomach rumble when I thought about it. I couldn't believe how brutal its death must have been. I felt angry and sad in equal measure. Had he killed it there, in our back garden? It was horrible.

'The kids OK?' Neil asked.

'Both asleep. Slept through it all.'

Neil had an old towel and a bucket of water. His dressing gown had a wet patch on it, the towel dripping as he lifted it to the wall. He dabbed at the words. It didn't seem to make much of a difference.

'I'll get a scrubbing brush,' I said. 'I think there's one under the sink.

It took us the best part of an hour to get the words off the house and the windows. And even when we had finished you could still see an outline of the words.

'It might look better when it's dried off a bit,' Neil said.

I hoped he was right.

It was fully daylight now. I wondered if any neighbours had spotted our bizarre house-cleaning exploits as they got ready for work.

I was too frazzled to care.

Our knuckles and fingers were red. Partly from the paint, but mostly from bleeding where we had scraped them on the brickwork. At times we had been working like demons, scrubbing and scraping and towelling. Fuelled by anger and feelings of violation. We were determined that the kids wouldn't see this. Or even any trace of it.

As he rubbed away at the last remnants I could see that Neil's look of fear had gone. He was ready for the fight now.

'Do you think it really was a message for the police?' I said.

He didn't answer straight away. He opened his mouth, as if to say something, then shut it again.

He didn't look up from rubbing away at the brickwork.

'What else could it be?' he said.

End of subject.

Part of me wanted to tell him about the dreams. About him, about the younger woman and about the girl. But I couldn't bring myself to do it. I was fed up with talking about my dreams and I certainly wasn't in any kind of mood for a major confrontation about whether he was seeing someone else or not. After all — they were just dreams — although, the woman had looked familiar. I wondered if it was someone he worked with, someone that I may have met briefly.

In truth, she was probably nothing to do with Neil. She had been alone at a table, writing. Neil wasn't there at all. And she hadn't looked surprised to see me. She had looked scared. It was different.

The brickwork where the words had been looked almost normal now.

BACK OFF CUNT.

Why would the attacker write that — and why the fox? What significance did that have? Neil had been going to say something else when I'd asked him if he really thought it was meant for the police. What was it? A confession?

It occurred to me that perhaps the message was meant for Neil. A jealous husband or boyfriend. Was that possible? I had been pretty much "missing" as a wife recently, either drinking, freaking out or crying. And now with copious amounts of soft paraffin rubbed under my nose and struggling to develop and maintain an additional personality. Maybe he'd started looking elsewhere.

If he had, I would kill him.

But Neil wouldn't do that to me. He had always been my solid granite. We were concrete. He wouldn't do that to me.

I felt goosebumps on my arms, and shivered. A gust of wind pushed against me.

Over the fence, in the next door garden, I heard the early morning birds screeching at each other. Although now daylight, the sky looked mean. Dark blue and black, heavy with moisture. Next door had left a sheet on their washing line and it flapped furiously in the wind. What on earth possessed them to leave washing out in weather like this? Neil went back indoors.

I noticed my breath, misting before my eyes and I felt my shoulders rise and fall with each breath. My chest expanding, filling with air. I became aware of me. I felt like I was seeing myself for the first time in ages. Looking down on myself. Seeing me for what I was.

I pulled a tissue from my dressing gown pocket and rubbed

away the remainder of the *Vicks*. I raised my head up, stared hard at the brickwork then looked up at the sky. I shut my eyes and mentally shouted "Bring it on".

If Neil was seeing someone else — that was his problem. I needed to sort myself out. If he was there to help, so much the better, if not — I could do it myself. I needed to be there for Michael and Rose and I wanted to be there for Neil.

Most importantly I wanted to be there for me.

I was back, I was in control and I was angry.

I told Anne to fuck off.

CHAPTER NINETEEN

It was still early in the morning, but the day was definitely with us. I pulled my dressing gown tighter and headed inside, flicking a fleck of red paint from under one of my fingernails. A fairly pointless exercise as both hands looked entirely red.

Inside the house, Neil was sifting through the dishwasher. He was looking for a bowl. I got a couple of spoons from the cutlery drawer and told him to grab a bowl for me too. We hadn't sat down to breakfast together for as long as I could remember. Years probably. Either he was going to work, or I was getting the kids ready, or one of us was running late and had to skip breakfast altogether.

We sat at the table, opposite each other. Both with our crunchy cereal and cold milk. Both with our red and still bleeding hands. He looked like he needed a makeover. A shave and shower at least. And perhaps an extra couple of weeks of sleep. I guessed I probably looked as bad. Maybe even worse.

'Whatever is going on here,' I said. 'We'll get through it. We always do.'

He looked weary. 'I know,' he said. 'I know we will.'

I was pleased he wasn't wired up to a polygraph. There was no way he would have passed on that statement.

'I'm serious, Neil. I've been fucked up for the last few weeks. I know that. But this has been the last straw. I'm not going to take any crap anymore,' I realised I had raised my spoon like a baton. Or a knife. 'I am going to fight this to the end. If my mind is going shit on me, I'm going to find a way of getting it back again. I am not going to let this…' I hesitated, hunting for the right word. I'm not sure that I found it, '…this madness ruin my life. I'm too strong for that. We're too strong for that.'

My face felt hot and flushed.

Neil reached over and lowered my hand. The one holding the spoon. He smiled.

'Concrete,' he said. 'You can't break through concrete.'

'Damned right,' I said. 'I'm going to find a counsellor.' I surprised even myself. 'The doctor suggested it might help. He said that soldiers, sometimes, and people, that have suffered from post-traumatic stress, often find it helpful to see a counsellor,' I said.

Neil raised both eyebrows. For him that signified major surprise (or acknowledgement; or understanding; or being impressed. A multi-functional movement).

'I'll ring the doctor and ask him who I should go to.'

Neil nodded. Multi-functional eyebrows still raised (impressed I think).

'I'm doing this, Neil. This is where it all ends.'

After I got the kids off to school and Neil had sloped out of the door to work, I rang the health centre where Doctor Jones practised. At first I got an automated system, then an unhelpful receptionist who sounded even more pissed off with life than me.

In the end, I practically demanded to be put through to Doctor Jones. It worked.

'Mrs Marsden?' he said, 'Is everything OK?'

'Everything is fine' I said. 'When I came to see you you mentioned a counsellor to me. You said it might be worth me going to see someone?'

'Mr Connell,' he said. 'Would you like me to contact him for you, talk him through what has happened?'

'Or perhaps you could just let me have his contact details,' I said. 'I'd be happy to contact him myself. Is he local?'

He was. Less than five miles away from Saltford in a place

called Newton St Loe. I knew it well. Several of the children at school lived there. A lovely place. A little beyond our price range for houses though. Amazing what five miles will do to a house price.

After I'd showered and got cleaned up from the spray paint I dialled his number.

He answered his phone immediately and listened quietly as I explained what had happened, and that Doctor Jones had recommended him. He suggested that I come over for an initial meeting.

'I won't charge you for it,' he said. 'We need to make sure we get along with each other first.'

His accent was Irish. Soft and gentle. I wasn't sure if that meant he was from Northern Ireland or Southern. I opted for the South. Maybe I would ask him when we met.

'I have a free morning this morning,' he said. 'Would that suit you?'

Butterflies started up gymnastics in my stomach. Was I really going to see a total stranger and tell him what was going on inside my head?

'I can be there in half an hour,' I said.

As I drove to Newton St Loe the skies grew darker. And heavier. One or two raindrops splashed the windscreen, but nothing more. It was as though the clouds were holding onto it, almost to bursting.

I found his house easily. I had driven past it hundreds of times on the way to and from school. It wasn't quite chocolate-box perfect — but it was close. I parked up against the hedge bordering the garden and climbed out of the car. The butterflies I'd forgotten I'd had, kicked in again to remind me where I was and what I was doing. I took a shallow breath (I'd tried for a deep one), pushed open the waist-level metal gate and looked up at the house.

A beautiful grey-slate roof sloped down to a Victorian looking conservatory. The front garden wasn't large, but seemed well kept. Foliage and grasses were everywhere. A busy garden with unusual looking statues and shapes. A wheelbarrow had blown over in the wind and lay on its side in the grass. Leaves swirled around on the ground as the wind picked them up. Although I saw only a few birds, the song coming from the garden was almost deafening.

An old, wooden garage stood by the side of the house with its rickety looking double doors open. Inside I could see the shape of an old car. The large upside-down double "V" on the front grille told me it was a Citroen. It looked like it was from the war although I couldn't be sure.

I hoped to God that Mr Connell wasn't some flash twat with flamboyant shirts and lots of jewellery. The last thing I needed was a wannabe hypnotist messing with my mind.

Above the front door a wooden sign read "Elm Gables". With every step I took closer to the house I fought the urge to turn around and walk back to my car and drive home. *Complete stranger looking inside my mind.*

The front door opened while I was still a few feet from it.

CHAPTER TWENTY

A tall man with neat black hair.

He wore smart glasses, a blue sweater and brown corduroy trousers. His slippers were burgundy. I guessed his age to be about forty-six, but possibly as much as fifty. He was about the same height as Neil.

'Mrs Marsden?' he said, looking first at me, then up at the darkened sky.

I nodded and forced the best smile my nerves would allow.

'My name is Colin,' he said, soft Irish accent glowing. 'Colin Connell.'

I mumbled that my name was Christine and kicked the "wannabe hypnotist" thing into touch.

He motioned for me to come in and I entered a small hallway. My mouth felt dry and I managed a deep breath. Sweetness on the air hit my tongue. I smelled spices. Cinnamon and nutmeg. Hot-Cross-Buns. And coffee too. Fresh. The aromas and tastes were lovely. I wanted to stop, shut my eyes and savour it. I didn't.

As we walked through the hallway into the house I noticed a white bust on a small, semicircular half-table against the hallway wall. At the front it read "The Human Mind". The head was sectioned with black lines, each section named within it. Presumably the different parts of the brain. I wondered which section had brought me there.

'It's a phrenology head,' Colin said.

He was ahead of me in the hallway and he hadn't turned around. He wouldn't have seen me look at the bust.

'It's pretty much regarded as a pseudo-science now of course,' he said. 'But fascinating nonetheless.'

I guessed all his clients looked at it as they came into the house. It was practically the only thing in an otherwise quite bland, but lovely hallway. A couple of wooden shelves lined the wall, empty and clean. And a beautiful wooden staircase led to the upstairs of the house.

'Your house is lovely,' I said. 'Is it very old?'

He stopped at the end of the hallway between two doors and turned to face me. The door now behind him was open and through it I saw dark marble worktops and a cream coloured Aga. The doorway to his left was closed.

'It's nearly one hundred years old,' he said. 'Or so I'm led to believe. 'About the time of the first world war. It's not the oldest house in the village though.'

He turned the brass knob on the closed door, pushed it open and signalled me inside.

My immediate thought was that it was like a film-set front-room — out of a Second World War movie. I half expected to see an airman with a black Labrador sitting on a chair. It looked like a comfortable study with a small wooden desk by a window that overlooked the garden. A silver photo frame stood on the desk. I couldn't see the photograph in it as it faced the window. On the other side of the desk was a letter tray and between the two, a closed laptop. One wall was covered by bookshelves almost to the ceiling. The shelves were full. More books perched on a low coffee table in the middle of the room and still more on the three small armchairs positioned around it. An old clock hung on the wall opposite. Below that was a fireplace. I noticed a large, dusty cobweb strung across the grille. The clock hands pointed at 11:05. There was a strong smell of freshly sawed wood, or new sawdust. It wasn't an unpleasant smell, but was quite at odds with the decor of the room.

'Take a seat,' he said, although he didn't indicate which one.

I wondered if this was some sort of test. If I chose one seat over another would it mean that I was more bonkers than if I had chosen another one? Should I consider the wooden backed chair behind the desk by the window? Did he expect me to remove the books from the armchair for him?

'Any one is fine,' he said. 'Just throw the books on the floor. Can I get you a drink? Coffee, tea?'

'I'd like some water please, if you have it?'

He laughed. 'I think we can do water,' he said. 'Are you sure you don't want a coffee, I've just made some?'

'Just water please. Thank you.'

'How about a hot-cross-bun,' he said.

'I'm fine, thank you. I ate just before I came out.'

I would have loved one really, of course, they smelled so good, but I didn't want to be munching my way through a bun whilst telling a stranger about my problems.

He nodded and disappeared. I heard him clattering about in the kitchen.

I chose one of the two armchairs that had their backs to the window. I didn't want to be distracted by the garden. And it also meant I had a full view of the door. I wasn't sure why that was important to me — but it was. I carefully picked the books off the chair and placed them in a pile on the floor next to it. Then straightened the pile a little. The floor was dark wood with a green patterned rug taking up a large part of it. The coffee table was on the rug. It struck me how new the rug looked. Its newness looked out of place in such an old-fashioned feeling room. I wondered why Colin had had to buy a new rug. Had he murdered a client on the old one? Got rid of it because it was soaked in blood? Would I be his next victim? What the hell was I doing there?

I jumped as he came back through the door. He smiled and handed me a glass of water. He plonked his coffee on the table.

He picked the books off the armchair opposite mine, across the coffee table, and put them underneath it.

'What's phrenology?' I asked.

'The study of bumps,' he said.

I wasn't sure how to respond to that, so I went for the "Neil Classic" and raised my eyebrows.

'Specifically the bumps and contours of the head,' he said. 'For some time it was thought that you could tell someone's personality and character traits by feeling the bumps on their head. Raised bumps behind the ears meant a pickpocket, small bumps just here,' he rubbed a small part of the top of his head with his finger, 'signifies vanity and arrogance.'

He smiled as he did it.

'But it is mostly dismissed nowadays as a pseudo-science, akin to say — palmistry or astrology.'

'Hypnotism?' I said

He nodded, slowly. 'Hypnotism,' he said. 'That too.'

'Fascinating,' I said.

He sat back in his chair. I hadn't realised he had been leaning forward. Had he been examining me?

'Please relax,' he said.

I thought I was.

'The purpose of this,' he waved his hand to indicate the two of us, 'is to see whether we get along. If I'm going to try and help you it is essential that you feel comfortable here. And that you feel happy talking about things. This isn't right for everyone.'

I was about to point out that I didn't think it was right for me. But I thought about Michael and Rose. And Neil.

'I understand,' I said.

'You said on the phone that you were attacked.'

I nodded. I didn't really know where to start.

'Would you mind just telling me a little bit about yourself,' he said. 'Background, upbringing, what you do for a living, married, family — all that sort of thing.'

He smiled again.

I felt nervous. Like at one of those gatherings where everyone in the room has to introduce themselves and no one wants to be the one to go first.

  I didn't want to go first either.

CHAPTER TWENTY-ONE

I told Colin as much as I could about myself. That I was thirty-six years old, married to Neil (he was thirty-nine), had Michael (eleven) and Rose (eight).

'I'm a teacher at a primary school in Bath,' I said.

He just nodded.

To be honest I didn't feel much like a teacher anymore. Having not been into school for the past month, and having a dark harbouring penchant for hurting girls, made me feel like a fraud when I said I was a teacher.

I felt like a fraud as a wife and mother too.

'Are you married?' I asked him. 'Kids?'

'I have a daughter at University in Glasgow,' he said. 'I was married.'

Aha. A divorcee. I noticed he still wore a wedding ring.

Perhaps he needed some counselling himself.

'Divorced?' I said.

'My wife died in an accident just over six months ago,' he said.

My eyes involuntarily looked down at the new rug. I forced them up again.

'Oh, I'm sorry,' I said.

'She never regained consciousness. She died three days later.' His eyes sort of glazed over.

I didn't know what to say, so I went for the safe option — again.

'I'm so sorry,' I said.

He shook his head and brought his eyes back into focus. Time to move on.

He asked me about my upbringing. Schooling, parents and friends. I was amazed at how much of my life I had already packed away. Not forgotten about, exactly, but certainly packed in boxes and archived somewhere in my brain. Away from the dark bit.

Talking to him helped me to re-visit myself. Assess where I had been and what I had done.

'I went on a climbing trip to The Andes,' I said. 'Before I met Neil. I went with my previous boyfriend.'

It had been the most exhilarating thing I had done up to then. It was tough, cold, hard and fantastic. In fact that had been what convinced me that I had what it took to be a teacher. To be anything I wanted to be.

It also convinced me that I didn't want to be with my boyfriend. I think he understood.

'I met Neil about three months later. I had already gone into teacher training and he had just started at a bank.'

Talking to Colin made me feel like I was fifteen years younger, talking about my trip and about how Neil and I had met. All my current issues disappeared. Eventually I finished speaking.

'Thank you, Christine,' Colin said. 'And now can you tell me what has brought you here today.'

All my current issues re-appeared.

I told him about the skateboard attack. About my sense of smell going haywire. And I told him about the dreams. In fact, I told him all the things I had promised myself on the way over that I wouldn't tell him. I think he was surprised. Perhaps he might want to feel the bumps on my head to see if I was insane. When I told him that it had even crossed my mind that they might be premonitions he smiled, but did me the courtesy of trying to cover it with his hand. It made me not want to say what I had been going to say next.

I said it anyway.

'To be totally honest, I'm really scared that the bangs on the head have damaged something inside my brain. That maybe they have triggered something. I'm really scared that I am losing my mind. That I'm going mad.'

He didn't smile this time. In fact he looked quite serious.

'Severe trauma to the head can cause brain damage,' he said. 'Sometimes permanent, very often temporary — with swellings etcetera. But it would have been picked up at the hospital and you would have been told about that as a possibility. Were you told that there was damage?'

'No, but it could have been missed. The bangs to my head might have weakened something in my brain that has subsequently snapped or broken or whatever it does. The dreams seem real to me. More than just dreams really. More like real life. It's very scary.'

'Dreams are not unusual after a traumatic incident,' he said. 'In fact most people have them. But they usually relate to the incident itself. Your dreams seem to be about something unrelated. Something shocking and traumatic in its own right, but still apparently disconnected from the original incident.'

He stood up and walked behind me to the desk. I didn't like not being able to see him, so I turned around. From a drawer he pulled a small pad and a pencil. It reminded me of school.

He came and sat back down again.

'What do you think?' he said. 'Would you like us to take this further?'

'Do you think you can help me get my mind back again?' I said. 'Get a handle on these dreams?'

'I think we can make inroads. I'm not sure if I can stop these dreams entirely. But we might be able to gain some understanding that will help to diminish them. At least diminish the impact they have on you.'

'Then I would like to take it further… are you OK with that?'

He smiled. 'Of course. I think it would be very beneficial.'

I assumed he meant for me.

'I have to ask, I'm afraid,' he said. 'Have you been referred or will you be paying privately?'

My face grew suddenly hot. I hadn't even considered money. I don't know what I thought was going to happen, but I hadn't taken into account that I would probably have to pay for counselling. I didn't know what to say.

He read the confusion on my face.

'I can call Dr Jones for you if you like,' he said. 'I'll ask him what he thinks about your case.'

I managed to construct a sentence — of sorts.

'What would be the cost?' I said.

'If he feels you should be referred, then the cost is covered by the NHS. At least for a certain period anyway. If you come as a private patient my normal charges are £45 per hour. Each session is an hour.'

Now I let him read the shock on my face.

'We couldn't afford £45 an hour,' I said.

'I understand,' he said. 'Because this is a PTS incident, a post-traumatic-stress case, I would reduce the charge to £30 a session. Would that be more manageable?'

'A bit,' I said.

'Let's see what Trevor Jones has to say about you first, shall we? Then we'll take it from there.'

He wrote down my mobile number, home number and email.

'The mobile is the best one to get me on,' I said.

As we stood up I looked at the clock. It was 11:55am. I couldn't believe that 50 minutes had gone so quickly. Or that I had opened up so much about such a lot of my life. I guessed it was probably a good thing.

On the way out, I paused at the bust.

'Pseudo-science?' I said.

'Almost certainly,' he said. He smiled again.

I heard a bump. It came from upstairs.

"My daughter is at University. My wife died recently".

I looked up at the ceiling in the direction of the noise.

'Mathilda,' he said. She's probably knocked something over again. She's my cat.'

'Lovely,' I said.

I hated cats. I was surprised I hadn't sniffed her out when I first came into the house. Odd, I thought.

Colin opened the front door for me. The rain had finally got its way and was pouring from grumpy looking clouds. The wind was still horribly strong and it beat the raindrops hard against the side of the house.

'How far is your car?' he asked.

'Literally just on the other side of the hedge. I'll be fine.'

Colin reached out his hand. I shook it.

'Nice to meet you, Christine,' he said. 'I'll be in touch as soon as I've spoken to Doctor Jones.'

'You too,' I said. 'Please call me Chris.'

The rain slammed against the windscreen as I drove away from Colin's house. I put the car lights on, even though it was only lunchtime. The sky was almost black in places. Birds flew high, they looked like they were being blown along on the wind. Hundreds of them, as though they knew it would be safer for them on the wing than in the trees (or wherever else they rested). I could almost smell the electricity in the air. The few pedestrians that had ventured out, or been caught out, didn't bother with umbrellas. It was too windy. Their heads down, coats wrapped around them, they moved as quickly as they could to wherever it was they were going.

I didn't want to go home. Even after just under an hour with Colin I had loads going on inside my head. It had taken me back. Back to nice places. I wasn't stupid. I knew that everything could seem better when you looked back on it.

But it had calmed me. Given me a warm feeling, a secure feeling.

I decided to go and see Mum and Dad.

CHAPTER TWENTY-TWO

Mum and Dad lived about thirty five minutes away. A place called Banwell, just east of Weston-Super-Mare. A beautiful place surrounded by woods and streams.

Being with Colin had started to unpack some of the archived boxes of memories I had stored away in my mind. There was a big box for Banwell. I had loved growing up there, and the house and area still held many happy memories for me.

Even with the rain hammering down and the wind howling, the place looked good. I remembered trying to build a shelter in the woods during a massive thunderstorm. I had wanted to stack up a fire and cook sausages too, but Mum, quite rightly, pointed out that the rain would put the fire out. It had felt like an adventure right on our doorstep.

I pulled the car into the drive and saw Dad's car. They were in.

Within five minutes I had used the loo, brushed my hair and sat down with Mum and Dad and a hot cup of coffee. Mum sliced the top off a packet of biscuits and tipped them onto a plate between us. I saw a couple of side dishes newly washed up on the drainer by the sink. They must have had an early lunch.

'How's it going, love?' Mum said. 'You look great.'

Dad nodded.

'I feel pretty good, actually,' I said. 'I have moments, of course. But I think I'm turning things around.'

I told them about what had happened the previous night. The spray paint and the mutilated fox (although I didn't tell them exactly what had been written on the wall). I told them a little about how Neil was looking. I didn't mention that he had been home late from work.

'You know when I went to see the doctor the other day?' I said. 'Well at the time he mentioned, because I had been through a traumatic incident with the attack, that it might be worth considering going to see someone else — a counsellor.'

'Do you think that would help?' Dad said. 'You seem to be coping really well.'

If only he knew.

'Actually, I went to see someone this morning,' I said. 'Before I came here.'

Dad looked at Mum. Mum reached for a biscuit.

'I've been having these, sort-of dreams and visions. They're not about the attack, but they have only happened since then. Also my sense of smell has gone pear-shaped.'

I felt a mini convulsion in my stomach, as though I was about to cry. *Hold it together, Christine.*

'The dreams have been horrendous. Violent and vicious — but also incredibly real. I have felt the wind blowing against me, and smelled the air. I've heard the noises.'

Fight back the tears!

'I have honestly felt like I've been losing my mind. It's been so real and it's like I've had no control over my thoughts. No control over my mind at all. At times I've felt like I'm going mad.'

I hoped that neither of them would come and put their arms around me and tell me that everything would be fine. That would send me off immediately and I was pretty proud of myself up to that point for not crying.

'You should have told us, Chris,' Mum said. 'We would have been there straight away. We can help you.'

A single tear trickled from my right eye. I rubbed my eyebrow and wiped away the tear at the same time.

'This chap I saw this morning, Colin, seems really good. He was recommended by Doctor Jones. He deals with these sorts of cases quite a lot I think.'

Dad reached for a biscuit too.

I looked out of the kitchen window to take my mind off my emotions. White clouds stood out against the dark sky. Rain still pummelled the earth.

Mum and Dad shifted their posture a little. I knew one of them would ask the question I had been dreading.

It was Dad.

'What sort of dreams are they?' he said.

For the second time that day I didn't know where to start.

'To be honest, Dad, I feel ashamed. I'm almost too embarrassed to talk about them.'

'You can't help your dreams, dear,' Mum said. 'They are just dreams.'

'But these aren't just dreams, Mum. They're different to that.'

My eyebrow itched and I rubbed my knuckle across it. I felt a dull thud starting up in my leg.

'I hurt people,' I said. 'In the dreams. Girls. I attack and hurt them.' I looked down at the table. I couldn't bring myself to make eye-contact with my parents. I didn't want to look at the biscuits either, they seemed too jolly for what I was talking about.

'I do horrible things to them. I think I may even kill them.'

My mum started to say something. Probably a repeat of "you can't help your dreams, dear", but I carried on talking.

'And they aren't just dreams. I thought I actually saw one of the girls at home. On the stairs — like a vision or something. And when I saw her, a wind blew. In the front room. A wind that was strong enough to blow my hair back off my face. There were no doors open and no windows. And she looked at me from the stairs. It was terrifying.'

My dad reached out and held my hand across the table. I still didn't look up.

'There was a smell too. A sweet, sickly smell that I can't identify. I always smell it when the visions and dreams come.

Always the same. And we had Oli and Abi over with the kids recently. The kids raided our wardrobe and dressed up in our clothes, used make-up — the whole works. When they came downstairs I freaked out. Josie looked just like one of the girls in the visions. One of the girls I had hurt. And the wind and the smell came right on cue. It was awful.'

My mum reached out and took hold of my other hand. It felt like we were at a seance.

'There are things happening to my mind over which I have no control. I am really, really scared.'

Almost as one, Mum and Dad stood up from their chairs and moved in close to me, one on each side. I felt their arms around my shoulders, hugging me. No words, just love, from them to me. My stomach was convulsing uncontrollably and my tears splashed onto the table.

It felt like I cried forever, although it was probably only a few minutes. But a few minutes was all it took to turn me into a wreck. My nose had run, my make-up had run and I felt exhausted. I just wanted to sleep. I wanted to shut my sore eyes and just sleep, held by my Mum and Dad. No words — just love.

'I'm sorry,' I said, eventually. 'I can't believe how much I cried.'

'It all needed to come out, love,' Mum said. 'You do need to let things out you know. It doesn't do any good keeping them bottled up inside.'

I tried to smile and wiped some of the snot from under my nose. I really needed to get tidied up.

'Do you want a biscuit?' Mum said.

It made me laugh.

'Do you mind if I make myself a sandwich,' I said. 'I suddenly feel starving.'

'You go and sort yourself out,' she said. 'I'll make you a sandwich. Ham OK?'

'Thanks, Mum. That would be lovely.'

When I stood up from the table I realised my heart was pounding, almost at double speed. And as Mum moved her hand from my shoulder I could see she was trembling.

CHAPTER TWENTY-THREE

The sandwich was on the table waiting for me when I got back from the bathroom. And a large glass of water. The biscuits were gone. And so were Mum and Dad. I could hear them in the front room. I knew Dad was reading the newspaper. He always rustled it as he read. I guessed Mum was either knitting or reading. I couldn't hear any talking.

The sandwich was great — just what I needed. I looked up at the kitchen clock. It was wrong. It said it was just after half past two. I wasn't sure, but I thought the time must be closer to 1 o'clock. I had only been there for about half an hour, and the roads from Newton St Loe had been pretty clear. I'd left Colin's at about midday so I would have arrived at Mum's and Dad's about 12:30. I made a mental note to mention it to them when I had finished eating.

I dipped a finger in the glass of water and put the cold, wet finger against my eyes. It soothed them, took away some of the heat from all the crying. I did it again, and then again.

After I finished the sandwich I hunted for the biscuits. They were in the bread-bin. I grabbed three and munched my way through them too. Mum called out from the front-room.

'Everything alright, dear?'

'Lovely thanks, Mum. Just having a biscuit.'

When I got to my last biscuit, I wandered through to Mum and Dad. He was reading, but Mum was just sitting there. No book and no knitting.

'I think the kitchen clock is a bit out,' I said. 'It's fast I think.'

'Your dad will look at it,' she said.

Dad put the paper down and nodded.

'How are the kids bearing up?' he said. 'Do they know about all these dreams and stuff?'

'No, of course not. I wouldn't put that on them. I think they're OK. I have been a bit distant and distracted recently, but I think I'm getting back on track now. You know what kids are like. Very resilient.'

'And Neil?' Dad said.

The tone of his voice was saying something, but I wasn't sure what.

'Neil knows,' I said. 'He seems a bit tired. I think he's got a lot on at work at the moment.'

'I meant, is Neil making sure you and the kids are OK. Is he there for you?'

'Of course he is, Dad. Neil is always there for us. You know how good he is.'

I sensed a reaction from Mum, but she didn't say anything. Perhaps I had imagined it. My mind was hardly in a great place.

'And what about school, dear,' she said. 'Is everything going OK for you back there?'

My eyebrow itched again.

'I'm not really back there at the moment. They want me to take as long as I need to get better. I stay in touch, and I did go in a couple of weeks ago, but I just feel it's better to not be there at the moment — until I know what's going on inside my head. Not with all the kids there.'

'You might find it's the normality you need?' Mum said.

'I will soon, Mum. I'm almost there I think.'

'And what about the Deputy Head job?' she said. 'Shouldn't you know by now?'

'I think they're just giving me more time, you know. Margaret spent a considerable amount of time persuading me to go for it in the first place. I'm sure she's just making sure I'm fit and well before adding to my responsibilities.'

I hoped I was right. I hoped that nothing had changed since all of this started. Mum's brow creased. It felt like it was the right time to leave. I had already given them enough of a burden with my sobbing in the kitchen. Now I was adding to it by giving them an opportunity to worry about my job too.

'It'll all be OK,' I said. 'I think I just needed to come here, to talk to you both. It all somehow seems much better now. You know, now that I've let it all out.'

They weren't stupid. I knew that. But they were kind enough to take what I was saying.

'Anyway,' I said, 'I really ought to make a move. Need to get tea ready. Be there for the kids. For Neil. Thank you for the food and for the shoulders to cry on,'

'We're always here, Chris,' Dad said. 'Just pick up the phone — any time, day or night. You know where we are.'

I ran to the car while Mum and Dad waved from the front door. It was still raining hard. I tried to avoid splashing through the puddles that had formed on the drive.

As I turned the key in the ignition a buzzer sounded. The petrol warning. I needed to re-fuel.

But that didn't make sense. I had had more than half a tank in there that morning, I would have used hardly any going to Colin's and then not much to Mum and Dad's.

I looked at the clock. It was nearly ten minutes to three.

And that didn't make sense either.

I looked back at the front door. Mum and Dad were still there. Still smiling, still waving. But their movements looked odd. Their arms juddered as they moved. Every turn of their head seemed staccato. It was as though I was looking at an old home movie.

My heart started pumping faster.

The pain in my leg intensified and I picked up a smell of something through the car air-vents. Although I knew it was a smell, it felt more like a physical sensation. My nose prickled. Smelling-salts?

I had no idea. I wasn't even sure if I had ever smelled smelling-salts before.

I gripped the steering wheel hard. In reality, I wanted to rush back indoors, shake Mum and Dad out of the old movie, and feel their love again. I needed them to let me know that everything was OK.

I gripped the wheel even harder as though through it I was getting a grip on myself.

"Don't let go, Christine," I said, my mouth barely open.

I forced a smile and a wave, and put the car into reverse. Slowly, their movements came back to real-time. As I pulled out of the drive my nose stopped prickling and my heart-rate dropped.

Along the main road, the pain in my leg was the last physical thing to disappear.

But I knew I had a problem. The clock on my dashboard was telling more or less the same time as the kitchen clock had, the one I had thought was wrong. The time on my phone agreed with both.

My heart rate pumped up again.

Less petrol than there should have been, and much later than I thought it was.

I shivered and turned the heating up.

And I realised that something had happened.

Somehow I had "lost" an hour and a half between leaving Colin's, and arriving at Mum and Dad's.

It made sense, now, that they had already had lunch and washed up. It made sense that I had been so starving hungry. It made sense that the kitchen clock had said the time it had. It hadn't been wrong. That all made sense now.

But the missing chunk of time from my day — that didn't make any sense at all.

CHAPTER TWENTY-FOUR

In my mind I tried to retrace my journey from Elm Gables. I had looked at the clock as I'd left, and it had definitely been almost midday. I wondered whether that clock had been wrong. I worked back further.

I went through breakfast, the kids going to school, Neil driving off to the bank.

I had a definite time for speaking to Doctor Jones as his phone-in time was only a fifteen minute slot before he started surgery at 9am. I had spoken to him at 8:45am.

Then I had showered. Tried to wash all the red paint and blood off my hands. Made an effort to look half human, and then come back downstairs to ring Colin Connell. It usually took me an hour to get ready. I may have taken a little longer this morning.

I had checked the weather forecast on the TV, grabbed a coffee and then picked up the phone. I remember telling him that I would be half an hour. As I slammed the door on the way out I realised I had meant to take an umbrella just in case. So I had to come back in for that. His clock had been right.

I pulled the car into a lay-by and sat back in the seat. I left the engine running to keep the warm air blowing gently on my feet. I turned the wipers off and let the rain cover the windscreen with circular psychedelic patterns.

Where had I gone between leaving Colin's house and pulling up at Mum and Dad's? I had obviously driven a lot. The fuel-gauge was almost on empty. I had definitely used at least half a tank. I wasn't sure exactly how many miles that represented but I guessed it must have been nearly 100 miles. The most I should have travelled was about 25 miles. Where the hell had I gone? Had I met anyone, or just driven? How could I not remember?

A large splat of rain slammed against the car roof.

It had been raining when I'd climbed into the car outside Colin's, and it had still been raining when I'd pulled up at Mum and Dad's.

I remembered some of the journey. I hadn't just zoned out and "woken up" in the driveway next to Dad's car. I remembered thinking back to my childhood as I came into Banwell. Thinking how lucky I had been to grow up there — with the parents I had.

I had been fully aware during that part of the journey.

The front of my head started pounding, just around the scar. The concentration seemed to be confusing me rather than clarifying things. I shuddered as a frightening thought hit me. Colin had been very keen for me to have a drink at his house. I'd said no to the coffee, but he almost insisted I have something. Could he have put something in my drink? I did drink all of the water. Had it tasted funny? I couldn't remember. I felt cold.

I flicked the wipers on and they squeaked across the windscreen. I decided to stop thinking about what had happened in the missing time. I used to tell the kids in my class that if they couldn't remember something, like a name or a date, they should think about something completely different. Invariably the thing they were trying to recall would come to them as soon as they stopped trying to recall it. I hoped that would work for me.

I pulled back out onto the road and looked out for a petrol station.

When I turned the car into our close I saw Margaret's car parked against the pavement outside the front of our house. She was sitting in the driving seat, she looked like she was reading.

I glanced at the dashboard clock. It was almost 3:30pm. Michael and Rose weren't due home for another half an hour. My heart started beating faster again. Something had happened to Michael or Rose. Why else would Margaret come to see me herself? Unless it was about the Deputy Head position. Perhaps they had come to a decision. Both options put even more pressure on my heart-rate. The throbbing pain in my head kept time with it. I wondered how long she had been waiting for me.

By the time I had driven the car onto the driveway, Margaret had climbed out of her car and started walking up the drive towards me. She held a hand up in front of her face, a small barrier to the rain.

She smiled at me as I got out of the car. I smiled back.

'Margaret?' I said. 'This is a surprise. Are Michael and Rose OK?'

She smiled again but didn't immediately say anything.

'Margaret?'

'Christine, they're fine. Don't worry. They haven't had an accident.'

She looked at the front door.

'Sorry,' I said. 'Let's go inside. This weather is awful.'

As we walked into the house the smell of paint hit me. I looked at Margaret but she didn't seem to have noticed. She had taken her glasses off and was wiping the raindrops from the lenses. As we walked into the living-room the smell of the paint was so intense that I expected to see that the offensive words we had scrubbed off the outside of the house that morning had seeped through the wall to show as a mirror image on our living room wall.

It hadn't.

The house felt cold. I asked Margaret if she wanted to take her coat off, but she shook her head.

'I'm not staying long, Chris. Just a friendly visit to see how you're doing. And to chat about a couple of things.'

It was always so difficult to extract what Margaret really meant when she said things. Her tone was nearly always even. As a result, most people had no option but to take what she said at face value. But my mind was shooting possible meanings all over the place.

'A couple of things?' I said.

'And to see how you are, Chris.'

Well, I've just been to see a counsellor, just had offensive language spray-painted on my house and I just lost an hour and a half and over a hundred miles that I can't remember at all.

'I'm fine,' I said. 'Shall we have a coffee? You have time for that, don't you?'

She nodded and smiled.

While the kettle hissed, I switched the heating on. I felt goosebumps all over my back, and my hair was damp from the rain.

As I stirred the coffees I tried to calm myself down. I slowed the stirring to a more sedate speed and breathed out slowly.

By the time I put the mugs on the coffee table I was pretty sure she wouldn't spot the slight tremor in my hands.

'How are you feeling, Christine? Are things going OK for you?'

'Definitely on the mend,' I said. 'I saw the doctor not long ago, and spoke to him this morning in fact. I think he's pleased with how things are going.'

'And your head? Is it healing nicely?'

I pushed my hand through my hair, pulling it back off my forehead.

'The scars are getting less noticeable by the day,' I said. 'The one on the back of my head isn't much more than a raised line now.'

Margaret frowned as she looked at my forehead.

'It's still quite red around the edges isn't it,' she said. 'It looks painful.'

I dropped my hand and let my hair fall back over the scar.

'It really is fine,' I said. 'I hardly even notice it anymore. I'll be right as rain soon. I keep on at the doctor to let me come back to work.'

'We all miss you, of course,' Margaret said. She took a sip of coffee.

I knew there was a "but" coming.

'And the children miss you terribly. But you know us. We soldier on through. That's why we're such a good team, Chris. We all adapt, we are all there for each other.'

Once again I couldn't read whether Margaret was really saying something else. *Face-value.*

'I can't wait to come back,' I said. I'm looking forward to seeing all the kids again. Putting all of this behind me. Onwards and upwards, you know?'

She took another sip of coffee. It amazed me that she could drink it so hot. I hadn't even touched mine yet.

'I was thinking about when you come back,' she said. 'I was wondering what would be best for you, to make coming back as easy as possible.'

I reached for my coffee. Too hot to drink but somehow, held in front of me, it felt like a barrier. Protection of sorts from what might be coming my way.

'Oh it's such a terrible shame that all of this has happened, Chris. A terrible shame. It always amazes me how a single event can cause ripples to travel so far and so wide. It's horrible that you were attacked. Awful. But it also has additional repercussions. Obviously it affects you personally, but also Neil and Rose. Michael. The school.'

Why had she mentioned Michael separately?

'The governors feel so sad for you too,' she said. 'They all think very highly of you, as you know.'

I lifted the mug of hot coffee to my lips and blew gently across it.

'It's really unfortunate that this has all come at this time,' she said.

Unfortunate?

'Just when we seemed to be moving forward with the Deputy Head position, gradually moving things into place.'

Aha!

'The governors were very keen to bring that to a conclusion at the end of February, have everything in place by the beginning of March. And then all this.'

She waved her hand in front of her. I blew across my coffee again.

'And now there's another problem too.'

I stopped blowing and put the mug down.

'Another problem?' I said.

'Chris, I'm sorry — but Michael got into a fight today.'

I sat up in my chair.

'A fight? You said he was OK?'

'He is OK, Chris. But he quite badly hurt the other boy — Harry Shaw.'

'But Harry is Michael's friend,' I said. 'He would never deliberately hurt him. It must have been an accident.'

'Christine, the reason I came round personally is that this isn't the first time. He's been in trouble a fair bit over the past couple of weeks. This was just the most serious of them all.'

I couldn't imagine Michael fighting anyone. That wasn't his nature at all. He didn't even bully Rose, and she was his "annoying little sister". If anything, he would protect people. Stand up for them.

'Perhaps he was trying to break up a fight,' I said. 'Maybe he was trying to protect Harry.'

'Michael started it, Chris. He was waiting for Harry in the playground and just launched an attack on him.'

My head felt like it was filling with water. I couldn't think clearly at all.

'Is Harry OK?' I said.

'He had to go to hospital for a check over. His nose was bleeding and his eye had a lump under it. I haven't heard back from the hospital or his parents yet. I'm sure he'll be fine. But I'm not sure what we are going to do about Michael.'

I felt a surge in my stomach. Adrenalin pushed its way through my body.

'It's unforgivable,' I said. 'I'm so sorry, Margaret. He can't go around fighting. I'm so sorry.' I tried to sound calm, but I wanted to kill Michael.

'I know it's not like him, Chris. That was part of the reason I came round. Have you noticed any changes in him at home recently?'

I squirmed in my chair. My cheeks felt hot.

'He's still too young for the "terrible teens" to be kicking in,' she said. 'How has he been here, at home?'

I felt ashamed that the only thing I had noticed about him was that he had looked tired. It was horrible to hear from someone else what I should have been seeing for myself.

'He's been looking a bit tired,' I said. It felt like a pathetic comment, but it was all I had.

Margaret raised her eyebrows.

'I know you'll want to talk to him,' she said. 'I have spoken to him at school, reminded him that his mum is a teacher there, and that he needs to set a good example. I asked him to explain his behaviour but he seemed reluctant to talk to me. I didn't want to push it because he's your son. We all appreciate that you have gone through a terrible time. Perhaps if you and Neil speak to him, he might be more forthcoming.'

'I'll speak to him straight away, as soon as he gets home. Do you want me to keep him off school at all?'

She didn't answer immediately. I watched her lips squeeze

tightly together.

'I think a good talking to will do the trick,' she said. 'Obviously we'll be keeping a close eye on him. And the sooner you're back with us the better for us all.'

'Of course,' I said.

'And you may want to consider a quick phone call to Harry's parents, just to see how he is. I've brought their number for you.'

'Of course,' I said again.

'The governors are seriously having another look at Matthew's application,' she said. 'They have interviewed him again and seem more interested than before. He is a good candidate, Chris, and he's been at the school for a good while. Longer than you.'

She put her coffee cup on the table.

I followed suit.

'Margaret, when the Dep. Head proposal first came up, I had no interest in it whatsoever — you know that. But it was you who persuaded me that it would be a good idea. And after a lot of thought, I agreed. You know how much I can bring to the school, you know how dedicated I am. All this is just a blip. I'll be back soon, I'll talk to Michael tonight, sort it all out. I'll give Harry's parents a call. I'm pretty much at the end of all this now.'

'Christine, I'm sure all of that is true. But the governors want stability. The school needs it. No decision has been made yet. They have already gone way beyond the time-frame they originally wanted. They are giving you lots of leeway. I'm just letting you know that they are under pressure too. Be thankful that they all know you. They understand your situation. But they have to think of the school too. For them, school-life goes on every day. The school has to be their first consideration. That's why they are the governors.'

'I understand,' I said. 'And I will be back as soon as I

possibly can.'

'I know, Chris.' Margaret stood up. 'And I can't wait.'

I walked Margaret to the door and waved goodbye as her car disappeared out of the close. My eyes glazed over. Rain splashed against my face. Cold, spiteful droplets. It brought me back into focus. Margaret's car was long gone.

I pushed the front door gently shut and listened to the latch locking home.

Michael fighting; Matthew moving in on the governors; and me unable to account for an hour and a half of my day.

I strode to the kitchen. The just-in-case bottle of wine was upright in the cupboard next to the clock. I pulled it out, slammed it on the work top and unscrewed the lid.

CHAPTER TWENTY-FIVE

I emptied the entire bottle down the sink. Even the smell of it turned my stomach. As the last of it swirled down the plughole I saw Abi's car pull up outside. She saw me at the kitchen window and waved. The back door of the car opened and Rose and Michael climbed out. The rain was easing off a bit. Abi didn't get out, just waved again and smiled, before driving off. She must have passed Margaret's car on the way. I wondered whether she knew about the visit. Maybe that was why she didn't come to the door herself.

The empty wine bottle clattered as I dropped it into the bin. I knew I should have put it in the recycling, but throwing it in the bin seemed more symbolic to me — and that was what I was after.

I was furious with Michael, embarrassed on behalf of Rosie, and utterly ashamed that I hadn't noticed.

He's been in trouble a fair bit over the past couple of weeks.

I felt as though it was as much my fault as it was Michael's, but he had to be told. There was no excuse for fighting.

I opened the front door just as the kids got to it. Rosie rang the doorbell anyway.

I gave a smile and rubbed my eyebrow. Damned itch.

'Hello, Mum,' Rose said. 'Are you feeling any better today?'

I told her I was. Much better.

Michael mumbled "hello" and walked past me to the living-room. I heard the telly come to life as I hung up Rose's coat.

'Have you got any homework today?' I asked her.

'I think so,' she said. 'Only a little bit.'

'Well if you go up to your room and get it done straight away, we'll do something nice for tea, OK?'

'Maccy D's?' she said.

'We'll see.'

'Does Michael have to do his now too?'

'I'm just going to go and talk to him about it now. So up you go. Quick as you can, OK?'

As she charged upstairs she shouted back down.

'Maccy D's please.'

Michael didn't look up as Rose ran through. Nor as I came and sat down in the armchair opposite the sofa where he had slouched. I reached for the remote and switched the TV off.

'I was watching that,' he said.

He still looked tired. But I could see he was agitated too. Full of energy, but too exhausted to do anything with it. He lifted his chin, looked like he was preparing for a fight. With me.

'Have you got anything you want to tell me?' I said.

'What do you mean,' he said. Flicking his eyes to the blank TV screen.

'Look at me, Michael!'

He looked. Shocked.

'What happened at school today?'

'Nothing,' he said. 'Anyway, what do you mean?'

'How's Harry?' I said.

Silence.

'Michael, what's going on? You know it's wrong to fight. And this isn't even the first time. It's not like you. What happened?'

'They've all been horrible to me at school,' he said. 'Calling me names and things. Even Harry.'

'Mike, you know that's what happens at school. Name-calling isn't something you should fight about. You know that. Me and your dad have always told you not to worry if that sort of thing goes on.'

'It's everyone,' he said. 'All the time.'

'Mike you should have come to me, or Dad. If you had spoken to us about it we could have sorted it all out for you. You've always come to us in the past. That's why where so good as a family, we all talk to each other about things.'

He went to say something and stopped himself.

'What?' I said.

'Nothing!'

'Mikey, talk to me. That's what I'm here for.'

He looked me in the eye now.

'That's just it,' he said. 'You're not here. Since you got attacked it's like you haven't been here at all.'

Tears filled his eyes. He tried to wipe them away with the back of his hand.

'You and Dad,' he said. 'It's like you've all gone quiet. I know you're here, in the house, but it's not like before. We aren't all talking to each other. Dad doesn't talk to you, you don't talk to Dad. And no one seems to be talking to us.'

I knew he meant Rose and him. And I knew he was right. My eyes were stinging. He spotted the tears and it made his worse.

'They were all being horrible about you, Mum. They were saying you were ugly. Calling you scarface, saying you had horrible marks on your face and that you would always be ugly now.'

He asked me if I thought you were still beautiful.

'Even Harry said it. He was my friend, Mum. And even he said it. 'I'm sorry that he had to go to hospital. But he shouldn't have been saying those things about you. None of them should.'

I held my arms out to Michael and he virtually leapt from the sofa to me. I held him tight, hugged him. We both sobbed.

The third stair creaked.

'What's wrong?' Rose said.

'Come here, darling,' I said. 'Everything is fine.'

'Why are you both crying?'

Michael immediately tried to pull away from me. Nothing could be worse than crying in front of your little sister.

Especially if you are hugging Mum at the same time. I held onto him with one arm and reached out to Rose with the other. She joined us in the hug, a look of bewilderment on her face.

'I'm so sorry I've not been myself,' I said. 'You kids and Dad are everything to me. I couldn't have got through any of this if it weren't for you guys, and I haven't been there for you. I'm so sorry.'

'You have been here, Mum,' Rose said.

Michael looked at her. She stared back.

'You're always here,' she said.

'Since the accident I've had so much on my mind, that I just haven't been the same. And there's no excuses for it. We're an island, us Marsdens, and we all protect each other. If ever I go quiet again — tell me. Better still — tickle me.'

I squeezed them both around the middle. Both of them squirmed. They both knew what was coming.

The tickling was just what we all needed. I wished that Neil had been there for it too.

It felt as though it had been pouring with rain, and now the sun was out, drying up all the puddles, warming everyone through.

But even during the tickling I had seen a dark cloud. Full of something bad.

As we had tickled each other, above the squeals and giggling, I had felt my arms getting stronger again. Surges of power pumped through them. And for a moment I had wanted to pick Michael and Rose up, one in each hand, and toss them against the living-room walls. The feeling had passed through my mind in a heartbeat — in, and then straight out again. It was so quick that I barely had time to register it. And of course I instantly doubted that I had even had the thought in the first place.

But I knew I had.

There was something else too. A voice. Not like a whisper and not like a thought. More like a feeling. But it shocked me. It wasn't a noise from the kids, and it wasn't a sound from outside. It came from within my head. I'm not sure what it said. It wasn't me, physically.

It sounded like a man's voice, but it also sounded like me, internally.

At first I had thought it was the thief who mugged me. I panicked that he had got into the house, even though we had changed the locks. And then I thought it might be Neil, home early and hiding somewhere.

But it wasn't. It definitely came from within me.

And it came just before I had the feeling of wanting to fling my children against the walls.

CHAPTER TWENTY-SIX

While the kids finished their McDonald's at the dining table, I sat on the sofa and shut my eyes. I tried to find a happy place. A place that was quiet and calm. In my mind I went through what had happened that day. I wanted to pinpoint my biggest challenges. I wanted to develop a strategy for overcoming those issues and I needed to work out which problem to attack first.

It was possible that Colin had drugged me at his house. He hadn't explained how his wife had died, he had practically insisted I have a drink or something to eat. And he had a new rug.

Of course it was possible. But it wasn't probable.

He'd seemed like a nice guy. He was recommended by Dr Jones. And I was experiencing extraordinary paranoia.

So something else had happened to me, resulting in me not remembering an hour and a half and close to one hundred miles of driving. I had to account for it — but I couldn't.

So that was probably challenge number one.

Michael had problems at school as a direct result of me being a shit mum. I could deal with that one immediately and as far as Michael was concerned I had probably already made inroads with the tickling and the Maccy D's.

The Deputy Head job was just one of those things. Of course I still wanted the job, but I had other, more important things to deal with first. I would get back to school as soon as possible. If I was the right person for the job — then I would get it.

I had already decided not to drink. I wasn't going to use any sort of substance to fool my nose into not smelling things and I definitely wasn't going to try to develop any additional personalities.

When I thought about Neil I felt butterflies in my stomach. I wasn't sure what was going on with him. It could just be the pressure of work at the bank — but it could be so much more too.

And the dreams. They were still an issue I had to deal with. Along with the ongoing pain in my leg with no bruise and no mark.

I caught my breath when I remembered the feeling of power in my arms when I'd tickled the kids, but also the desire to hurt them. To fling them away from me against the walls. And then the voice. Unclear, dripping with hatred and inside my head. The voice of a man.

Missing time.

Dreams and visions.

Physical changes and feelings of power.

Wanting to hurt my children.

Hearing voices.

I had a big problem. It scared me. It scared me a lot.

I saw my word-puzzle book on the floor under the coffee table. My electronic dictionary sat on top of it. My hands were shaking again as I picked up the dictionary. I typed in a word and started reading the definition.

My concentration was broken by the sound of a key scratching at the front door.

Neil.

He was in before I managed to switch off the dictionary and close the lid.

'Hello,' he said.

I shut the lid and put the dictionary down beside me. Neil looked at it, then at me.

'Are you OK?' he said.

I stood up and walked over to him.

'Of course. How was your day? You're a bit late again?' I looked into his face. He still had dark bags under his eyes, his nose looked red. I couldn't make out if his eyes were bloodshot or not.

'Work,' he said. 'You know how it is.'

'You should have let me know.'

I breathed in through my nose as we kissed. Tried to play detective with my sense of smell. No alcohol as far as I could tell. A spicy aroma — perhaps a tikka sandwich for lunch. And something else. Was it perfume? I couldn't be sure. Really not sure at all. But it was possible.

He nodded in the direction of the sofa.

'What were you up to?' he said. 'You looked very guilty when I walked in.'

'I was just looking up a word in my dictionary. For one of my word-puzzles.'

His eyes moved to the puzzle book, still closed and still under the table. Then he looked straight at me. I blushed.

'How are the kids?' he said.

'Just finishing a McDonald's. I wanted to treat them tonight. I thought you and me could have something quick from the freezer. And I've got stuff to talk to you about too.'

His shoulders dropped slightly and he forced a smile. 'Great,' he said. 'Let me just get a drink first.'

I heard Michael in his room, destroying planets on Playstation. Rose curled up in front of the TV watching a DVD.

In the dining room, behind closed doors, Neil and I chewed our way through a cook-from-frozen Chinese meal for two. I told him as much as I could about my day, about Colin Connell, about Mum and Dad and about Michael. I didn't mention the missing time or the unexplained mileage reading.

As soon as I mentioned the fight, Neil opened his mouth to shout upstairs for Michael to come down. I stopped him.

'He was protecting me,' I said. 'And Rose.'

'How on earth was he protecting you? You weren't even there.'

'Not so loud,' I said. 'They'll hear you.'

'I need to give that boy a damn good talking to.'

I explained how other children had been rude about me. Calling me ugly and scarface. How it had been affecting Michael, and presumably Rose too.

'That will be why he asked me if I thought you were still beautiful,' Neil said. His voice softer now.

I nodded.

'I tried ringing Harry's parents earlier, but they must have been up at the hospital. I'm going to call them again after we've eaten. Find out how he is. Maybe offer to go round there and talk to them.'

Neil nodded.

'I still need to talk to Michael as well,' he said.

'Why don't we sit down and talk to him together,' I said. 'Before bed?'

'OK,' he said. 'Together.'

He put his chopsticks down and wiped his mouth. 'And what about paying this Connell bloke? Do you think it's worth it?'

'I'm not sure what to make of it at the moment. I'll give the doctor a call in the morning and talk it through with him. It will give me a chance to find out if Colin Connell has spoken to him yet.'

'If we have to pay for it, we have to pay for it,' Neil said. 'It's important to get you better, Chris. We will always find a way.'

I reached over the table and touched his hand.

'Let's see what the doctor says first,' I said.

After we'd finished eating we loaded up the dishwasher together and threw away all the empty food containers. I told Neil to go and spend some time with Rose in the living-room while I called Harry's parents from the phone in the kitchen.

Yes, Harry was fine really. A bit shocked and bruised. We know how sorry you are Christine. Yes, it might be helpful to visit. No — I'm not sure it would be a good idea to bring Michael — I'm sure they'll sort it out between them back at school. In about twenty minutes? Yes, that will be fine. See you then.

What a relief. Harry was OK and his parents were still talking to me. I put the phone down and opened the kitchen door.

Rose was still sprawled on the sofa, still watching the film. Neil was sat in the armchair looking down. Open in his hands was my electronic dictionary. He looked confused. I felt my heart bump. The dictionary always switched on to the last word that was looked up. As I walked into the room, Neil stared up at me.

I could see by his expression that he had read it.

Insane - in a state of mind which prevents normal perception, behaviour, or social interaction; seriously mentally ill.

CHAPTER TWENTY-SEVEN

I ignored Neil's expression. He ignored mine.

'How's Harry?' he said.

'I'm going over there now. He's OK, but they said they would like me to come and see them.'

Neil put the dictionary down beside him, still open.

'I'm not sure how long I'll be,' I said. 'You're OK with the kids aren't you? If I'm not back in time, be gentle with Mikey. I have already spoken to him and we really should do it together.'

'I'll be good,' he said.

I leaned over and kissed him goodbye, but I could feel him holding back.

When I stepped outside into the darkness the rain had stopped but huge clouds scudded across the sky. I pulled my coat tight around me and shivered. The car would take a while to warm up, so I put my collar up and climbed in.

I drove through the damp streets and prayed that I wouldn't "lose time" again. I didn't have enough petrol for a start.

I rubbed my eyebrow and thought about what I would say to Donna and Mark Shaw — Harry's parents. I hadn't taught Harry personally, but I had taught his older sister, Petra, a few years earlier.

I felt so embarrassed and ashamed. But not of Michael, although he was the one who actually attacked Harry. I knew that really I was the one to blame.

I was starting to worry about being able to get a grip on things. I had always thought of myself as proactive and capable. The Mighty Atom. But now I was starting to wonder.

It seemed that everything I tried was being usurped by my own mind and body. I had tried *Vicks* to mask the smells;

Anne to disguise my personality; doctors for the pain in my leg; and a counsellor for the shit in my head. It felt as though every corner I turned, something else was waiting for me. Something I hadn't bargained for.

I already knew that I currently had no idea how to combat the unusual strength that pumped through my body at certain times. I was pretty sure I had no idea how to deal with the male voice that seemed to have appeared in my head. And I seemed to be able to do as much about my feelings of violence and aggression as I could about my dreams.

The car splashed through a huge puddle in the road, showering water against the side of the car and the pavement.

That missing hour and a half. I had given it a lot of thought. The way things were going, I felt that there was a strong possibility of it happening again. I had already determined that I would be ready for it, and that if I couldn't stop it happening, I would at least be aware of it after the event.

It occurred to me that I might be able to get a handle on it if I used a calendar or diary, split into hours, or half hour slots. I could put a tick against every half hour or hour to confirm that I was "still there".

It might help to keep me focused on where I was and what I was doing every half hour of the day. If I printed it out from my computer I could fold it up and keep it with me all the time.

My plan was that this would keep me firmly in real time. But if I did "disappear" I would at least have a record of it by the missing ticks on the page.

It seemed to make sense. I decided to ring Dr Jones first thing in the morning and talk to him about the missing time, see if there was anything he could do. But the half-hourly tick record would be my own defence against it. It would give me a degree of control. And I wanted that.

The lights were all on at Harry's house. I thought it would be impertinent to park in their driveway, so I pulled the car up against the pavement outside. As I locked the car and walked toward the house I saw a shadow disappear from an upstairs window, the curtain swayed.

Mark Shaw answered the door. His face was pale and blotchy, his smile weak. His hair was messed up and he still wore his suit, tie missing, and top few shirt buttons undone. He looked completely different from when I had seen him before at Parent's Evening. Over his shoulder, in the living-room, I saw his wife, Donna and their 14 year old daughter, Petra. Donna signalled something to her daughter, who stood up with all the theatrics of a teenager and disappeared. Moments later I heard loud clomping up the stairs.

The journey home was as uncomfortable as the meeting with Harry's parents had been.

For some reason, I couldn't get rid of the dream I had been having. The wind, the girl, the smells and the violence.

I wasn't having the dream, I just seemed to be replaying it on a continual loop in my mind.

I turned the radio on and sang along to any songs that I vaguely knew, I opened the window and tried distracting myself with different smells. I started "dancing" in my seat as I drove. But it kept replaying, again and again. Like when there's a song stuck in your head, and no matter what you do to try to distract yourself, it always goes back to it.

It wasn't scaring me either. It just kept playing over and over. I felt like it was trying to ingrain itself into my brain cells, even more than it already was.

I resorted to swearing along to the music. And when the music stopped, I swore along to the DJ.

By the time I pulled into our driveway I had goosebumps all over me from the open window and a sore throat from all the singing and swearing. In my mind, I was still hurting the girl.

I checked the clock on the dashboard before turning the engine off. Nearly 10pm. I hoped that Neil had been OK at dealing with the kids. Especially Michael.

I pushed the front door key in the lock as quietly as I could. I guessed that Neil would have gone to bed already.

Before I managed to turn the key in the lock, the front door opened. Neil looked about as good as Mark Shaw had a couple of hours earlier.

'How did it go,' he said.

'Oh, you know. OK.'

He stood aside as I walked in. I shook my coat off and let it fall to the floor. Neil bent down, picked it up and hung it over a hook.

'You've not even had your shower,' I said. 'I thought you'd be in bed by now.'

He didn't smile.

'I wanted to wait up for you. See how it went with Harry's parents. Also I spoke a bit to Michael.'

I frowned at him. I had told him to go easy on Michael.

'I didn't get angry with him. We just talked,' he said. 'And to be honest, Chris, I think you and I need to talk too.'

My heart jumped. Neil never wanted to talk. Not about anything. Even when his father died he still didn't feel the need to sit down and have a good talk about it.

I stretched my neck back and moved my head from side to side. If someone had offered me a massage and a hot chocolate right then I would have killed for it.

I realised that the loop in my mind had stopped playing.

'I need a drink first,' I said.

'We haven't got any.'

'I meant a coffee. At least let me get a coffee. And a couple of paracetamol.'

On my way through to the kitchen I noticed that my

electronic dictionary was back under the coffee table, on top of the word-puzzle book.

I wished I hadn't washed that last bottle of wine down the sink.

CHAPTER TWENTY-EIGHT

Neil hovered about while I made a coffee. I thought he'd get me the headache tablets, but he didn't. I got them myself, gave him a look, and plonked down on the sofa.

He remained standing.

'How are you doing, Chris,' he said. 'I mean really. No bullshit.'

Wow! That was direct.

'I'm fine, Neil.' I waved my hand in as dismissive a way as I could. 'Tell me what happened with Michael.'

Neil's expression didn't change. He wasn't buying the "Michael" gambit.

'I told you,' he said. 'Michael was fine. What's happening with you? I know I didn't get the full story over dinner. And when I walked in you looked guilty as hell — on your dictionary of all things.'

I stared straight ahead and pretended to sip my too-hot coffee.

'I'm sorry, Chris, but I had to see what you were looking at. I checked the puzzle book when you were out. *Insane* isn't in it!'

I almost came back at him with "*Well you keep coming home late and going to bed early. What the hell is going on there? I had a dream about you, you know. And another woman!*". But this wasn't the time for that one. He had already told me he had a lot on at work and I knew he would just repeat that again. And he was right. I hadn't been as honest as I could about my day.

OK. Let's see if he could take it.

I looked him in the eye.

'The only things I didn't tell you were about the journey from the counsellor's to Mum and Dad's,' I said. 'And a couple of things that happened when I got home.'

Still Neil's expression remained steadfast. A slight eyebrow flicker because he wasn't sure what was coming next, but nothing more.

'I told you all about the counsellor, all about Mum and Dad and all about the chat with Margaret.'

Neil nodded.

'And I told you about the talk with Michael, why he was fighting, and that we had a massive tickle afterwards.'

He nodded again.

'I didn't tell you I was looking up certain words on my dictionary because I was embarrassed. And scared.'

'Scared of what?' Neil said.

'Scared of what you might think,' I said.

'What happened on the journey to your mum and dad's?' he said.

'That's part of the problem,' I said. 'I don't know.'

'Chris, come on. You have to be honest with me. I can't be here for you if I don't know what's going on.'

I looked away from him and rubbed my ear.

'That's what I'm saying, Neil. I lost some time. I set out from the counsellor's at about midday and I didn't get to Mum and Dad's until about 2pm. But I went straight there, as far as I know, and I didn't realise that I had got there so late. I thought it was about half-twelve.'

'I don't understand what you're saying,' he said. 'You drove around for a bit, or stopped off or something on the way?'

'I'm not explaining it very well,' I said. 'Basically, I had some sort of blackout, or something, between the counsellor's and Mum and Dad's. But it wasn't a proper blackout. Although I don't remember anything about it, I was still driving. According to the fuel-gauge I think I drove about one hundred miles — and I don't remember any of it.'

'Chris, that doesn't make any sense. Perhaps you were just thinking about stuff. God knows you've got plenty going on to think about. You probably just had your mind on other things. I've had that before — where you're driving and you suddenly become aware that you can't remember the last few miles. Your mind has just been on other things. I think that's normal.'

'A few miles, Neil? I can cope with that. But a hundred miles? That's not normal.'

Neil clicked his fingers, as though he'd suddenly solved everything.

'You might have a fuel leak,' he said. 'I'll get it checked out.'

He had a point. I hadn't considered a leak. That would certainly explain all the missing fuel.

'But what about the missing time? The hour and a half?'

'Maybe you really did fall asleep,' he said. 'Perhaps you were mentally exhausted after the counsellor and you pulled over on the way to your mum and dad's. Perhaps you just don't remember doing it.'

I felt stupid. But I also felt like I was right.

'It seemed very real,' I said. 'I don't think I fell asleep.'

'And you said something happened at home?' he said.

'While I was tickling the kids, I heard a voice. Inside my head, Neil, I heard a voice. It was real and it was definite. It sounded like man's voice. Or at least a voice that was deeper than mine. It felt like it came from me. Like it *was* me in some way.'

'A voice? What did it say?'

'I don't know. I couldn't make out the words. I also felt immense power and strength going through my arms. I felt incredibly strong.'

'And this was while you were tickling the kids?' he said.

I nodded.

'Maybe it was an adrenalin rush. You know — the blood pumping around your body from all the laughing about and tickling. I don't know what to say about the voice. If you were all laughing and screaming…?'

'Neil, I know what you're trying to do, and I'm grateful. But these things did all happen. I don't think they can be just explained away, and I think it's dangerous to ignore them.'

'Dangerous?'

'I have no idea what is going on inside my head. But every time I try to deal with it or combat it, something else happens. I used to have a degree of control, but at the moment I feel like my control is severely limited.

'I know you're trying to make me feel better by coming up with explanations for the things that are happening to me, but the truth is, I am slowly losing my mind.'

'But you're not going insane,' he said. 'A knock on the head doesn't send people insane.'

'Well what the fuck does it do then, doctor Marsden?'

That changed his expression.

'I don't know,' he said. 'But I think that you should go and see the doctor again.'

'I'm going to see him in the morning. I'm ringing him first thing.'

'Chris, I'm only saying what I think. I really don't believe you're going mad and I don't think you're losing control. I *do* think you are suffering from stress, and that's completely understandable.'

He shuffled down next to me on the sofa and sort of wrapped his arms around me. I pulled back and he tried to pull me close.

I held back some more.

'You're not going mad, Chris. I guarantee it.'

I wished I'd stopped to get a bottle of wine on the way home.

CHAPTER TWENTY-NINE

The following morning was heavy with mist. Damp, rolling curtains of it moving slowly around the streets. I was pretty sure I could smell the sea on it, even though we were fifteen miles or more from the nearest wave. I wondered if it had rolled all the way down the A4 from Avonmouth. All sounds seemed to have been deadened, like when it snowed. But the birds still screeched their morning greetings to each other (if that was what they were). It bothered me to think that the birds might not be able to find all their usual places in the mist.

I had climbed out of bed before anyone that morning. I made them all a packed-lunch and cooked everyone a hot breakfast. They had all looked at me with bewildered expressions — especially Michael.

Neil and I barely spoke. But only because we were busy doing other things. When we kissed goodbye he told me to be careful. I told him I would be.

Michael pulled Rose's ponytail while she was putting her arms into her coat. She squealed and pushed back into him, he tripped over his school bag and burst into laughter. If Rose had been going to complain, his falling over stopped it dead in its tracks. She laughed too. The tickle really had done them some good. Michael quietened down a little as he said goodbye. He looked suddenly preoccupied.

'You know Harry probably won't be in today,' I told him.

'Are you sure he's OK?' Michael said.

'I told you, he is fine. I saw him last night. He had bruises and bumps, but he's OK. I even got the feeling that he felt a bit guilty about it himself.'

'He was calling you names,' Michael, said. 'But I didn't mean for him to go to hospital.'

'Michael, just make sure that nothing like that ever happens again, no matter what names people use. As long as you're sorry and as long as you don't do it again, everyone will be fine — I promise.'

'OK?' he said.

'The teachers know that it's not normally like you to do anything like that. In a few weeks it will all be forgotten about. And I'm sure you and Harry will be fine too.'

'When are you coming back to school?' he said.

I shook my head. 'I'm not sure, Mikey. Very soon, I hope.'

He looked happier as he chased Rose to the car. He would be fine.

At 8:30am I printed off a page of time-slots from my computer. They were divided into half hours, and each time had a line next to it to write in appointments. I ticked from 6:am, the first time on the sheet, to 8:30. So far, so good. I folded the sheet and put it in my handbag, along with a pen.

When I rang him during his surgery phone-in at 8:45am, Doctor Jones said he could see me straight away.

I drove as quickly as I could through the thick mist and heard my name called out by an electronic voice as I stepped through the health centre's automatic door.

Although I was probably his first patient of the day, Doctor Jones' room smelled as though hundreds of sick bodies had already passed through it that morning. The air was stale and poorly. I wanted to tell him to throw open a window and let something fresh in. I was thankful that I wasn't his last patient of the day. No wonder doctors were off sick all the time.

He nodded at the chair in front of his desk. As I sat down I looked from him to the window, several times, willing him with my mind to open the damn thing. It didn't work.

'You said on the phone that you think you've experienced a blackout,' he said. 'A period of time that you can't remember

— is that right?'

'That's right,' I said. 'I lost about an hour and a half yesterday after going to see Mr Connell.'

'You know, the human mind is a remarkable thing,' he said. 'It recognises when we are highly stressed or overwhelmed and often switches into "protection" mode. Almost like an auto-pilot. Have you ever experienced a moment when you're driving and you suddenly realise that you can't remember the last few miles?'

I wondered how much trouble I would get into for punching a doctor on his first appointment of the day.

'My husband said the same thing,' I said. 'This was different. It wasn't like that.'

He sat back in his chair and smiled.

'What was the last thing you remember doing?' he said.

'I remember leaving Colin Connell's house, climbing into my car and looking up at the sky. The sky was dark, with big, heavy clouds. It had just started raining really hard and I wondered if there might be lightning. I think I could smell the lightning.

'There were a few people about and I noticed that none of them had umbrellas. And then I decided not to go home, but to drive to Banwell to see my mum and dad.'

He wasn't making any notes as I spoke. I think I thought he should be.

'And then I remember coming into Banwell and thinking back over my childhood. Being with Mr Connell had started me thinking about things I hadn't thought about for ages.'

'You said that you "lost" about one and a half hours. But also that you drove almost one hundred miles that you can't recall?'

I nodded.

So did he.

'To have driven that far in that amount of time, you must

have been averaging about 65 miles per hour.'

I hadn't thought of that.

'That seems a little on the fast side,' he said.

I couldn't argue with that. I wondered if I had been caught on a speed camera somewhere. Or even whether I had been pulled over by the police. I couldn't remember a damn thing, so anything was possible.

'Are you absolutely sure it was that distance? Or indeed if it was only an hour and a half?'

'I can't be a hundred percent sure about the distance. I hadn't pushed in the mileage thingy at the start. I'm only guessing by the amount of fuel that had gone. The fuel-gauge said nearly empty and I'm pretty certain I had over half a tank when I'd started out that morning.'

Doctor Jones pushed his chair back and reached up for a large book on a shelf over his desk. It looked like a directory to me, but I assumed it was full of medical stuff.

'Had you eaten anything prior the this "blank" period?' he said.

'I'd had breakfast,' I said. 'Then I rang you and you gave me Colin Connell's number. I didn't eat anything else after that until I got to my mum and dad's. And I was starving.'

'What had you eaten for breakfast?'

'Just cereal. And a coffee.'

'Had you had anything else to drink — other than the coffee?'

'I'd had several coffees,' I said. 'We were up pretty early. In the early hours really. We had an intruder in the garden, and then the police were called. It was all a bit stressful. So I'd had a few coffees to keep me going.'

'Nothing else?'

I wasn't sure how to broach the subject of Colin Connell's virtual insistence that I drink or eat something. Doctor Jones had recommended Connell personally. But perhaps the doctor was thinking along the same lines I had, that maybe I had eaten or drunk something dodgy.

'Mr Connell gave me a drink,' I said. 'Practically insisted. He must have thought I looked thirsty. Offered me food too.'

'But you didn't have any?'

I shook my head.

'Only a glass of water. I wasn't really hungry at the time,' I said. 'I think I was a bit nervous.'

'OK,' he said. 'Let's have a look at you.'

He picked up one of those wooden lolly stick type things they put on your tongue while they look down your throat. He also grabbed one of those torchy eye things that seems to double up as an ear thing too. Medical terminology was never my strong point.

The throat examination was over in a moment. I think we both knew there was nothing wrong with my throat. But he spent more time hovering around my ears. And even longer staring into my eyes through the torchy eye thing.

'Have you had any problems with the wounds?' he said. 'Are they still healing OK?'

I was going to say "Well you're the doctor — you tell me". But the timing wasn't right.

'I think they're healing fine,' I said, trying not to blink at the bright light still shining in my left eye from a distance of about ten millimetres. He moved it back across to the right eye again.

'And are you feeling generally well at the moment? Have you had any dizzy-spells or feelings of nausea?'

'I still have this pain in my upper left leg,' I said. 'There's still no bruising there, and there are no marks or scratches either — but the pain is definitely there. It's a dull ache practically all the time, but every now and then the pain intensifies. Sometimes for a prolonged period and sometimes just a sharp stabbing pain.'

At last he switched the bright light off and I squeezed my eyes shut for a few seconds. When I opened them Doctor

Jones had disappeared. Then I felt hot breath on the back of my neck. Instinctively I jolted forward, almost out of the chair, and spun around.

'I'm sorry,' he said. 'I just need to examine the wounds on your head. I didn't mean to startle you.'

I blushed. 'Sorry. I had closed my eyes after the torch thing, and when I opened them I couldn't see you. Then I just felt breathing behind me. It made me jump.'

I sat back in the chair. Calmed myself down.

'I need to feel around your neck and also your head too,' he said.

"Phrenology — it's pretty much regarded as a pseudo-science now"

'Very often,' he said, 'blackouts are caused by a lack of blood reaching the brain. So for some people, if they stand up too suddenly it can cause a minor blackout. Also diabetics can be prone to them, and those with low blood pressure.'

As he spoke I felt his hands pressing in at the base of my skull around my neck. His fingers felt smooth and dry. He pressed hard and I winced. He didn't apologise.

'I need to see if there are any obvious signs of blood loss or internal bleeding. I know you've already had an MRI for all this, but it is possible that something small may have been missed. If it's been building up over the last few weeks it may be the thing that's causing you the problems. If there is something near the surface, I might be able to feel it on your head.'

He felt around my head a bit. I stared at the closed window again. Perhaps the lumps on my head would convey my desire for fresh air.

'That all seems OK as far as I can tell,' he said. 'Can you roll your sleeve up and we'll just check your blood-pressure.'

For some reason I hated the blood-pressure thing. As soon as he wrapped it around my arm I tensed up. I knew it wasn't painful, but feeling my veins throbbing against the sleeve as the air is pumped into it makes me feel on edge and uncomfortable. I always feel like they pump too much air in, so it's really tight and then they leave it pumped up for too long, letting it out too slowly. Perhaps I'm a wimp. Although I'm fine with needles and spiders.

The air hissed as he slowly let it out.

'Let's have a look at this leg of yours,' he said. 'If you would just hop onto the examination bed.'

I rolled my sleeve down and blushed again as I pulled my trousers half way down.

'Where does the pain seem to be?' he said.

I put my hand over the area that hurt.

'It feels like it's right at the surface,' I said. 'Although there's nothing there to see. Maybe I damaged it inside when I hit the ground?'

'It is possible that there is some nerve damage,' he said. 'If you are feeling something on the surface, but there's nothing there.'

'Sometimes it feels deep in there too. Could that still be nerve damage?'

He felt around the area I had pointed to.

'It's possible. Does this hurt.'

'It's no more than the dull ache at the moment. Pushing it seems to have no bearing on whether it hurts or not. It just comes when it wants to.'

'This was x-rayed at the time wasn't it? And it came back fine.'

I didn't know what to say to him. So I just looked at him.

'OK, if you would get dressed and come and sit back down.'

I pulled my trousers up and shuffled over to the chair again.

He sat down and looked into his big medical directory, turned a few pages.

'I think perhaps we should get you to the hospital again,' he said. 'It might be prudent to have another brain-scan.'

'No problem,' I said, zipping up my boots. 'I think that would be a good idea too.'

'I think we should do it sooner rather than later. Perhaps we should get you there straight away.'

He turned to his computer monitor and tapped a few things on the keyboard.

'Do you have time to go there now?' he said.

'Is it Bristol or Bath?' I said. Both were more or less the same distance from home, but Bristol was slightly better for parking.

'It's up to you, but Bristol might be a good option. I'll need to ring them.'

He asked me to "park myself" in the waiting-room while he contacted the hospital. He said he would come out personally to get me when he was ready. For ten minutes I flicked through a caravan magazine that was almost as old as Rose.

The waiting room door squeaked and Doctor Jones walked towards me. He held a sheet of paper in his hand.

'They can see you straight away,' he said. 'I explained your symptoms and what happened. If you hand this to the reception when you get there, they'll put you in the right direction.'

He handed me the sheet of paper. I wasn't sure if I was supposed to look at it or not. I decided not to.

'They will write to me, of course,' he said. 'But please feel free to call if you have any additional questions that I might be able to help with. And we should then make another appointment once they've seen you, and once we know where we are.'

I thanked him and headed out to the car. Outside it felt like the mist was clinging to me as I walked. I could almost feel my hair turning to ringlets with each step. I climbed into the car and turned on the engine. Then I read the letter from Doctor Jones.

The patient, Christine Marsden, has presented with possible blackout. No external trace of bleeding to the cranium or behind the eyes. Brain-scan may show up something further. Patient suffered wounds to head approximately 5 (five) weeks ago. Seems to be healing satisfactorily. No previous history of dizziness or blackouts. Possible brain damage?

I folded the letter and put it on the passenger seat, turned the heaters on full-blow, and steered the car out of the health centre car park.

CHAPTER THIRTY

It pissed me off, every time I had to visit the hospital, that I had to pay for parking. It hadn't always been like that. When Michael was born parking there was free. Then, when Rose came along all they asked for was a voluntary contribution (for the car parking). Now it was obligatory and patrolled. I wondered what happened to all those with an ongoing illness who had to come to hospital regularly — it must have cost them a fortune.

The mist was still horribly thick and all I could see in the parking attendant's hut was the dark shape of someone moving about as little as possible. As I begrudgingly pushed a few of the lowest denomination coins I could find into the ticket machine I hard-stared over at the hut. I'm sure they couldn't see me through the mist, but perhaps they could feel my venom.

I handed the letter from Doctor Jones to a young lady behind a reception desk. Although she wore a medical looking uniform, I didn't think she was a nurse. She briefly glanced at the top of the letter (without reading the rest of it) and handed it straight back.

'You want down there,' she said, pointing. 'And then go to the right. See the reception there.'

I walked down the corridor in the direction she had pointed. Although I had been for an MRI scan before, none of this looked familiar. The last time I had been through the scanner was when I had just been attacked. They had wheeled me there from my ward.

I turned right and saw another, smaller reception area. A dozen or so chairs had been arranged around the desk to form a waiting area. Although it was not yet 10am, most of the chairs were occupied.

I handed my letter to the grey-haired lady behind this desk. She didn't look like a nurse either. She read the entire letter and then put it onto a pile of other papers in a letter tray. She asked me if I would like to take a seat and wait for my name to be called. I thanked her, and sat down.

Perhaps it's being British. Or perhaps it's just being human — but no one seems to like sitting next to anyone else in a waiting room if they can avoid it. If it had been possible, I guarantee that there would have been at least one empty chair in-between everyone sitting there. Apart from couples, we all sought our own space.

I had no such luxury of choice. I picked a chair. On my left sat a young mother, bouncing a baby gently up and down on her leg. To my right, a big man, made even bigger by the fact that he had kept his outdoor coat on. He shifted a bit as I squeezed down as tactfully as I could. But he didn't look at me or make any sound of acknowledgement. Once seated, I noticed the usual pile of magazines perched on a small table. I decided not to bother. It wasn't worth the hassle of disturbing the big guy again just to read a crummy old magazine. Instead, I took the time-sheet from my handbag and updated it. I had to make myself do it every half hour, not just when I remembered.

The baby, bouncing on the young mother's knee, started coughing. It sounded as though it had a forty-a-day habit of the strongest cigarettes money could buy. The mother patted its back as it bounced. One more hacking cough and the baby threw up on its mother's bouncing knee. Not a lot — but enough to make me regret my choice of seat.

The MRI was worse than I remembered. It was noisy and made me feel restless. I hadn't remembered it taking so long last time either. It wasn't painful at all — apart from the noise, but I was grateful when they finally pulled me out again.

I was directed back to the receptionist who told me that they would contact my GP with the results as soon as they had them.

The whole thing had taken nearly two hours from parking to leaving. The mist had started to disperse as the sunlight forced its way through to the damp earth. I updated my time-sheet.

When I pulled into our drive at home I checked the clock on the dashboard. Nearly midday. It felt as though the time-sheet was almost becoming a habit as I instinctively reached for it. Lunchtime. A drink, some food and maybe even a sleep.

I settled for water and a sandwich. Sunlight stretched across the work surfaces in the kitchen as I made my lunch. I could feel its warmth on my hands. Too nice for a sleep.

I finished my lunch, drank down another glass of water and decided to go for a walk. I didn't want to think about anything. I didn't want to try to analyse or make sense of anything. I just wanted to feel my legs working, breathe in fresh air and feel the sun's rays on my face.

I put a tick against 12:30pm on my sheet and dropped it, and the pen, back into my bag.

Although the sun was doing its best, it was still chilly outside so I grabbed my coat from the hook by the front door, reached for a scarf too and stepped out into the early afternoon sunshine.

I had no real plan of where I was going. I just wanted to be a hippie. I wanted to hear the birds, feel the breeze and the sunshine and taste the air. I might even smell a flower or two if I had the opportunity. I headed out of our close and turned left — away from the direction of the town and heading towards the local park and woods. My strides were large. My arms swung vigorously, fists clenched and I pumped air into my lungs Almost immediately I heard the birds, felt the breeze and smelled the smells. I loosened my scarf a little. It tickled against my neck. The cool air soothed the tickling. I breathed in deeply through my nose.

What was that smell? It didn't smell right. It smelled sweet. Sickly. The wind picked up and blew my hair. Something pulsed through my arms. I tried to reach into my bag. The time-sheet was just a quick grasp away. But my arms pulsed again, straightening and strengthening.

The heavy mist came from nowhere, blotting out the sun and swirling around my body. Moisture dripped from my face and I felt like I was choking as I breathed in through my mouth. There was so much moisture in the air I thought I would drown. I tried again for the time-sheet. Tried forcing my hand to my bag. I reached the opening, drowning from the moisture, pushed into the bag. And my damned leg stabbed me from deep inside the bone.

The muffled sound of ringing reached me. What was that? It didn't sound like my mobile. Why didn't anyone answer it. It must be coming from somewhere near. How else could I hear it.

Of course I couldn't answer it. I couldn't even move. Couldn't move my legs, my arms. Couldn't move my eyes or my mouth. I wasn't breathing.

That damned ringing.

I gasped for air. Sucked it in. It was as though my natural breathing mechanisms had been switched off. I had no idea for how long. But now, at last, someone had just found the switch and flicked them on again. Just in time.

And with the new breath came clarity.

It was as though I had just climbed out of my skin as a new me. Like leaving a dream for consciousness.

This wasn't a dream. I wasn't unconscious. This was real.

I was in Rose's room. Standing over her bed, looking down at her pillow. Weak sunshine strained through her bedroom window and bounced off the carpet and walls.

My left arm hung straight down against my body. The fingers of my left hand outstretched. My right hand was behind my back. Gripping something.

The phone stopped ringing downstairs and I heard the "beep" as the answer phone kicked in.

I brought my right hand from behind my back. My knuckles were blotchy, red and white, from holding it so tightly. It was a face flannel, dripping wet. It was a spare one. Not one that any of us used. I must have got it from the airing cupboard. And then wet it. And then walked into my daughters bedroom with it hidden behind my back.

A groan gurgled up from deep in my throat as my stomach churned. Both my knees gave way and I thrust the wet flannel to my mouth. I stopped the sick from coming out. Swallowed it back down again. My throat burned. My eyes stung.

I looked over at Rose's digital clock — 2:25pm. My stomach turned over again and I felt cold along my shoulder blades. This time the flannel didn't stop the vomit from hitting Rose's floor.

I crawled on my knees as quickly as I could to the bathroom, lifted the toilet lid and stuck my head over the rim. But no more sick came. I closed the lid and pulled myself up onto the seat.

I sat quietly for at least five minutes, trying to work out what I had been doing in Rose's room. Why I had been looking down at her bed and pillow, and why I had been hiding a wet flannel behind my back?

Obviously it made no sense. I pulled a wodge of toilet paper from the roll and wiped my mouth. Then pulled some more and wiped my eyes. I dropped the flannel in the sink and went downstairs to find a cloth, a bowl of water, and some carpet shampoo for Rose's room. My legs shook a little as I walked down the stairs. When I reached the kitchen, the phone started up again. It made me jump.

'Hello?' I said.

'Hello — is that Christine?'

'Yes?' I said.

My throat still stung from the burning sensation caused by the vomit. I regretted answering the phone because it hurt to talk.

'Christine, it's Donna Shaw — Harry's mum.'

Oh God. This was all I needed. Some new problem with Harry or his parents. I held the phone in one hand and reached for a glass from the cupboard. I needed some cold water. I had a feeling this was going to be a long call.

'Hi, Donna,' I said, trying to sound as bright as I could. 'How's Harry? Is he feeling better today?'

'Oh, Harry's fine,' she said. 'To be honest, I think he could have gone in today, but I thought a couple of days would be good. Let the dust settle. Actually I think he wanted to see Michael, let him know that everything is OK — you know?'

'He's a lovely boy,' I said. 'I'm pleased he's OK.'

I ran the tap as quietly as I could and filled the glass when the water felt cold on my finger. I managed a quick sip.

'I was ringing to see if you were OK?' she said.

'Me? I'm fine. Just a bit of a dry throat at the moment,' another quick sip, 'but I'm fine really. Thank you.'

'It's just that I saw you earlier today and wondered if you were OK?' her voice faltered slightly. There was a hesitancy.

'Where was that?' I said. 'Did I not look OK?'

No reply. Had she not heard the question?

'Donna?'

'Well... it was outside our house? When you were there... earlier?'

'Today?' I said.

'About two hours ago,' she said. 'At least, I thought it was you? You were sort of in the shadows of the trees on the opposite side of the road. That was you — wasn't it? I recognised the car first. You looked like you were looking up at our house. I waved from the window but I don't think you saw me. By the time I came out to talk to you, you were gone.'

I didn't know what to say. I couldn't get my mind around what she was telling me. I couldn't deny it — because I had no idea if it was true or not and I couldn't acknowledge it as fact for the same reason.

'Oh, do you know,' I said, 'I don't know if I'm coming or going at the moment. I was so worried about Harry. But I am pleased he's on the mend. It's really lovely of you to phone as well. It's so nice to know that there are people out there looking out for you.'

I wanted her off the phone now. I needed to think.

'And you're sure you're OK?' she said.

'Donna, it's so kind of you. But yes, thank you, I'm fine. And thank you so much for letting me know about Harry — please do pass on my best wishes to him, and Michael asked after him this morning. He really feels dreadful about it.'

She told me that she was pleased I was OK, and then put the phone down. I half expected her to ring back for clarification of whether it really had been me or not. But the phone stayed silent.

I finished my glass of water and refilled it. I needed to find my time-sheet, if only to confirm what I already knew. I had lost time again. I had apparently driven again, and I had no memory of any of it. Again.

The time-sheet wasn't in my handbag. The pen was — but it was snapped in two. Thick blue ink dribbled from one half of it. My handbag was a mess.

I eventually found the time-sheet in my car. It was on the back seat, screwed into a tight ball. I brought it into the house and unravelled it as carefully as I could. I smoothed it out onto the dining table. All the time slots were ticked up to the 12:30pm mark. The next three entries 1:00pm to 2:00pm were marked too. But not with ticks. Each time indicator had been scored through so vigorously with the pen that the paper had torn. On the lines next to the obliterated times was a word. It looked like it had been scratched onto the page with the broken pen. It too had ripped the paper, and at first it was difficult to make out. But I think I already knew what it said.

"Bitch".

CHAPTER THIRTY-ONE

No sooner had I read the ruined time-sheet when the front doorbell rang. I glanced up at the clock. It would be the kids, home from school. Although my handbag was sticky and inky I shoved both the time-sheet and the pen back into it and chucked it onto a dining chair. As I opened the door to let the children in I noticed Abi locking her car and walking up towards the house. I didn't think I could cope with another conversation but I waved and manufactured a smile, which I hoped was both welcoming and reassuring.

'Are you OK, Mum?' Rose said. 'Have you had a good day?'

I kissed her on the head and told her I had. Michael gave me a high-five, which I took to mean that he was feeling better about himself already. The kids dashed past me, and charged upstairs. I wondered where Abi's children were. As I moved towards her to give her a peck on the cheek she baulked.

'Are you OK?' she said.

'I'm going to punch the next person that asks me that,' I said, smiling again.

'It's just that you look...'

She stood back and examined my face. It was very disconcerting.

'Look what?' I said.

'You just look like you're not very well. Like you've been poorly or something.'

Rose screamed. And I heard a bump coming from her room, followed by hurried footsteps.

Even before the scream stopped I realised that I had forgotten about the vomit on her bedroom floor.

'I'm sorry, Abi,' I said, backing away from the door. 'I spilt something in Rose's room earlier — I was just going to clear it up when you arrived.'

'Do you want a hand?' she said.

'It's fine really, it will only take me a minute.'

I heard Rose running down the stairs. It sounded like she was crying.

'Sorry, Abi. I'll give you a call. Later on. Is that OK?'

Rose was starting to shout now — in a moment she would announce that someone had puked on her floor. Abi looked over my shoulder at the commotion.

'Thanks,' I said. 'For bringing them back. I'll call you.'

I held my hand up like a phone to my ear and pushed the door shut as quickly as I could without being rude.

As I turned round, Rose bashed into me, her face wet against my jeans.

'Someone's been sick in my room,' she screamed. 'It's all over my carpet.'

I heard her brother coming down the stairs now. He would have run in to her room to see what all the fuss was about and then come down to make some gross comment about it.

'I'm so sorry, darling,' I said. 'I was just going up to clean it when you got home. I was a bit poorly when I was in your room earlier. It will all be fine. I'm so sorry.'

Michael decided now would be a good time to stir the commotion up even more.

'What were you doing in her room anyway?' he said. 'Have you been in my room too?'

Rose stopped crying and looked up at me.

'What were you doing in my room?' she said.

'I was just dusting it and airing it a bit. I open the windows in the house every now and then, just to let the air in. So it's all nice and fresh for us.'

Rose turned her head to look at Michael. He nodded at her.

'It's disgusting,' she said. 'Please will you get rid of it.'

'I'm going straight up to do it now.'

'I thought you said you were OK today?' Rose said.

'I was OK. Just apart from that one little thing.'

'It doesn't look very little.'

'I'm going up now, Rosie. Why don't you see what's on the telly while I sort it all out.'

No wonder she had screamed. It looked much worse on her carpet than I had remembered. And the smell was horrendous. It was a wonder she hadn't been sick herself.

By the time I'd finished rubbing away at it, and squirting carpet shampoo over the area, it looked pretty good. Cleaner than the rest of the carpet. I opened her bedroom window and left the door ajar.

When I got downstairs she was watching a cartoon.

'Leave it for a bit to dry,' I said. 'About half an hour should do it.'

'Is it all gone now?' she asked.

'It's all gone. I'll vacuum once it's dry. You'll never know it was there.'

A stupid comment, I know, and she gave me a frowny look to say as much.

I threw the cleaning cloth in the bin and put the bowl in the sink in the kitchen. I had just finished washing and drying my hands when the phone rang. My heart jumped. What on earth else had I done in the missing time? I wanted to let the call go to answer phone, but I heard Rose already on her feet and heading for the extension. I grabbed the phone.

'Hello?'

'Hello? Is that Mrs Marsden?'

Soft voice. Irish accent. Reassuring.

'Mr Connell?' I said. 'How are you?'

'I'm fine, thank you. More importantly, how are you?'

For some reason his question shocked me. Perhaps he had spoken to Doctor Jones. But I didn't think the doctor would tell him about my blackout. Surely that was confidential. I could tell him I had just been sick on my daughter's bedroom carpet. It occurred to me that I might have driven to his house as well as Donna's in the new missing chunk of time?

'I'm fine too.' I said.

'OK. I did try ringing your mobile number first, but it went straight to voice mail.'

I had no idea where my mobile was. I didn't remember seeing it in my ink covered handbag. I scanned the kitchen to see if it was lying around somewhere. It wasn't.

'I'm not sure where my mobile is. It's probably run out of batteries somewhere. Sorry about that.'

'I've spoken to Trevor Jones at the Health Centre. We had quite a long chat about you.'

Oh shit.

'Really?' I said. 'What about?'

'Just about whether or not you were to be referred or not. We both felt that, given your circumstances, it would be appropriate to refer you.'

'OK.' I said. I wondered what he was referring to when he said "circumstances". 'So what does that mean then?'

'Well, it means that you can come and see me, and the cost will be covered for you. We agreed that an initial period of ten weeks might be suitable. We can then review it after that. Normally ten weeks is plenty.'

My blood raced a bit. At one point I had considered Colin Connell as a potential murderer and a possible suspect in drugging me. I knew that those considerations were all highly dubious and based solely on a chaotic imagination, paranoia and fear. But nevertheless, once you have thought of someone in that way, it's hard to see them any different.

'That's... great,' I said, trying to sound like it really was.

He obviously picked up on my tone.

'If you've second thoughts,' he said 'or if you'd prefer not to come to see me, we can arrange for you to see someone else. Of course you don't have to have counselling at all if you'd rather not. We would recommend it, but the choice is yours.'

'When were you thinking of starting it,' I said.

'The sooner the better. I have a slot tomorrow at 10 o'clock if that suits. And then at that time every week. We can always give it a try, and if you find that it's not helpful then we can just stop at any time.'

Shit.

Come on, Christine.

'Tomorrow at ten is absolutely fine,' I said. 'Do I need to bring anything with me?'

'Not really,' he said. 'You might find it helpful this evening to write down everything that's been happening since you were attacked. All the things you've felt, physically, mentally and emotionally. If you can put dates against each item it would help you to get a good picture of what you've been feeling. Also, if you've any questions you might want to ask me, you can jot them down too. You don't have to do this, of course, but it may help. And if you do, you don't have to bring your writings with you, I don't need to see them, unless you want me to. It's just to help you get everything down.'

Perhaps he wasn't a murderer after all. And maybe he hadn't tried to drug me. He sounded nice. More importantly, he sounded professional.

'Thank you, Mr Connell,' I said. 'I'll see you tomorrow at ten.'

'No problem,' he said. 'And please do call me Colin.'

Neil was late home again. Almost forty-five minutes. He hadn't rung me. I didn't know if he had texted because I still couldn't find my mobile. He kissed me on the cheek. I smelled no alcohol. No trace of spicy food. And no perfume. In fact, he smelled a bit like he had been exerting himself. Not sweaty and not body odour, but maybe one level below that.

As his lips and nose touched my face I shuddered. His face was icy cold.

'You're freezing,' I said. 'Where have you been?'

He dropped his briefcase on the floor by the shoes and coats and took his overcoat off.

'Nowhere,' he said. 'Apart from work, and driving home. Did you get my text?'

I put my hand against his cheek. He moved his face away.

'You're face is so cold,' I said. 'What on earth have you been doing?'

'I haven't been doing anything. I had the window open on the way home, just to get some air. I did text you to say I was still having to work a bit late.'

'I'm not sure where my mobile is. I must have put it down somewhere. I think it's out of battery. You didn't ring.'

'Because I sent you a text.'

As greetings go, I knew this wasn't a very good one. I really wanted to ask him how his day was, and for him to ask me about mine. I wanted to tell him about my visit to the hospital, the MRI, that I blacked out again, that I was apparently hanging around outside Harry's house and that I had been sick in Rose's room after "waking up" there with a wet flannel hidden behind my back.

I wanted to tell him that I was booked in to see Mr Connell the next day. And I wanted to tell him that I (or someone) had scored through my time-sheet and written the word "Bitch" on it.

And part of me knew that the real Neil would want to hear about those things too. But he wasn't the real Neil at that moment. And I certainly wasn't the real Christine.

But I knew that we were both strong individuals, and that we had been even stronger together. And right then, our strong wills were stopping us from communicating.

Rose broke the impasse.

'Mum was sick in my bedroom today,' she said from behind the sofa. 'I nearly stepped in it when I got home from school.'

She poked her head over the sofa and smiled at Neil.

'Oh no,' he said 'poor Mum.'

He looked at me, and this time his face showed more than just eyebrow movement. Despite his comment to Rose, I saw no concern or sympathy in his eyes. His brow furrowed and the sides of his mouth drooped slightly. He looked like a man who had just been told he had lost the race. Even though he had given his all, given his very best, it had not been good enough.

'Come into the kitchen,' I said. 'I'll make us a coffee.'

I told him about my day. I hadn't seen him so animated for a long time. He listened intently, made appropriate sounds with his voice, generally at the right times, and he seemed (at last) interested and concerned. He seemed particularly concerned, even worried perhaps, when I showed him my time-sheet, and I think he had to stop himself from saying something when I told him about looking down at Rose's bed. I don't think he was entirely worried just for me.

At one point, he reached out for my hand.

Being The Mighty Atom, I held it together pretty good.

'I'm not going to let bloody insanity get the better of me,' I said. 'Just let it bloody try.'

Neil returned my smile of defiance with a smile of something else. Pity, I think.

'I mean it,' I said. 'I'm not going to let some bastard with a skateboard fuck up my life.'

Neil's eyes flickered at the comment. His face seemed to momentarily change colour. It was so fleeting that I wasn't sure if it reddened or whitened. It was as though someone had temporarily knocked him off balance. Less than a second later, he was back.

'What's this Colin Connell like?' he said.

It sounded a little like he was changing the subject.

'He seems nice,' I said.

Neil raised his eyebrows.

'Not in that way,' I said. 'He seems like a nice person. He has a daughter in University and his wife died in an accident about six months ago.'

'What kind of accident?'

I pictured the new rug in Colin's study.

'I have no idea,' I said. 'I didn't think it was right to ask.'

'Well, he'd better not try anything funny. Or *he'll* end up having a bloody accident.'

CHAPTER THIRTY-TWO

I woke up in the night. But only because of Neil snoring. I stayed awake long enough to realise that I should make a note of my mileage reading every time I got in and out of the car, along with my time-sheet. Then sleep took over again.

In the morning, the first thing I heard was the beeping of Neil's alarm clock.

I felt pretty good. Refreshed almost. I couldn't recall any horrible dreams or visions, I had no dream-fuelled feelings of suspicion towards Neil and I didn't stink of vomit, booze or *Vicks*.

And I remembered deciding to write down my mileage as I got into or out of the car. Not a bad night really.

Before going to bed I had done as Colin suggested and written down everything relevant I could think of since being mugged.

I jotted down details of the dreams; the sense of smell; the visions; the wind and the noise; the girl on the stairs; Josie at the barbecue; Rose's room; being outside Harry's house; the paint on the back of the house; and, of course, the blackouts.

I decided I would let him see the list if he wanted.

On another sheet of paper I wrote down all the things I had done to try to combat what was happening to me. Drinking; determination; *Vicks*; Anne; my time-sheet; my mileage record; seeing Doctor Jones; and, now, seeing him — Colin.

Reading the list I felt guilty. There must have been more I could have done. I must have missed something.

I would let him see this list too. See if there was anything else he could suggest.

When Michael and Rose had gone, and Neil too, I printed off

a new time-sheet for the day. I added a section on it for writing down the car mileage.

Before leaving the house I ate cereal and an apple. I drank coffee and filled a sports bottle with water. That was coming with me into Colin's house.

I ticked off all the times that had already passed and kicked myself for not having printed this out the night before so I could tick it off as soon as I got up in the morning. In the car I wrote down the overall mileage the car had done. I realised it wouldn't do any good just to press the journey mileometer to zero. If I could write "Bitch" and screw up my time-sheet, it was a fairly safe bet that I could push the mileometer button whenever I wanted. I was pretty sure that I couldn't change the overall mileage record, however, whether I was conscious or not.

I scribbled next to the nearest half-hour time slot: 37,867 and made a note of the actual time and the date. It occurred to me that it might be prudent to add my potential destination too, so I wrote Colin Connell underneath the date.

It was another grey and cloudy day, but so far there was no mist and no rain. I could smell no electricity in the air.

I pushed back a thought in my mind. Tried not to think it at all. But I knew it was there. A dream free night, no horrors anywhere in the house, an improvement in the weather and control of my time and mileage. Could it all be over?

On the drive to Colin's house I must have checked every minute as it went by and every mile as it flicked over on the mileometer. Everything seemed normal as I pulled up against his hedge. I grabbed my handbag and bottle of water and pushed the car door open. I'd made it, without anything weird happening (apart from checking every minute and mile).

As I walked his path to the front door I noticed that the wheelbarrow was no longer on its side. The garage doors were closed, hiding the old car from view. And I heard no birdsong.

His front door creaked slightly when he opened it. I hadn't noticed that the last time.

'Hello Christine,' he said.

'Hi, Colin.'

He moved back into the entrance hallway and I followed him in, squeaking the front door shut behind me. I smiled as I caught site of the phrenology head.

'Pseudo-science, remember?' Colin said. 'Don't get too chummy with him, he'll only let you down.'

The smell of coffee had reached me before the front door had even opened. I gripped my water bottle.

'Just go through into the study,' he said. 'I'm just getting a drink. Do you want one?'

I held up my water bottle and shook it. The water sloshed around inside.

'I'm fine, thank you. I have some water with me.'

I thought he looked a little surprised.

'No problem. I'll be in in a minute. Sit anywhere you like.'

The study looked tidier than it had the last time I was there. The books were more ordered, although still stacked on the floor, and all the seats were available. I noticed that the silver photo-frame on the desk by the window had moved. I heard Colin making a drink in the kitchen. He sounded well occupied. Instead of sitting straight down, I moved over to the desk. I figured that if he came in now, I could get away with the pretence of looking out of the window at the garden. Looking down at the photo-frame I saw that it held a colour photograph. The colour seemed to be faded, probably because of sunlight beaming through the window, although there was none at the moment.

A man, a woman and a girl. All sitting on the floor, all smiling. Colin looked younger in the picture. It was difficult to be precise, I guessed it had been taken about five years earlier.

The girl, presumably the daughter now at university, looked more like her mother than like Colin, but I could see his expression in her face. The woman looked comfortable and happy. She had straw coloured hair, quite long and wavy. It looked very natural, as did the whole sitting. They all had their arms hung over each other's shoulders. It made me feel very sad.

I jumped as I heard a noise at the door. Colin was already halfway in with his coffee. He looked over at me as I blushed.

'That was taken about three and a half years ago,' he said. 'We had all just got back from the holiday from hell. It was supposed to be sunny Spain, but they had floods and all three of us got sick. The only reason we had the picture taken was because it was already booked for that day and already paid for.'

'You all look great,' I said. 'Very happy. You wouldn't know that you'd been ill.'

'My daughter, Ruth, put the picture in the frame for me for my 50th birthday. Before she got the frame I just had the picture perched up on the bookshelf by the window. I think the sun caught it a bit. It's a shame really.'

'What was your wife's name?'

'Louise. Louise Jane Connell.'

He looked past me, through the window at the garden. I wished I hadn't asked her name.

'I'm sorry,' I said. 'Neil always says I'm nosey.'

'Your husband,' Colin said.

I nodded.

'How does he feel about you being here today?'

He's jealous and threatening.

'He's fine,' I said. 'We just want to get everything back to normal again. So anything that helps is good. So he's good with it.'

Colin indicated the armchair that I had sat in before and we both sat down.

'Did you feel it worth making any notes before coming today, or would you prefer to just take it as it comes?'

I reached into my handbag and pulled out both sheets of paper. I checked which one was the "problems" sheet and handed it across the coffee table. There was a small stain of dark ink from the mess I'd tried my best to clean up in my handbag. I ignored the stain.

'I've written down everything I think that's been relevant since the attack. There's quite a bit I'm afraid. And it's a bit all over the place.'

Colin's eyes flicked over the page of scribble. At one point his brow furrowed. A moment later his eyebrows raised. Then he pursed his lips and blew a gentle flow of breath through them. He didn't speak at all. When he'd finished reading it he handed it back to me.

'Do you have a pen?' he said.

I pulled one out of my handbag.

'If you can remember,' he said, 'can you put rough dates against these things that have happened. Maybe put the date you were attacked at the top of the page. I understand the first blackout was after you came here the day before yesterday, but if you can put the date down for that too it would help.'

I thought and scrawled over what I had written. I think I had it pretty much spot-on date wise. I handed the sheet back to Colin.

He picked up an A4, hard-backed notebook from the coffee table and opened it up, like a book. A silver pen rested between the pages.

He put my sheet on the left-hand side of the notebook and started writing on the blank page on the right. Again he was silent.

He clicked his pen and looked up at me, then past me, and then back down to the notebook again, writing some more.

'Last night I had no dreams at all,' I said.

He looked up at me and nodded. Back to his writing.

His eyes were narrowed, his mouth tightly shut. His face seemed total concentration. It gave away nothing of his thoughts. I felt a flutter in my stomach. Perhaps I had been too honest, too open. Presumably he was in touch with social services through his work. Local authorities perhaps. Would I be considered a danger to others? From what I had written it was clear that all was not well inside my head. Were Michael and Rose at risk? What was he scribbling down in that book of his? A help note? An SOS? The first draft of a letter to social services?

The flutter in my tummy grew great flapping wings.

He stopped writing and looked up from his notebook.

'Had you ever experienced any of these things, or anything remotely like them, before?'

I had thought this through a hundred times. I had tried to think back over childhood nightmares and dreams, tried to remember if I had ever blacked out in the past — if there had ever been any "lost" moments. I was convinced there were none.

Although I knew the answer, I didn't speak straight away. I wanted him to realise that I was taking this seriously and that I was giving everything proper consideration. I looked up to a corner of the ceiling and furrowed my brow. After a few seconds of "concentration" I looked back down at him.

'Never,' I said. 'I have thought and thought so much since the attack, ever since the first dreams started coming, but I don't ever recall having had anything like them in the past. I've gone back all through my childhood and I can't recall a single event that's even remotely similar.'

He nodded.

'What do you think about the attack?' he said

'What do you mean?'

'I mean, when you think about what happened to you, what do you think? How does it make you feel? If you were looking back on it as a mere observer, rather than being involved, how would you regard it?'

I wasn't really sure what he meant.

'Well... it hurt,' I said. 'It caused me a lot of pain. And when I think of it I feel angry — although sometimes scared. I wonder if the person that did it has a family, whether he might be a young dad or not. I try to imagine how he felt after he did it. Whether he felt guilty and sorry or whether it gave him a buzz, made him elated. It's crossed my mind that he might have been a pupil of mine once, not that I have any reason to assume that he was, but it intrigues me.'

Colin nodded again but said nothing. It felt like he was asking me to continue.

'That's about it, really,' I said. 'Obviously I wish it hadn't happened, but I can't turn back the clock. It's made me much more wary when I go out, or go to the front door. I find myself looking around a lot more now, checking to see who is nearby. And the sound of skateboard wheels on the pavement makes goosebumps come up on the back of my neck.'

'The first dream,' he said, 'was approximately two weeks after the incident — is that about right?'

'I think so. I was due to go back to work the next day, so just over two weeks since the attack. I was looking forward to going back to the school, seeing all the kids again. They sent me so many cards. It was lovely. And then the night before I was due back, I had the dream.'

'In the two weeks between the attack and the first dream, had you had any dreams or blackouts or odd experiences at all?'

I shook my head.

'None,' I said. 'Apart from my sense of smell.'

'Tell me about that.'

'I noticed that smells seemed more intense and stronger while

I was in the hospital in the days after the attack. They kept me in for almost three days and some of the smells were just too much for me. I'm sure that was why I was sick so much. Too many intense smells.'

'And this was the only one of these "symptoms" you experienced almost immediately?'

I nodded.

'And this acute sense of smell hasn't diminished at all since then?'

'As far as I can tell,' I said. 'I suppose I have got used to it a little, but it's still as strong as ever. When I fill the car up with petrol I have to hold a sleeve or handkerchief over my mouth and nose. It's as though all the smells are a hundred times stronger, so even nice smells, like roses, are sometimes too strong for me.'

He tapped his pen against the notebook.

'This may sound like an odd question,' he said, 'but do you blame the attack for what's happening to you now?'

It didn't sound odd. It sounded bloody stupid. I wondered if it was a trick question. If somehow by answering it a certain way I would ensnare myself in his "contact social services" trap.

'Of course,' I said. 'Is that wrong?'

He smiled.

'Not at all. But not everyone who suffers from post-traumatic-stress is able to pin their difficulties on the actual event that caused them. It can be difficult for some to see the link to something that happened weeks or months ago to what they are experiencing now.'

'I have no difficulty at all,' I said. 'It's very clear to me that the attack is what's caused all of this.' I waved my hand in the direction of my sheet of paper on his open notebook. 'The problem I do have is that I can't see how it's post-traumatic-stress that's at the root of it all. I don't think I have that. I think it's something else.'

He picked up his pen again and made a note.

'What do you think it is?' he said.

'I think that I received two quite heavy bumps to my head. One from the skateboard and one from when I hit the pavement.' I lifted a handful of hair to show the scar on my forehead. 'I honestly believe that some sort of damage has been done inside my head. I know that I've had scans and examinations and tests — but I think that something has either been broken or torn. Some sort of protective lining or something inside my brain. It literally feels like a curtain has been torn off an area that was previously secret. And now it's open and all these horrible things are coming out of it. I now have dreams about hurting young girls, I see visions of girls on my stairs and now my mind seems to continually replay these horrors, ingraining them ever deeper. And whatever I try to do on the outside to combat it, doesn't seem to have any effect inside. I can't mend the tear.'

I heard the scratching of his pen as he wrote.

And the latest "event",' he said, 'was yesterday when you blacked out and ended up in your daughter's room?'

'It was as though I just came to. I had gone out for a walk to clear my head and then came to in Rose's room.'

'Did you go into your son's room at all?'

'I don't know. I didn't check afterwards to see if there was any evidence of me having been in there. I didn't think of it. Michael hasn't said anything since, so I guess I didn't.'

'And prior to that — you went to your son's friend's house — Harry?'

'Yes. His mother rang me to say I had been sitting outside in the car looking over at their house. Apparently she waved and I ignored it. Then she came out, and I had gone.'

'Was Harry at home, do you know?'

'As far as I know. She had said she was keeping him at home

for a couple of days. But she didn't mention whether he had seen me outside as well as her.'

Colin sat back and tapped the silver pen again. He said nothing.

I felt that I had said as much as I could.

When he spoke again it was in a much quieter voice. It unnerved me.

'Christine?' he said. 'Does Harry have a sister?'

CHAPTER THIRTY-THREE

Colin's question had shocked me. There was an inference there that hadn't occurred to me. I had assumed that if Harry's mother really had seen me outside her house, I had been there because of Harry. That something in my subconscious had been worried about him and that I had gone to make sure he was OK.

I hadn't thought for one moment I might have driven there because of Petra.

If I was feeling bad for having opened up to Colin, that one realisation made me feel a whole lot worse. It begged the question — who had I gone to see during my first blackout?

The biggest part of me refused to believe that I would be spying on or stalking young girls. But the evidence of the dreams, and being in Rose's room, needed addressing. A small part of me had to accept that, sickening though it was, it was possible.

Colin spent the rest of the hour asking me about my childhood, particularly school friends. He asked me whether I had been bullied at school, whether there were any girls who were nastier than the others. When I told him my school days were fine he said that maybe something had happened that was so painful that my mind had shut it off. Perhaps it wasn't physically possible for me to remember it. Was there anyone else I could talk to about that time? Perhaps my parents might remember something?

When I left his house my mind was spinning. I couldn't string any coherent thoughts together and I forgot to write down the mileometer reading. I didn't remember to do it when I got home either.

I felt grubby. I considered having another shower, but

instead I pulled a blanket from the airing cupboard, grabbed my pillows from the bed and settled down on the sofa in the living room. I just needed some space in my head. I needed to stop thinking. Sleep was the only way I could achieve it. I had no alcohol left in the house. I ticked off 11:30 on my time-sheet.

As I drifted off to sleep, my thoughts diminishing slightly, I remembered that during the tickling session I had wanted to hurt both the kids, not just Rose. I found this comforting.

Several raps on the front door woke me up. I couldn't understand why they weren't using the doorbell. A thud pulsed through my forehead and temples. I thought about ignoring the front door and hunting instead for some paracetamol. As I stretched my body under the blanket my invisible leg pain twanged.

The knocking at the front door came again. Loud and forceful. I swung my legs out from under the blanket and ruffled my hands through my hair in an attempt to wake myself up. A glance at the clock told me I had been sleeping for less than an hour. It was 12:15.

Before opening the front door I checked that the safety chain was across. I also made sure there was a closed umbrella next to the shoes, just in case I needed to defend or attack. I thought that whoever was the other side of the door would have heard me shuffling to open it, but apparently they hadn't. Another set of very loud raps made me jump.

I opened the door slightly less than the safety chain would have allowed. As I peered through the tiny gap I saw the uniform of a police officer. My heart took an extra beat.

'Mrs Marsden?'

A female voice.

'Hello,' I said.

'PC Stephanie Chalmers, Mrs Marsden,' she said. 'May I come in?'

I shut the door slightly and pulled the safety chain from its lock. When I opened it again I recognised the police officer. She was on her own. She had been the pretty one at the hospital straight after I had been attacked. She was still pretty. She held a shopping bag.

She looked at my hair, then the rest of my face.

'Are you OK?' she said.

'I was asleep,' I said. 'Is everything OK?'

'May I come in?' she said.

I stood back. As we walked to the living room I asked her again if something was wrong.

'Everything is fine, Mrs Marsden,' she said. 'I may have some good news for you.'

I caught my breath.

'Have you found him?' I said. 'The man who attacked me?'

My eyes felt as though they had doubled in size. I took a deep breath — and involuntarily held it.

'No,' she said. 'Not yet. But we are still working very hard to do just that.' She pointed at the sofa. 'Can we sit down?'

I gathered the pillows and blanket into my arms and dumped them in the dining-room.

She sat on the sofa, I chose the armchair. She pulled the shopping bag onto her lap, put her hand in and looked up at me. She looked as though she was about to do a magic trick. Maybe pull a rabbit out of the bag.

'We think we have your handbag.'

I recognised it before it was all the way out. She didn't hand it to me — just held it up, like she was displaying it to prospective purchasers at an auction.

The bag looked dirty and scratched. A smell of damp and mould hit me. I reached out for it.

'Is it your bag?' she said, pulling it back from my outstretched hand.

'Yes,' I said. 'At least, I think it is.'

She let me take hold of it. The strap felt cold.

'Am I allowed to look inside?' I said. 'Has it been… checked for fingerprints or whatever?'

'To be honest, Mrs Marsden, we're not likely to find anything of much use on it. It has been handled since it was found. There's nothing inside it.'

I looked anyway. Two chewing-gum wrappers and a pencil. I couldn't remember ever putting a pencil in there.

'I don't think the pencil is mine,' I said. 'Has that been checked?'

'We wouldn't get anything off that either I'm afraid. Of course, it's possible that you put it in there and forgot about it?'

It sounded like she was trying to put the idea in my head. Almost as though she was forcing the idea on me.

'It is possible,' I said. 'But I don't think I did.'

'Can you confirm that the bag is yours? Now that you've looked inside?'

I nodded.

'Yes, it's mine. Where did you find it?'

'Actually, a council worker found it. It was in some bushes by the bus depot. They were trimming the foliage back and saw it tangled in the undergrowth. As you can see, it looks like it's been there for some time.'

I turned the bag over in my hand. Obviously it was ruined. I could add it to my ink-soaked current one.

'Did they find anything else?' I said. 'My purse, or keys?'

'Nothing else was handed in,' she said. 'We can get a beat officer to check it out just to make sure.'

'When was it found?'

'Yesterday morning, I believe. This is the first opportunity we've had to get it round to you.'

I couldn't believe that they hadn't already checked to see if there was anything else of mine in the bushes. And I found it hard to get my head around the virtual certainty that they hadn't even checked the bag for fingerprints, or DNA or whatever they needed to do.

'Is there any likelihood that you'll catch the person who attacked me?' I said. 'I mean, on a scale of one to ten — is it likely?'

She folded her shopping bag and stood up.

'As I said, we're still working on the case. You never know what might turn up. Sometimes we get lucky.'

I felt heat rising up my neck. My eyes narrowed and the venom glands on my tongue opened up in readiness.

'Lucky?'

'It only takes one mistake from him and we could have him,' she said.

'One mistake? You mean like "leaving my ransacked handbag around for weeks in a public place" type of mistake?'

'I'm afraid I really need to go, Mrs Marsden. I'm pleased we have been able to return your bag to you. Should anything else turn up, or if we find the suspect, we will, of course, be directly in touch.'

I know my neck was flushed red. I could feel it. I showed her to the door and thanked her for bringing the bag back to me. I pushed the front door shut — probably harder than was necessary. I slammed the safety chain back into place. On the way back into the living-room I kicked a slipper that had dropped off the shoe rack.

I put my hands on the back of the sofa and leaned into it, stretching my neck and shoulder muscles. My body felt too tense. Pushing against the back of the sofa helped. It drew some of the tension out from me. The sofa absorbed it. I stretched my legs out one at a time, flexed my arms and elbows. Each movement pulled more of the tension out from my heated body. I pushed my head back and breathed out slowly through my nose. A few minutes passed. The red heat on my neck withdrew. My heart rate normalised.

'Fucking Cunts,' I said aloud. 'Bastard Fucking Cunts.'

Of course, now that I had some perspective, I could see that the case wasn't as important to the police as it was to me. For them, it was simply a mugging. I had been injured, of course, which made it a bit more serious, but it was essentially just a mugging. Just. So apart from the injury, all that happened was that my handbag was nicked. Now it had been returned. If they just happened to find the chap that did it — then all well and good. If not — well hundreds of crimes went unsolved every month. Many of them much more serious than mine.

So to them — the police — it was already an old case. Not even a thorn in their side anymore. Just a pile of unfinished, but probably already filed away, paperwork.

But to me, it felt as though my life may never be the same again. It had been, at least temporarily, shattered. I felt as though an axe hung over my head, waiting to come down on me, waiting to take control of my mind altogether. I feared losing my children. I feared hurting them, physically and mentally. I feared losing my husband. And I feared myself. From one moment to the next I had no idea what I would do. My life was no longer something over which I had complete control. Something else had crept in, through the dark torn curtain. A monster — which, to me, seemed alive with evil — was roaming my brain, looking for the next area to claim for itself.

I felt scared. Petrified in fact. And in that moment, leaning forward against the back of our sofa, tension oozing from my body, I thought about suicide. I know it is regarded by some as "the coward's way out", but at that moment it felt like an act of courage and selflessness. I was filled with anxiety of what had become of me, and horrified about what might still be to come.

I used to be The Mighty Atom. I still was. And I couldn't

find anything to beat these things that were happening to me.

I wasn't feeling sorry for myself. In fact, as all the tension dissipated, I felt stronger and more lucid than I had done in weeks.

I had time to write letters to Michael and Rose. And to Neil. One for Mum and Dad. They would see it as an act of bravery too. I would explain that I had tried every other weapon and that this was the ultimate one. The one that couldn't fail.

I had options. The Clifton Suspension Bridge seemed too dramatic, but there were other places. I didn't want to inconvenience anyone else, although if I landed on the skateboarder that would be a bonus. A feeling of calm came over my body, as though I was being covered in velvet or silk. I knew it was the right thing to do — and I felt at peace.

The peace was shattered by the phone ringing.

CHAPTER THIRTY-FOUR

It was Neil.

'Just phoning to see how you got on this morning,' he said. 'At Colin's.'

The emphasis on his name said it all. It was nice to hear from him — even if it was only to check up that nothing untoward had happened with the counsellor.

'It was pretty intense,' I said, and then regretted my choice of words.

'Intense?'

'I mean, it brought up a lot of issues. To be honest, it gave me even more shit to think about. I thought the idea of counselling was to make you feel better, not worse.'

'What sort of things?' Neil said.

I didn't really want to talk about them again.

'Just stuff to do with the dreams and what happens after a trauma. He asked whether I was bullied at school. That sort of thing. It's all fine though.

'Anyway — the police found my handbag. They dropped it round a short while ago.'

Silence on the other end of the line.

'Neil?'

'That's great,' he said.

He sounded distracted. I wondered if anyone else was with him in the office. I didn't want his colleagues hearing how fucked-up his wife was.

'Did they catch the bastard that attacked you?' he said.

'Not yet. I don't think it's much of a priority anymore. They said they might get him if they "get lucky".'

'I've got to go,' Neil said. 'I may be working late again. I'll see you later.'

The phone clicked off before I even said goodbye.

I hadn't seen Neil jealous for ages. Years, probably. It was a side of him I didn't like. But at the same time it made me feel wanted. Like sweet and sour at the same time. Maybe it stemmed from guilt. Perhaps he had something to hide.

I gave myself a massive bollocking for considering suicide. I had far too much to live for, and I was way stronger than anything happening to me.

If I really was going mad, losing complete control of my mind, I was sure that there were ways to deal with it outside of myself. I would be medicated, perhaps given a room at some sort of hospital. Did they even have institutions like that anymore? Maybe, if I was sufficiently sedated, I could still live at home. Carers would surely be available to make sure I was OK. To make sure I wasn't hurting anyone. If I was safe, they wouldn't take Michael or Rose from me. After all, Neil would still be there. He still had control of his mind.

But did I really want a life like that? Medicated. Sedated. Monitored.

Of course not.

I picked up the phone and dialled a number. It answered on the third ring.

'Hi Dad. It's me.'

Dad sounded tired, a bit muffled.

'Are you and Mum both in?' I said. 'Can I come and see you?'

The kitchen clock said it was five past one. I grabbed a banana and an apple, picked up my inky handbag and headed out to the car. I made a note of the mileage this time, ticked off 1pm on the time-sheet and switched on the car radio. If I had something tangible to listen to it might hold me in the present.

As I drove I noticed things around me. A red coloured roof on a white painted house; trees swaying in the wind; a woman whose coat blew open as she walked, its belt flapping wildly. I paid more attention to the road signs, played games with the number-plates of the cars coming the other way. Made up stupid sounding meals from the letters on the licence-plates and used the numbers as the amount they had paid for their meal. Worms, Triffids, Maggots, Yaks and Goldfish — and you paid £809 for it!

It helped me to concentrate on the "now". Gave my hellish mind something else to think about. I quite enjoyed the journey.

Dad's car was in the drive. I drew up next to it. Mum was at the front door as I clambered out of the car, having just ticked off 1:30pm on my time-sheet and noting down my mileage.

'Your dad's a bit under the weather,' she said.

We kissed, and I hugged her.

'What's wrong with him?'

'He's just a bit run down, dear. We're obviously worried about you. I think it's got to him a bit.'

Shit. They needed this visit like a hole in the head.

'Sorry, Mum. But I won't stay long. I just needed to talk to you both about something. Just test your memories a bit.'

She flinched.

'I could come back when he's feeling better if you like.'

A shadow loomed up behind her.

'Come in, Chris,' Dad said. 'I'm fine. Just a bit tired, that's all.'

I followed Dad into the living-room. Mum wandered off to the kitchen. I could smell the coffee and milk already in the mugs, waiting for the hot water. I could smell that the kettle had already been boiled once too.

'How are you really, Dad?' I said.

He flopped down into his armchair, his back to the window. The light shone through his grey hair making it look thinner and more sparse than it really was. For the first time I saw him as looking older. It stirred something in me that I didn't want to think about.

'I'm fine, Chris. Really. It's just tiredness. What with all this stuff that's happened to you. It's a worry for us. I'm just not sleeping great at the moment. But our concern is for you.'

Mum walked in, the coffee mugs clinking in her hands. She held out a mug for me.

'And how are you, Mum? Are you OK?'

'Oh I'm fine, dear. As your Dad says — we're both worried about you. But we're OK in ourselves.'

All three of us sipped our coffee. I heard the wind blowing outside, saw a few leaves fly past the front window.

'They found my handbag,' I said. 'A council workman found it as they were trimming some bushes along the high-street.'

'Was there anything in it?' Mum said.

I shook my head. 'I don't think there's much chance of them finding the bloke who attacked me either. I got the impression that it was more or less on the back burner — unless they get lucky.'

'I don't know what's wrong with our society today,' Dad said. 'It feels like we all have to look out for ourselves. We certainly can't rely on the police anymore. Too busy handing out speeding tickets.'

Mum raised her eyebrows. Gave him one of her looks.

'Well that's what it feels like,' he said. He pointed his hand at me. 'Someone gets attacked — hospitalised — and the police do nothing. It's been nearly two months since it happened and they haven't even found a suspect. Not one. What the hell are they doing? It's not like she lives in the crime capital of the world. They can't be that busy.'

Mum ignored his rant and looked toward me.

'I'm sure they're still looking, dear,' Mum said. 'They keep these things open all the time, don't they?'

'I don't know, Mum. I'd like to think they would, but I just don't know.'

Dad had a bit more colour to his cheeks now. Perhaps a regular outburst about something was all he needed to aid his recovery. He sat more upright in his chair. Now the light from the window gave his head a slight glow around the edges. With a little imagination I could visualise a sort of halo. Actually it needed a lot of imagination.

'I went to see that counsellor chap again this morning.'

'Oh, Christine.' Mum said.

'Actually it brought up quite a lot of stuff. It was pretty helpful, I think, to see things from a different perspective.'

'What did he say, Chris?' Dad said.

'I think he was trying to establish a link between me being attacked, and some of the dreams I've been having since then. He was trying to make sense of them — or rather, get me to make sense of them. Personally I can't see that these particular dreams are linked directly to the attack, although I do think that the attack has caused me to have them.'

'What do you mean?' Mum said

I rested my coffee on the arm of the sofa and itched my eyebrow.

'I mean that the dreams are as a result of the attack — but they're not about the attack. I'm not reliving the attack or wreaking revenge on the bloke that did it. That's not what the dreams are about. But I absolutely believe that the attack has in some way triggered the dreams that I've been having.'

Dad nodded. He sat forward in his chair.

'But the counsellor was trying to get me to establish a link that would explain the dreams and connect them directly to the attack in substance.'

Dad coughed quietly.

'It would make sense if there was a link of some sort,' he said.

'It would help enormously,' I said. 'And it would make me feel less of a danger to people. Less of a risk.'

Mum made a noise that was a cross between a laugh and a snort.

'Chris,' she said. 'How can you say such a thing. You're no danger to anyone.'

I didn't want to tell her about the blackouts, about being in Rose's room, about hanging around outside a pupil's house — and about not being aware of any of it. I could see they were finding it hard enough to cope with my situation already, I had no wish to make it harder still.

'I know, Mum,' I said. 'But it's a bit scary, you know, having dreams about hurting people, vulnerable people. It just makes you worry. Makes you wonder what you really are capable of.'

'Well we know you, darling,' she said. 'And you're just not like that. You're not that kind of a person.'

Up to the point of the attack, she was probably right. I wasn't that kind of person. But since then, my mind had changed. Sometimes it felt as though my whole physiology had changed. I wasn't sure that I was the person I used to be. I wasn't really sure who or what I was at all anymore.

'Colin, the counsellor, asked me about my childhood. He asked if there was anything that happened to me.'

Mum's face grew pale. Dad's flushed pink. I noticed his hands clench into fists.

Their physical reactions surprised me. The back of my neck prickled.

'What do you mean, Chris?' Mum said.

'He asked me if I had been bullied by anyone at school. Or whether a group of girls had hurt me in any way. I told him that I had had a great time at school. Lots of friends, no problems at all. That's right, isn't it?'

'Of course it is,' Mum said. 'You loved school. You were sad to leave, you worried that you wouldn't see all your friends again.'

The colour seeped back into her face. I looked at Dad. He

nodded.

'As far as we know,' he said. 'You never had any problems at school. Certainly not with other people. You might have been a bit late with your homework a few times, but never a problem with friends.'

As if in reaction to Mum, the colour in his face slowly drained back to normal. His hands relaxed.

He let out a nervous little laugh. Mum followed suit. They both looked like they had dodged a bullet.

'Colin said that sometimes our minds protect us from pain. He said that it's possible for something to happen to us, physically or mentally, that is so painful our mind literally forgets it. It sort of wipes it from our memory. He wondered if anything like that happened to me, and whether you might remember it because I can't — my brain has wiped it.'

They looked at each other and shook their heads.

''There's nothing from your school days, Chris,' Dad said. 'I'm sure we would remember if anything nasty had happened to you. We really would.'

'I don't like thinking like this,' Mum said. 'It somehow seems to taint something that was good. You had a lovely childhood. We all had such fun. You weren't bullied, Chris. You were so popular.'

I felt deflated, and that surprised me. I had known all along that nothing had happened to me at school. And the only reason I had come to see Mum and Dad was because Colin had put the idea in my head that something may have happened that seemed so bad to my young self that my brain wiped from my memory. I hadn't believed it. But subconsciously I had obviously hoped for it.

'It would make sense,' I said. 'If I had been. It would help explain why I was dreaming about hurting girls. School-age girls. It would mean that as a response to the skateboard attack I was fighting back in my mind to something that had already damaged me before. Something that had hurt me or caused me pain, something more significant than the skateboard attack.'

'I'm sorry, love,' Mum said. 'I really am.'

Shit, shit, shit, shit, shit.

'What about outside of school?' I said. 'Did anything happen to me outside of school?'

'Chris,' Dad said. 'We're really sorry, darling. Nothing happened to you when you were that age. And nothing since, as far as we know.' He managed a weak smile. 'Maybe there's another link that we just haven't thought of yet?'

CHAPTER THIRTY-FIVE

I pulled my car door shut in Mum and Dad's drive, and held back the tears. I couldn't believe how much I was letting this get to me. I ticked off 2:30pm on the time-sheet and checked the mileage to make sure it hadn't changed since I had been inside. It hadn't.

Mum and Dad watched me pull out of the drive. Now I could see that they both looked older, not just Dad. It made me realise how precious time was. But also how cruel and relentless it was too.

I wondered why we gave ourselves time. Why we gave ourselves the means to measure it. Hours; minutes; seconds. Days; months; years. Why had we imposed those things on ourselves? They imprisoned us. Reminded us every moment that our lives were unstoppable. We couldn't pause time. As each measurement passed, our lives decayed. We grew another year older, and another, and another.

I drove the car through the streets and thought about removing time — taking all the measurements away. I was no longer thirty-six years old. I was one life. I was living one life, and at each moment, I was at a certain point in that life. I wasn't old, or young. I had no years — time measurement didn't exist anymore. For a moment I felt a rush of adrenalin pump up from my stomach and flow through my body.

I felt free. Unrestricted by time or age. If I didn't mark off the years anymore, did away with birthdays and anniversaries, perhaps I could pause time. I wouldn't age in the conventional sense. I would just be living my life. My one life.

I checked the clock on the dashboard. I was still there, in "real" time. Then I put my hand over the clock. Blotted it from my vision. I think if I could have removed it from the dashboard at that moment, I would have. I would have happily thrown it out of the window.

I wondered whether I could persuade Neil and the kids to do away with time. If not for themselves, perhaps just for me. Just my time. The excitement filled me up. Although I was strapped into my car seat, I felt taller, healthier, like I could live forever. I smiled. I smiled at the cars coming past me in the opposite direction and I smiled at the people walking around the streets. I didn't know if any of them could see me smiling at them. I didn't care. I felt so happy. Felt like I hadn't felt since the attack. Since before the attack. I wondered what I looked like. How silly my huge grin looked.

I checked the road and then looked at my grinning face in the rear-view mirror.

There was a woman in my car.

I felt like I had been smashed in the chest with a railway sleeper. My foot instinctively hit the brake. I saw her in the mirror, behind my reflection, on the back seat staring out of the window.

My head froze, I couldn't move my neck or any of my upper body. I felt like I was paralysed. I couldn't look away from her in the mirror. She turned her head slowly to look at me. My heart strained to break out of my paralysed body. I could feel it beating against my chest. My head felt like it was being covered with a dark sheet, as though it was being crushed down by an outside pressure. I felt like I was losing consciousness.

And the woman in the back screamed at me. She raised her hands in front of her face, protecting herself, and she screamed at me. My body was suddenly loose. My arms grew strong and my eyes grew livid. The voice in my head forced its way through. Pushing me, urging me. I wanted to kill her, I wanted to pummel her until she died.

I turned around and returned the scream, at the same time

raising my right fist, clenched and full of fury, ready to be unleashed on the bitch. I was ready to kill.

And she was gone.

The car had come to a standstill by now. Thankfully I had somehow pulled it over to the side of the road, and although it was annoying for the cars coming up behind me, they could still get past.

I put my hand up to my forehead. It was clammy. I pushed my hair back and stretched my neck. My heart was still pounding out of my chest and my throat had a painful tingling sensation from my scream. In fact it had probably been more like a roar than a scream. A horrible growling sound with enormous power behind it.

I released my safety belt and turned off the engine. I shut my eyes and stretched out my legs as far as I could. I didn't feel like getting out of the car.

My legs were shaking. Almost as though they were shivering. A fast, vibratory shake. And I realised that my whole body was shaking in the same way, as if suffering from the after effects of an electric-shock.

Or had I been outside in the cold for a long time?

I looked at the clock — 2:51pm. I hadn't lost any time at all. I was still there.

While my heart was still pumping double-time I decided to take another look on the back seat, just to make sure I really was alone. I sat low in my seat so that my head came below the top of the seat-back. I peered around the side. No one.

No sign of anyone.

But something was on the seat. Right in the middle, where the woman had been sitting. My mobile phone.

I reached back for it. It felt warm in my hand. I pressed the unlock buttons. The screen flashed on immediately. I checked the battery bar at the top of the screen. Full battery. There were six missed calls, a couple of text messages and one voicemail. I dialled the number. It was Neil, telling me he was having to work late again. So he had rung me.

Four of the missed calls were from our home number — presumably me ringing my mobile to try and find it. The other one was from Margaret at the school. I assumed it was before her visit about Michael fighting at school.

I put the phone on the passenger seat and started the engine.

I wasn't sure how much more of this I could take on my own. I was convinced that I needed more help. I thought about driving directly to see Doctor Jones, or perhaps Colin, just to see if there was anything else they could do for me. I felt shocked that I had gone from such a joyous high to what felt like the depths of hell in a split second. I wondered how much a body could take before the organs started to go wrong. Was it possible that I could get a heart-attack from all this?

The thought of having a heart-attack behind the wheel of my car made me feel sick. I could imagine what sort of damage I would do if I was driving. I decided that it might not be safe for me to drive the car anymore. I had wanted to use my bicycle more anyway. It would be good to use the bike. I could get fitter, help the environment and, hopefully, be less of a danger to others.

As I drove, and my heart found a more healthy rhythm, I thought about the woman in the back of my car. I knew she wasn't there now, and I knew she wasn't physically there at all. But she was real. I replayed what I had seen. The woman, behind me, sitting in the back. There had been something funny about the back seat. I hadn't noticed it at first, probably due to the terror of seeing the reflection of a woman in my car. But now I remembered. I had seen in the mirror the top of the back seats behind her. They had been white, they looked like leather. All the seats in my car were dark grey, and they were material, not leather.

There was one other thing about the woman. Something I

had tried to direct my mind to ignore. But I couldn't ignore it.

I knew her.

And I think she knew me.

It was the woman from the dream. The one who had been sitting at the table, writing. The one who had looked scared when she saw me, and closed her writing book.

And now, having just seen her close up in my car, in daylight, something else hit me. A realisation that made the hairs stand up on my arms. She looked like me.

A lot like me. Perhaps several years younger. But although she looked younger, there was something old about her. I couldn't figure it out.

For a moment it crossed my mind that perhaps it was me. Perhaps I was seeing a different version of me, maybe someone I could have been if I had taken a different path in life. Maybe it was me if I hadn't met Neil, hadn't had Michael and Rose.

Maybe it was a vision of a bleak life that I had somehow avoided. Maybe it was a good thing. Maybe it was showing me how lucky I had been — how lucky I was now. Maybe.

I had stopped shaking, or shivering, or whatever it was my body had been doing. I wanted out. I wanted to go somewhere completely different. Somewhere where I could get my head together in safety. Where I wouldn't be worried about hurting anyone. My long ago trip to the Andes came to mind.

I had pushed every sinew and limb on that trip, had challenged my body and my mind, and in doing so I had found contentment and peace. At the end of each day trekking I had felt relaxation like never before. And a pure clarity in my mind that I had missed ever since.

I wanted that again. I needed it. I wondered how I could make it happen.

I slowed the car before turning into our close. I think I was nervous of who, or what, I might find waiting for me. But there was no one there. No Margaret, no police and no attacker.

I made a note of the mileage, ticked off 3pm on the time-sheet and grabbed my phone. I had a quick look in the glove-box to see if there was anything I needed. I wasn't planning on being back in the car until my head was sorted. Then I checked the boot. Only my wellies. I grabbed them, slammed the boot shut and locked the car.

For a split second I thought I saw her back in the car again. The shape of her head, her long hair blowing gently. But it was nothing more than the shadow of me. I was still alone.

I dumped my wellies inside the front door and made straight for the kitchen. The car keys jangled in my hand. I wasn't sure what to do with them. Bearing in mind that I had driven during both of my blackouts, it seemed sensible to hide them somewhere. But obviously, if I hid them, I would know where they were. I filled the kettle with water and reached for the decaf. I found a couple of semi-stale chocolate biscuits in the biscuit-barrel and grabbed both of them.

I sat down at the dining table with my coffee. The biscuits were gone before the kettle even boiled. The keys swung back and forth on my finger and I tapped them with the other fingers. I could always get Neil to hide them somewhere. But I would probably find them anyway. I knew how his mind worked. He wasn't very imaginative. And what if I had another blackout between now and him coming home?

I needed to do something immediately. Then the simplest of answers came to me. Neil had a spare set of keys to my car, as I did for his. Just in case either of us lost our key, or locked it in the car by mistake, the other one would be able to come to the rescue. And that was the answer. I took the house keys off my bunch and went out to the car. I unlocked the doors with the electronic key fob, opened the passenger door and clicked "lock" on the key fob. All the door locks thudded into place. I put the keys in the glove-box, shut the passenger door again and watched the indicator lights flash to confirm that the doors were all locked and the alarm set.

Back inside the house, I opened a small window in the living-room, finished the rest of my coffee and sniffed the air. Nothing too horrendous. The fresh air from outside was slowly making its way around downstairs. I found my time-sheet and ticked off 3:30pm. I felt as though I had scored a little victory with the car keys. But I knew there was something else I had to do too.

I marched into the kitchen, picked up the telephone and dialled the health centre.

CHAPTER THIRTY-SIX

After hanging up from the health centre it took about three minutes for an uneasy feeling to well up inside me. I started thinking that perhaps it hadn't been such a great idea to lock the keys in the car. What if I needed to get away in an emergency? What if there was a problem with the kids and I needed to get somewhere faster than my bicycle would take me?

I pushed the doubts back down and told myself that life was full of "what ifs?". What if I hadn't been attacked? What if I wasn't blacking out? What if I wasn't slowly (or bloody quickly) slipping into insanity?

The "what if?" questions disappeared as soon as the doorbell rang.

Michael and Rose.

I opened the door. The children looked up at me and rushed in, shouting "hello" as they flew past.

Abi stood at the doorway, Jessica and Josie stood behind her. They looked nervous. Abi smiled.

'How are you doing?' she said. 'Got ten minutes for a coffee?'

My heart sank. I loved Abi, but I didn't want to have to go through everything that had happened.

But then — what are best-friends for?

'Of course I have,' I said. 'That would be lovely.'

Abi stepped inside, kissed me on the cheek and squeezed my arm. Jessica and Josie brushed past me and clumped up the stairs. Michael and Rose were already bumping around up there. No screams, thankfully. None of Mum's vomit or weird stuff to deal with today.

'Come through to the kitchen,' I said.

I put the kettle on and we both leaned back against the worktops. Abi folded her arms. She spoke quietly.

'I've not seen much of you lately,' she said. 'Not since the barbecue.'

I folded my arms too.

'Things have been a bit... hectic,' I said. 'You know? They found my handbag.'

'That's great,' she said. 'Where was it?'

'Just on the high street. It had been dumped in some bushes or something. Nothing in it, of course.'

'Any news on the person who attacked you?'

I shook my head. 'I don't think they'll get him, to be honest,' I said. 'How are you?'

'Chris,' she said. 'Come on. We've been best friends for years. You don't get away with it that easy.'

'I mean it,' I said. 'How are you?'

'Michael and Rose were talking to Josie and Jess in the car, about you being sick in Rose's bedroom. I didn't overhear — they were practically shouting. They all had a laugh about it.'

I put my hand up to my eyebrows, rubbed a finger along one of them. I felt my face blush.

'Chris, it's OK. But don't go through all this on your own. That's what I'm here for.'

The kettle boiled and the switch clicked off. I turned away from Abi and made the coffees.

'I was just sick,' I said. 'I had been in Rose's room, just tidying a bit and opening the windows. The sickness just came on — all of a sudden. I had got a cloth to clean it all up when the phone rang. Then you guys arrived home, it was all too late by then.'

'Have you been to the doctor?' she said.

'Several times. In fact I've just made another appointment for tomorrow morning.'

She tapped a finger against the kitchen cabinet.

'How's Neil?' she said.

I turned to face her again. Looked into her eyes. Tried to detect what was going on behind the question.

'What do you mean?' I said.

'How's he dealing with what's gone on? Has he been able to take any time off? Time to be with you?'

Her voice hadn't changed at all. She didn't blush and she didn't pale. Just a straightforward question.

'Actually he's been working late a lot,' I said. 'Obviously he's "there" for me, mentally. But he's really busy at the moment. Something going on at the bank.'

Abi nodded. Her expression showed sympathy. For me? Or for Neil?

'How are the wounds healing?' she said.

I lifted the hair from my forehead, tilted my head down so she could get a better view.

'Is it painful?' she said.

'Occasionally. It just comes on every now and then.'

'Josie mentioned that Michael had a spot of bother at school,' she said.

I felt like I was on the defensive every time Abi opened her mouth. I felt like I had to either justify or deny things. Things that were happening to me, and my family. Abi was my friend, for god's sake. Why was I so bloody paranoid and defensive? *She* wasn't the enemy. *I* was.

'Let's go into the dining-room,' I said. 'We can talk there.'

And how I talked. And cried. Her too.

I told her about the dreams. Explained why I had freaked out at Josie at the barbecue. I told her about the girl on the stairs, the offensive writing on the side of the house and about going to see a counsellor.

She asked for a glass of water when I told her about the blackouts. And she sat in silence when I mentioned the tickling, with the voices and the feelings of power and evil.

I showed her my time-sheet. Then I showed her the one with "Bitch" scrawled on it, the one from the day I was sick in Rose's room. And I told her about the damp flannel hidden behind my back and the phone call from Harry's mum to say I had been waiting outside their house in my car, and then disappeared by the time she came out to see me.

By the time I told her about the vision of the woman in the back of my car she was sobbing almost uncontrollably. I found a tissue in my handbag and handed it to her.

'Oh Chris,' she said. 'I'm so sorry.'

I realised then how inadequate some words are. And how special some people are.

I reached across the dining-table and took hold of her hand — just as Neil had done with mine a couple of nights earlier.

'Abi, I'm sorry,' I said. 'You're right. I should have spoken to you. I should have asked for your help even. I'm sorry.'

She stood up and walked around to my side of the table. I stood too and we hugged, wet cheeks and occasional convulsive crying — together.

It helped. Helped a great deal.

'And I've been fighting back too,' I said. 'You know me — I haven't just been taking this shit.'

She laughed about the *Vicks* under my nose. She laughed too about my attempt at being Anne, although her laugh didn't sound quite as sincere as before.

'Good idea with the time-sheet and the mileage,' she said. 'And seeing the counsellor too. What's he like?'

'His name's Colin,' I said. But he seems nice, as a counsellor. I think he killed his wife.'

That brought the genuine laugh back. I didn't tell her that I was being serious. Just took the opportunity to laugh too.

We both snuffled and wiped our eyes and noses with tiny bits of tissue. I had no doubt that my face looked every bit as streaked with makeup as hers. Probably worse. We wouldn't have looked out of place as backing singers for *Kiss*.

'Another coffee?' I said.

We resumed our original places in the kitchen, leaning back against the work-tops. This time, I noticed, both our arms were by our sides. I rinsed my cup and grabbed a clean one for Abi.

'Why don't I spend some time with you?' she said. 'It's daft for you to be on your own during the day and for me to be on my own during the day somewhere else. If we're together we can be there for each other.'

'What on earth would I be there for you for?' I said. 'It would be all one-way. You don't need me?'

'You'd be surprised,' she said. 'You always make me feel happy. Always bring a smile to my face. You're so funny.'

'What if something happened to me while you were here?' I said. 'I have no idea what I do or where I go when I blackout. I don't think I'm safe to be around. Seriously.'

'Well you're obviously safe enough to see the doctor, and to see the counsellor. And Neil and Michael and Rose. And your Mum and Dad.'

She had a point.

'But I think it's getting worse,' I said.

'All the more reason for us to be together,' she said.

She had another point. But so did I.

'I think something happens to me physically when I have these blackouts. I don't mean just the fact that I'm blacking out. I mean that I think my body changes. I think I become stronger somehow. More aggressive. If you look at the time-sheet with "Bitch" written on it, you can see how aggressively that was written. And that's my writing, nobody else. It looks almost as though it's been scratched onto the page. And the crossing out of the times have gone right through the paper.

'And even when I haven't been blacked out I have been aware of changes in my body. My arms growing stronger when I was tickling the kids was horrible. I felt enormous power — but not in a good way. And this morning, when I saw the woman in the back of the car, I wasn't blacked out then. I wanted to kill her. Literally. I roared at her, I heard a voice and I prepared myself to kill her.'

Abi smiled — just.

'I'm not as weak as you think I am,' she said. 'Anyway, I can always carry a panic alarm with me.'

We both laughed. A nervous sort of laugh.

'You might need one.'

'What time is your appointment tomorrow?' she said. 'I can come with you. I'll just sit in the waiting-room while you go in. Then we can go for a coffee afterwards.'

I hesitated.

'I'm not sure what's going to happen,' I said. 'In the back of my mind I half thought that they might send me to hospital.'

'Well I'll come with you there too. I'll take a book and hang around while they do whatever they need to do. Then we'll have a coffee.'

'I sort of meant — to stay. I thought they might want to admit me to hospital.'

Abi looked as though I had just spoken to her in Mandarin.

'I was going to tell the doctor about the vision in the car. Also about the feelings I had toward Michael and Rose. I thought it was better to come clean about it all. I don't think I can get through this safely without medical help. And I don't just mean medicines. I think I need the health system to start fighting for me too.'

Now Abi looked like I had slapped her.

'Do you think you really need to mention Michael and Rose?' she said. 'I mean, you haven't actually hurt them at all. On the contrary, you've given them even more love than before.'

'When I'm conscious, I care for them. I make sure they're safe and protected. And that's why I'm going to mention it to the doctor. At the moment, I'm conscious, therefore I want to make sure they're going to be OK. I know that anything can happen to any of us at any time — that's life. But there is one thing that may be a danger to them that I can do something about — me. When I'm blacked out I have no idea what I feel or what I do. But the visions and experiences I've had have been too scary. I wanted to hurt the kids while I was tickling them. I heard a voice, and then I wanted to hurt them. That's not normal.'

Abi opened her mouth. I knew she was about to protest, about to say that everything would be fine, that she would be with me.

I didn't give her a chance to speak.

'And this morning,' I said. 'When I saw the woman in the car, I would have killed her. I know I would, Abi. I had the strength in me, but I also had the will. I wanted her dead and I would have done it, without even thinking about it.'

Abi shook her head, but said nothing. What could she say. She folded her arms again.

I thought she looked like one of my children at school who had been told they couldn't sit next to their friend in class that day.

'I would love you to come with me, Ab. But I just don't know what's going to happen. If they admit me to hospital you might have to take a whole stack of books to read.'

'What time is your appointment?' she said

I wondered if anything I had said had got through to her.

'It's at 9:10am,' I said.

'I'll be here at 8:50am,' she said.

'Abs, did you hear anything I just said to you?'

'All of it,' she said. 'I'll be here at ten to.'

I opened my mouth to protest. She didn't give me a chance to speak.

'Chris, if I'm not here to give you a lift, how the fuck else are you going to get there. You can't go on your damn bike.'

CHAPTER THIRTY-SEVEN

Abi and the kids stayed for tea. We all had beans on toast. Not much of a meal, but quick and easy.

Neil walked through the front door at 5:30pm. Right on time.

A shitty thought zipped through my head. *Perhaps he was on time because he wasn't seeing anyone tonight. Abi was with me.*

Shitty thought. She was my best friend and he was my husband.

He looked taller than he had for several days. Brighter and more awake too. He smiled when he saw me. And when he realised Abi and her children were here the smile took on a different characteristic. False. I'm sure Abi and the kids wouldn't have recognised it. But I did. He was disappointed that they were there.

'You're early,' I said.

Looking at me, genuine smile again.

'I told them I had to get home on time at least once in a blue moon,' he said. 'Something smells good, what is it?'

'I had a professional come in to cook tonight. It's beans on toast.'

'Ah,' he said. 'It smelled better than that.'

'I can ask the chef to do you some if you want. I think we still have another tin.'

'I'll pass on that. Have we got anything in the freezer?'

'Go have a look. I'll break it to the chef.'

Neil dropped his briefcase by the sofa and stuck his head round the dining room door. He gave and received all the requisite greetings and stomped off to the kitchen. I heard him turn on the tap and open the freezer door.

As I stood in the living room, next to Neil's briefcase, for a moment it felt like summer. I felt light and warm. The Neil I loved was back, and laughter belted out from the dining room.

If I put all that had happened out of my mind and ignored the ache at the top of my leg, I could feel normal. And, for a brief space in time, I felt whatever normal was to me. My own version of it.

I wanted Abi and the kids gone, Michael and Rose in bed, and just the two of us sitting down together. I didn't care what we did. Eat together; watch telly together — anything. As long as it was just us, together.

Abi read my mind. I heard her raise her voice over the top of the kids.

'Come on Jess, Jose. Finish up now. It's getting late.'

All four kids protested. I would have expected nothing less.

'No really,' she said. 'We must be going. Dad will think we've deserted him.'

I heard Josie shout "We have", and they all laughed again.

I walked back into the dining-room and sat back down to my now cold beans on toast.

'You don't have to go,' I said.

Abi looked up and smiled at me. She nodded.

'Come on kids,' she said. 'See who can be the first to get their coat on.'

She really was my best friend.

In less than five minutes she managed to calm them all down and have them ready by the front door.

'I'll see you at ten to nine,' she said.

Josie overheard as she jumped off the the front doorstep.

'Why is that?' she said.

'Me and Christine are going for a coffee,' she said. 'And don't be so nosey.'

In the flow of fresh air that spilled in from outside, I smelled Abi's perfume. Not deliberately. But it came to me, entwined with all the other scents coming my way. I had smelled it before. On her, of course, but on someone else too. My immediate thought went to Neil. But that was unjust. It wasn't him. It was the kids. Michael and Rose. Presumably from where she was giving them a lift every day. I realised I hadn't even thanked her properly for all the lifts. I decided to pop out to the local shop and find some chocolates for her. I glanced at my car in the drive and remembered the keys locked inside.

Abi had been right. Cycling to the doctors would be a bit crap. I could do it, of course, and it wouldn't take too long, but if the weather was poor, or if the rush-hour traffic was still hanging around, it would be a complete pain in the backside.

And I couldn't even cycle to the shop tonight. I had no lights on my bike.

I heard the microwave beeping in the kitchen and smelled Neil's tea. Chicken Biryani. I closed the front door and walked through the living-room towards the kitchen.

Neil was just peeling the plastic back from his meal. He hadn't got a plate ready. Or a knife and fork. I opened the cupboard and took out a plate.

'I'll just warm this up for you,' I said.

'I was just going to eat it out of the packaging,' he said.

I put the empty plate in the microwave and switched it on.

'It only takes 30 seconds,' I said. 'Cavemen eat Biryani out of the package, not bank workers.'

'Cavemen are so hungry,' he said, 'they don't even bother microwaving it in the first place.'

I enjoyed these stupid conversations. I knew Neil did too. It was like a game of silly verbal tennis, with neither of us bothered who won.

'Do you want me to wash your loin cloth?' I said.

He made a stupid face.

'It doesn't really need it,' he said. 'I've only had it on since Christmas.'

'I know,' I said. 'I can see your baubles.'

I took the warm plate out of the microwave and handed it to

him. He turned it upside down over the microwave meal and inverted the plate and packaging together. I couldn't believe that not even a morsel fell to the floor. The entire meal, sauce too, rested dead centre of the plate.

'Hah!' he said.

'Baubles,' I said.

Neil was happy to drive us to the shop. Michael and Rose were happy to stay at home for five minutes.

I opened the passenger side window and checked the air outside. It was OK, so I left the window open. Neil gave me a sideways look, which I ignored. He reached over and turned the heater up.

'So why have you locked your keys in the car?' he said. 'On purpose?'

'I'll tell you on the way,' I said.

He looked at me with a stupid grin on his face. Presumably mirroring how stupid he thought I was for deliberately locking the keys in the car.

'It's great that you were back on time today,' I said. 'Really great.'

He smiled again.

'How was your day?' he said. 'How was the counsellor?'

Jealousy again?

'How long have you got?' I said.

Another stupid grin. 'Just about until we get to the shops.'

'The counsellor was fine,' I said. 'Really good, in fact. I think it's highlighting things for me though.'

'What do you mean?'

'I mean, I'm not really sure that what I have — if I actually have anything — is post-traumatic-stress.'

Neil kept his eyes on the road. But I knew he was listening.

'The bangs on the head have caused these dreams and visions, I'm sure of that. But the dreams and visions are not about the attack. They are about something else. The counsellor asked me if I had been bullied by a girl or a group of girls when I was younger. Obviously I hadn't. But he said that maybe I had and my mind had erased it as a memory, because it was too painful.'

Neil let out a single laugh. Shook his head.

'What?' I said.

'It sounds like he's making it up to me,' Neil said.

I felt as though I should defend Colin, but didn't.

'It kind of felt like that to me too,' I said. 'But I knew what he was getting at. And to be honest, if I can find an answer to all this, then I would be very happy. So I went with it. I drove to my mum and dad's to see if they could remember anything from my childhood.'

'Really?'

'Neil, just listen. Don't make any comments, please.'

He looked over at me. His face lit up from the oncoming headlights. He raised his eyebrows.

'Obviously they confirmed what I had said. That there was nothing in my childhood at all. Nothing. In a way I was disappointed, not to be able to pin everything on some long forgotten event. But I knew, at least, that there was nothing wrong with my memory.'

Out of the corner of my eye I saw Neil half turn his head to say something. Then he stopped and looked back to the road ahead.

'On the drive back home,' I said, 'I started thinking about time. Started imagining a world without it. I started to feel pretty happy. Had some of my confidence back.'

I could feel Neil bristling to say something, but he still kept quiet. I wondered whether I should continue with what I was going to say. But what the heck. If my best friend could deal with it I was pretty sure my husband could. At least he should.

I told him about the woman in the back of my car. Told him

about my ferocious feelings and how I was ready to follow them through. I told him about every aspect of the blackouts. And then I told him about Rose's bedroom and about the feelings I had felt when I tickled the kids.

I told him everything that was on my mind and from my mind. This time I didn't cry. I must have let that all out with Abi.

I was surprised when he pulled the car into a lay-by. He left the engine running, presumably because I still had the window open. He turned in his seat to face me. He looked tired again.

'And I'm worried about you working late,' I said.

He sighed and his jaw tightened.

'What are we going to do, Chris?' he said.

That surprised me too.

'What do you mean?' I said.

'What's happening to you is seriously wrong. None of this should be happening. None of it is normal.'

At last. I was finally getting through to someone.

'Exactly,' I said.

'So we need to do something to make it all better,' he said.

'I'm seeing the doctor again in the morning,' I said.

His head dropped and he clenched his fist against the steering wheel.

'For fuck sake,' he said. 'How many times have you seen the doctor now? And what has he done for you? Not a damn thing. Your life is fucked at the moment. Mine too. And if you're now hearing voices that are telling you to hurt the kids or kill people. What the fuck, Chris? What the fuck?'

It wasn't like him to swear so much. Every swear word felt like a sting.

'I've been doing everything I can to overcome this,' I said. 'Everything within my power, everything I can think of. And to be honest I feel like I've been doing it alone.'

'What does that mean?'

He knew very well what it meant.

'You've not been here, Neil,' I said. 'You've not been here during the day and you've been working fucking late most nights. So what the fuck do you suggest I do?'

'I'm doing the best I can too,' he said. 'I still have to work. I can't just drop everything and stay at home all the time. Life just isn't like that.'

'Well my life just isn't like it used to be,' I said. 'I didn't asked to be attacked. And I sure as hell didn't ask for all this shit to be happening to me. What else can I do — other than go to the doctor? When we're sick, that's what we do. And I know I'm sick.'

He didn't say anything.

'And you don't *have* to work late. You could leave at the normal time. Even if you brought work home with you, that would be better. At least you'd be here.'

'You know we aren't allowed to take work home. Everything has to stay within the bank. You can't just bring people's bank details home and start working on them.'

'Well it's funny that you're having to work late just when I need you most at home.'

His fists clenched tighter on the steering wheel.

'What do you mean — funny?'

'You know what I mean. How do I even know you're at the bank?'

He slammed his fist on the dashboard and swore. His teeth were so tightly clenched that it sounded more like hissing than words.

His face screwed up and his eyes narrowed. He leaned forward towards me.

'I have to fucking work,' he said, still hissing. 'If you don't trust me, come and wait for me to fucking finish.'

He backed off slightly.

'And then maybe I'll come and wait for you when you see your fucking counsellor,' he said.

I closed my eyes and stretched my head back.

'Oh for god's sake.' I said. 'I'm seeing a counsellor because I'm trying to get better. The doctor recommended him. I didn't choose him. I would be more than happy for you to come along. Be my guest — if you can get any time off work.'

A huge lorry sped past us, headlights on full beam and sounding its horn. The noise was deafening, the lights blinding.

'Fuck off,' Neil and I shouted in tandem.

The lorry passed and we both sat in silence while the heat from our argument dissipated.

I looked out of the open window, watched the moon disappear and reappear from behind the clouds. I heard Neil tapping his wedding ring finger on the gear stick.

I wound the window up and he stopped tapping.

'What are we going to do about the kids?' I said.

CHAPTER THIRTY-EIGHT

I hadn't meant it as an ambiguous question.

I had felt, as soon as the argument had died, that we were back to normal again.

Perhaps Neil wasn't finished arguing, or maybe he genuinely misunderstood.

'I want them,' he said.

'What?'

'I want them.'

'I mean what do we do with our kids, together. You and me. How do we protect them from me? I'm not suggesting that we separate!'

I was shocked at his matter-of-fact answer about the kids when he thought I was talking about a split. Why hadn't he fought back at me, pleaded with me to re-consider?

'Oh,' he said. 'I thought you'd had enough of me. Of us.'

'And all you could say was "I want them"?' I said.

'I was trying to brash it out,' he said. 'Trying to make you think I wasn't bothered.'

'Well it worked,' I said.

At last he unclenched his fist. A car flashed past us, and for a moment I thought I saw tears in Neil's eyes.

He reached over for my hand, squeezed it. I put my other hand on top of his.

'Flippin' idiot,' I said.

'Bloody twonk,' he said.

I wiped my eyes. Perhaps I hadn't spent all my tears after all. And when he thought I couldn't see, Neil wiped his. He opened his door and climbed out. A few seconds later he was at my door. He opened it, unclipped my safety belt and helped me to my feet. We hugged each other in the cold air for a long time. One car beeped its horn as it sped past.

The break-up and make-up over with, the atmosphere in the car was much lighter. I opened my window only a little, and Neil had the heater only on low. A few minutes passed in silence.

'I am worried about the kids though,' I said. 'And I'm really not sure what to do about it. Abi said she'll come and spend time with me during the day, but I'm a bit scared about what I might do to her.'

'Do you really think you might do anything to her?' he said. 'I know you're worried, but you haven't actually hurt anyone yet. It's not in your nature to hurt anyone.'

'I know it's not. But my nature seems to have changed. I'm not the me I used to be. The point is, I think that there is the potential for me to hurt Michael or Rose. If we're really blunt about it, based on the dreams and visions I've been experiencing, and the fact that I ended up in Rose's room, she would seem to be the one most in danger.'

'From her own mother?' Neil said. 'Really?'

'Neil, I know it doesn't sound possible. But I really don't seem to have control over my mind or body at certain times. Something happens to me. Despite my best efforts and all my fight, something just waltzes in and takes over.'

Neil shot a quick glance at me, then back to the road.

'When you had those feelings,' he said. 'When you were tickling the kids. You said you heard a voice?'

'It sounded like a mans voice. I thought it might even be you, that maybe you'd come home early. But it wasn't. It came from inside me. And the power I felt in my arms and the hatred in my heart — it was like a tidal-wave. I had to fight the urge to hurt them. I could see myself throwing them away from me. Throwing them against the wall. I really do think I could have done it.'

'And what stopped you?' he said.

'What?' I said.

He chanced a longer look in my direction. Long enough for me to see his smile. Perhaps more of a smirk. He looked very pleased with himself.

'So what stopped you?' he said. 'What stopped you from crushing our kids against a wall? What was it?'

I opened my mouth but nothing came out.

'I don't know,' I said.

'Think about it.'

I didn't know what he was getting at. His voice sounded as though he had made some fantastic discovery.

'Well,' I said. 'Nothing stopped me. The moment just passed.'

'Did it?' he said. 'That's not what you said earlier.'

I thought for a moment.

'I didn't say what it was earlier. I don't know what it was.'

Another look, another smirk. If I didn't guess or if he didn't reveal what he knew soon, we were in danger of crashing.

'What are you getting at?' I said.

'You said "I fought the urge to hurt them".'

I looked at him. Was that it? That was what all these smirks were about.

'What?' I said.

'Chris, you fought the urge to hurt them. The moment didn't just pass. You fought. You managed to override the voice, the power and the feelings of anger...'

'Hatred,' I said.

'OK, hatred. But you overcame them. You were strong enough to fight them. Where the kids were concerned, their safety, their wellbeing, you were too strong for the "other" you. You won.'

The smirking made more sense now. Perhaps he was onto something.

'Is that what I said? That I fought the urge?'

'Word for word,' he said. 'That's exactly what you said.'

I thought about it. Took myself back to the tickling and tried to replay it in my mind. I tried to summon up the same feelings, challenged the voice to come back. The memory wasn't so clear. Had the moment passed? Or had I overcome it myself? I wasn't sure.

'You can control it,' he said. 'When it comes down to it, you are in control.'

If that was the case, what did it mean for all the other things that were happening? If I could control my urges at that moment, could I simply take control of the other things too? I wasn't sure that I could apply it to my dreams — even I wasn't that clever. But the visions, perhaps.

'What about when I blackout?' I said. 'How can I take control of that when I'm not even aware of where I am or what I'm doing?'

'Does anything happen to you before you blackout? Are there any signs of what is about to happen?'

Obviously I had given this an inordinate amount of thought myself.

'Nothing that I can think of,' I said. 'The first time it happened, on the way to Mum and Dad's, I wasn't aware that anything had happened at all. If I hadn't noticed the time on their kitchen clock, I would probably still be unaware of it today.

'The second time I was walking along the road toward the woods. I think I thought it became misty, and there might have been a smell, but I get smells all the time. And it was a misty day.'

Neil didn't say anything. He probably wasn't smirking either.

'For all I know,' I said. 'I have blacked out before now and not even known about it.'

The thought hung with us both. It scared me. I'm not sure

what it did to Neil.

'Maybe the Mum and Dad time wasn't the first,' I said. 'Or maybe there were more before the walking one. Maybe even since then.'

'But you were aware when you "woke up" in Rose's room,' he said. 'You knew then, without seeing a clock, that it had happened again. You were aware of becoming conscious again.'

'But I wasn't the first time. What does that mean? That the blackouts are getting worse? Better?'

'I don't know,' he said. 'Maybe just different. Or maybe you're getting used to them, getting more control or awareness or something.'

I sniffed in the air from outside.

'I am going to talk to the doctor,' I said. 'About the kids.'

'What do you mean? Talk to him about what?'

'I think I should be honest with him. If I need help, medication of some sort, they need to know what they're dealing with.'

'You're not going to tell him about wanting to hurt them?'

'I think I should,' I said.

'No way, Chris. No way. You start talking about wanting to hurt the kids and what's the doctor going to do?'

'Hopefully, help me,' I said. 'Prescribe medicine — maybe even admit me to hospital.'

'Sorry, Chris, but I think you're way off with that. Way off. He's going to alert social services.'

'He can't do that,' I said. 'Doctors have to take an oath.'

'The Hippocratic oath,' Neil said. 'Not an oath of secrecy. Any mention of kids getting hurt and they'll be onto social services before you've even left the surgery.'

'What if I ask to be admitted to hospital? What if I tell them that you're at home for the kids and that I need to be hospitalised.'

'But I have to work, Chris. I might be at home for them for a few days. Maybe even a week or so. But what then? What happens when I have to go back to work? If you've got yourself admitted to some hospital somewhere what would we do. That would traumatise the kids anyway, you being in hospital.'

'But I might hurt them, Neil. Maybe not when I'm conscious, maybe I can fight it then. But when I'm blacked out I'm not aware of a damn thing. I can't fight then.'

'What about your mum and dad?' Neil said. 'Why not have the kids stay with them? Just while this is all sorted out.'

I shook my head.

'Mum and Dad are already going through it. Dad's not well and Mum looks worn out. And that would cause even more disruption to Michael and Rose if they have to live there. It would be a hassle getting to school, they wouldn't be near their friends. It would just be a nightmare.'

'Well it would be a damn sight more of a nightmare if social services came and took them into care because their mum says she might hurt them and she should be hospitalised for their protection.'

'But if I explain everything to him,' I said. 'Talk it through with him, ask his advice. If I'm completely upfront and honest with him, he wouldn't need to contact social services.'

Neil shook his head and slowed the car to a stop.

'If someone came to you,' he said. 'And said that they thought they might hurt their two young children, what would you do?'

I thought about that the entire journey home.

CHAPTER THIRTY-NINE

The dreams came to me again that night.

I already thought they had reached the heights of realism, but I was mistaken.

This time, the wind and roar had diminished slightly. The mist was less thick.

This time I could hear voices. I could see things more clearly.

My arms felt chilly, and the light in the sky seemed low. It felt like early evening or late afternoon.

I was waiting. Hiding behind gorse bushes. On the ground I had spread out a pale blue sheet. A bottle lay on the sheet. Not a wine bottle, but a smaller, brown bottle. Like a medicine bottle. There was a small white cloth next to the bottle. It looked wet.

I peered out from behind the gorse. A patch of mist cleared and I saw her. She was dragging something behind her, walking up the hill towards my hiding place.

Mist swept in and covered her again. I took the opportunity to come out from behind the gorse. I ran up the hill a little way. Away from the girl. Then stopped, turned around and started walking very slowly back down towards her.

I could hear her talking. Her young voice. Speaking to someone. Talking to the thing she was dragging along. I couldn't make out what she was saying. It sounded muffled. Like I had something in my ears.

A clear patch as the fog swept skyward, and there she was. Startled to see me at first. She faltered, slowed down a little. Then she smiled and came towards me. She had a dog with her. That was what she was dragging. A fat, reluctant dog.

I wasn't surprised. I had expected her to have a dog. It shuffled along behind her. Obviously not used to much exercise.

She was a little further up the hill than I thought she would be. Almost past my gorse hiding place. I extended my stride to close the gap between us.

We met slightly uphill from the gorse. A feeling of excitement filled my body.

We talked. My voice sounded muffled like hers. My voice sounded different too. A different tone. Deeper. But not unfamiliar.

I bent down to her dog. Patted it. It revolted me.

I listened carefully. Were there other voices? I didn't think so. It felt like we were alone. Just us. And her revolting, fat dog.

I pointed over at the gorse bushes. I laughed and told her something. She laughed too and spoke to her dog.

We moved towards the bushes. She seemed very happy. Quite at ease. But I felt the adrenalin rising with every step we took.

Now she stopped. A few feet short of the gorse. I was pointing away from it. Pointing up the hill. She looked in that direction as I disappeared behind the gorse.

The bottle and cloth were in my hands. The cloth was dripping wet now. I dropped the bottle and kept hold of the cloth.

The girl turned back to me. Came closer to the gorse. I reached out to her with my empty hand and held the other, with the cloth, behind my back.

She stepped into the hiding place, still dragging her dog behind her.

I slammed her down to the ground with all my weight on top of her. She struggled against me as I pushed the cloth over her face and mouth. She forced her head from side to side, desperate to breathe, but I pushed the cloth harder against her, covering her nose and mouth.

Her fat dog started barking and snarling at me. I punched out at it, but it was at the end of its lead, still attached to the girl's wrist. I couldn't reach it. I thrust my elbow into the side of the girl's head, it seemed to stun her. Then I turned my body and kicked out at the dog. I caught it full on its jaw, shifted my body a little more and kicked again. Another powerful blow to its head. It went limp and slumped to the ground.

As I moved my body back over the girl I heard another noise. It sounded like glass. Breaking glass.

Moments later a searing pain shot through my upper leg. I pinned the girl down with one arm and thrust my other hand down to the pain. Something was sticking out of my leg. The pain felt hot and cold at the same time. I pulled whatever it was out of the wound. Was it the bottle? Had she broken the bottle and stabbed me with it while I was kicking her dog? 'BITCH'.

The wound felt deep and ragged. It made me feel even more powerful. I looked down at her face, already bleeding from my attack. I stroked her hair off her forehead. Smiled at her.

Raped her.

Killed her.

For minutes I laid my full weight on top of her still body. Got my breath back, calmed myself down. I heard short breaths coming from her dog, but did nothing about it.

The pain in my leg felt warm. Not too uncomfortable, but sticky and raw. I rolled off the girl onto my back. The roar and the wind was there. And a smell. A sweet, sickly smell. The mist and wind would carry it away. Disperse it, clean the hiding place. Nature would work on my behalf to hide my toil. Nature was pure. Nature cleansed everything.

The mist cleared above me. The sky looked momentarily clear. I felt warm all over. Content. The dead girl lay beside me. Her injured dog still puffing breath at the end of its lead.

When I woke up my hand was already down at my leg.

Rubbing the invisible wound. I didn't feel distressed or scared. I felt calm. It was as though I had woken with some new perspective. I had somehow stepped away from everything and was able to see the events of the dream in a less involved way.

Yes, it had been me. Yes, I really had raped and killed a girl. But the dream had brought clarity. It explained the pain in my leg.

I knew it wasn't physically (or mentally) possible for me to have done the things I had done to the the girl.

Something was happening to me. I was having these dreams for a reason and I knew they had to mean something. I just had to figure out what.

Once Neil was dressed and ready for work, I told him about the dream. The full details. I also reminded him that I was going to see the doctor that morning.

'Please don't mention the kids,' he said. 'I really don't see how any good can come from it.'

Abi said almost exactly the same thing when she arrived at ten to nine.

I managed to avoid giving either of them a proper answer.

As it turned out, I didn't mention it to the doctor. I didn't have to. I had already decided on my next course of action.

The most important thing to me was Michael's and Rose's safety. Like any mother, I would do anything I could to keep them safe.

I didn't think they would be safe being taken away from Neil and me. If they were in care, we would have no way of protecting them.

And I still thought that it would be too disruptive for them to stay with my parents.

I had thought about asking Abi if she and Oliver could have

them to stay for a while. I knew Jess and Josie would love it as much as Michael and Rose. But it wouldn't be fair on Abi. I'm sure she would have said yes. And I'm sure she would have meant it. But it would have been just as disruptive to her as it would have been for my parents.

I still felt that the best thing to do would be to remove myself from the picture. I was the potential danger, and it made sense to distance the kids from the source of danger as much as possible. I had already ruled out suicide for the time being. I was too determined to get my life back, to go down that route. But I would keep it in reserve as my final weapon — if needed.

I had decided, instead, to speak to my mum and dad. Dad had been poorly, Mum tired. If I could stay with them, I would be able to look after them, put their minds at rest and be a safe distance from the kids.

If I could work with the doctor and the counsellor, find a way of developing the additional strengths I needed to combat the dreams and feelings, then I could mend myself. Make myself a stronger person.

It would mean asking Abi to look after the kids until Neil got home. But perhaps Neil could change his hours a little to get back sooner.

It wasn't a great plan. It meant putting on Abi and Neil. I wasn't overjoyed at the thought that Abi would be the first person to see Neil after he finished work. And it meant that I wasn't going to be around as much for Michael and Rose. But I had to think of their overall safety. If there was even the remotest chance that I might hurt them, I had to do everything I could to stop it.

Me staying with Mum and Dad for a while seemed like the least worst option out of a very short list of shitty ones.

When I told the doctor about my idea he was all for it. As long as I could still go to see Colin, he felt it might be beneficial.

'Almost like a holiday,' he said.

I was going to ask him what sort of holidays he went on, but stopped myself.

'We've still not had the results back from the last MRI,' he said. 'Have you experienced anything more?'

'Well, I think I had another blackout episode,' I said. 'And the dreams are still coming. And I thought I saw someone that wasn't really there.'

He raised his eyebrows and nodded. I didn't know what it meant.

'And I have heard a voice.' I said.

'Do you feel like hurting yourself?' he said.

I wasn't sure how to answer that one. If I said no would the next question be about hurting others?

'I don't think so,' I said.

The doctor nodded again.

'I think we can perhaps change the dosage of your tablets, perhaps look at additional things too. And I think it might not do any harm to request a psychiatric assessment. How would you feel about that?'

'Do you mean now?' I said.

He smiled.

'We would need to request an appointment first,' he said. 'It might take a week or so.'

'I'm not sure,' I said. 'What would it involve? What would happen to me?'

'Well, we might not need it,' he said. 'It can be very tricky deciding whether someone should consider an assessment or not. There are guidelines, of course, but there are also degrees of experience. In other words, you might only be experiencing mild symptoms of psychosis, brought on temporarily by the head injury, or it could run deeper.'

I felt like I was on dangerous ground here. As though things were running away from me a little. I needed to bring them back. My goal was to be medicated sufficiently to give me time to fight this, but not come across as so mad that I needed to be sectioned. Having never been in a position like this before, I wasn't entirely sure how to play it. It was clear I was having problems. I needed help to diminish them. But I didn't want to become a zombie, drugged up to my eyeballs and unable to function at all.

'Would you say that you have had some sort of experience every day for the last 7 days?' he said.

'Yes.'

'Do you feel like people are talking about you? Saying things behind your back?'

'No,' I said. 'Not at all.'

'Do you think that people are watching you, or following you at all?'

'No, of course not.'

'But you say you are hearing voices, and you are seeing things which aren't there.'

I nodded but said nothing.

'Is your sense of smell still playing up?'

'I don't really hear *voices*,' I said. 'It's *a* voice. And I can't really make out anything that is said. It's a muffled sound really.'

'How are you getting on with Mr Connell?' he said.

'Fine. I'm sure it's helping me to get a handle on things. It probably helps to give me some perspective.'

He pursed his lips and tapped the end of his pen against them.

'These episodes you describe as "blackouts",' he said. 'I think it is safe to say that what you're experiencing is memory loss.'

I gave him a look.

'In a way it feels a little like sleepwalking,' he said. 'The sleepwalker wakes up, and can't remember anything he or she has done. In a similar way, you are doing things, perhaps going places, perfectly normally, but you have a sudden and immediate memory loss. In other words, you effectively 'wipe out' a proportion of time that has just passed. It gives you the feeling that you have been doing something in an unconscious way, when in fact you have probably been behaving perfectly normally.'

I wondered how driving a hundred miles somewhere or sitting in my car outside a pupil's house or being in my daughter's bedroom with a damp flannel behind my back could be described as perfectly normal. But I said nothing.

'Let me have a look over your notes, and I'll maybe consult with a couple of my colleagues,' he said. 'It will all be confidential, so don't worry. Then I'll contact you in a day or so to see how you're getting along.'

'Ok,' I said.

'Will you be at your home address?' he said. 'Or will I need to take your mother and father's details?'

I gave him Mum and Dad's address, and my mobile number.

I stood up to go.

The doctor looked awkward. He was about to say something but hesitated.

I stood by the chair and looked at him.

He found his voice.

'Just one more question,' he said. 'I'm sorry, but I have to ask. Is there any history of psychosis or mental illness in your family?'

CHAPTER FORTY

As I walked back into the health centre waiting room, Abi stood. She looked concerned.

'Everything OK?' she said.

'Of course,' I said. 'Fine. Let's go.'

She took my arm. I felt like an invalid being helped to the car. I didn't take my arm away.

'Coffee?' she said.

'Please,' I said. 'But let's go somewhere not too near. I need to get my thoughts together.'

Abi drove and said nothing.

Something was bothering me.

It wasn't the question about mental illness in my family. I told him that there was none. I thought that Mum and Dad were totally transparent, what you saw was what you got. And as far as I knew, their parents and siblings were too. If they were hiding any kind of mental issues they were making a damned good job of it.

But before he'd asked the question, while I sat listening to him drone on, something had clicked into place in my mind.

I opened the car window a little and breathed in. Abi still said nothing, allowing me the time I needed.

The sky was turning the colour of milky charcoal. No doubt more shitty weather on the way.

Come on Christine — think.

A splat of rain hit the car windscreen. I watched it spread out. Watched it drip down the glass.

And it came to me. The little bit of something that had stuck to my mind, fluttered.

The wet flannel. When I had woken up in Rose's room, I had the wet flannel behind my back.

In the latest dream I had covered the girls face with a wet cloth.

Goosebumps popped up on my back. I had been re-enacting the dream — with the flannel, in Rose's room. But I hadn't had that dream yet. And the pain in my leg was from a wound inflicted by the girl as she fought me. She used the bottle that I had taken and hidden in the gorse. Either it had broken in the struggle, or she had managed to smash it herself, and she stabbed me with it. But I'd had the leg pain ever since the skateboard attack, not just since this dream.

I shivered. I felt as though someone was watching me. I glanced over at Abi, but she was looking for somewhere for us to stop.

Now I knew what the flannel and the pain in my leg were, but what did it all mean? Was this something that was going to happen in the future? Was I going to kill Rose? Did someone I know intend to go out killing young girls?

'Is over there OK?' Abi said.

She was pointing at a small coffee shop I had not been to before. It was tucked between a betting shop and a bank.

'Great,' I said.

Perhaps my dreams were actually nothing more than my mind trying to make sense of the feelings and actions that had already happened to me.

Perhaps my dream concocted the attack in order to make sense of why I had an inexplicable pain in my leg. Perhaps the cloth in the dream was only there to help explain why I had a wet flannel behind my back in Rose's room.

And perhaps all of the dreams, visions, voices and sensations were simply my mind fighting back after being attacked. All the memory loss, all the horrors that I had felt. Perhaps they really were all nothing more than my brain, swollen and bruised since the injuries, fighting its way back to normal and fighting the attacker that I was unable to fight in real life at the time.

Abi parked the car against the pavement.

'My treat,' she said.

The coffee shop was empty of customers, but had two staff behind the counter. The smell of fresh coffee beans was glorious. We ordered our coffee and sat down at a table by the window. A suited businessman strode in and asked for an expresso and a muffin to take out. Once he was gone, the only noise came from the street outside and the clanking of coffee pots and mugs in the shop.

'So how was it?' Abi said.

I realised how shallow my breathing had become. I took a deep breath and blew the air out of my mouth slowly.

'I may have to go for a psychiatric assessment,' I said.

Abi tried to keep the shock from her face. She obviously didn't know what to say.

'He's going to look through my notes and talk to colleagues. Then he'll let me know.'

Abi found her voice.

'Do you really think you'll need that?'

I shook my head.

'I have no idea, Abs. Perhaps it's just what I need.'

She took a sip of her coffee. Hid behind the mug for a moment.

'Did you mention Michael and Rose?'

'No. You and Neil thought it was a bad idea, and to be honest, so did I. I think I just wanted to make sure they were safe, so perhaps I wasn't thinking quite straight.'

Abi smiled.

'I'm pleased,' she said. 'I'm sure you did the right thing.'

'I have made a decision about what I'm going to do though,' I said.

She put her mug on the table. Steam drifted up from it.

'I'm going to go and stay with my mum and dad for a bit. If they'll have me.'

'OK?' she said.

'That way I know I won't be any harm to Michael or Rose.'

'What about your mum and dad?' she said.

She had spotted the flaw in my plan.

'I know,' I said. 'But I've been thinking about this. I don't think I'm much of a danger to adults. All the dreams and visions and feelings have been directed towards children.'

The clanking behind the counter stopped and I realised how awful my last sentence had sounded. I lowered my voice.

'Apart from the woman I thought was in my car, nothing else has had anything to do with adults. I don't know, maybe it's to do with the fact that I was attacked by someone relatively young.'

Abi picked up her mug and sipped.

'I just need to know that the kids are safe,' I said.

'Why not come and stay with us for a while?' she said. 'We'd be happy to have you.'

I thought about Oli. Thought about the hassle I would be to them both. And I thought about Josie and Jess.

'It wouldn't be right, Abs,' I said. 'Thank you for offering, but I would worry about Josie and Jess.'

She thought for a moment.

'Why don't I have Michael and Rose stay with us then?' she said. 'Josie and Jess would love it. It makes sense. I pick them up and take them into school anyway at the moment. Why not have them stay?'

'I knew you'd offer to help, Abs. But it would be a real hassle for you and Oliver.'

Abi sat back in the chair and laughed.

'What hassle?' she said. We have a spare room that they could both use, or Rose could go in with Jess. Seriously, Chris, it would be easy to do. Then you know the kids are safe and you don't have to put your parents through anything.'

She leaned forward across the table.

'Besides,' she said. 'I would need to look after them until Neil got back from work anyway.'

'I thought I would ask Neil if he could change his working hours a little. Just for the time being. Just while I sort out my head problems.'

Abi shook her head.

'No offence, Chris, but can you really see the bank being compassionate? They're a huge organisation. I can't see them taking into account the needs of an employee's wife, can you?'

I felt like I was on the brink of caving in. I had been sure that my original idea of staying with Mum and Dad had been the right one. But now I wasn't.

'What about Oli?' I said.

'Chris, it'll be great for us all. You know what the kids are like when they're together. We never hear or see any of them. It will make our lives easier.'

'I would give you money for board and food and stuff. And I can get Neil to come over and get their washing. Or I could cycle over and get it.'

Abi looked for all the world like she was going to throw the last of her coffee in my face.

'We're friends, Chris,' she hissed. 'Fuck off.'

'Well you must let me do something,' I said.

'You can. You can make sure you get better. And do it quickly, otherwise I'll keep your children.'

I reached across the table and squeezed her hand.

'Thank you, Abi,' I said. 'I don't know what I'd do without you.'

With her free hand she pointed her forefinger down her throat and pretended to be sick.

I kicked her under the table.

'When do you want to do it?' she said.

'Well, I was going to ask Mum and Dad and Neil tonight, and arrange it for tomorrow. Is that too soon?'

'The sooner the better,' she said. 'Get them over and let the fun begin.'

I was still squeezing her hand. She moved it away.

'Another coffee?' she said.

I shook my head.

'I think I need to get home. Start washing some of the kid's clothes, sort out towels and things.'

Abi grabbed her handbag and finished her coffee.

'I'll help,' she said. 'I'll stay with you until it's time to get the kids.'

I made sure I kept myself busy for the rest of the day. While I was waiting for the washing machine to finish, I ironed shirts and skirts. I made us lunch and coffees and Abi helped go through the kid's wardrobes to find the clothes I thought Michael and Rose would want to take.

Ever since the journey home I had been wanting to broach the subject of how long the kids would be staying with Abi. I'm sure she was wondering too. But neither of us brought it up. I had no idea how long it would take me to find a solution to my loss of mind control.

When it came to picking-up-time from school I had to mention it.

'I don't know how long this is going to take, Abi. I have no idea at all.'

'Don't worry,' she said. 'I'm happy to have them for as long as it takes. Months if needs be.'

'Of course I need to run all this by Neil,' I said. 'He might knock it dead in the water. He won't want the kids away for long, I'm sure. Maybe it will spur him into trying to sort something out with his work.'

'Do you want me to mention anything to them when I pick

them up? Or do you want to talk to them yourself?'

'I think I'd like to wait until they're home. I'd like to sit down with them both and tell them.'

Abi picked up her handbag and rummaged around for her car keys.

'I'll leave my bag here,' she said.

When she was gone I opened a few more windows in the house. I took the opportunity to walk into every room and breathe in the atmosphere. Our bedroom still smelled of hairspray and deodorant from the morning. Michael's room smelled vaguely of socks and damp. Rose's bedroom still smelled of the carpet shampoo.

But in each room there was also the smell of the people. With my eyes shut I would have known who inhabited each room, just by the smell. Not the smell of the things in the room, but by the smell of themselves that was indelibly present.

I opened the airing cupboard and pulled some clean towels out for them to take. They smelled fresh and felt warm. I looked at the spare flannels. The sight of them made me think about Doctor Jones. How long would it take for him to make a decision about the state of my mental health? It felt like some things were now out of my hands. I hated the feeling of not being in control over my own future. I felt a surge of anger, and then power. But not the nasty power that I had been feeling of late. This was a "just" power. A "determined to win" power. Whatever it took I was going to beat this thing. I was going to fight it with everything I had.

I thought back to my trek up The Andes. Reminded myself how strong I could be. I remembered obstacles that I had overcome, determined not to be beaten.

I thought about Rose's birth. How hit-and-miss it had felt. The cord wrapped around her neck, having to time my pushing so as not to cause her any additional problems. I had willed her to be OK. I had concentrated my mind so hard it made my head hurt. She would be OK. I didn't realise until afterwards how common it was for a baby's umbilical cord to become wrapped around its neck.

And I thought about when Michael had stopped breathing when he was only two years old. I had been at home alone with him. Neil was at work. I left him in his bouncy chair while I went into the kitchen to prepare his food. While I was doing it, something made me want to check on him.

His face was blue and his eyes bulging. There was no breath coming in or out of him at all.

My instincts kicked in. I picked him up, checked his throat, patted his back and prayed like hell. I switched into auto-pilot. It seemed like it took forever, but in a few seconds I had him breathing again. The hospital checked him over and he was fine. So I knew I had dealt with tough things, frightening things, in the past.

I focused back on the flannels. I was strong enough. I knew I was.

A breeze blew in through Michael's bedroom window and rattled his blinds. I felt a chill on the back of my neck and instinctively turned around to look. There was nothing there. I closed the airing cupboard door and peeped around Michael's bedroom door. The blinds vibrated in the breeze, motes of dust swirled off them and spun around his room. I made a mental note to clean his room while he was away.

I wondered whether I should shut his window. Then a noise made me jump.

It was only a dog. Barking in the distance, its bark distorted on the breeze and somehow enhanced as it passed through the vibrating blinds.

The fine hairs on my arms bristled. I felt once more like I was being watched. I turned again to look.

The dog-barking intensified. The gentle breeze from the

window turned to a gust. It blew one of Michaels books off the window sill. I stepped into his room to pick it up and shut the window, but something stopped me just inside his doorway. Another noise.

But this wasn't the dog or the rattling blind. It was much closer than that.

It came from downstairs, at one of the open windows.

CHAPTER FORTY-ONE

My heart froze and I held my breath. I stood at Michael's bedroom door like a statue, trying to open my ears to every sound. As quietly as I could I breathed in through my nose, tried to smell if the house had changed.

Another noise. The creak a window frame makes as the window is pulled wide open.

I needed a weapon.

A quick scan of Michael's room gave me nothing.

I knew that Neil's length of broom handle was by his bed. But I didn't want to move further along the landing, giving away the fact that I was upstairs.

I heard the jangling of keys.

Were they my old keys? I had been expecting the attacker to come and try to use them on my car or house. Since we had changed the locks, he wouldn't be able to get in. Unless he climbed through an open window.

I cursed myself for being so stupid as to come upstairs, leaving windows open downstairs.

What did he want? Was he looking to steal things? Or was he after something else? Was he after me?

A bump from downstairs. Something landed on the kitchen floor. Something heavy. Like a person.

I was surprised I heard it over the thumping of my heart. But I had to act. I had to do something. A rage started burning inside me. I thought of how David Banner became The Incredible Hulk when he was angry. I was angry.

I turned to leave Michael's room. I dropped all but one of the towels I had taken from the airing cupboard. This was to be my weapon.

A footfall. Not mine. He was walking about. He wasn't

rummaging through things, he was just walking about. He was looking. Looking for me.

I unfurled the folded towel, held one corner and let the rest hang free. I twisted it around by moving my wrist in small circles. The towel wrapped around itself, looking more like rope with each twist. When it would twist no further I took the bottom end and brought it up to the top. It wasn't much, but it would still hurt if I swung a powerful and accurate shot against the side of his head.

I had a score to settle.

A scratching sound drifted up the stairs. Like metal on something more dense.

I moved towards the top of the stairs. The floorboards creaked slightly as I walked. They seemed deafening to me, but I couldn't remember ever hearing them creak when I was downstairs, and Neil or the kids were upstairs. I hoped that the intruder heard nothing.

As I reached the top of the stairs and looked down, a shadow moved against the living room wall at the bottom of the stairs. He had walked past the stairs, but not come up. I wondered if he had heard the creaking floorboards. Perhaps he was choosing to bide his time. Choosing to wait for me to come to him. He would certainly have the advantage of seeing my legs coming down the stairs before I would see him. I wondered if he was armed with something more dangerous than a skateboard. I suspected he was.

I had a rolled-up towel.

Another shadow on the wall. He was still walking about, not hiding. Unless there were two of them. Or more.

I heard the dog barking again. I hadn't shut the window in Michael's bedroom.

From outside I heard the sound of a car pulling to a stop. Car doors slamming and children's voices.

My children's voices.

They were back from school. I had lost track of the time and they were about to walk in to find an intruder in their home.

I roared. Screamed and roared. And I charged down the stairs as fast as I could without falling over.

I leaped the last four steps and raised the towel above my head in the most threatening way I could.

Over the noise I made I thought I heard banging and scraping coming from the kitchen. There was no one in the living room. But I was certain I glimpsed another shadow disappear from the wall near the kitchen.

I ran full pelt at the kitchen, still screaming, still roaring. I slammed the twisted towel against the door frame as I rushed in.

The kitchen window was wide open, as far as it could go. The pot-plant that once sat in the sunlight of the window sill lay on its side on the worktop, soil spilled from the pot. The saucer it had rested on was broken.

I virtually threw myself at the open window and craned my neck in every direction to try to catch sight of the intruder. But I saw no one. Not a sign. I had launched myself onto the worktop and now saw that my trousers were damp from the upturned plant. My hand was muddy from the soil. And I must have banged my elbow on the window sill as I now felt electric-shock-pulses of pain shooting from my elbow to my hand. My fingers tingled.

I squeezed the towel as hard as I could. Fuck, fuck, fuck.

I wanted to scream even louder. I felt like punching holes in the wall. I smashed the towel against the worktop. Sent the already unhappy plant crashing to the floor.

I knew that if I had the attacker in my grasp, I would have ripped him to pieces. Starting with his face, I would have torn him apart with my bare hands.

I so wanted that.

The doorbell rang.

I heard Michael and Rose and Josie and Jess. They all screamed, shouted and laughed as though they were arriving for a birthday party.

I rubbed my tingling elbow and jumped off the worktop. I used the towel to quickly gather up the broken pot and scattered soil into a corner of the kitchen and went to answer the front door.

All four children ran straight past me and banged up the stairs. Abi stood at the front door looking at me. She looked confused.

'Are you OK?' she said.

I stepped out of the house and past Abi. I looked around for the intruder. But he was gone.

'Did you see him?' I said.

'Who?'

'The man who attacked me. He was just here. He came into the house through an open window. I was upstairs and I heard him. I managed to chase him away.'

I realised I was talking much faster than normal and my voice seemed to have automatically tuned to a higher pitch. I probably sounded like a cartoon character.

Abi looked around, then looked hard at me.

'Did you see him?' she said.

'I chased him away. I ran down the stairs screaming at him and he ran away. He went back out of the kitchen window. You must have seen him, Abs. I heard you arrive in the car, that was what spurred me into action. You must have seen him.'

Abi shook her head.

'We need to call the police,' she said. 'You can give them a description now. They'll be able to get fingerprints from the window. They might even have him on file somewhere already. Are you OK?'

I was shaking vigorously. It was probably a mixture of fear

and anger. It felt like ninety percent in favour of anger.

And maybe it wasn't fear. Maybe it was humiliation or embarrassment.

'I can't give them a description,' I said. 'I didn't really see his face.'

Abi followed me into the house. She shut the front door behind her.

'Oh,' she said. The disappointment in her voice was obvious. 'Did you manage to get any new details about him? They might be able to do something even from a description of his clothes or his height.'

I felt my face flush with heat.

'I'm not sure that I saw any of him at all,' I said. 'I saw his shadow on the wall. A few times. But I didn't physically see him. He got away before I caught him.'

Abi looked as though she was struggling to find the right question.

'Did he say anything?' she said. 'Did he talk to you, or shout?'

I shook my head. I could see where this was going.

'He was here, Abi. I heard him come in the window. I heard the rattling of keys. And I heard him walking about downstairs. I saw his shadow, several times. He was here.'

Abi nodded.

'I think you should ring the police,' she said. 'Tell them what happened. Get them to come round and check the window for fingerprints. If he was inside your house, Chris, they have to do something about that. They can't just ignore it.'

I walked to the kitchen to fetch the phone. Even as I walked, the doubts about what I had heard and seen started flooding my mind.

I hesitated before picking up the phone. I dialled 999 and kicked some stray clumps of soil over to the broken plant in the corner. I told myself to lower the pitch of my voice. Slow it down a little. Sound less like a cartoon and more like a human being. A believable, normal human being.

Part of me hoped they wouldn't answer the phone.

They answered on the third ring.

CHAPTER FORTY-TWO

Abi looked up at me as I walked back in from the kitchen.

'What did they say?' she said.

'I didn't ring them.'

'Why?'

I wasn't sure what had made me hang up as soon as they answered.

'I'm not sure,' I said. 'Something just made me think about it all again. I don't want to come off as some crackpot who contacts the police every time I see a shadow or hear the wind blow.'

Abi said nothing. Happy to let me convince myself that I had done the right thing.

'And you're right,' I said. 'I couldn't give them a description. Couldn't tell them anything I hadn't told them already, other than the guy has a shadow.'

She nodded.

'And I'm sure he wouldn't be stupid enough to leave fingerprints anywhere. He probably wore gloves. What's the point?'

In the kitchen the phone rang. I knew who it was. I let it ring. Abi looked at me, then over my shoulder at the kitchen.

'I'll just let it go to answer-phone.' I said.

'Do you want me to get it?' she said.

I rushed back into the kitchen and grabbed the phone just before the answer-phone clicked in.

I spoke to the police as quietly as I could, tried not to let Abi overhear. Tried to reassure them that everything was OK and that I had called through to the emergency services in error. Yes — I had thought I'd needed the police, I thought I'd seen someone in the house, yes — everything was fine now, no — I wasn't under duress, no — I wasn't alone in the house, I had a friend with me.

I realised I probably sounded even more like a crackpot than if I had just spoken to them in the first place.

When I walked back into the living-room, Abi pretended to be busy listening out for the children upstairs.

'That was the police,' I said. 'I must have dialled the number before putting the phone down. They were just ringing to make sure everything was OK.'

'Oh?' Abi said.

'I told them everything was fine, that I had rung them by mistake.'

'Did you tell them about... anything?' she said.

My eyebrow tickled. I tried to ignore it, but couldn't.

'I said that I had thought someone had got into the house, but that it was probably just the wind. Because I didn't see anyone or hear any talking, I think they were OK with that. They just wanted to make sure everything was OK and that I wasn't being threatened by anyone. They did ask me if anything was missing.'

Abi looked around the living-room.

'And is there?'

I shrugged.

'I don't know. I haven't had a chance to look. I don't think anything has gone. If there really wasn't anyone here, nothing will be gone.'

'It might prove, one way or the other, if someone was here,' she said.

I couldn't think of anything of value in the living-room apart from the TV and DVD player, and they were obviously still there. The computer was in the dining-room, and that hadn't been taken either. I couldn't see the intruder legging it down the street with a kettle or a microwave, but I checked them both just to make sure.

By the front door, all the coats and shoes were where they should have been, apart from the kids' dumped in a pile as they'd stampeded through. My crossword books still lay scattered on the sofa. Even my mobile phone was where it had been, on the coffee table in front of the TV.

My handbag remained in a heap in the corner of the armchair. I opened it up and looked inside. My purse was still there. Nothing seemed to be missing at all. I even found myself looking up at the central light fitting and counting the light-bulbs.

And while I checked, I replayed the event in my mind. From when I'd heard the first noise to when I had charged down the stairs, screaming. I had smelled nothing different. But there had been a bump. The flowerpot? Blown over by the wind? But there had also been a scraping sound. Metal against something. A jangling of keys. I couldn't explain that so easily. And the shadows on the wall. I had been lucid enough to prepare a weapon out of a towel, conscious enough to negotiate the stairs — at speed. Aware enough to hear Abi and the kids arrive outside. On this occasion, I didn't think my mind had been playing tricks on me.

'I didn't see him,' I said.

Abi nodded.

'I know,' she said.

'It must have been my imagination?' I said.

Once again I prepared tea for everyone. Abi stayed with me until Neil arrived home. Once again he was late. He didn't look very pleased to see me, and he made no effort to be particularly friendly towards Abi. This time he definitely hadn't texted or rung me. Apart from a brief hello, he walked upstairs. I heard our bedroom door close. Quite firmly.

Abi graciously left for home almost as soon as Neil walked in. She knew we had a lot to talk about. I told her I would ring her later or talk to her in the morning when she came to pick up Michael and Rose. She let herself and Jessie and Jose out, and I didn't go to the front door to say goodbye. Instead, I left Michael and Rose to finish their tea and went upstairs to find Neil.

I tapped on the bedroom door. He didn't answer, so I opened it.

He looked up as I walked in. He was sat on the bed, legs dangling over the side, shoes still on. He had loosened his tie, and his neck was flushed red, as though he had been rubbing it with a rough towel. His face looked grey, and sweat dotted his brow. I wondered if he was going to be sick.

'Are you OK?' I said.

He wiped some of the sweat from his forehead. His eyes were bloodshot. I wondered if he was drunk.

'I feel a bit shit,' he said. 'Like I'm coming down with something.'

He ran his hand over his hair, pushed it back as if it was long and lustrous and not short and neat.

I reached over and put the back of my fingers against his brow.

'You do feel a bit hot,' I said. 'When did this come on?'

He hesitated, as though I had asked him a trick question.

'Neil?'

'About lunchtime,' he said. 'I've just felt a bit off all afternoon. And tonight, on the way home, I started feeling worse.'

'Didn't they notice at work?' I said. 'They should have let you go early, not made you work late again.'

He blushed.

'It was after I left, really,' he said. 'That was when it really started coming on.'

I sat down next to him. The bed bounced slightly.

'Let me get you something,' I said. 'You should take some paracetamol, bring your temperature down a bit. And I'll get you some water. Are you hungry?'

He shook his head and the bed bounced in time to the movement of his head.

'Not at the moment,' he said. 'I might just lie here for half an hour or so. Just with the lights off. I won't sleep. Just rest my eyes a little. I think it will help.'

I kissed his cheek and stood up as gently as I could.

'I will get you some water though,' I said. 'And those tablets.'

I closed the bedroom curtains as he kicked off his shoes and lay back on the bed.

I wondered if I would get a chance to talk to Neil before the kids went to bed. Although I had hoped to have them safely with Abi by tomorrow, I couldn't speak to them without talking it through with Neil first.

I stopped off at the bathroom cabinet to find the tablets and took the box downstairs with me.

As my foot hit the bottom step the front doorbell rang.

I hurried to the door so that it wouldn't ring again and disturb Neil. With the box of tablets in one hand I slid the safety chain into place and opened the door with the other. The chain did its job and the door stopped moving when it had opened just a few inches. Through the gap I saw the doorbell ringer's car at the end of the drive. My heart sank low in my chest then rose again, beating faster than I wanted it to. As well as feeling like some dark, malevolent sinkhole had been sucking down whatever sanity I'd once had, I was now starting to feel persecuted as well.

It was a police car.

CHAPTER FORTY-THREE

I thought about leaving the safety chain where it was and attempting to carry on a conversation through the barely open door. But it *was* the police.

'I'll just take the chain off,' I said, and shut the door in the officer's face. The chain stuck and it took me longer than I liked to get it undone. I cursed under my breath until if finally came free. I opened the door.

'Mrs Marsden,' the officer said.

Although he hadn't said my name as a question, I didn't recognise the young man on my doorstep.

Outside was dark and a faint light from inside the house lit up his face. I was struck by how young he really looked. Not much older than Michael really. He certainly didn't look old enough to drive. I couldn't help looking past him to the police car to see if his mum had brought him. Another officer sat in the passenger seat. He didn't look like anyone's mum.

'Hi,' I said.

'May I come in,' he said.

I knew that that wasn't a question either.

'Of course,' I said, and stood back from the door to allow him in. 'Go through to the living room.'

I didn't really want Michael and Rose to see the police. Things were eventful enough as they were. But I knew I couldn't very well have a chat by the front door without things seeming a little odd.

I shut the front door and walked after the officer. He stopped a few paces in and turned to me. He glanced at the packet of tablets in my hand.

'Headache?' he said.

'They're for my husband. He's come home from work not

feeling very well.'

'Mr Marsden?' he said.

I nodded.

He glanced around the room, staring at things as though he was assessing the house for purchase. The police radio strapped to his left breast crackled. Male voices chattered. The words made no sense. The young boy ignored the chatter.

'We had a call,' he said. 'Came through as an emergency.'

I breathed out, unaware that I had been holding my breath.

'That was me,' I said. 'It was an accident.'

He looked at me, his eyebrows raised.

'An accident?' he said. 'Was anyone hurt?'

I wasn't sure if this was police humour, or whether he was being serious. As a result, I didn't know how I should answer the question. I hesitated.

He somehow managed to raise his eyebrows even further.

'Mrs Marsden?'

Michael and Rose were still in the dining room, arguing about something. Probably nothing.

'I rang the number by mistake,' I said. 'Someone has already rung me back. I explained it was a mistake.'

He looked around some more.

'You mentioned something on the phone about an intruder,' he said. He stopped looking around and stared directly at me. 'Was there one?'

I felt like I needed a drink of water. My throat felt raspy.

'I thought I had heard someone,' I said. 'I was upstairs, and I thought I heard someone downstairs.'

'Did you have a look?' he said.

'When I got to the top of the stairs I saw a shadow at the bottom — thought I saw a shadow. So I ran down the stairs, shouting.'

One corner of his mouth twitched upwards. He forced it back down again.

'Then when I got downstairs, I thought I saw a shape running to the kitchen. Another shadow, really. I ran as fast as I could but when I got into the kitchen there was no one there. The kitchen window was wide open and a plant had been knocked off the window sill.'

'Did you see anyone outside?'

I shook my head.

'He was gone.'

'He?' he said. 'I thought you said you didn't actually see anything more than shadows?'

'Not *him*, then,' I said. 'Just whoever, whatever. Anyway, I thought that perhaps I might have imagined it. I picked up the phone to ring the police, but then reconsidered. I must have already dialled the number. I'm sorry, I didn't mean to.'

It sounded like the argument in the dining room was starting to die down. I had no doubt that the children would be charging through the living room at any moment, either to watch TV or to go up to their rooms. I wanted the police boy gone as soon as possible. I wanted to go upstairs and talk to Neil and then I wanted to talk to the kids. I did not want to be explaining yet another police officer in our house.

'So it really was nothing,' I said. 'I'm so sorry to have caused you any trouble. But I'm very grateful that you came round to check that everything was OK. Thank you.'

My heart rate increased again. I wasn't sure that I was handling this particularly well. The police officer looked unimpressed.

'I think I should have a quick look around,' he said. 'Just to make sure.'

This really wasn't going the way I had hoped. A vein in my neck started throbbing.

'This was ages ago,' I said. 'Really, there's no one here. And nothing is missing. I've checked the whole house.'

'Where is your husband, Mrs Marsden?' he said.

I felt like this was running away from me.

'He's ill, upstairs. I was just getting him a drink of water and some tablets.'

I shook the box of tablets. The sound of rattling pills I had hoped for didn't materialise. I must have looked faintly ridiculous. Or worse.

'All of those tablets?'

A heavy pulse started in my invisible leg wound. It kept a beat all its own, completely out of kilter with the throbbing of my neck vein and the pounding of my heart.

'Of course not,' I said.

The young police officer's posture changed. He seemed to hunch down a little. His eyes narrowed and he looked around again. But this time his head movements were quicker. It was as though a bomb had gone off nearby and he was hunting around for the perpetrator. His hand reached up to his radio and he turned his mouth towards it.

'Mike, do you want to come in here a second,' he said.

At first I thought he was speaking to Michael. A bizarre conspiracy theory sped through my already spinning brain.

It felt like no time had passed from him speaking into his radio, to there being a knock at the front door. Not loud, but loud enough to demand attention.

'My colleague, Mrs Marsden. Would you let him in please.'

The heavy pulse in my leg became something more. I felt jagged broken glass twisting and pushing into me. Now that I had seen the horror of the dream with more clarity, so the pain became more defined. Inside my leg I felt flesh and muscle becoming reshaped and deformed as the shattered bottle stabbed and turned.

Perhaps it was because I now knew what had caused the pain, or maybe it was the reminder of what I had been doing when I was stabbed — whatever it was, I cried out.

Instantly I felt my forearms changing. Becoming stronger.

Although I was in my own living room, I felt as though I had been transported back to the wild place with the gorse. An enormous rage grew within me.

At the back of my mind I heard more knocking at the front door.

Stay here Christine. Stay here.

I fought my mind. Battled with it to regain control.

The knocking grew louder.

My vision blurred in and out. My left leg with the wound, crumpled under me. I didn't fall.

Through the blur I saw the young police officer reach again for his radio. He moved closer to me. I grabbed hold of his shoulders to stop myself falling to the ground.

His voice grew louder, he was shouting into his radio. Or was he shouting to someone else.

I heard another voice. I knew I had to fight. But I didn't know whether to fight the voice or the police officer. Confusion swirled around me. I had to fight back. The police officer must be attacking me. He must be trying to catch me. Trying to arrest me. I have to fight back.

I can hear crying. The police officer is shouting somewhere else now. As I cling onto him, he is waving his arm about, pointing. He's shouting to get back. But I can't. I need to stop him. But he's not shouting at me. I recognise the crying. It is Rose. Michael is shouting at me now. It was a conspiracy. But he's shouting out 'Mum, Mum, Mum. Please stop.'

I cry out again as the pain in my leg intensifies. It is stinging, as though someone has just squeezed lemon juice into the open wound.

I have to escape. I have to get away from the police. I can't kill them with Michael there. He'll see me. He'll tell his dad.

My ears tingle and wind rushes around them. The wind drowns out all the voices, all the shouting. All except my voice. The voice inside me. Steady, calm and commanding. I feel what it wants. I don't need to understand the words. I feel them.

It becomes darker. A mist has come down. A dark mist. And the noise of the wind diminishes. No voices from the world, no sound at all.

Just the tuneful hum of the voice inside me. Nothing more than a whisper now. Nothing more than a suggestion. A hint.

CHAPTER FORTY-FOUR

'Christine?'

Who was that? The back of my head hurt. I moved my fingers and they touched carpet. I was lying on the ground. On a carpet.

'Christine, can you hear me?'

I didn't recognise the voice. I was scared to open my eyes. I didn't know what I was going to see. And it felt like an explosion of pain might burst into me if I opened them too soon.

I tried to nod my head without moving it.

A hand squeezed mine.

'Squeeze my hand if you can hear me.'

I squeezed.

I squeezed my other hand at the same time. There was something in it. I squeezed again. The box of tablets.

I felt something moving on my chest. Sliding across it from one side to the other. I decided to risk opening one eye. A little.

It was difficult to focus with just one eye, so I opened the other one too.

A man and a woman were crouched down by my side. Both dressed in green. Both paramedics.

The woman slid a stethoscope across my chest. Either my heart was on the move, or she was listening for something else.

The man said my name again.

'Christine? How are you feeling?'

He smiled at me. His voice was calm. Comforting.

I smiled back.

'I'm OK,' I said.

Apart from the back of my head, I felt no other pain. I

wanted to touch my leg wound, but I knew it wasn't there. I made a move to sit up.

'Wait just a moment, Christine,' the man said.

He restrained me with a gentle hand. I had no desire to fight back.

The woman took the stethoscope from her ears and nodded to the man.

'OK,' he said. 'You can sit up now. But slowly please.'

As I moved, he moved his arm under my body to help. I felt another arm come under me from the other side. It was Neil. He looked like he had completely recovered from the illness that had laid him out on our bed when I had left him upstairs earlier. I wondered how much earlier that had been.

'How long?' I said.

'Just a few minutes,' Neil said.

Even in my slightly confused state, a few minutes didn't make sense. Not unless the paramedics had been waiting outside our front door — just in case I had some need of them.

I heard the crackle of a radio. The police officer. The noise came from the stairs. I looked over and saw a larger, older police officer than the one who had been questioning me earlier. Neil looked up at him.

'Well, everything seems OK,' the officer said. 'There certainly isn't anyone else here.'

Neil thanked him.

To my left the young police officer appeared from the dining room. I noticed a red mark on his cheek. He walked directly over to me.

'How are you feeling?' he said.

I could see the red mark was blood. His cheek bore a scratch. I wondered what else I had done.

'I'm OK, thank you,' I said. I ran a finger along my cheek and pointed up at his scratch. 'Was that me?'

He touched the scratch with a curled finger and smiled.

'It was me, actually,' he said. 'When you collapsed I tried to hold you, and use my radio at the same time. I scratched myself as I reached for the radio. My wife's always telling me my nails are too long.'

Old enough to drive and old enough to have a wife.

'Did you know there is soil and fragments of broken crockery on your kitchen floor?' he said. 'And what looks like a hand smear mark on the kitchen window?'

The male paramedic reached down to my wrist and started monitoring my pulse. I wondered if this was standard paramedic procedure once the police started asking questions and they were on the scene. Was it some sort of rudimentary lie detector. If my pulse went up — I was lying. If it went down — the truth.

I thought *good luck to him* with my pulse.

'That was the plant pot,' I said. 'I mentioned it earlier? The hand marks on the window were probably me, when I looked out of the window, then tried to pull it back shut again.'

He glanced at my hands, but said nothing.

For the first time since becoming fully conscious again, I saw Michael and Rose sitting quietly on the sofa, both looking at me. I smiled at them and made a move to stand up. Neil held me fast and looked at the male paramedic.

'I think we just need to take you into hospital,' the paramedic said. 'Just to give you the once over.'

If he was still monitoring my pulse, he would certainly feel something now.

'I'm fine,' I said. 'Really. I don't need to go into hospital. I just need a glass of water. Really, I am fine.'

The male paramedic looked over at Neil, then the young police officer. Then back down at me.

'It's always advisable, if the patient has lost consciousness, to have them looked at,' he said. He looked at his wrist watch. 'It probably wouldn't even take long. We would certainly recommend it.'

My pulse hammered up a notch or two more. I was scared. Something inside me was screaming at me not to go into hospital. Not even for a check up. I knew I was already on the edge — or even perhaps slightly over it. It would only take a quick call to Doctor Jones, or a brief look at my recent medical history, to realise that I might have serious psychological issues.

Although I had already considered turning myself in to be hospitalised only that morning, I felt as though things had changed. I was already sorting out the children's safety by having them stay with Abi, and it now seemed essential to me to sort myself out. I didn't want to be kept in a hospital. There was every chance that if I was committed to an institution of any kind, the future for Michael and Rose would, almost overnight, become darker and more uncertain. With a mother committed, and a father working, what future for the children? What would the social services make of it?

I looked at Neil and tried to speak to him through my eyes. At first he didn't seem to get it.

'I think it wouldn't be a bad idea, Chris,' he said. 'Just to make sure you're OK.'

I intensified my eyes so that they went from speaking to screaming at him. Why were men so bloody stupid sometimes?

'Unless,' he said, 'you really do feel better.'

At last. I smiled at him and turned to the paramedic. He looked again to the young police officer.

'It might be for the best, Mrs Marsden,' he said.

I sat up straight and did my best to look as calm and happy as possible. As though I was sitting on a picnic rug on a summer afternoon, rather than recovering from some sort of breakdown on my living-room carpet.

The female paramedic spoke.

'We need to make sure that there is nothing more serious happening to you,' she said. 'It's not that common to have a blackout without something triggering it. And you are still recovering from a couple of head wounds, it really would be sensible to come along.'

Why were women so bloody stupid sometimes?

Surely she could understand. I didn't want to lose my children. What woman would? Could she not read my eyes either?

'I think she seems OK,' Neil said.

I squeezed his hand. My pulse slowed a little. I breathed a little easier.

'I am,' I said. 'Really, I am fine.'

It was with some reluctance that the paramedics left. They told me that it was essential to ring them should I have any ill effects at all, no matter how trivial they might seem. Particularly with my vision and balance.

The police officers seemed even more reluctant. In fact they were almost like petulant teenagers when they finally walked out through the front door. They gave us no advice of what to do should anything take a turn for the worse. I got the feeling that they would be overjoyed to never hear from us again. At that moment, that suited me too.

I tried to reassure Michael and Rose that I was fine. We sat and cuddled. We laughed about how young one of the police officers had been. And that he scratched himself while reaching for his radio.

Michael looked at ease. Rose still slightly on edge. We cuddled some more.

Neil brought me a large glass of water. He really did look very well now. I wondered what had happened to stop him feeling ill.

After ten minutes of cuddles and laughs, I told the kids to go up and get ready for bed, and to come down when they were both ready. I figured that would give Neil and me at least twenty minutes talk time. Michael would get distracted on a video game, and Rose would play out some sort of search and rescue story with her cuddlies.

'I'm pleased you're feeling better,' I said to Neil. 'Thank you for being there for me.'

The first ten minutes of our chat were taken up with me trying to explain what had happened with the police officer. Why they had come round in the first place, and why it had been so essential for me to avoid hospital. Neil listened to everything I said. He heard it all. I'm not sure he understood. I told him more about the intruder I thought had broken in through the kitchen window. The scratching noises I had heard and the shadows I had seen. Then I told him about the kids staying with Abi for a while.

At first, he was adamant that Michael and Rose should stay at home. But I think he misunderstood the reasoning behind it. I explained it all again.

'Do you really think it's necessary though?' he said.

I ran over it a third time. A shortened version.

It was much easier telling Michael and Rose. The excitement grew in them as the prospect of staying away for more than one night sunk in. It was only later, when I said goodnight to Rosie in bed, that she started crying.

'I don't want to go away,' she said. 'I'll miss my bedroom and all my cuddlies.'

'You can take your cuddlies with you,' I said. 'And you'll only be sleeping there. You can come here after school if you like, with Abi. But I'm going to be staying with Nanny and Grandad for a few days because I need to rest and get better.'

'I want to stay with you at Nanny's,' she said.

I kissed her on the forehead and brushed her hair back with

my hand. She didn't like the feeling.

'Mum!'

I smiled and pulled my hand back.

'You'll have such a lovely time,' I said. 'I love you Rosie Lee.'

By the time I plonked myself down on the armchair in the living-room, I felt exhausted. I looked over at Neil and he closed the TV guide and tossed it onto the coffee table. I climbed up from the armchair and joined him on the sofa. He put his arm around me.

'I'm so sorry about all this,' I said.

'Don't be so bloody stupid,' he said.

'I just don't know what's real and what's imagined anymore,' I said. 'I was convinced there was someone in our house earlier. But I didn't actually see anyone. Even when I looked out of the window I saw no one.'

Neil pulled me into him.

'You've gone through so much,' he said.

'We're all going through so much,' I said.

I pushed my head back into his arm, eased some of the tension from me into him. I knew he wouldn't mind. That was what he was there for. We were both there to help ease each other's tension. I squeezed my eyes tight and breathed out. Neil's body was warm against me. My mouth formed a tiny smile and I determined once again to feel bright and cheerful.

But when I opened my eyes I was staring at the bare wall behind the TV. A chill I couldn't stop crawled over my upper back, starting at my spine and prickling its way out to my shoulder-blades and beyond.

I shouldn't have been looking at a bare wall. There should have been a picture there. A picture of us, celebrating our tenth wedding anniversary.

There was something missing after all.

CHAPTER FORTY-FIVE

'I have no idea,' Neil said when I asked him if he knew where the missing picture was.

I thought about going upstairs to ask Michael or Rose if they had knocked it off the wall or hidden it, but I knew they wouldn't have.

Neil and I spent twenty minutes lifting the furniture, turning cushions, moving tables. I even rummaged through the bin.

We tried to remember the last time we had actually been aware of the picture. Neither of us could remember for sure. But we both agreed we were more likely to notice it not being there. We concluded that it hadn't been missing for long.

'Do you think we should call the police back?' Neil said.

'No way,' I said. 'What good would it do anyway? They can't fingerprint something that's not there.'

'The window,' he said. 'With the hand mark on.'

'I would die if they did it and it turned out to be me. When I jumped up on the side to look out of the window, I would definitely have put my hand on the glass for support. I just don't want to take the chance.'

Neil nodded.

'Why would anyone want to steal a photograph of us?' he said.

It was a good question. For which I could only think of one answer.

'So he knows what we look like?' I said.

My back prickled again.

I couldn't understand why someone who could break into our house with apparent ease would want to take away a photo of us. Surely if he wanted to hurt us, he would do it in the house, not try to recognise us somewhere else and then do something.

Unless it was just to torment us. To make us feel like we were being watched wherever we went. And why Neil too, or was it just my photo he wanted? Once again I felt like somehow I was dragging Neil into something he didn't deserve to be in.

I imagined the attacker outside the house right at that moment, watching. He would have seen the police come, then the paramedics. And he would have watched them all go. Without me. He knew I was still inside. Knew we all were.

Why was he doing this? Had he meant all along to do more than just steal my handbag?

I wondered again whether he might have been an ex-pupil of mine. I racked my brain to think of anything I might have ever done to make a pupil really pissed off with me. I couldn't think of anything.

But if this was a long-term plan on his part, vengeance, or some sort of vendetta, I must have done something in my past.

Colin had asked me if I had ever experienced anything like this before. I started to wonder if I had, in fact, blacked out before. If I had done something to upset this person, if I had hurt them, that might explain why they were getting back at me now.

I wondered where it would all end.

Once again I felt like I should apologise to Neil. I hugged him instead.

'When are you going to your mum and dad's?' Neil said.

'I haven't rung them yet. But soon I hope.'

Neil looked at the floor and nodded slowly. He looked vulnerable.

'Maybe I should stay here,' I said.

He shook his head, looked up at the gap on the wall that used to hold our picture, and turned to me with a poor attempt at a smile.

'I'll be at work most of the day. It wouldn't be good for you to be at home on your own.'

'Abi will come and stay with me.'

He shook his head again.

'Chris, that could be putting you both in danger, unnecessarily. It's pointless.'

'You'll starve,' I said. 'You'll be like a lost kitten without me.'

'I believe they have invented meals that you can simply cook in a microwave,' he said. 'And I think if you turn the tap on, water comes out. You can drink that.'

'You won't have anyone to help you drink.'

He punched me gently on the arm.

'And if that's how you're going to fight an intruder, you've got no chance.'

'Give them a call,' he said. 'It'll do you good. Them too, probably.'

I made two calls. The first one was to Abi to make sure it was OK for the kids to come over the next day after school. She had spoken to Oli, and he thought it was a great idea. I didn't tell her about the police and paramedic situation. Nor about the missing photo.

The second call was to Mum and Dad. At first Mum was concerned that something had happened between me and Neil.

'We're fine,' I said. 'Really. I just need to get away for a bit, try to get my head straight. My friend, Abi, is having Michael and Rose for an extended sleep over, Neil's got a lot of work on. It just means I won't be banging around the house on my own. As long as it's OK with you?'

Of course it was OK. They were my mum and dad.

In the morning I held back the tears and said goodbye to Michael and Rose. I didn't want them to go off to school having seen me cry. Rose managed to keep a check on hers too.

'Have a fantastic time with Josie and Jess,' I said. 'And be good.'

They promised they would, and ran out to Abi's car as though they were in a race.

I noticed that Neil's eyes had been red when he'd hugged them goodbye before he left for work.

After he said goodbye to them, he held me. I cried a little.

'I'll call you later,' he said. 'Around lunchtime.'

He never usually called me at lunchtime. Or anytime, from work.

'Be careful,' I said.

'I'll kill anyone who breaks into our house,' he said.

'I meant with the microwave meals and working the tap.'

At 10am Dad arrived to pick me up. I had packed enough clothes and make-up for a week, although my suitcase felt as though it was heavy enough for a month. Dad threw me a look as he hefted into the boot of the car.

'It's not as much as it seems,' I said.

In the car Dad sniffed and snuffled. I desperately wanted to open the window, but I didn't want to make him feel worse.

'You're still not feeling well?' I said.

'I'm OK,' he said. 'I'm pleased you're coming home for a bit. You can help your mum look after me. I was thinking of hiring a servant anyway.'

We both smiled.

'Maybe we could get a bit of fishing in,' I said. 'If you're feeling up to it.'

His smile grew broader.

Although I had brought my daily time-sheets, I hoped that being with Mum and Dad, in a different environment, might make the blackouts and dreams less frequent. Maybe even stop them completely. I was due to see Colin again in a few days and I wanted to be able to tell him that things were calming down.

Mum was waiting at the front door as Dad pulled into the drive. Dad insisted on lugging my suitcase. He struggled with it up the steps to the front door and I wished I had packed less things.

As usual, Mum had already boiled the kettle in readiness for our arrival. An unopened packet of biscuits sat on the kitchen table. I thought I could smell baking too. Fairy cakes.

Dad took my suitcase upstairs to my old bedroom. I followed him up and helped dump it on the bed. It always surprised me how small my room seemed compared to my memories of it from childhood.

'Do you mind if I open the window?' I said to Dad.

'Of course not,' he said. 'It's your room.'

'I'll just unpack,' I said. 'I'll be down soon.'

He sniffed and snuffled his way downstairs, joining Mum in the kitchen. I heard their muted voices drifting up to my room.

'Thank you for having me to stay,' I said.

The three of us were sat at the kitchen table, hot mugs of coffee and sweet biscuits in front of us.

'I've made some cakes,' Mum said. 'But they're too hot at the moment. We'll have them later.'

That was her way of saying it was OK.

'I won't stay too long,' I said. 'Just a short break really. Try to make sense of things.'

'You can stay as long as you want,' Dad said. 'You know that.'

'We know you're safe when you're with us,' Mum said. 'We like that.'

'I'm safe anyway,' I said. 'It's just my mind that does odd things at the moment.'

Doctor Jones' question about any history of mental illness in our family popped into my head.

I already knew that there wasn't, but an enormous urge welled up inside me to ask the question anyway.

Butterflies flipped in my tummy. I didn't need to ask. It might only serve to upset Mum and Dad. Why upset things when I already knew the answer?

'I went to the doctor again,' I said. 'He asked me all sorts of odd questions.'

Mum took a bite of another biscuit, Dad put his coffee mug down on the table. My butterflies fluttered even more.

'What sort of questions?' Mum said.

'Questions about my mental state.' I pushed the handle of my mug a few inches. Twisted the mug around. 'About whether I had experienced any sort of mental breakdown in the past. About whether I felt like hurting myself, or others. He said he wanted to consider whether I should be sent for a full psychiatric assessment.'

'Oh Chris,' Mum said.

'In a way it was quite funny really,' I said.

I grabbed a biscuit and took a tiny bite.

'I mean, he even asked me if there was any history of mental illness in our family. Can you believe that?'

I forced out a dismissive laugh. Even to me it sounded hollow.

'What did you tell him?' Dad said.

'She would have told him there wasn't any, of course,' Mum said.

'Exactly,' I said. 'That's exactly what I said.'

'How serious does he think your condition is?' Dad said.

I took another tiny bite of the biscuit.

'I don't know. Fairly serious I suppose. If he's considering sending me for an assessment.'

I looked at Dad. Looked into his eyes. I thought I saw something there, but I couldn't work out what it was. He held my gaze for a moment then shifted it to Mum. She stood up and went to check on the fairy cakes.

'They're still too warm,' she said.

'I was right,' I said. 'Wasn't I?'

'Of course you were right, dear,' Mum said, her back to us both.

The fairy cakes smelled good. But now I smelled something else too. Tension.

'Dad?'

'What happens if the doctor decides you need to go for this psychiatric assessment?' he said. 'What happens after that?'

'I don't really know,' I said. 'I suppose it's possible that they will give me additional medication, or I might have to stay somewhere where they can keep an eye on me. But I'm only guessing. My big concern is Michael and Rose. If I'm assessed as having some sort of mental disorder I'm worried how that might affect Michael and Rose. I don't know if social services would get involved.'

My cheeks grew warm as I spoke. My voice struggled to keep an even tone, and my eyes felt watery.

'I'm scared that they might take them away from me.'

Mum turned from the cakes.

'Darling, that wouldn't happen,' she said. 'You're a wonderful mother. That would never happen.'

I stood up and threw my arms around Mum. I heard the scrape of Dad's chair as he rose from the table.

'Chris,' he said. 'No matter what happens, we love you. We always have loved you, right from day one. And we always will love you. You were our only child. You have always been the most important thing in our lives.'

'Roy!' Mum said.

'Your mum and I were overjoyed when we had you. You have made our lives worth living.'

An uncomfortable feeling crept over me. I felt like Dad was

telling me something other than what he was saying. I searched between the lines, but couldn't fathom his meaning. It was obviously putting Mum on edge too.

'Roy!' she said again.

Dad stared at Mum, his eyes narrowed. His lower lip was shaking, it looked as though his shoulders shook too.

He looked into my eyes. A deep and penetrating stare. But not angry. He wasn't showing me anger. His eyes were full of sorrow.

He turned away and strode towards the front room. Before he turned, I saw something else in his eyes.

Tears.

CHAPTER FORTY-SIX

Seeing my dad shaken and tearful had wrong footed me. I had never seen him cry before. I needed to get my bearings again.

He and Mum obviously had something they needed to sort out between themselves. And I needed time to think.

'Are you OK here, Mum? If I go and finish unpacking?'

'Of course, dear. You go ahead.'

Her face was pale, her lips tight and showing only marginally more colour than her face. I couldn't tell if she was angry or scared.

On the way upstairs my arm brushed against one of the photos on the wall. It was of me and Dad. I must have been about twelve years old. Dad was in his fishing gear, I had tried to dress like him.

I remembered the day. Damp and cold. I held a tiny fish in my hand and flashed an enormous grin.

Dad's grin was even bigger, although he had no fish to show.

Straightening the photo, I continued up to my room. Once inside, I shut the door then opened it again, just a couple of inches, fell onto the bed and stared up at the ceiling.

The open window blew a draft to the door, causing it to creak as it moved slightly.

I was sure that Dad had wanted to tell me something.

His questioning about what would happen if I was assessed with some sort of psychiatric disorder had jarred me. Mum's reaction to him was out of character. They normally gelled together seamlessly. Rarely discordant, rarely at odds. But something had definitely shifted between them in the kitchen.

I ran through what he had said again and again, desperate to find a hidden meaning.

But perhaps the meaning wasn't hidden at all. Perhaps it was more obvious.

Maybe there was something in my past that I either didn't know about or had forgotten.

Or maybe there was something in my parents' past. Something that Dad felt ready to share with me, but that Mum wanted him to keep quiet about. A hidden secret of madness in the family?

My mind whirred, as though someone was turning a handle against it around and around, like a butter churn, trying to make something solid out of the sloshing liquid of my thoughts. Memories and flashbacks flipped around inside my head. I thought of all the relations I had met. I thought about my grandparents. Had I missed something in one of them? I remembered the silly things Grandpa used to do. Was that more than just silliness? Had Grandpa been mad?

The pictures spun ever quicker, I could almost hear the flickering noise as each one popped up before me, only to be replaced instantly by another.

Although Dad had only spoken a few sentences, the air had felt heavy and tense. Tense enough for Mum to react almost immediately to what he was saying. She knew the meaning in his words. The meaning that I couldn't see.

I could hear her downstairs, moving from the kitchen to the living-room. She shut the living-room door behind her.

I laid as still as I could. Made my breathing shallow and opened my ears.

At first there was nothing.

Then I heard Dad's voice. Muffled, of course, through the closed door and the ceiling. He coughed, or sneezed. I wanted to give him a hug.

Mum's voice was louder. Still muffled, but more shrill than Dad's. Somehow easier to understand. It always had been like that. When I was little I used to lie awake listening out for their voices downstairs. Occasionally I would hear Dad laughing at something on the telly. But mostly, it was Mum, her voice carrying upstairs to my room. When I was scared of monsters and ghosts, I found it comforting to hear her.

Hearing her voice now only brought with it anxiety and questions.

A small child materialised in my mind. A boy.

I have no idea where he came from, no idea who he was. But my mind soon found a reason for him.

"You were our only child. You made our lives worth living."

It had seemed an odd thing for Dad to say.

But what if that wasn't true? What if I wasn't their only child?

The whirring pictures in my mind, until now consisting of real people and genuine memories, gave way to darker scenes. Mind-made scenes.

The boy.

Was he a long-lost brother? My sibling, perhaps born before me? A disturbed child? One with problems of the mind?

No doubt it took a disturbed mind to come up with such an alternative background. However, disturbed mind or not, the idea grew in stature and reality.

Had the child died in his early years? Before I was born? Or had he lived? Did he live still?

Was HE the one attacking the girls?

And now my heart raced. I had discovered a hidden secret of such horror that I couldn't string together any coherent thoughts at all. Sweat erupted over my body and heat burned from every pore.

There was madness in the family. I had a sibling who was insane. A psychotic killer of young girls. And I shared his genes.

If the mad sibling was in an institution somewhere, that would surely be my ultimate destination too. What would happen to Michael and Rose? To Neil?

My life started to unravel, keeping pace with the unravelling of my mind. Tears tickled the side of my face and dripped onto the pillow. I clenched my fingers into the duvet and held on, trying to stop myself from spinning away.

Downstairs Mum's voice grew more shrill, Dad's voice became louder.

I felt a cold breeze blow across my face from the open window.

For the first time in my life, as far as I could remember, I was aware of my parents arguing.

I latched on to every sound and nuance. Tried to hold firm to the voices. I didn't want to think about the other mad child that had been hidden from me. Couldn't bear to think about it. He had already cursed my future.

Mum and Dad were now shouting at each other. Louder and louder, still muffled, until a full and clear sentence reached me. My mum's shrill shouting had reached the point of understanding.

'*She doesn't have to know!*'

I held my breath. Stopped it where it was in my lungs. Held it there, waiting for the next words to fly upstairs to me.

But instead, the living-room door opened. Dad's heavy footsteps stomped along the hall and the front door was pulled open and slammed shut.

I heard his footsteps in the drive, then nothing.

Through the open living-room door I heard Mum sobbing. Gentle cries, but not controlled or managed.

I listened to her forever. She didn't stop. I closed my eyes and breathed in time with her sobs. My fingers still gripped the duvet. I don't think I could have gone to her, even if I had wanted to. I wanted her voice to make me feel better. To protect me from the monsters and ghosts. But her crying gave them permission to be there. She wasn't protecting me anymore.

When I awoke, my bedroom door was closed. The window and curtains too. I opened the window.

I had no idea who had been in the room.

The bedside clock said 4:30pm. I had slept for approximately five and a half hours.

My throat was dry and my eyes sore. I needed to wash my face and have a drink.

When I got downstairs the first thing I spotted were Dad's shoes at the bottom of the stairs.

I could hear that the television was on in the living-room.

I drank two glasses of water at the kitchen sink. As I turned the cold tap off I thought about Neil, on his own. *Microwave meals.*

When I pushed open the living-room door, they both looked up at me. All seemed quiet between them. For a moment I wondered whether I had dreamt it all. Perhaps there had been no argument. Perhaps Dad hadn't stormed out of the house.

But Mum's eyes told the true story. Red rimmed and puffy.

I sat down on the sofa. Mum was sitting in the armchair to my left, Dad in the one to my right. A familial triangle.

Dad forced a smile. He shifted about in his chair. I noticed his head twitch.

'How are you, dear?' Mum said. 'You obviously needed that.'

So it was her who had been in my bedroom.

'I didn't even know I was tired,' I said.

'Neil rang while you were asleep,' she said. 'He's going to give you a call later, after dinner.'

'Was he OK?' I said.

'Fine, I think. He just wanted to make sure you got here OK.'

I nodded. One of the rare occasions he rang me from work, and I was asleep.

'Shall I get us a drink?' Mum said.

Dad stood up and walked over to the television. He switched it off at the set, rather than using the remote control that had been resting on the arm of the chair he had just pulled himself out of.

'Chris,' he said. 'Darling. We need to talk to you.'

I tried to stand up, but some invisible force kept me pushed back into the sofa.

'I'd love a drink, Mum,' I said.

Mum stood up.

'Diane,' Dad said quietly. 'We need to speak to her. We need to do it now.'

My shoulders and neck tensed. Every slight movement I made was in staccato. Although I had just drunk two full glasses of cold water, I felt as though I needed a gallon.

The pump of my heart was more obvious and more intense than I had ever known it before, pounding against my ribcage. My stomach constricted.

I thought of the time I had been sent to see the headmaster at school. I had thrown another girl's plimsole through the window of the gym. The window had broken and the girl's plimsole had ripped. Waiting outside the headmaster's office had been one of the most frightening moments of my schooling.

And now I waited for my parents to speak to me.

I already knew what they were going to say. I was simply waiting for the judge to pass sentence after the jury had already found me guilty.

"Christine Marsden. You have been found guilty of insanity, as your brother was before you. Your children will be taken from you and you will be deprived from ever seeing them or your husband again. You will be sent from here to an institution from which you will never be freed."

Dad cleared his throat with a ragged cough. Mum put her

hand to her mouth. I drew in as large a breath of air as I could manage. I hoped to God I wouldn't pass out.

'Chris, love,' he said. 'Your mum and I love you more than anything. We have only ever wanted to give you the very best life you could have.'

His voice broke and stuttered, like an engine dying. He managed to keep it going.

'We just wanted to pour our love into you. And no matter what happens. No matter what you decide to do, and no matter what you think of us, please know this. We have always loved you.' He brought his trembling hand up to his temple. His cheeks flushed red. 'We have always had your best interests at heart, and we will always love you for the rest of our lives.'

I shook violently on the sofa. Tears streamed from my eyes and the air barely made it to or from my lungs. I felt like a child again, desperate to be somewhere happy. I couldn't bring any words from my mouth. None came to my mind.

Through blurred eyes I saw Mum crying into her hands. Dad shook as he fought to control his voice.

I had never before been hurt by my Dad. But now, as he spoke, one word pierced my heart and tore into it, ripping my soul away as it passed through me.

CHAPTER FORTY-SEVEN

Certain words carry with them the full weight of their meaning for all to understand. Cancer; murder; rape; death; insanity. Every right-minded person feels the unease and distress that these words bring whether they have personally experienced them or not.

But "adopted" isn't such a word.

"Adopted" passes most people by, leaving them no more touched by it than by the breeze of the day.

'Your mum and I — we adopted you as a baby. You are adopted.'

Seconds after hearing it stutter from my dad's lips I choked. An enormous pressure pushed down on every part of my body. I felt crushed by the air around me, compressed so that I could take no air into myself. A ceaseless head-rush made everything spin. I struggled against the pressure. Blood surged to my limbs and muscles and I forced myself up out of the sofa. I pit myself against the pressing air and pushed through it to the downstairs toilet.

I retched and cried.

I felt as though my life was a lake into which my father had just thrown the word "adopted" like a pebble. As it hit the surface I had immediately felt the first ripples, but I knew that slowly the pebble was sinking. Deeper and deeper. It would soon hit the bottom where it would lay, irretrievable and unchangeable, forever. It would become part of me.

After a few minutes, the retching subsided. The tears too. My mind regained some focus and I thought about the two people I had known as my mother and father. Neither had followed me to the toilet. They both remained in the living-room.

The two people I thought I could always trust. The people I thought would never have a reason to lie to me.

And yet they had been proficient and consistent liars for all these years. Every birthday and Christmas. Every personal moment shared with them. They had been nothing but deceivers of the worst kind.

All the talk about "always loving me" and "you made our lives worth living". Just words. No real love at all. How could there be? They were liars. People who love you don't lie to you. People who love you don't deceive you your whole life.

A vicious heat rose from my chest and shoulders, spread over my neck and up to my head. Humiliation burned through me. I had been the last to know. Everyone had been laughing at me. Talking about me behind my back. The nasty little secret that I knew nothing about.

I slammed my fists against the toilet floor. Banged them hard, again and again.

'No, no, no, no, no, no.'

Perhaps it was a joke. Perhaps they were trying to make me feel better about the madness in some way. But that made no sense. My mind was bullshitting me.

'Shut up, Christine. It's no joke. They've been lying to you your whole life.'

I stormed out of the toilet and charged upstairs, knocking photo frames off the wall as I went.

Me and Dad — fishing.

I heard them smash against the floor, but I didn't look back.

I kicked the bedroom door shut behind me and dived onto the bed, face down.

And I screamed. Into the duvet, I screamed and roared. I shouted and cried and I wailed and thrashed like a baby.

I tasted sick in my mouth and spat onto the bedroom floor. I didn't give a fuck about them and their house anymore. Fuck them.

I curled up in the duvet, wrapped it around me and curled as tight as I could. I pulled it over my head. Every part of me was hidden. Hidden from monsters and ghosts. Hidden from the world. Hidden from my mum's shrill voice downstairs. Hidden from Dad's low mumble. Hidden from them both. Mum and Dad.

I thought about all the physical characteristics I shared with them. My dad's eyes; Mum's nose; Grandad's chin. All of these were nothing but coincidence. I had been so blind. I could see that all of these likenesses had been exaggerated. The reality was, I didn't look like any of these strangers. Michael didn't have Grandma's wicked grin. Rose didn't have Auntie Jane's dimple. In fact, Michael and Rose didn't have real grandparents from my side of the family at all.

And now the pebble hit the bottom of the lake.

I felt it thud into the tectonic plates on which my life had been built. It caused such a seismic shift that all of my memories, all of my experiences and all that I had held to be true and to have been built on such solid foundations, began crumbling and crashing down with a relentless and awesome disintegration.

None of my relations were related to me. All of them had helped perpetuate the lie. Every one of them knew the truth. How often had they had to be reminded to be careful not to say anything? To not let the dreadful secret out from its dark hiding place inside their heart?

Why had they all chosen to conspire against me? I had been a small child, for god's sake. What harm had I done? Why wouldn't they have told me?

When I was eleven years old, I had known a boy at school who was adopted. He knew. He wasn't ashamed of it. He wasn't bullied because of it. Why was he told by his "parents" and why was I not told by mine? What was their purpose in hiding the truth from me?

An urge to leave the house welled up inside me. I looked around the room for my mobile phone. I wanted to ring Neil and have him come and pick me up. It was downstairs, in my handbag.

I needed desperately to get away. Away from this house and away from these people.

I pulled the duvet off me and grabbed my suitcase. I had already hung some of my clothes on hangers and folded others into drawers. Now I tore them from the wardrobe and hurled them into the suitcase. No order and no care.

The bedroom curtains fluttered in the breeze from the open window. The curtains separated in the middle and I caught a glimpse of the back garden. The old swing frame was still there. The swing came off it when I was a child, but I persuaded Mum and Dad to keep the frame so I could still climb on it. Dad's old shed stood beyond that. Dilapidated now, but as a child I had thought it a wonderful place. He used to clear all the garden tools out of it in the summer so I could use it as a den. The three of us even slept in there a few times. I used to worry that spiders would crawl into my hair during the night, but Dad told me that the woodlice would eat the spiders before they got anywhere near us.

Deceivers and liars?

If only they had told me. If only I had always known, like the boy at my school. He was fine. I would have been fine too.

Hundreds of kids were adopted. Thousands, probably. Some had difficulties, I knew that, but Mum and Dad were good people. They would have made it alright.

But they didn't tell me.

If I had known, I could have dealt with my current situation differently. I would have had more time. Time to find my real parents. Perhaps I would have made contact with them anyway by now. Then I would know if there had been any mental illness in the family. In my family.

The curtains stopped moving as the breeze died.

I looked around the room. My bedroom. I had always loved

it. It was the first room at the top of the stairs.

'That's because you're the most important person in the house.' Dad had said.

When I got older, I realised it was just because it was the middle-sized bedroom of the three. They had the biggest, then I had the middle-sized. The small bedroom was always just a place for laundry.

But that still didn't prevent me from feeling important.

Some of my books still sat on the bookshelf. My old teddy sat next to them. He looked like he was smiling.

I stopped throwing clothes into the suitcase and opened the bedroom door. Just a few inches. Then I sat on the bed.

I shut my eyes and kicked my legs, just like I used to do when I was smaller and my legs couldn't reach the floor. I listened for voices. No low, mumbling. Nothing shrill. All three of us were quiet. All of us alone in the same house. All consumed by raw thoughts that had not existed before now.

I opened my eyes and looked through the crack in the door. There were no ghosts or monsters out there. Nothing dark or evil waited for me. Just empty hooks on the wall where the photo frames had hung before I knocked them off.

Me and Dad — fishing.

I did have a childhood. A good one. Whenever I hurt myself, those personal moments of pain, Mum had been there, wiping away the blood, sticking the plasters down, smudging away my tears. And she protected me from the monsters and ghosts without even realising it, just from her voice drifting up the stairs. She helped me through all the embarrassing things I had to go through as a teenager, and as a young woman. She helped me to feel less embarrassed.

They had virtually thrown a party when I dumped my old boyfriend and met Neil.

And they poured their love onto Michael and Rose. Filled their hearts with love.

Even now, I knew they were there for me.

They had re-opened the door of their home to me. A home I had not lived in for almost twenty years, and they made me feel as though I had been gone no more than a day. The same bedroom, the same house, the same them. It was as though their lives had been on hold, waiting for me to come back. To make the family unit whole again.

They had always been good people. Always. But even good people can't be good all the time.

If Roy and Diane, good people, and good parents, had kept something like this from me, there must have been a reason for it. Just as there was a reason for the old swing frame still waiting in the back garden, and my old teddy bear still smiling at me from the bookshelf.

CHAPTER FORTY-EIGHT

I wanted to go downstairs. I still felt embarrassed and humiliated. But I had to move things forward. I had to overcome my feelings and find out the truth

I let the lid of the suitcase fall back onto the bed and stared down at the jumble of clothes inside. I thought back to when I used to pack in a hurry to go and sleep at a friend's house. Or if the three of us went to stay anywhere. Mum would always ask if I wanted her to check my packing. I never did.

I opened the door and walked to the top of the stairs. The photo frames were still scattered on the floor. At least one of them had broken, and glass sparkled on the carpet.

I carefully stepped over the frames on the way down. I didn't stop to pick any of them up. That could wait.

The living-room door moved silently as I pushed it open.

Mum and Dad were sat together. Mum in the armchair and Dad perched on the arm. His hands rested on her shoulders. Their faces were blotchy and damp. I wondered how much they had cried.

Dad stood up and Mum looked up at me. They both seemed awkward, unsure of themselves. I felt the same way too. Family. The pressure that I had felt in the room before, had evaporated completely. I felt no tension.

I realised I was staring at them. Trying to look into them, but also trying to see them on the outside for the first time. Like meeting a stranger. I couldn't do it. I couldn't sufficiently remove myself from my recognition of them to see them in any other way than as my parents.

I had no doubt I could generate dislike. Perhaps even hatred. But what would that achieve? And how long would it last? It wouldn't help me. And now was the time in my life when I needed help more than ever.

The air in the room grew still. As though time had paused and was waiting for us to catch it up.

Dad caught up with it first and started it moving again.

'How are you, Chris?' he said. 'Are you… OK?'

I thought I would cry, or run to him. But I did neither. I sat back down on the sofa and put my hands on my knees.

I opened my mouth to speak but my throat and vocal chords weren't yet ready for speech.

I swallowed, straightened my back and rolled my shoulders, and took another run at it.

I thought my first question would be "Why didn't you tell me?". It took me by surprise when I spoke.

'Thank you,' I said. I swallowed again. 'Thank you for my life.'

Mum burst into tears again. Dad moved towards me but I held up my hand. He hesitated and stayed where he was.

It's funny how things come back to you out of the blue. Mum was always one to sit down to talk, probably so she was at the same level as the person she was talking to. She must have felt comfortable with herself that way. Whereas Dad was a pacer. He couldn't sit still for long. If things were unresolved he would be on edge until the problem was sorted.

He wasn't able to sit down now. This problem wasn't sorted yet.

'I feel ashamed,' I said, 'and embarrassed and humiliated. I feel like I was lied to my whole life. That everyone knew about it but me. And I feel utterly broken-hearted.'

I closed my eyes and waited for the excuses to come. The reasons why they had lied to me. What would they tell me to wash the guilt from their hands? Which other could they blame for their deceit?

'We're so sorry, Chris,' Dad whispered.

I tightened the grip on my knees, tried to control the surge inside me. A nerve in my neck reacted to something.

'Sorry?' I said.

Dad said nothing.

Was sorry supposed to wipe it all away? Did the word sorry carry enough power with it to obliterate that other word — adopted?

The pebble was already a part of me. It was there for good. In reality, it had always been there, I just hadn't known about it.

'Sorry?' I said again.

My legs shook. I gripped my knees tighter still. I opened my eyes and gave the surge that had been building up in me permission to do its worst.

'For fuck sake! What the fuck do you mean by sorry? How can you say sorry and think that somehow that makes it alright? How does that make things alright?'

As I screamed out the first few words, Mum jolted up in her chair. Dad's head twitched back and to the side, as though he had just taken a punch on the cheek.

I wiped the spittle off my chin with as much dignity as I could muster. My throat was raw.

'Sorry isn't enough,' I said.

I looked down at the carpet. Focused on the fibres, the pattern. As a child I had pretended that the pattern was a country lane leading to a secret world. I followed it with my eyes now. It didn't feel the same.

I didn't hear my mum move from the chair. But a warm hand touched the back of my neck. I let it rest there, massaging my neck. Her hands had always been slender. Now her hand felt almost bony. But her touch was soft. I reached up and rested my hand on hers. Lay my head to the side, touching my cheek on our hands.

'Shall we go for a walk?' she said.

I nodded.

It had seemed that many of our talks and decisions had been made on walks. Talks about schools and teachers; talks about holiday destinations; talks about friends and boyfriends. All three of us seemed at ease outside. Words seemed to flow more easily, as though the cool natural air really was blowing away the cobwebs in our minds.

The sky was darkening, turning the evening into night. Our coats were ruffled by the wind as soon as we stepped from the front door. I pulled mine tight around me. As we walked down the drive, Mum put her arm through mine. I let it stay there.

The pavement by the road was fairly narrow, so Dad walked ahead of us. But soon we left the road, and the pavement opened up. Dad dropped back level with us and walked next to Mum. We must have walked almost half a mile before she spoke.

'Me and your dad wanted children very much,' she said. 'Back before you were born we had tried to have a child. But back then, things were different. Not like they are today. Today they can give you pills and medicines to help you conceive. They can give you fertility treatment. Back then, none of that existed.'

She paused, as though waiting for a memory to fully arrive in her mind.

'I did get pregnant, once,' she said.

I saw Dad take her other hand.

'But it just wasn't to be, I suppose. It was OK. Me and your dad loved each other. That was what kept us going.'

She squeezed my arm as we walked. We turned down the path to the woods. The rustling leaves sounded as though they were welcoming our approach.

'But because we wanted a baby so desperately, we decided to look at other options. We had so much love in us, it seemed like the right thing to do, to have a baby. We hadn't known anyone else who had adopted, but we found out as much as we could about it.

'It wasn't so long ago that they were sending babies, whose parents couldn't look after them, to Australia. It broke my heart to see pictures of these tiny children going off to another country. No parents to wave them off. Not knowing what they would find when they got to the other side of the world.

'And when I lost... when we couldn't have a child naturally, it made me think of all those little children that had been sent away because there hadn't been anyone in this country to look after them. It seemed so unfair.

'Obviously they had to make sure we were suitable people. They looked into our backgrounds, our finances. Did we smoke? Did we drink? All sorts of things. It was as though they were trying to make it as difficult as possible for people to adopt a child. But they had to get it right, you see. They couldn't hand over a child to just anyone. So even though it felt like they were trying to put us off, we carried on. We were determined. Just like you are. I think you got that from us.'

A shiver passed across my neck. I squeezed my arm against Mum's. The leaves in the trees mellowed and turned their noise to nothing more than whispers.

'Eventually we were approved. And when we saw you, oh Christine — you were the most beautiful thing we had ever seen. Your beautiful brown hair and your beautiful brown eyes. You were so lovely. We couldn't believe it. You were so little. Just three months old when we got you.

'When your dad held you in his arms for the first time he looked like he had won the pools and the lottery all at the same time. I don't think there was a prouder man anywhere. You were like all our Christmases come at once. A precious little jewel. And from that moment, we've never stopped giving thanks that you came to us.'

A gentle breeze brushed against my face. It cooled the wet

streaks on my cheeks. I felt the air ripple over the scar on my forehead.

I didn't want to ever let Mum's arm go. I felt as though she was holding me up. I was sure I would collapse if it weren't for her solid, bony arm entwined with mine.

For the entire walk we had all been focusing ahead. None of us had looked at each other. That was the way with walks. That was probably why it was easier to talk. We just focused on where we were going and what we were saying. Expressions and facial reactions didn't get in the way.

But now I turned my head to her and looked into her face. And I saw her for what she was. A kind, loving, generous woman.

A woman I was proud to call Mum.

Above us and around us the cold air moved through the trees. A huge block of wind pushing its way towards us.

Mum's face softened, became fuzzy. Misty. I moved my hand across my eyes to wipe away the tears. But there were none to wipe.

Dad had disappeared in the mist. Mum was slowly joining him. I shouted to them, screamed for them to keep a hold of me. But they never heard me. The roar around us smothered my voice.

I was alone. But I knew the girl would be there soon.

CHAPTER FORTY-NINE

Apparently I had lashed out at my mum. It was only Dad pulling her back from me that prevented me from hurting her.

So then I had launched myself at them both, knocking them to the ground.

And then I had run. Away from them, into the woods.

They called my name and searched for me for over an hour. While they were looking for their lost child, I was killing someone else's child. And her dog.

The same thing. Same as before. Re-living the same moment. Stifling my cry as she forced the broken bottle into my leg. Slamming a rock against the side of her face and kicking out at her fucking dog.

And then dragging the bodies. Hers lifeless, the dog's, still whimpering with life.

Neither of them talked of calling the police. Or an ambulance. Their only thought was for me.

They didn't leave until they found me.

Eventually they did. They said I had been building a makeshift shelter from fallen branches and foliage.

They both came to me, despite my earlier attack, and stood by me as I worked. I heard and saw nothing. They said I appeared feverish and determined. Concentrating only on my work.

I didn't remember building any kind of shelter in my "dream". There was a gap between dragging the bodies, and ending up back in the gorse hiding place. I had no idea what I had done with the bodies.

Perhaps I had built some sort of shelter and hidden them in it. I had no idea.

There was an even larger mind gap between being in the gorse and waking up to reality, so that when I eventually "woke up" I wasn't at first aware of where I had been inside my mind.

I heard Mum's voice first. She wasn't talking to me. She was speaking to Dad. Then I heard his mumble.

I turned to them both. I held a broken branch in my right hand. The scar on my forehead stung. I wiped the sweat from it, dabbed it with my sleeve. I brushed some of the leaves off my hair.

They stopped talking and looked at me, probably not sure whether I was back or not.

'You didn't hold onto me,' I said. 'I screamed for you to hold onto me.'

Mum came to me and stroked my hair, brushing a few more leaves from it.

'Shall we go home?' she said.

I dropped the branch I had been holding and nodded. I wasn't sure what time it was, or even what day it was. And I couldn't remember how we had all come to be in the woods. Home sounded like an excellent idea.

They walked either side of me on the way home. I felt as though I was being marched somewhere. Protected on either side. At one point, Dad took my hand. It was warm and rough. Firm. It felt like a dad's hand should feel.

By the time we reached home I had recalled the details of the nightmare that had come upon me in the woods, and Mum and Dad had told me everything that had happened in the real world.

'I'm so sorry,' I said. 'For lashing out at you. And for pushing you both over. I wasn't aware of any of it.'

They looked at each other.

'It wasn't you, Chris,' Mum said. 'We knew that. You wouldn't do anything like that.'

A chill hit the back of my neck.

Mum pushed open the front door and I felt the warm air on my cheeks as it escaped from the house. The chill stayed with me.

I couldn't explain the blackout. The last one had occurred when the police officer had been asking me stressful questions in my own living-room. I could understand that. Stress can have a tremendous impact on the body.

But this time? My heart had been warm. I had been feeling nothing but tremendous love for my mum. I had wanted to hold her and thank her over and over again. To tell her I understood, as a woman and as a daughter. I had wanted to lift her up into the light and make her know how special she was. Stress was nowhere to be seen.

But still it came. The nightmare and the killing came. It was as much a part of me as the pebble now lodged inside me. And it was letting me know that it was still there. It didn't matter what emotion I was feeling, whether flying through blue, summer skies or fighting through dark, poisoned brambles, it was still there — lying inside me.

'I need help, don't I?' I said.

Dad sat in his armchair, I lay on the sofa. Mum, in the kitchen, filled the kettle and no doubt went on the hunt for a packet of biscuits.

'I think you do, love,' he said. 'They can't let you be like this. It's not right. It's not fair on you.'

I told him where I had gone during the blackout. What I had done.

'And I get them more often now,' I said. 'Sometimes I don't even blackout and it still plays in my head.'

Mum walked in with coffees and biscuits. She must have had an endless supply somewhere because it was yet another new packet.

I wanted to talk to them. I had so many questions. But I didn't know the right language to use. Whatever I said would hurt. *Real* parents; *proper* family; *genuine* relations; *actual* grandparents.

None of it sounded right. None of it gave Mum and Dad the regard they deserved. They all sounded like words designed to sting.

'There probably is madness, isn't there?' I said.

'Chris, there are things you can do nowadays,' Dad said. 'It used to be that adopted children and their natural parents would never expect to find each other.'

Natural parents. Less sting.

'But now,' he said, 'you can access original birth certificates, look up history and so on. I think there are even services that talk things through with you. Help you to find out about your natural family.'

And now I wanted to protect him. I wanted to tell them both that they were my proper parents. That they were my real and genuine family. And those same words that had sounded so spiteful in my mind just a few seconds earlier, now sounded beautiful and restorative.

'Can I ask you something?' I said.

I didn't look at either of them. Left the question in the air for whoever got to it first. Or whoever felt they could avoid answering the least.

I know that they knew what the question was going to be. It was the elephant in the room. The one question that had been there from the start, but that we had all avoided.

'Ask whatever you like,' Dad said. 'We'll answer everything we can.'

And so it was Dad I turned to. I held my eyes to his and steeled myself.

'What was the reason behind you not telling me that I was adopted?'

I expected him to stand up and start pacing. All he did was sit forward in his chair. He looked over at Mum, the merest glance. She returned his look with a flick of her eyes. Permission granted.

'Back then,' he said. 'Parents who adopted were told that there was never any possibility of the adopted child being approached by their natural parents. All ties were completely cut and there would never be any communication. It was the same for the adopted child. Unless the adoptive parents decided to tell the child that they were adopted, that child would never find out by any other means. And even if the child was told, they would never be able to find out about their natural parents.

'For some parents, who were giving up their child, this was almost like a guarantee that there would never be any comeback. They could move on with their lives and allow the child to move on with theirs. It was felt important for both natural parents and the adopted child that the split should be absolute and irreversible.'

He sat back in his chair. He looked like he needed to sleep for a week. I had forgotten that less than an hour ago I had attacked him and Mum. He swallowed and leaned forward again.

'They changed the law a few years ago,' he said. 'It opened up the way for adopted children to find out more about their natural parents. Gave them the right to find out about them. Goodness knows what effect that must have had on some of the parents who had tried to get on with their lives, tried to build a new life.

'You see, some parents who gave their children up for adoption wouldn't have spoken about it to anyone else. After giving up their child they may have moved somewhere new. May have tried to forget about it all. They may have got married, may have changed partners, may even have had more children.

'Some parents had no choice. They were encouraged, perhaps even coerced into giving up their child. Single mothers would have been told that giving up their child for adoption was the best thing they could do for their baby. Especially if they came from a poor home or a broken family.'

He sat back again, swallowed some more. He took a sip of coffee. And shut his eyes. When he opened them again they were watery.

'Your mother and me had decided, even before we had you, that we would tell you that you were adopted, right from the word go. We had read about how to do it: Tell you when you're in your cot; talk to you about it as we push you in your pram. We felt that the best way was just to be open. Having you come to us felt like the most natural thing in the world.

'When we told the adoption people that we planned to tell you about the adoption they didn't seem at all surprised by that. They told us that usually they don't advise either way, they just leave it up to the new parents. But then we had a visit from a care-worker. She had been heavily involved in your case. She gave us no details at all, but she insisted that it might be better not to tell you about your adoption.

'Obviously we kicked up a bit about it, but we didn't want to rock the boat. We'd already set our hearts on you and we were terrified that someone might take you away from us. She seemed so insistent, that we agreed not to tell you. And we kept our word. There were so many times we wanted to tell you. It was almost as though opportunities would pop up. But we had promised.'

He coughed. Mum and I hadn't said a word while Dad spoke. We had barely moved. Now we both reached for our coffee.

I wondered what on earth had compelled a care-worker to insist that I be kept in the dark. Had my circumstances been so awful that they had to be hidden from me?

'I think you really need to try to find out about them,' Dad said. 'Your natural parents. I think it's important. For all sorts of reasons.'

'I wouldn't know where to start,' I said. 'How do I go about it? Do you know what my original name was?'

'All we know is that it was Christine,' Dad said. 'They never told us your original family name. I think that's all part of the separation thing. No one knows. Just like your natural parents wouldn't have known you were coming to us. The only name that was ever mentioned was your name. And we wanted to keep that name for you. It had been given to you at birth and we felt it was yours to keep. We had no right to change it.'

My mum cleared her throat. Like a gentle little cough. Her hands were shaking a little as she put her coffee mug down.

'I think I might know,' she said. 'I think I know what your family name was.'

CHAPTER FIFTY

Dad started coughing. Choking, almost. He gasped for air, as though something had gone down the wrong hole.

He swigged his coffee and the coughs became less vigorous and less frequent. He was flushed red from the neck up.

'What are you talking about, Diane?' he said. 'We were never told their name. Never.'

Mum stroked her knee, as though she was rubbing something off. She didn't make eye contact with either of us.

'That time the care-worker came to see us,' she said, 'when she told us we shouldn't tell Chris she was adopted, she brought a folder with her. Can you remember it?'

Dad shook his head.

'She had already been with us for quite a while,' Mum said. 'We were all in the living-room and she needed the loo. Because of what she had just told us, that we couldn't tell Christine about the adoption, you said you needed a drink of water. You had both left the room and she had left the folder on the table.

'I told myself I shouldn't. But I felt hurt that we couldn't follow our original plans. It wasn't her fault, I knew that, but I wondered why she had been so insistent.'

Dad shook his head slowly, before bowing it. He gripped the bridge of his nose between his thumb and forefinger.

'I knew I didn't have long. I heard the tap running in the kitchen, and the loo hadn't yet been flushed. So I looked.'

Mum raised her eyes to mine, then to Dad, his head still bowed. He mumbled her name.

'I know it was a risk,' she said. 'But I had to know.'

'What did it say?' I said.

'There were several sheets of paper, but I only had time to

really just scan the top sheet. Besides, I didn't want to disturb the pages too much in case she noticed when she came back in.

'There was lots of writing, most of it typed, but some of it written in ink. There were several signatures too. But two names were in bold. I thought, at first, that they were just the names of some of the officials that needed to sign these things. You know, to say that everything is OK. You usually need lots of people to approve things. But it dawned on me that two of the surnames were the same. Well, I thought that would be too much of a coincidence, having two officials with the same name. So I assumed they were the names of your mother and father.

'I didn't have time to read any of the other stuff that was written there, so I was no closer to finding out why she wanted us to keep your adoption from you, but I remembered the names. That much I did get.'

She lowered her gaze again and went back to rubbing her knee.

I waited for her to continue, but she said nothing.

'Mum?'

'I'm just thinking, dear,' she said. 'I want to make sure I get it right.'

I looked at Dad. He had looked up and seemed to be holding his breath.

'Lapton was your family name. L-a-p-t-o-n. And then there were two names. The man's name, presumably your father, was easy to see. It was Richard. But your mother's name, that was difficult to read. It was something like Amelia — but it wasn't quite that. I think it was spelt differently. Like A-m-e-l-i-e. So Amelia but with an "e" on the end instead of an "a".

'I don't know if it was a spelling mistake or not. It was more difficult to correct on a typewriter if you made a mistake. But the surname was definitely Lapton.'

I played around with it in my head. Christine Lapton. It

sounded slightly off, like it wasn't quite right. Lapton sounded odd to me. Lapton, Lapton, Lapton.

'Richard and Amelia?' I said.

'Definitely Richard,' Mum said. 'And I think Amelia — but possibly with an "e".'

'Diane,' Dad said.

'I'm sorry, dear,' she said. 'I would have told you, but I felt so guilty. And if I had made a mistake after all, and they really were just officials, what would have been the point of giving you the names? You would have been guilty too. At least this way it was only me who would have been in trouble if it had ever come out.'

'But after all these years?' he said. 'You never said anything.'

'When would I have, Roy? When would have been the right time? There was no point. Not until now.'

'Are you sure it was Lapton?' I said.

She nodded. 'Definitely. I knew I wouldn't ever forget the name.'

I wanted to say Christine Lapton out loud, just to hear what it sounded like in the open. But I was conscious of how it might make Mum and Dad feel. It carried so much more with it than just a name.

'Did you see anything else?' I said. 'Anything at all? Anything about their state of health, any mental illnesses, anything?'

Mum shook her head.

'As I said, I only had just a short amount of time. I had no time to read anything else at all. Just the names.'

Richard and Amelia or Amelie Lapton.

'Do you know where in the country I came from?'

Dad shuffled in his chair.

'We picked you up from a large building in London,' he said. 'You were brought to us there. But you could have come from anywhere in the country.'

'There was nothing on the sheet I saw,' Mum said. 'Only the London address of that building.'

I wondered where the mad Laptons came from. What was my heritage?

'There must have been mental illness in the family,' I said. 'That was why they asked you not to say anything, so that I'd never find out. And that must have been why I was taken for adoption in the first place. They must have taken me away from them, because they were mentally unstable. They weren't suitable to look after me.'

My mobile phone rang. I grabbed it out of my handbag. It was Neil. I wanted to tell him everything. Blurt it all out. About the adoption, about the mental illness and about my real name. But I couldn't even put it together in my own mind yet. I sent the call to voicemail.

'It was just Neil,' I said. 'I'll talk to him tomorrow.'

Dad climbed to his feet and stretched his arms above his head. The stretching made him cough.

'So what do you want to do, Chris?' he said. 'What do you want us to do? We'll help you in whatever way we can.'

'I wish you had the Internet here,' I said. 'I suppose I would start by looking up the name Lapton and see what it came up with. Then I could also look to see if there are any organisations that help adopted children to locate their natural parents. That's assuming they're both alive of course.'

'There's no reason to think they might not be,' said Mum. 'Your dad and I are pretty fit and healthy and we were relatively old when we had you.'

'You weren't old,' I said. 'But if they had a mental illness — maybe that affects your health in other ways too. Maybe they had a shortened life because of it.'

Dad started pacing.

'Do you want to go home?' he said. 'So that you've got the Internet? And Neil, of course.'

'I think I'd like to stay here tonight. If that's still OK with you?'

Dad stopped pacing.

'And I'm really hungry too,' I said. 'Have we got anything to eat?'

Mum stood up.

'We always have something,' she said.

We ate in the kitchen. If Neil had walked in on the conversation over the lasagne he would have known nothing of the day's events and revelations.

No matter how old I got, I always felt like I was a small child when I sat down to eat with Mum and Dad. Presumably it was the same for everyone. Their parents were always going to be parents no matter how old the children got.

I had opened the kitchen window, and a gentle breeze blew in from the night. Even in the darkness there was life outside. Occasionally a bird would call. Something would rustle through the leaves on the lawn. Dad's face had regained some of its natural colour, Mum's eyes wider now that some of the puffiness had left them.

But we all looked tired. Like we'd spent the day travelling. I just wanted my bed. I was sure I had only enough energy to finish eating and stumble up the stairs. The continual whirring in my mind was on pause. If I never had another thought, I would be happy.

'Do you still go fishing, Dad?' I said.

He wiped some sauce from his bottom lip.

'Every now and then,' he said. 'Although I don't really have anyone to go with anymore.'

I looked over at Mum.

'Could we all go?' I said. 'Sometime soon?'

CHAPTER FIFTY-ONE

By the time I sloped up to bed, someone (presumably Mum) had cleared the broken photos from the stairs. I'd forgotten about them and realised I hadn't apologised for smashing them. I wished I had.

I spent the night slipping in and out of sleep.

I wasn't disturbed by dreams or visions, but my new name came and went like a flickering light.

I tried to imagine what my natural parents might look like. I thought about Michael and Rose. What physical characteristics would they have inherited from these people? What if the madness had passed to them too? Did it work like that?

I turned in bed, first on one side, then the other. I moved my arms and legs to try to find a comfortable position. I lay on my back, then my front. I lay with my eyes open, then shut. I was so tired I would have happily gone to sleep forever, and yet I felt as though I could get up and run around the house to burn off energy.

Eventually the birds outside greeted the new day with raucous chatter. The sun broke through the curtains and I followed the slow laser of light as it inched across my bedroom wall.

I was grateful for the end of such an uncomfortable night, but would gladly have accepted another eight hours to try again.

I texted, then rang, Neil.

He was running behind for work and didn't have much time.

'We need to meet for lunch,' I said.

'I can't, Chris. I'm so busy at the moment. I don't think I have the time.'

'Make the time, Neil. This is very important. I'll be outside at

1pm.'

He sighed. A sigh tinged with a growl. I imagined his eyebrows were raised significantly too.

'Make it 12:30,' he said. 'But I won't have long.'

Dad said he was happy to take me into town.

'I have things I can do there anyway,' he said. 'Will you want to come back here again afterwards?'

I hadn't really thought any further than lunch with Neil.

'It might be a good idea for me to go home,' I said. 'I can make a start on the Internet then, see what options are available. And tomorrow I have another appointment with my counsellor, although I might cancel that.'

'I'll be in town for about an hour,' he said. 'Then I'll come back to the bank and you can decide what you want to do then.'

I packed my suitcase with the intention of leaving it in Dad's car.

'Do you want me to make you a sandwich, love?' Mum said.

'I'll eat when I'm with Neil,' I said.

Neil kept me waiting for ten minutes. In fairness I had been five minutes early. We walked to a cafe a few minutes from his work. We ordered two coffees and two chicken and sweetcorn baguettes.

When I first mention the word "adopted" the colour drained from Neil's face. His eyebrows went way beyond raised. It fazed him so much that he knocked a great glug of coffee over the table. I had never seen him so shocked.

I told him everything I knew about the adoption; the names; the insistence by the care-worker that I shouldn't be told; the possible mental illness. I told him how much Mum and Dad loved me. I told him that, yes, of course I was pissed off with them at first, but somehow it all seemed to make sense now. I felt even more of a unit with them now.

I told him that I had lashed out at my mum and pushed them both to the ground. That I had then blacked out for about an hour.

We talked about my worry for the kids. If there was mental illness, would it affect them? Was it already in their genes?

He rang his work while we were in the cafe and told them he felt ill and wouldn't be back in until the morning. So now both of us were shocked.

'I'm not sure how long I've got, Neil,' I said. 'To find them, I mean. The doctor could ring at anytime and tell me I have to go for a psychiatric assessment. I'm sure if that happened I would be put away somewhere. I have to find them before that happens. At least then I'll know how the mental illness manifests itself, assuming it does exist.'

'I'll help you,' he said. 'We'll go through it together. We'll brainstorm and see if we can come up with ideas on how to trace them. We'll work on it as a team. I'm sure we'll find something.'

I rang my Dad's mobile, but it was switched off. I didn't bother leaving a message, I knew he would have no idea how to retrieve it. We ordered another coffee each.

'What about the kids?' Neil said.

'What about the kids?' I said.

'Are you going to tell them? About being adopted.'

'They aren't adopted,' I said.

Neil kicked me.

'I don't know,' I said. 'I was thinking of keeping it from them for thirty-seven years and then breaking it to them when they started going a bit doolally.'

'You won't have to wait thirty-seven years for that,' he said.

'Not if they're anything like their Dad,' I said.

He kicked me again.

I avoided answering his question about whether to tell

Michael and Rose. I was only just starting to get my head around it myself, so I had no idea what words to use when telling the children. I would tell them, of course. I couldn't very well fly off the handle at Mum and Dad for not telling me, and then not tell Michael and Rose.

We left the cafe at quarter past one. Dad was already hanging around outside the bank when we got there. I told him I was going to go home and Neil lifted out my suitcase.

I gave Dad the biggest hug, thanked him for everything. Thanked him for my life. I squeezed him hard. It made him cough. But he smiled through it.

Neil dumped my suitcase into his car, and we drove home.

Although Neil and I were home together, I felt uneasy. I kept him with me as I opened the windows downstairs. Made him wait outside the downstairs loo while I was inside. And I made him come upstairs with me so I could find a cardigan to put on.

'Has that missing picture turned up?' I said.

Neil shook his head.

'I've not looked for it,' he said. 'I've been busy cooking microwave meals. You have no idea how complex that is.'

I *Googled* the surname Lapton and immediately brought up dozens of sites inviting me to trace my ancestors or to start my family tree.

We both took turns, searching and researching. I discovered that one's natural parents are more generally known as birth parents. We looked at the agencies that were available to help both adopted children and birth parents to get in touch with each other. And I found out how to get hold of my original birth certificate.

I made initial contact with the local council to try to arrange a meeting to discuss my adoption and was told it might be possible to see my adoption file, once they had located it.

Every time I heard a noise outside, Neil would have to go and make sure that there was no one there. But he had to wait for me to come with him if it meant he was going to be out of sight.

After three hours on the computer I had to stop. I slumped down in the armchair. Neil chose the sofa. He put his feet up.

'Bring me twelve paracetamol, six gallons of cold water and a frontal lobotomy, please,' I said.

'You already had the lobotomy years ago, remember?' Neil said.

'I remember,' I said. 'It was to bring me down to the same social level as you.'

Neil dragged himself off the sofa and stood behind my chair. He massaged the back of my neck. I was pleased that it felt different to when my Mum had done it the day before. It took my mind off my pounding head.

'I am scared, Neil,' I said. 'About where this is all going. Even if I find my birth parents, that's not going to stop any mental illness if it's already inside me.'

'It might not be inside you,' he said.

'Where have you been the last couple of months?'

'But couldn't that just be as a result of your head injuries?' Neil said. 'It might not be a sign of anything more.'

I admired his optimism, but would have preferred the truth. Uppermost in my mind was the safety and future of Michael and Rose. I knew that Neil was the same. He would have thought about the consequences of me being mentally unwell. At the very least he would have wondered if it were true. My behaviour of late must have appeared more and more bizarre to him. He couldn't not be worried.

He stopped massaging and resumed his natural position on the sofa.

'I'm seeing Colin tomorrow,' I said. 'Do you want to come?'

I hadn't planned on inviting him until the question came out.

'It might be good,' I said. 'Then you will have met him, you'll know where I'm going, and you'll know the sorts of things we talk about. Then you won't be so jealous.'

'I'm not jealous.'

'So, do you want to come?'

'I've got work,' he said.

'You had work this afternoon,' I said. 'But here we are.'

'I don't think I'd get away with it again.'

'You won't know until you try. Anyway, you could always tell them you had to see a counsellor. That would worry them. They might decide not to throw so much work at you.'

'Isn't this all private though,' he said, 'what you and the counsellor talk about? Me being there might make things awkward.'

'It's only awkward if I say it is, and I'm the one inviting you.'

He propped a cushion under his head.

'I'll see how I feel in the morning,' he said.

'I might have changed my mind in the morning,' I said.

He reached for the cushion and launched it at me. For an ex-rugby player, it was a very poor shot. Even if I had been standing on the chair it would have cleared my head by at least a couple of feet. It landed on the sideboard in the corner, knocking over a vase of flowers. He ran for the vase while I ran for a tea towel.

'Pillock,' I said.

'I didn't want to hurt you,' he said.

He picked up the vase and fallen flowers. I mopped the water from the sideboard.

'It's gone down the back,' he said. 'It's dripping down the wall.'

'So what are you going to do about it, Einstein? Do you know where the other tea towels are?'

He lumbered off to the kitchen, vase in one hand, flowers in the other.

We passed each other on his way back.

'I'm going to stick this straight in the washing machine,' I said. 'You can put that one in too, once you've finished with it.'

I walked into the kitchen as Neil hefted his strength to moving the sideboard away from the wet wall. I shoved the wet tea towel into the machine and left the door open.

I noticed soil still on the floor from the plant.

'Neil,' I said. 'You could have at least hoovered that up.'

He shouted to me from the living-room.

'Chris. Chris, come here.'

'Don't change the subject,' I said. 'It would only have taken you a minute.'

Neil raised his voice. My heart went cold.

'Chris. You need to come in here.'

I ran into the living-room, wishing I had grabbed a knife first. Neil was red-faced. It didn't look like it was from the exertion of moving the sideboard away from the wall. He pointed at the wall behind it. As I drew closer I could see there was writing.

'Look,' he said. 'It's been scratched into the wall.'

I heard a scratching sound coming from downstairs.

Neil moved as I crouched down next to him. My pulse shot up. I pulled my cardigan tight around me and leaned into Neil and sat on the floor, not daring to move. The words on the wall explained the missing photograph.

"I KNOW WHAT YOU LOOK LIKE NOW".

CHAPTER FIFTY-TWO

'We've got to get out of here,' I said. 'We need to get out — right now.'

Neil put his hands on my shoulders.

'Chris, calm down. We need to think about this first.'

'What is there to think about?' I said.

I stood up and pointed at the writing.

'He knows what I fucking look like!' I said. 'We have to get out — now.'

Neil stood in front of me and took my hands. He looked into my eyes and made sure I looked into his. 'If he was going to do something here, in our house, he wouldn't have taken the picture. He wouldn't have needed it. This is just a warning of some sort.'

'A warning about what?' I said. 'He was the one who attacked me. What the fuck have I ever done to him? I don't even know what the bastard looks like.'

Neil squeezed my hands.

'Chris, don't worry. I'm here. We're here together. No one is going to come here. If they do... well, they won't.'

'What are we going to do?' I said. 'This has to come to an end, somehow. We can't go on like this.'

'We should call the police,' Neil said. 'This is concrete evidence. They have to take notice of this.'

I shook my head.

'I don't want the police here again, Neil. Not after what happened the last time. I lashed out at my mum and dad yesterday. God knows what I would do to the police. They only have to start asking a few questions and I flip out.'

'I could talk to them,' Neil said. 'On my own.'

'That would just come across as weird. And besides, how

would you explain how you found it. No policeman in the world is going to believe that you were casually tidying behind the sideboard when you happened to come across some writing scratched into our wall. They'll probably think it was me. That I was the one who wrote it while experiencing a blackout. I'm the one who is going round the bend, remember?'

Neil turned from me and looked again at the writing on the wall. He mumbled something under his breath.

'What did you say?' I said.

'I wonder why he put it behind the sideboard,' he said. 'We might not have found it for years. Maybe never.'

'Maybe he thought we'd look behind there for the missing photo.'

'But the photo wasn't on the sideboard,' he said. 'It was on the wall. It makes no sense.'

'Neil, the bloke's a psycho. He's not supposed to make sense.'

We took photos of the writing, with our phones and with the camera. Close up, to get the detail, then further back to include the sideboard. If it ever needed to be put before the police at least we had evidence from the actual night. They could always come and see it in the flesh if they needed to, but the digital pictures all had the time and date attached.

We both had a microwave meal for tea, and water from the tap. It wasn't so hard.

We didn't exactly brainstorm about our next move, but we each put forward one or two ideas. Neil thought about installing a burglar alarm and perhaps even cameras.

I thought about buying a guard-dog or setting up some sort of laser tripwire in the garden.

'And I thought my cameras idea was a bit O.T.T,' Neil said. 'Do you know which shops sell laser tripwires?'

'It was just an idea,' I said.

'Why don't I go and look at burglar alarms tomorrow

morning while you're in with your counsellor?'

'Why don't you come in to the counsellor with me, then we'll both go and look at burglar alarms afterwards?'

I let Neil think on that and went to the kitchen to phone Abi. She was out, but I spent a few minutes talking with Oli and thanking him for putting up with my kids. And then I spent ten minutes talking to Michael and Rose. I could hear giggles and laughter in the background and both of them sounded breathless. I was amazed that they came to the phone at all. I told them I loved them.

'Gotta go,' Michael said.

'I miss you, Mum,' Rose said.

'Miss you too, darling,' I said.

In the morning Neil rang his work and told them he was still sick. He told them he was "going to see someone" that morning.

'You're going to see someone?' I said. 'What does that mean?'

'It means that they will think I'm going to see a doctor about being ill, when in fact I never mentioned the doctor at all. I didn't lie, and they will come to their own conclusion. It's not my fault.'

He then insisted that I phone Colin to make sure it really was OK to bring him along. It was.

As Neil drove us to Newton St Loe I could tell he wasn't himself. He barely said a word. I had expected to feel quite at ease that he was coming with me, but butterflies flitted about in my tummy and perspiration dotted the back of my neck.

'Stop here,' I said. 'Against the side of the hedge. That's his house there.'

Neil climbed out of the car and rolled his shoulders.

'He obviously earns a lot of money,' he said.

'Not from me,' I said.

Colin opened the door before we reached it. Something about

him looked different, but I couldn't work out what. He shook hands with Neil and they both smiled introductions to each other.

We followed him through the hall. I was surprised to see that the phrenology head was missing.

'I've had a tidy up,' he said, showing us into the study. 'Moved a few things out.'

There were no books on the floor, none on the chairs, and the whole room looked bigger. I couldn't smell any sawdust either. Only a slight chemical odour. Cleaning fluids.

'No head?' I said.

'Sorry?'

'Your phrenology head,' I said. 'It wasn't there.'

'Oh that,' he said. 'It got broken.'

'It's all pseudo-science anyway,' I said.

Neil looked at me.

As Colin followed us into the study the sunlight reached his face. Now I could see what was different about him. He had scratches on his face. Not deep, but visible. Several in a line, as though from a woman's fingernails. His eyes were rimmed red. He reached out his hand to point us to the seats and I noticed a bandage just visible on his wrist under the sleeve of his jumper.

'Sit yourselves down,' he said. 'Can I get you both a coffee?'

We said yes to the coffee and sat down on an armchair each. I reached out and held Neil's hand as he looked around the room, taking it all in.

'It'll only be for an hour,' I said.

'I'm OK,' he said. 'It's all good.'

I was pleased that Neil had come. Colin's scratches and bandaged wrist had only heightened my feeling of unease that had started up in the car journey. And he seemed to be taking too long in the kitchen to make just a couple of drinks.

I wondered what had made him tidy up, and why he had

needed to use cleaning chemicals in a room that previously had looked like it had seen nothing more than a quick flourish from a duster — infrequently. I wondered about his wife's accident.

'We could always go,' I said. 'Leave now. We could say I suddenly felt ill or something.'

'I'm fine,' Neil said. 'Seriously.'

Colin walked back in. He had three coffees and a plate of flapjacks. I reached out for one, then hesitated. What if he'd made them himself? Neil reached past me and grabbed one, no hesitation. It made me feel a little easier.

It turned out that Neil and Colin had something in common. They both had played, and both still loved, rugby.

In fact at one point I started to think the session was entirely for Neil's benefit rather than mine.

But Colin listened as I told him about the adoption and the blackout. He asked about Doctor Jones, and how things were progressing. I explained that I was still waiting for the results of the latest MRI scan and that Doctor Jones was consulting with colleagues about whether I should be sent for a psychiatric assessment.

'And how do you feel about that?' Colin said.

I told him. About my worries for the children if I was locked up in some desperate asylum somewhere. He laughed. Neil did too. I hadn't meant it as a joke.

'Do you think a psychiatric assessment is necessary?' Colin said.

'Do you?' I said.

He smiled. 'I asked first.'

'The honest truth is — I don't know. I'm worried about how I am and about what's going on inside my head. And now I'm worried that I really do have mental illness in the family. A family I have no knowledge of, no idea of their history, and no idea how to get in touch with them. And if I do have to go for an assessment, how long do I have before they put me away somewhere? Time is of the essence.'

'The language you're using, Christine, may not be helping you. You won't be "put away somewhere" or "locked up in an asylum". Those things just do not happen. You may be required to stay in hospital for a short time while they ascertain what may or may not be wrong with you. But the chances are there's nothing wrong with you at all and you'll be straight home again.

'If you think of this as people trying to help you to get better, rather than anyone wanting to put you away somewhere, it might help you to feel more positive about it.'

Neil shifted in his chair. 'Is there any chance that this could still all be as a result of the mugging, rather than a mental illness?'

Colin nodded. 'Of course,' he said. 'Christine suffered serious head trauma. Very often injuries like this can change a person's personality completely. Usually just temporarily, but in some cases permanently. The brain swells up inside the skull and that's when problems can occur. The swelling goes down over time and generally the person comes back to how they were before the injury. But sometimes more damage has been done inside the brain. That's why MRI scans are so important.'

He glanced at me but continued talking to Neil.

'I also believe that Christine is suffering post-traumatic-stress syndrome as well. Although she doesn't feel that the incident has affected her in that way, I believe that, on a subconscious level, it has. And stress has a very powerful impact on us. On both the mind and the body.'

Neil nodded and looked over at me. Colin turned to me.

'I do think it would be beneficial to try and find out a little of your family history, if you can. From a medical point of view it could give some pointers and may discount certain things. I deal with quite a few people who have either been adopted or given a child up for adoption. I also have colleagues that advise with adoptions and getting in touch with birth parents. I know that, for some, it can be quite a difficult thing to do. It brings its own set of potential worries for both sides and it needs to be handled carefully.'

He smiled.

'If you decide you do want to go down that path, I would be happy to put you in touch with someone. They could at least direct you to the best person to talk to if they can't help.'

When Colin spoke, I found myself getting lost in his voice. A lovely soft accent and intelligent speech. I could see why he was a counsellor. Even Neil had warmed to him.

But when he wasn't speaking, when I was just thinking about him, or looking at him, something else happened to me. Something prickled my mind, as if saying *beware*. And his house too. It didn't feel warm. It didn't feel secure. And it didn't feel safe.

I had no idea if that was my swollen brain making things up. It might even have been as a result of the mental illness that potentially ran through my genes.

His friendly manner and gentle tone just seemed too good to be true. There were scratches on his face for a reason. The broken phrenology head and the bandaged wrist hiding under the jumper all had a story to tell.

And his study smelled so chemically clean.

CHAPTER FIFTY-THREE

Neil had been completely taken with Colin.
'He seems like a really nice bloke,' he said.
'Just because he likes rugby that doesn't make him a nice bloke.'
'I thought you liked him?' he said.
'Will you come with me again next time?' I said. 'I'd like it if you were there.'
'I don't want to detract from what he's doing for you. And I'll probably be working anyway.'
'What if I made it for a time when you weren't working?'
'It's up to you. I'm happy to come if you want me there.'
We drove to the D.I.Y store in town and checked out the burglar alarms. They didn't do laser trip wires. They had security cameras though. We bought wireless versions of both.
It took us three hours to get it all fitted at home. The picture quality of the camera was shocking. The intruder alarm was excellent. We spent twenty minutes playing with it, standing in various places in the house, and then moving to set the alarm off. I half expected a knock at the door from our neighbours or the police.
Neil made us a couple of sandwiches for lunch and we sat in front of the T.V watching our new security camera in action. After a few minutes it made my eyes hurt. We turned the T.V off.
'I think there's something funny with the counsellor,' I said.
'With Colin? He seemed fine to me. Seemed nice.'
'When I was first there,' I said. 'The very first time, he mentioned that his wife had died. He said she had died in an accident, but he didn't say what. Then, as I left, there was a noise upstairs. He had told me the house was empty. He said

it was a cat, but I never saw it.

'And then today, he had changed things in the study. Things had been moved and tidied. There was a smell of chemicals, like from cleaning stuff. And he had scratches on his face. And did you see the bandage on his wrist? I think there's something going on there.'

'What sort of something?'

I didn't know what to say. I knew he would laugh at me if I said what I really thought — that Colin had killed his wife and was now attacking his patients.

'I just think it's odd about his wife; odd that he said the house was empty but there was someone upstairs; and odd that he had scratches and had cleaned the study.'

'I thought he said the noise upstairs was a cat.'

'I never saw a cat,' I said. 'And more importantly, I never smelt a cat. My sense of smell is so strong I could have smelled body odour on a flea on a cat.'

Neil smiled now. A crooked smile which trembled slightly on one edge.

'So you think that maybe she isn't dead,' he said, 'and he's got her trapped upstairs. But she escaped down the stairs and there was a fight. That head thing you were talking about got broken and she scratched his face and hurt his wrist. Maybe he got blood on the floor in the room we were in.' His smile broadened. 'Or maybe he killed her in there.'

I blushed and looked away from Neil. He noticed the blush.

'I do understand,' he said. 'It must all look a little odd. But I really don't think he's that sort of person, do you? I mean, he seemed really nice.'

'And really nice people don't kill their wives?' I said.

I realised how stupid the comment was as soon as I had said it.

'No, they don't,' he said. 'Not if they're really nice.'

He had lost the smirk.

'Is that why you want me to come with you?' he said. 'Just in case he's really a psycho.'

I shook my head.

'That wasn't why I wanted you there today. But while I was there, I had such an uncomfortable feeling about him. I really would feel happier if you came. Or I could just stop going, or find someone else to see. I don't know if Doctor Jones knows anyone else.'

'To be honest, Chris, Colin rang me earlier, on my mobile. He wants me to come with you too. After you told him about how you blacked out and attacked your mum and dad, he's a bit worried in case he needs me for protection. He thinks you might be a psycho.'

I whacked him around the head with a cushion and fell into him.

'Help,' he said. 'I'm being attacked by a psycho.'

I tickled his ribs and made him squeal like a girl. He struggled and squirmed, but he couldn't get away. I was relentless.

He loved it really.

The next day, Neil went back to work.

Abi came round and spent the morning with me, making sure I didn't blackout or do anything too weird.

Every night for the next four, I had the dreams. And every day I couldn't get the memories of them out of my head.

I wanted Michael and Rose back. I missed them desperately, but Abi assured me they were having the time of their lives. I told her about the adoption but asked her not to say anything to the kids just yet. When she came around each morning she helped me look into trying to find my birth parents.

We searched census records, birth records, marriage records. We looked on as many of the social networking sites that we could think of. And I spent what felt like a fortune ordering certificates and gaining access to certain on-line records.

We spent several hours checking all the information we had, then cross-checking names with dates and places.

At the end of it, my head pounded, but I knew we had made progress. My heart fluttered when I considered what we now had. It really did feel like I had a chance of finding them. All I could do now, was wait for the ordered certificates to come through, which would then confirm or dash my hopes.

On his first day back at work, Neil didn't have to work late. He picked up a takeaway on the way home and we ate it together, laughing about how crap our new security camera was.

But every other day that week, and the first two days of the following week, he was late home. The smell of alcohol kissed me before he did. I found it difficult to get through to him. Often I would have to repeat things to get an answer. He looked as though he was turning something over and over in his mind.

Obviously I asked him what was going on. But he blamed it all on work.

One evening I noticed a bruise by his ear. He told me he had walked into a lamp post.

The next day he was home on time. Perhaps even slightly early. He virtually crept in the front door. He seemed odd. On edge. His voice was quieter than usual when he spoke to me.

'Are you... OK?' he said.

'I'm fine. How are you?'

'Good. How was your day?' He hesitated to make eye contact with me. It was like he was holding back. As though he was waiting for me to say something. Not just anything — but a specific something.

'Neil, what's wrong?'

He took his coat off and hung it up. He seemed to relax a little. He smiled. Sort of.

'Nothing is wrong,' he said. 'Everything is fine.'

'I know I'm paranoid,' I said. 'But I'm not bloody stupid. What is the matter?'

'It's just work, you know. All the usual. Have you done much today? Been out? Sat in front of the telly?'

'I've been searching on-line for more information about the Laptons. I've not had a chance to go out, or watch the telly. In fact I was just thinking of switching on the news.'

He grabbed my arm. He looked desperate.

'Let's eat,' he said. 'And maybe have an early night.'

As we ate, he laughed at every silly little thing I said. His voice alternated between a virtual whisper and a bellow. His movements were jerky and exaggerated.

After we had eaten and put the dishes in the dishwasher he ushered me through the living-room to the bottom of the stairs.

'Are you sure you're OK?' I said.

'He smiled and nodded.'

'It's too early for my shower,' I said. 'Let me just flop in front of the telly for a while first. Let my dinner go down.'

He checked his watch and hesitated.

'What channel?'

'Anything. Just while my food goes down.'

He grabbed the remote control and switched the T.V on. He flicked through the channels and stopped on something about the countryside.

'I like this,' he said.

We watched it until it finished. Neil kept hold of the remote the whole time, not even putting it down on the seat next to him. When it was over he switched the T.V off and looked at me.

'Let me just watch the news headlines,' I said. 'Then I'll have my shower.'

His eyes widened. He blushed.

'Let's not watch the news tonight,' he said.

He gripped the remote with both hands.

'I haven't seen any news all day,' I said. 'I only want to see the headlines.'

'We're just starting to feel better, Chris. You know how depressing the news is. Why don't you go and have a shower and I'll get you a coffee and a choccy muffin.'

'I don't want a muffin,' I said. 'And I don't really want my shower yet. If you don't want to watch the telly why don't you go up and have your shower?'

His jaw tightened. His eyes closed slightly.

'Are you angry?' I said.

'I just think that we can do without the telly once in a while.'

His voice grew louder as he spoke. His tone moved up the scale at the same time.

'Neil?'

He slid the back off the remote-control and flicked the batteries out onto his hand.

'Neil!'

'All I wanted was a nice relaxing night. For us to get ready for bed and have a peaceful time.'

He definitely wasn't relaxed or peaceful.

I went over and wrenched the remote from him. He still clenched the batteries in his other hand. I put the remote down next to him on the sofa and held his empty hand.

'Neil, I agree,' I said. 'It would be lovely to relax, and lovely to have an early night. And you're right, we are starting to feel better.'

His battery hand relaxed slightly.

'But I definitely don't want a muffin or a coffee.'

He softened slightly.

'Are you sure about the choccy muffin?' he said.

'I'm sure.' I grabbed my handbag and headed off to the stairs. 'But I am going to have my shower.'

The shower was warm, but hardly relaxing. Neil's odd behaviour spun around in my mind. His reactions during dinner had been bizarre. And in all the time I had known him, he had never had a problem with watching T.V.

After my shower I dried off and slipped on my pyjamas and dressing gown. I reached into my handbag and pulled out my mobile phone. I flicked through the apps and touched the one for BBC News.

Neil looked startled to see me standing on the stairs. I had deliberately avoided the third stair.

'That was quick,' he said. 'Everything OK?'

The pain in my thigh sparked. My arms felt like they were getting bigger, more muscular. I stopped them from shaking.

'Chris?' he said.

I could see something start in his eyes. It looked like panic. I noticed the batteries from the remote control dumped beside him on the chair. My neck twitched and a fizzing sensation shot through me. I put my hand against the wall for support. Neil stood up.

'Chris?' he said, again.

I held my mobile phone up to him.

'What the fuck is going on, Neil? What the fuck is going on?'

He hesitated. Wasn't sure whether to come over or not. I knew he wouldn't be able to read the detail of what I was showing him on my phone from where he stood, but he would have seen the BBC logo. The fact that he stayed where he was told me he already knew which article it was.

'What do you mean?' he said.

'I mean, what the fuck is going on? Why didn't you want me to watch the news, Neil? What was the reason for that?'

He held his hands out to his side.

'I thought it would be nice for us to have an early night,' he said. 'Miss out on the telly for once.'

I stopped myself from throwing the phone at him.

'Bullshit,' I yelled. 'Why didn't you want me to see this?' I said, thrusting the phone in his direction.

'I don't know what you're talking about,' he said. 'I don't know what that is.'

I read the headline out to him. It was already burned onto my memory, so I could see his reaction as I spoke.

"Families distraught as two teenage girls go missing"

I watched Neil sink back onto the sofa.

CHAPTER FIFTY-FOUR

Something didn't feel good here.

Two young teenage girls had gone missing from their homes in Bridgwater, a little over an hour away from our house. According to both sets of parents, the girls had left for school as normal that morning. Other pupils told police that they had seen the girls chatting and laughing as usual and that they got on the bus to school together. They sat together, but they normally did anyway, and nothing seemed out of the ordinary.

The teachers that took the girls for lessons had all been spoken to and they confirmed that both girls had been present that morning, but they had both handed in notes from their parents to say they needed to leave at lunchtime. None had realised at the time that the notes had been produced by the girls themselves with forged signatures.

The families became worried when neither girl arrived home at the normal time. They made many calls to the girls' mobile phones and left increasingly frantic messages on the voicemail. Neither of the phones were answered. The police were currently sifting through CCTV footage to see if there were any sightings of the girls. No one had yet come forward as having seen them.

As I read the article, in the bedroom after my shower, a pain shot down from my head to my heart. The girls weren't much older than Michael. The parents no different to me and Neil. And their children were missing.

My brain tingled, as though electricity hummed through every cell. I felt my head growing warmer on the inside. I gulped for air and fought back the welling tears. What had I done? How could I have allowed this to happen?

I knew it was my fault. The missing girls were dead, I knew

that already. Both horribly murdered. Abused and killed. They had to be. I had seen it all. All of my visions and dreams had told me this was going to happen. They had all been premonitions — and I had done nothing to warn people. I had allowed it to go ahead.

The tingling in my brain spread through every vein and sinew of my body, and chilled. A thought thrust into me with such force that I felt it through my whole body. What if I hadn't just allowed it to happen? What if I had made it happen? What if it was me who had done it?

I checked the time and date on my phone. Then double checked it against the bedside clock. I hadn't blacked out. I surely hadn't blacked out? How would I have got to Bridgwater? I didn't have the car keys. Where was I earlier today? Had Abi been with me the whole morning? I couldn't remember.

My heart pounded in my chest and my breathing came hard. The scar on my forehead throbbed and I put my fingers to it. Ran them along the ridges. Felt the lumps. And the bumps. *Phrenology.*

If Bridgwater was only an hour or so from our house, it would be virtually the same from Newton St Loe.

From Colin's house.

I flicked through the story on my phone and searched for similar items. I hunted around the website looking for articles about attempted abductions, especially from the previous week, around the time that Colin had scratches on his face and a bandaged wrist.

I couldn't find anything. Maybe it just hadn't been reported.

I picked up a leaflet I used to bite down on when I put my lipstick on, and wafted it in front of my face. Although my body was covered with goosebumps, my face was burning hot. I could have done with a more substantial leaflet.

I tried to remember what Colin had been like on my previous

visits. The missing wife, and daughter. The unseen cat. Despite the fact that I was blacking out often, it may still have been him that drugged me on that first visit.

And why had Doctor Jones specifically recommended him? I had no real idea about Colin Connell's credentials. I was only going on the word of another person. I had seen nothing for myself.

And was it really believable that Colin was seeing me for free? Had Doctor Jones really organised that, or was he getting something out of it too? Both him and Colin Connell seemed to know each other pretty well. I didn't know what kind of man Doctor Jones was. Did he have a wife? Was she missing too?

I worked back in my mind over all the visits I had taken to the doctor. Was there anything that I had missed? Anything weird or unusual? I wasn't sure. I recalled his examination of me, his breath on the back of my neck. What had he done to me whilst I had my eyes shut?

He had felt my head too. Felt the lumps and bumps. Was there some connection between him and Colin over phrenology? Was I just part of some bizarre experiment? And why was the phrenology head now missing from Colin Connell's hallway?

Presumably the doctor lived around here. It would be more than possible for him and Colin to drive to Bridgwater.

I thought again about hearing the thump upstairs at Colin's house. The thorough cleansing of his study. I wanted to search his house, to look upstairs and hunt through all the rooms, find out what was up there — who was up there. And did he really play rugby? Or was that just to put Neil at ease?

And Neil was at ease. He thought he was a nice bloke. They had seemed very friendly, Colin and Neil.

I didn't like where my mind was taking me now. I put the leaflet down and shook my head, tried to clear it. But the thought had already started. There was no stopping it.

Maybe Colin and Neil weren't meeting for the first time. A conspiracy of three. The doctor, the counsellor and the banker.

Don't be stupid, Christine!

I picked the leaflet up again. Flapped it vigorously.

But Neil had been working late. Over an hour late some evenings. He had a bruise on his face. He looked awful. And he didn't want me to see the news. He didn't want me to see that two girls were missing.

I shot a look at the bedroom door. Strained my ears. Was he coming up the stairs? Was that the third stair creaking?

I looked for his cut-down broom handle. I saw it leaning against the wall by his side of the bed.

Neil had turned almost aggressive when I'd told him I wanted to watch the news. And he had practically insisted that I come upstairs for a shower.

What had happened on that night I stayed at Mum and Dad's? What had Neil really done when I wasn't at home?

I racked my brain for clues. Retraced the incidents of the past couple of months. The writing on the wall outside. That wasn't Neil, he was with me in bed. But Colin? The doctor?

And the "intruder". Neil has a house key, could it have been him. He was the one that "found" the writing scratched into the wall behind the sideboard. How did he know to look there? And why had he not bothered to look for the missing photo? Was he the one that took it?

Everything was spinning out of control in my mind. Thoughts and questions overlapped each other, followed by bizarre answers to questions I hadn't even thought of. The room felt as though it was on fire. I loosened my dressing gown. I needed a drink, my tongue stuck to the roof of my mouth, it was so dry.

Calm down, Christine.

I knew I had to confront Neil. I had to find out what was

going on.

I pulled my dressing gown tight around me. Got back to the missing girls story on my phone and stepped as quietly as I could to the top of the stairs. I heard no sound coming from the living room. The T.V was still off.

I had vaguely thought that I would plan my immediate "next move" based on Neil's reaction to me pointing out the article on my phone. If he had run at me, I would charge back up the stairs and grab his broom handle. If, instead, he had denied everything I would prepare myself for a prolonged period of arguing and questioning. If he had confessed to everything — well, I wasn't sure how I would react to that.

So watching him just sink back onto the sofa threw me a little.

'Neil?' I screamed.

He put his head in his hands.

The hysterical tone in my voice persisted.

'Neil! What the fuck is going on?'

When he raised his head up to look at me, I expected to see tears, or embarrassment, or shame. But there was nothing. Even his eyebrows weren't telling me anything.

'Calm down,' he said. 'Stop screaming.'

The only way I could stop screaming, and therefore give the impression of being calm, was by not saying anything at all. And, under the circumstances, that just wasn't possible.

'I can't calm down,' I screamed. 'You need to tell me what the fuck is going on, right now.'

He sat back into the sofa. Stretched his arms out along the top.

'Nothing is going on,' he said. 'I don't understand what you mean by *what is going on?*'

'Why didn't you want me to see this?' I said. 'Why were you keeping it from me? What is going on that you don't want me to know about?'

He frowned.

I shook.

'How did you know to look behind the sideboard to find that writing? How long have you known Colin Connell? What's going on with Doctor Jones? And why didn't you want me to know about these missing girls?'

If there was a sudden shortage of "stupid" pills, I knew why. Neil had obviously taken the lot. His expression changed from perplexed to total confusion (stupidity).

I crossed my arms and waited for an answer. I had spoken in a language he was familiar with — it shouldn't have been too difficult.

CHAPTER FIFTY-FIVE

Neil closed his eyes and rested his head on the back of the sofa. I stepped from the last stair onto the living-room carpet. I was still ready to run back upstairs if I needed to.

With his eyes still shut, he slowly sat up straight and brought his hands onto his lap. He was moving so slowly, it was like watching him in slow motion. My pulse quickened.

He stood up, still in slow-motion, eyes still shut and turned in my direction, as though he was on a slow-moving turntable.

When he opened his eyes, my heart stopped. I put one foot back on the stairs and made ready to run. His eyes pierced into me. He looked as though he wanted to tear me to pieces. I had never seen his eyes so still. They burned with hatred.

I tried to stop my voice from trembling. Tried to keep it calm and even.

'Neil?' I said.

I steadied my leg on the stairs. Tensed the muscles so that I was primed. So that my leg would stop shaking.

Neil clenched his fists and sucked in the air. His face turned to a scowl and his mouth opened.

'What the fucking hell are you talking about?' he yelled.

I covered my ears with my hands. Spittle flew from his mouth as he shouted. His face turned a deep red. Each word was separate and distinct.

'For fuck sake, Christine. What the fuck are you going on about?'

I moved my other foot onto the first stair, backed away from him slightly.

He closed his eyes again, leaned forward and screamed, louder than anything I had ever heard coming from him.

The scream lasted until he ran out of breath. Then he turned away from me and kicked the sofa. He punched the cushions, over and over, swearing with every punch, then he threw them across the room.

None of them at me.

He launched himself against the sofa, tipping it onto its back. And he kicked the base of it, rupturing the material underneath. He dug his hands into the rupture and ripped it wide open. Tore at it like a maniac, pulling enormous strips of stringy material away from the sofa.

He screamed again.

'Fucking hell!'

He turned to me, and pointed.

But he said nothing, just held his hand out straight towards me for a few seconds.

And then lowered his arm and his head.

I saw the cloud move from him. The redness left his face and the rippling aggression dissipated. His shoulders hunched forward and his head sagged down even further. He looked about six inches shorter than he had just a few seconds earlier.

Neither of us spoke.

I sat down on the creaking third stair and Neil stood where he was, hunched and sagging.

I was aware of my heart pounding. Not too fast, but very strong. I didn't feel breathless, but I did feel as though I had just run for several days non-stop. All my limbs ached and tingled. I wanted to sleep. I wanted to be at my mum and dad's house, in my old bedroom, asleep.

'I don't get it, Chris.'

Neil had raised his head, but the rest of his body remained as it was. The burning hatred had gone from his eyes, leaving only despair in the ashes.

'I really don't,' he said.

I looked down at my feet and thought about what to say.

'I don't know what you were accusing me of,' he said. 'But

you really have got some issues.'

I looked over at him.

'You didn't want me to see this story,' I said. 'About the missing girls.'

He shook his head.

'Of course I didn't. You've been on a knife edge since you were attacked. And all the things that have happened since — the horrific dreams; the writing on our walls; your blackouts. All of that, has only made things worse for you.'

He walked over to the shattered sofa and pulled it back up the right way. He retrieved the nearest cushion, put it on the sofa and sat down.

'I knew,' he said, 'that if you heard about these missing girls, especially the fact that it's not a million miles from where we live, it would affect you. It's potentially just what you've been dreaming about. I didn't know how it would affect you, but I knew it would.'

He put a hand to his forehead and lowered his eyes.

'And what with your blackouts…'

He hesitated and looked away from me.

'… well, even you don't know where you've been going, what you've been doing during them.'

I stood up. The recognition of what he was saying slapped me across the face.

'Did you think I might have done something to them?' I said.

He shook his head, but had already taken one too many milliseconds to answer.

'Of course not,' he said. 'But who knows where you've been? And you obviously thought I had something to do with it.'

I didn't hear him. He had taken hold of my heart and crushed it between his hands. The room grew bigger. I was Alice, shrinking, having just sipped from the bottle labelled "drink me". If my own husband thought I was capable of taking these poor girls, what about my mum and dad? What about Abi and my friends? What about the school? And what about the police? Would they all suspect me?

Neil's voice broke through my thoughts.

'And I was obviously right,' he said.

'Right?'

'Not to tell you. You've completely gone off on one since you found out. I have no idea what you were going on about with Colin Connell and the doctor. I have known Colin Connell since you took me to see him. I have known the doctor ever since we both started going to see him.'

He stood up and gestured towards the sideboard.

'And as for knowing where to find the writing on the wall. How the fuck would I know it was there. I found it, that was all. I had no idea it was there until I found it.'

He threw his hands up in the air.

'For fuck sake, Christine. If we can't even trust each other, what the fuck can we do?'

I had been thinking the same thing.

I looked around at the cushions scattered on the floor. The ripped material from the base of the sofa.

Whatever it was that had burned inside Neil, he had taken it all out on the furniture. But the hatred in his eyes had been for me. Pure and direct. I shivered as I thought about what might have happened if the sofa hadn't been the closest thing to hand. If I had been standing next to him when he lost control.

'What's happening to us, Neil?' I said.

He raised his eyebrows and shrugged. This time his eyebrows spoke volumes. It was my fault.

All of the problems, all of the arguments and all of the pain. It was all my fault. Not Neil, not Michael or Rose, not even the bastard who attacked me in the first place.

It was all me. I was the one creating the pain. I was the one creating all the uncertainty and chaos.

I was the one with the mental illness creeping slowly through the cells of my brain.

'I didn't ask to be attacked,' I said. 'I didn't want any of this. And I can't help what my messed up mind is doing to me. I'm trying to fight it, but it keeps coming back with more. I don't know what else I can do.'

He shrugged again.

'And if you weren't working late all the time,' I said, 'maybe we could do more together.'

He looked away from me. Looked down at the floor.

'I've still got to work, Chris,' he said. 'Life still goes on you know. We can't stop everything.'

'I still might get the Deputy Head job,' I said. 'That comes with more money.'

He looked up at me again. I could see in his eyes that he didn't think there was a chance in hell of me getting that job.

'It's not just about the money,' he said. 'It's about keeping things together too. It's about keeping our —,' he stopped for a moment, searched for the right word, then continued anyway. 'It's about keeping our sanity. For your sake, for mine and for Michael and Rose. Living life helps to do that. Even a boring, bank life. While all this other shit is going on, work helps to normalise things. Keeps an anchor in the real world.

'I know you didn't ask for any of this, Chris. None of us did. But it's happening, and mostly it's happening to you. The kids can't help you, and although I want to do everything I can, I'm not sure what I can do — other than keep our life going. So somehow we have to keep a hold of real life. That's what I'm trying to do. Trying to hold onto it for the both of us.'

I walked over to the sideboard and ran a finger along the top of it. I didn't look back at Neil.

'So you didn't tell me about the girls because you thought I had done it — during a blackout.'

'Chris, I didn't tell you because I didn't want you to get upset about it. I have no idea what's happening inside your head at the moment. But it's not right and it's not normal. I want to keep as much stress away from you as possible.'

'I thought you had done it,' I said. 'With Colin Connell and Doctor Jones.'

'They may have done,' he said. 'But I work in a fucking bank.'

I turned to look at him. He looked directly at me.

'What are we going to do?' I said.

'I don't know, Chris. But I think Michael and Rose should come home, and I think you need to get some more help as soon as possible.'

CHAPTER FIFTY-SIX

Far from the air being cleared after our bust up, a fog of unresolved problems drifted between us.

I still couldn't believe that Neil had thought I had something to do with the missing girls — even though the same thought had come to me earlier. And he couldn't believe that I had suspected him of being involved.

Seeing as I was the one that was potentially going insane, I thought that his suspicion of me was the greater of the two crimes. I was entitled to see things skewed.

As a result, I slept in the bed, and he slept on the damaged sofa.

I made sure I had his sawn-off broom handle by my side of the bed.

It was nearly 2am when I heard footsteps coming up the stairs.

I reached out from under the duvet and felt the smooth wood of the broom handle.

He tapped at the door.

'Are you awake?' he said. 'Chris?'

I thought it unlikely he had come to kill me. I pulled my hand back under the duvet. But made a mental note of the angle I needed to shoot it out if it came to it.

We talked for just over two hours. Then Neil went back downstairs to the sofa and I stayed under the duvet.

In all the years we had been together, we had never had a "trial separation", and I wasn't about to start one now. But we both agreed that it might be good for me to get away for a bit. Good for us both.

But I really needed to be at home. I needed the Internet and I needed to try to maintain at least a tenuous grip on normality.

Neil had the bank. I had the home. School didn't seem like much of an option at the moment. And the silence from Margaret about the Deputy Head position was screaming volumes at me.

So I agreed to spend the nights with my mum and dad, and the days at home, probably with Abi.

I was starting to wonder how much our friendship could take. Not only was she looking after my children morning and night, but she was becoming my permanent unpaid minder during the day. She still insisted she was happy.

The morning after our argument, then early morning talk, Neil went off to work as normal. I showered, wandered through a living-room that Neil had obviously tidied after our chat, ate breakfast and debated whether I should ring Abi or not.

I didn't need to debate for long. The phone rang.

'Hello Mrs Marsden.'

It was Doctor Jones. Killer, or carer?

'Are you free to come and see me this morning?' he said. 'We have the results of your MRI scan back and I would like to go through it with you.'

'Is everything OK?' I said. 'Is everything still normal?'

He hesitated. Perhaps it was my use of the word "normal".'

'We aren't really able to discuss things over the telephone,' he said. 'And it's much easier to point things out to you as we speak. Can you get to see me as soon as is convenient?'

My stomach turned over.

'I can probably be there in about half an hour,' I said.

'That's fine. If you just go to reception when you arrive and they'll let me know you're here. I'll see you straight away, or if I'm with a patient you'll be my next one.'

My heart started pounding as I hung up from the doctor. A sensation trickled across my skin. Would I be walking into the surgery of a lunatic? A man who had joined forces with Colin

Connell, and possibly Neil, to abduct and kill young girls?

I wasn't a young girl. But surely I knew too much. What if Neil had contacted the doctor and let him know about my accusations the night before?

Neil didn't have to kill me to keep me quiet. He only had to let the doctor know, and he would prescribe something. Something to numb my ability for coherent speech or thought. Or something to keep me quiet for ever.

How did I know Neil had gone to the bank that morning? He may have gone straight to see Doctor Jones, or Colin Connell.

And what if I hadn't answered Neil when he'd tapped on the bedroom door in the middle of the night? Would he have assumed I was sleeping and done something to shut me up then?

Of course not. It would be too obvious. There were three of them to sort out any problem. That was why the doctor wanted to see me now.

The phone rang again. I looked at it. The caller number looked familiar, but my mind was spinning out with all the questions rushing through it. I couldn't place the number.

Was it the attacker? Had he got my number? Perhaps he was someone I knew. Someone like Neil.

I grabbed the phone.

'Hello?'

'Christine? Is that you?'

It was a woman. I knew the voice, but the face was still unclear.

'Hello,' I said again.

'Christine, it's Margaret. How are you feeling?'

I felt as though thousands of eyes were watching me. Like I was on a stage in front of thousands of people. All up in the cheap seats and all looking down on me. Their staring eyes pushing me into the ground.

'I'm OK,' I said. 'How are you?'

'I left a message for you on your mobile a while ago,' she said. 'I never heard back from you. I was just thinking that you and I haven't had a coffee together for a while. It would be useful to catch up with how you're doing. Let you know about things here. Perhaps I could come round and see you? I have a free morning today.'

How did she sound? Was she happy? I couldn't tell. If she had good news for me I would pick it up in her voice. But Margaret never gave anything away in her voice.

'I'm just on my way out to the doctor,' I said. 'I'm not sure how long I'll be there. Maybe another day would be better?'

'Today would be best for me, dear,' she said. 'I'll pop around at about 11 o'clock if that's alright. That should give you plenty of time for the doctor. I don't mind waiting if I have to.'

As someone who was battling to stay in control, the two phone calls telling me I had to go there, and I had to be here definitely knocked me back a bit.

I decided that the doctor wouldn't kill me in his surgery, and that I didn't have to take any medicines he gave me if I didn't want to. If he did prescribe something, I would look it up on the Internet as soon as I got home. If he tried to inject me with anything, I would refuse. I could always just walk out. I couldn't see him chasing me through the waiting-room brandishing a syringe, even if he was a cold-blooded killer.

In the taxi on the way to the health centre I talked to myself. Not out loud, of course, but quietly, in my mind.

Doctor Jones' surgery smelled different than the last time I was there. Not so much of sick bodies. More of chemicals. Cleaning chemicals. The blind across the small window was drawn shut. Natural light seemed desperate to get in, but the good doctor was determined it wouldn't. As I moved over to the seat in front of his desk I scanned the room for syringes. I sat down and pushed the seat slightly further away from the desk. Slightly further away from the doctor, and slightly nearer the door.

Having not located any syringes, I now found myself looking for evidence of phrenology.

And I wanted to open the small window.

Doctor Jones sat back from the desk. He flicked through some pages in a buff coloured folder.

'How are you getting on, Mrs Marsden?' he said. 'Any more blackouts or visions?'

I told him I'd had a blackout while staying with my parents. I forgot to mention the aggression I had shown towards them.

'And did you manage to speak to your parents about any mental illness in the family?'

I explained the whole adoption thing, and that I was in the process of trying to find my birth parents. I tried to sound nonchalant about it all. As though it wasn't suddenly the most desperate thing in my world.

He put the open folder down on his desk and moved his chair forward. He clasped his hands together and looked at me. He lowered his head so that he was peering at me over the top of his glasses. I could see the white pages from the folder reflected in the lenses.

'I wish you the very best of luck in finding them,' he said.

'Thank you,' I said. 'You mentioned you had the results back from my scan?'

He sat upright and pulled out a single page from the folder.

'Our brains are split into regions,' he said. 'Sections that deal with different things. Things like sight or hearing, or memory and recognition.'

I nodded.

'Your results are inconclusive,' he said.

He looked at the sheet in his hands and shook his head.

'Swelling of the brain is quite normal in these sorts of

situations. Trauma to the head, front and back. Quite expected. Over time, the swelling goes down. That's why it's useful to have ongoing monitoring of the situation. Your initial scan may show up the swelling, and any major internal bleeding, but often we see more as the swelling goes down. Hence the additional scans.'

He looked behind him at the blinds across the window. Then looked up at me.

I shivered.

'I would have expected your swelling to have gone down more by now. It doesn't mean that there's a problem, only that it's taking longer than some.'

I crossed my legs.

'Why would it do that?' I said.

He shrugged.

'Every case is different. Our bodies are different. And we all react differently to different things.'

'Of course,' I said.

'The report from your latest scan suggests that there may be something in your Frontal lobe and your Temporal lobe. Although, as I say, this is not conclusive. As the swelling goes down it may turn out to be nothing at all.'

Tiny pulses started up in my head as though highlighting the areas he was speaking about. I reached for the scar on my forehead and ran my hand gently from that one, to the one on the back of my head, now just a slight ridge under my hair.

'I don't know what the Frontal and Temporal lobes do,' I said. 'Does it have any effect on me?'

He tipped his head on one side, stretching his neck, then straightened it again.

'The Frontal lobe has many associations,' he said. 'Damage to that area can affect personality. Also motor skills. It can send mixed messages to your muscles and limbs and often comes out in violent or aggressive behaviour. Sometimes it can cause inappropriate behaviour, like rudeness or swearing. It can make it more difficult for the sufferer to plan or organise things.'

He looked into my eyes. I organised them not to react.

'And the other one?' I said.

'Temporal lobe damage can result in memory issues, a lack of recognition of every day things and can affect perception — hearing, vision or smell.'

He put the sheet of paper back onto the other pages in the file.

'It is also most closely aligned to schizophrenia.'

I shook my head.

'What does that mean?' I said.

'Schizophrenia describes a breakdown in the relation between thought, emotion and behaviour. Sufferers slowly withdraw from reality into a fantasy world, often terrifying and delusional. They may hear voices and see people that aren't part of reality. Or they may think that there is a conspiracy against them from other sources. They feel as though their perception is failing them, along with their mind.'

I realised I was rubbing the back and side of my neck. My hand came away damp. My chest barely moved from the shallow breathing. If the doctor pulled a syringe on me now — I was screwed.

He smiled.

'But that's only a possibility,' he said. 'We can't really see from this report whether there is damage to those areas or not.'

I forced myself to take deeper breaths.

He sat back in his chair and pushed it away from the desk. He reached over to another folder on the side-desk that held his keyboard and monitor.

'The thing is,' he said, opening the folder, 'I have been speaking at length with colleagues.'

He gave the impression of scrutinising the contents of the

folder. I knew he was just avoiding eye contact with me.

'And this really isn't something we rush into. The general consensus was one of "better to be safe than sorry".'

I gripped the underside of my seat. I saw it all now. The whole reason for getting me in there as soon as possible wasn't to go through my scan report, which in reality showed nothing. My brain was still too swollen — the doctor said so himself. The real reason was in the folder he held in his trembling hand. That was the syringe.

'We have agreed that you should undergo a psychiatric assessment.'

CHAPTER FIFTY-SEVEN

As I walked away from the health centre I almost got hit by a car. I hadn't seen it reversing. It's tyres screeched as it stopped, despite the slow speed it was moving. The driver gestured at me. He mouthed something.

I was finding it difficult to focus on the pavement as I walked. It was as though every other pedestrian was making a beeline for me. I found myself swerving out of the way of someone every few steps.

I had no idea where to go with this. I didn't know what my next move should be.

I felt like running. As far away as possible. But I didn't know where to run.

Doctor Jones estimated that my assessment would take place in approximately three weeks. Possibly sooner. He could try to chase it up if I preferred. Try to hurry it along.

I had to try to delay it.

I felt as though I was missing something. Some piece of hidden information that would enable me to escape from the pressure bearing down on me.

If I had a psychiatric assessment I would lose Michael and Rose, I was convinced of that.

Instantly a vision came to me. A home, a desolate cottage. Windswept and alone. We could all go there. Me and Neil and the kids. On an island somewhere. I had seen them on the telly. I knew they existed.

Somewhere we wouldn't be found. None of us.

I walked past a travel agents. Pictures of cruise ships and mountains filled the window.

I put my hand on the door handle to go in, but stopped myself.

What would I do if I was alone with the kids? What would I do to Neil? What on earth would I do to my own daughter? My beautiful Rose.

The vision of the desolate cottage for four became a wretched, self-imposed prison for one. What else was there for me to do? I had to protect the children. I couldn't let them be taken from me for being unstable.

But they would put me away, surely. Perhaps I had been wrong all along. They would take me away, not the children. They could stay at home. They could stay with Neil. With Neil and who else?

Then a peep of the "something" I thought I was missing showed itself. Something about the scans. Why had he been so dismissive of them? He wanted me to have an assessment. If the scans proved that there was some damage to my Frontal and Temporal lobes, I wouldn't need the assessment. My actions and dysfunction could be caused by the damage to my brain sustained during the attack.

I needed to see the scan results. I wanted another doctor to look at them. Or I could take them to the hospital and ask them to be explained to me there. I turned back to the health centre.

My heart pounded as the adrenalin pumped its way through my body. At once I could see a different future. One where I wasn't insane, just damaged by the attack. Why had the doctor been so desperate to have me assessed? Would they lock me up, just on his say so?

I strode through the waiting-room and made my way round to Doctor Jones' room. I pushed straight in.

An elderly woman looked up at me, then back to the doctor. Doctor Jones blushed and stood up.

'Mrs Marsden,' he said. 'Would you mind waiting outside please. I'm with another patient.'

'I need those scan pictures,' I said. 'I'd like to take them away with me please.'

The doctor apologised to the lady sat opposite him. He walked towards me and ushered me out of his room. We stood together in the corridor.

'Mrs Marsden,' he said. 'There are no pictures of your scan here. The pictures that were taken from your scan are assessed at the hospital by a physician specifically trained to interpret MRI scans. They then write their report based on what they see. The report is what is sent through to your GP.'

I realised how dry my throat was.

'I'd be happy to give you a copy of the report.'

I nodded.

'If you'd be kind enough to wait in the waiting-room, I'll photocopy it and bring it out to you after I've finished with my current patient.'

'Sorry,' I said.

He patted my arm and opened the door of his room. The old lady looked up at us both.

I read the report while sitting in the waiting-room. It told me nothing new. It was exactly as Doctor Jones had read it. It even used the word "inconclusive". I wondered how long it would take for the swelling to go down sufficiently for the scans to show things more clearly. I stopped myself from barging into his room again. Instead I asked at reception for a pen and some paper. I wrote a note to Doctor Jones requesting that I be sent along for another MRI scan before going for the psychiatric assessment. I signed the letter then handed the pen over to the receptionist. I took the note along the corridor to the doctor's room. I hovered around just outside the door. I could hear voices inside. I didn't want to piss him off by charging in there again, so I slipped the note under the door and left.

As I walked to the taxi rank I could see the pavement more clearly. People weren't walking into me, and I wasn't having to swerve. I didn't look in the travel agent's window as I strode past.

The taxi dropped me outside my house at 10:45. I could see Margaret waiting at the front door.

I paid the taxi driver and walked towards her. She tried to pull off a smile, but it didn't work out. She held her arms out to me as I drew nearer.

'Christine, how are you? You look wonderful.'

I tried a smile too, but obviously it just wasn't our day.

'You too,' I said. 'It's lovely to see you.'

She bustled inside as soon as the door was open. It was as though it was her house and I was her guest. I half expected her to offer me a coffee.

'Coffee?' I said.

She nodded. 'Please.'

She followed me to the kitchen. Although she gave the impression of concentrating on me, her eyes studied every area of the rooms we were in. She looked as though she was looking for something she had previously lost, but was embarrassed to be seen looking for it. She needn't have been embarrassed on my behalf. I had no idea what she was looking for. Perhaps she was wondering what the inside of a house looked like when it was inhabited by a woman who was slowly drifting further and further away from the shores of sanity.

I wanted to snap her out of it.

'Biscuit?' I said.

She stopped looking.

'Ooh yes please,' she said.

I realised as soon as I had said the word that I had no biscuits.

I poured two mugs of coffee and walked to the dining-room. Margaret followed. Neither of us mentioned the lack of biscuits.

'So really, Christine — how are you? You were just at the doctor?'

'I think I'll be ready to come back soon,' I said. 'Really soon.'

I couldn't make eye contact with her as I spoke. I hoped she wouldn't read the lies.

'That would be wonderful,' she said. 'It really would. How's Michael? He seems much happier.'

I rubbed my thumb and forefinger across my eyebrows.

'He's great. Really good.'

'I understand he and Rose are staying at Abigail's at the moment.'

I tried a dismissive throw of my head.

'They're just having a little fun holiday really. They love being with Abi's children.'

Margaret moved her coffee cup and leaned forward. I knew what was coming.

'Christine,' she said.

'I'll be back really soon,' I said. I sounded so desperate. 'I'm almost better, and I can't wait to be in school again. Back with the kids. I'm really missing them. There will be so much to catch up on. So much I must have missed. It's funny, isn't it, when you aren't there for a while you feel almost nervous to come back again. But I can't wait. I'm not nervous at all. It'll be ever so soon.'

Margaret sat quietly during my rant, allowing it all out.

'The governors have been in a very difficult situation,' she said. 'We were all desperate for you to come back as soon as possible. But only when you were better.'

'I am better,' I said.

Margaret held up a hand.

'It's been over two months now. And you know as well as

anyone how much happens in a school in two months. In two days even. It was simply becoming harder and harder to justify delaying making an appointment. The school needs a Deputy Head. Needed.'

I lowered my head to my hand and closed my eyes. I felt drained of energy, utterly exhausted.

'As you know, it was me that recommended you to the position in the first place. And I know that it was I who convinced you to go for it. I blame myself, really. I know that once you made your mind up try, you really wanted the job. I had talked you into it.

'It's just that Matthew has been there. Every day he's been there. He has been in on meetings, volunteered for clubs and after-school work. He has answered all of the governors' questions and more. His credentials, Christine, are not that different from yours. OK, he's not quite as experienced, and he lacks some of your qualities. I think we all know that if things had been different the governors would probably have been able to come to a different conclusion.'

I wiped the tears off my cheeks.

'Matthew is a good choice,' I said. 'He'll do a good job.'

Margaret reached across the table and held my hand.

'I'm so sorry, Christine,' she said. 'Truly I am.'

I smiled. A genuine one. Stroked her hand.

'It's for the best,' I said. 'It's probably the right decision for everyone really. Me too.'

Margaret patted my hand and squeezed it.

'Sorry about the biscuits,' I said.

We both laughed.

I stood up from the table and walked into the living-room to grab a box of tissues. As I moved, the phone rang. I wiped my nose on my sleeve and diverted to the kitchen to get the phone.

'Hello?' I said.

'Is that Christine Marsden?'

I didn't recognise the woman's voice.

'Yes,' I said.

'Mrs Marsden, my name is Mary Brookes. I am one of the Adoption Advisers at the district council offices. I am ringing to make an appointment for you to come in to see me. We think we have found your adoption file.'

CHAPTER FIFTY-EIGHT

I could hardly breathe as I showed Margaret to the door.

Before I learnt that Matthew had been given the position of Deputy Head, I had been so busy trying to reassure her that I was fit enough to come back to school that I hadn't told her anything about the adoption.

I didn't see any reason to change that after I finished talking to Mary Brookes.

'You think you have my file?' I had asked her.

'Normally we wait until the birth certificate and adoption certificate come through first, but because you knew both parent's names, this does seem like the correct one.'

'I can be there just as soon as I get a taxi,' I said. 'My car's off the road at the moment, it's waiting for work to be done on it.'

'Oh I'm afraid there's normally a two or three week wait for appointments,' she said. 'I was going to check your availability on that kind of time-frame.'

'I may not be here in two or three weeks time,' I said. I didn't want to tell her about the psychiatric assessment in case it made things more difficult for me. 'Is there any way I could be seen sooner?'

She asked me to hold on for a minute. When she came back to the phone she was slightly breathless.

'Could you come in tomorrow morning at 9am?' she said.

That was when my breathlessness started.

After Margaret had gone I decided to have a midday shower. I needed to think.

I stood with my back to the shower and tipped my head back. The warm water caressed its way down my scalp, sending delightful shivers over my shoulders and back. The water wrapped a blanket of warmth around me, soothing away the stress.

The embarrassment of not getting the job I had wanted still rumbled around inside me. I wasn't sure Matthew would be up to the job at all. He would no doubt muddle his way through, calling on everyone else to do things for him, then taking the credit when they were done. No doubt his number one priority would be sycophancy directed towards Margaret. That was one of the few things he was the ideal candidate for.

I felt for Margaret. It must have been difficult coming round to tell me. It was decent of her to do it face to face rather than over the phone.

Beneath the rumbling embarrassment lurked a much darker concern. I had only two or three weeks before I was to be examined for signs of mental instability. How did one make it through a psychiatric assessment unscathed? I had to find my birth parents as soon as possible.

And that brought me to Mary Brookes. From her voice, I pictured her to be in her early sixties, white hair and soft features. I had immediately felt comforted when she spoke. Reassured that I was in safe hands. Although it was the first time we had ever spoken she made me feel as though I was a cared-about friend.

And I realised that bubbling up, through the darkness and embarrassment, were feelings of excitement and joy. Like a new chapter of my life was opening. I hoped I didn't fuck it up by attacking her during our meeting.

I signed in at the district council offices reception a little before 8:45am. I was early. I had Neil drop me into town on his way to work. Despite our agreement that I would spend the nights at my mum and dad's, I had spent the night in my own home. My husband lay beside me in bed, but the gap between us was enormous.

I wished him a good day at the office, and as I slammed the car door shut he wished me a good day doing whatever I was doing.

I hadn't told him about the adoption file. I wasn't sure who he was at the moment. Wasn't sure who I was either. Something made me want to hold back from him. Not just physically, but mentally and emotionally too.

I still loved him. And there was something in his eyes when he looked at me. We had a lot. But I had made the decision to close down a little. He didn't need to know everything I was doing. Just as I was damn sure I didn't know everything he was doing.

The digital clock on the wall flicked over to 9:00 as a woman with blond hair and red framed glasses walked up the corridor towards the waiting area. Although there were at least six other people seated around me, she looked directly at me, and as she drew near enough, spoke my name.

'Mrs Marsden?'

She wore a green knitted cardigan and a brown scarf. I guessed her age to be about 45 years old. She carried a clipboard and a pale-green folder.

I stood up and smiled. She held out her hand.

'I'm Mary Brookes,' she said.

I shook her hand.

'We'll go through to meeting-room six.'

She didn't move immediately, and I wondered if I was supposed to know where meeting-room six was. Did she want me to lead the way?

But she turned and started off down the corridor she had just appeared from. I followed her, trying to look intelligent enough to find a room on my own if I really had to.

Meeting-room six had a hand-written "Do Not Disturb" notice on an A4 sheet of paper. Someone had drawn a smiley-face which actually looked quite sinister. I thought it might have been a warning of the consequences for ignoring the notice.

Mary pushed the door open and walked straight in.

The meeting-room was empty save for a wooden table and several chairs surrounding it. It was very clean. The blinds across the windows were open just enough to see daylight, but not enough to see the outside surroundings. The carpet tiles smelled new. The fibres scrunched underfoot. I wondered if Mary could smell them.

Mary offered me the chair at one end of the table, and she sat in one near me against the longer edge. It was a good position for eye contact and speaking, but not so good for me trying to look over at what was in her pale-green folder. It was almost as though she had planned it that way.

Although I had been completely wrong about her age and look, based upon our phone conversation, when she spoke to me a warmth started in my legs and moved with the current of the blood flowing through my body. Without realising it, she had instantly comforted me and turned my hidden pressure valve to open. Maybe she did realise.

She looked into my eyes. She was trying to read them. Or read me through them.

'Thank you so much for coming in,' she said. 'May I call you Christine?'

I nodded.

'This can be quite an emotionally charged time for those who were adopted. Seeing their file for the first time. Have you always known you were adopted?'

I shook my head.

'I only found out recently,' I said. 'It was a bit of a shock.'

She nodded slowly. I thought I saw her grip on the folder tighten.

'And how have you been, since finding out?' she said.

'OK, really. I was very upset at first, with my parents, you know, the ones who adopted me. But we're really good now. They had wanted to tell me right from the word go. But they were advised not to.'

Mary frowned. She sat back in her seat. She looked a little uncomfortable.

'By a relative?'

'By an adoption worker,' I said. 'A social worker or something. They said that normally it's up to the new parents whether they tell the child or not, but in my case they advised that I shouldn't be told.'

Mary shook her head. It looked like a little shiver.

'That's very unusual,' she said. 'Do you know the reason for that?'

'My mum and dad weren't given a reason. They were just told that it might be for the best. And as they didn't want to cause any problems, either for me or for the adoption, they did as they were advised.'

Mary held the folder upright in her hands. She touched the tip of her nose against the end of it. She lay the folder on the table and opened it. The flap on the folder prevented me from seeing the contents.

'There isn't very much in here I'm afraid. Were you expecting much?'

'To be honest, this is so new to me, I wasn't really sure what to expect. I thought that maybe there might be a letter from my birth parents for me, maybe something explaining why they put me up for adoption. I don't know if that sort of thing is normally in there?'

'Back when you were adopted,' she said. 'Your birth parents would have been told that there would never be any contact with you in the future. They knew they were giving you up for good. They wouldn't have been allowed to put in a letter for you. They would also have been told that there was no way that you would ever be able to trace them. It would be a new life for all concerned.'

I swallowed hard and tried to keep the tears at bay.

Mary noticed my efforts.

'Can I ask how your life has been?' she said. 'What are your parents like?'

Between sobs I managed to tell her how wonderful my childhood was and how loving and caring my mum and dad were.

'Obviously I have no idea what my life would have been like,' I said. 'But I have had a wonderful life.'

'That's lovely,' she said.

She meant it.

'And do you have any thoughts about the future?' she said.

'What do you mean?'

'About what you want to do with this new found information. Many adopted children want to try to find their birth parents, for example, although that's not always the best thing necessarily. Or they might want to find siblings if there are any.'

Brothers and sisters? That hadn't even entered my mind before now. Being an only child, I had assumed that that was how it was with my birth parents too.

'Don't brothers and sisters get adopted together?' I said.

'Sometimes. But often there is a large time gap between children. It's not always possible to home siblings with each other. And it's not uncommon, of course, for the same birth mother to have a different father for her other children.'

I was starting to build a picture in my mind. Of a desperate mother, mentally unstable, not able to keep her children or her partners. Endless children taken away from her, all with different fathers. Until eventually she was taken into care herself. Never allowed to have anymore children. Or partners.

'But of course, your parents were married,' Mary said. 'How much do you know about them?'

I shook my head.

'Nothing,' I said. 'My mother, I mean the mother that brought me up, thought she saw a sheet of paper with my birth parents' names on it. That's all I know. That and the fact that they were asked not to tell me about the adoption. I have been on the Internet looking up the names. But it's very difficult to pinpoint who is who. There are so many people with the same name.'

Mary patted something in the folder. Presumably a sheet of paper.

'The Internet can be so useful,' she said. 'But in cases of adoption, it can cause immense heartache. It's so easy to trace people, with just a few clicks. And then people go rushing in, arranging to meet up, or even just turning up unannounced. We would strongly urge you to come through us if you feel you want to take things further. We can make things easier for you and your birth parents. You must remember that they thought there was never any way you could find out who they were, let alone meet them. It could be very unsettling for them.'

I wanted to say *"Well they were the ones who gave me up. I'm the one who has been wronged. What about my feelings? I'm the one that matters here"*.

'Of course,' I said. 'I would never want to cause any difficulties for anyone.'

Mary smiled.

'Shall we begin?' she said.

CHAPTER FIFTY-NINE

Mary took a clear-plastic A4 envelope from the green folder. She pushed the folder to one side and took the first of several sheets of paper from the envelope.

A sudden prickle of panic came over me as I realised I hadn't brought a pen or paper.

'Will I need to take notes?' I said.

'These are all copies,' she said. 'You will be able to take them away with you when we are finished.'

I clasped my hands together on the table in front of me. Crossed my legs. Held my breath.

'There's not a great deal here,' she said. 'But we'll go through it anyway.'

She read out the first sheet, without letting me see what was written on it. Even when she had finished she didn't pass it over to me.

My birth mother was called Amelie. She was French. My father was Richard. He was English.

I sat in silence as she read. Tried to take it all in. Mentally record every snippet of information. I tried, simultaneously, to analyse it for signs of mental illness in my parents.

I weighed 7lbs 7oz when I was born. Blood tests taken on mother and child came back with negative results. There was no explanation of what they were negative for. And the sheet confirmed that my mother had a signed receipt for the Government Memorandum headed "Adoption of Children".

The officer that had written the report concluded that my mother had come across as a desperately sad woman. Only wanting the best for her child, Christine Lapton. Me. She was quiet and withdrawn, but with a genuine determination to make sure her daughter would be looked after.

There were possible issues with my father, Richard Lapton. He was a dentist with his own practice near Cawsand in Cornwall. He was not entirely in favour of the adoption. He had hinted that there were concerns with his wife's drinking. Although she was clear thinking in regard to the adoption, she did appear quite an awkward person, sometimes a little chaotic.

I was well looked after by her and up until the time of the review I was healthy and growing as expected.

Mary put the report face down on the table in front of her and pulled the next sheet of paper from the plastic envelope. I put my hands to my mouth and tried to look through a gap in the blind. Tried to take my mind off how I was feeling.

I didn't have to read between the lines to see that there was a problem with my mother. Awkward and chaotic, withdrawn, drinking. Desperately sad. I knew how she felt. I wondered if that was just the start of her problems, whether her symptoms became steadily worse. What would mine do? I had already been through the drinking stage. And withdrawn, chaotic and awkward seemed to be a part of my everyday life at that moment.

I wondered how my father had felt. Watching his wife disintegrate and seeing his child taken away for adoption. What did it do to him?

The second sheet of paper was headed up "Adoption Act 1958" and consisted of three statements. One from my current mum and dad, one about me, and one about my birth parents.

The statement from my birth parents showed their consent to the adoption, knowing that it was in my best interests to have different parents.

The statement about the mum and dad I grew up with talked about their intention to formally adopt me. And that during visits to their home by an officer of the Authority, I had appeared happy and well cared for, and to be making good progress.

The statement about me indicated that the child — Christine Lapton, was to be known as Christine Cooper. I was aged eight months and had a satisfactory medical certificate. I had been placed with the applicants (Mr & Mrs Cooper) and had been in their continuous care and possession since then.

I was shocked that everything seemed to have been summed up in such a short space. A new life in just three short paragraphs.

The next few sheets in the envelope were forms and court records. All the legal stuff. Most of it signed and written by officials.

And the last three sheets were headed "Guardian Ad Litem Enquiry — Adoption Act, 1958".

Three pages of questions and hand-written answers taken during an interview with my birth mother — Amelie Lapton.

It listed her nationality as French and her employment as a librarian. It gave details of her child, and her husband.

It gave her address as 18, Bay View Road, Cawsand, Cornwall.

One of the questions asked if she had freely consented to the adoption. She replied that she had. On what grounds? *Unable to provide a home for infant.*

Questions about her health followed. Normally healthy? *Yes.* Any history of serious illness or mental or physical disease in herself or family? *No.* Does the mother believe the child is normally healthy, physically and mentally? *Yes.*

Religion of mother? *Catholic.*

A section at the bottom of the last page was headed Remarks/Comments. It was blank.

Underneath that, the final paragraph explained the nature and permanent effect of an adoption order and that in giving her consent she fully understood that it would be irrevocable, and would permanently deprive her of her parental rights.

My birth mother's spider-thin signature called out to me from just below that paragraph.

Looking at it on a sheet of paper, it wasn't possible to see the pain or emotion involved. It looked cold and calculated. Simple and quick. It looked like a relief for everyone. Glad to be shot of the child. Not my responsibility anymore. Now I can get on with my life — without that burden.

I tried to put myself in her shoes, but I couldn't.

Would I eventually end up there anyway? Would the madness that forced her to give up her child, force me to give up mine? I wondered whether she had already experienced blackouts, or feelings of wanting to hurt people. Desperate times called for desperate measures, I knew that. But giving up your child?

Mary put all the sheets of paper back into the clear envelope and handed it to me.

'Do you know what you want to do now?' she said.

My mouth felt so dry I thought I might not be able to speak.

'I need to find them,' I said. 'It's quite urgent. I only have a few weeks at the most.'

Mary's expression turned to one of shock. I hadn't meant it to come across like it did.

'I mean, I was attacked a few months ago. I sustained fairly serious head injuries. And since then, I've been experiencing dreams and visions, blacking out often.

'The doctors have said that I now need to have a psychiatric assessment. And it's going to happen in the next few weeks. So obviously I have to find them before then. I have to find out if there is anything in the family, any history of mental illness.'

Mary pointed to the envelope now grasped firmly in my hand.

'There was a question about mental health,' she said. 'And the answer came back clear.'

I nodded. 'I know. But is it possible that she was trying to hide it? Or maybe she thought it was going to come on later? And there's nothing about my father.'

'It appears that he was in good health too,' Mary said. 'Judging by what we do know about him. A successful business. Presumably well respected in the area. His main concern seemed to be regarding your mother.'

'So that's why I need to find them. If I was taken into adoption because she was going insane, I need to know about it. All the evidence of chaos and confusion and desperation they talk about in here are exactly the feelings I have been experiencing. I don't want to lose my children. I don't want them taken away from me. So I need to find out for sure exactly what was wrong with my mother so that I can be prepared for whatever happens to me. I want to make sure my children are safe. But not by placing them up for adoption.'

Mary leaned forward, glanced in the direction of the window.

'Can you help me to find them?' I said.

She drummed her fingers on the table and pulled the now empty green folder towards her.

'There are certainly some things we can do to help. For instance, I can check to see if your birth mother and father are still alive. I can see if any death certificate has been registered with a GP anywhere. It doesn't always turn something up, but it might. At least that way you'll know if it's worth pursuing.'

'What if there are other children, or relatives? They might know if there is anything in the family. Would they be over in France?'

Mary shook her head.

'I'm sorry, Christine. I've no way of knowing where any relatives might be. There are a couple of adoption registers that you can go on. They may already have your parents on there. Since the law changed a good many birth parents and relatives have signed onto the registers in the hope that their children might start searching for them. It's a good place to start. There is a charge to go on them, but it's only a one off payment for administration. Once you're on, you're on for good. No more fees.'

'Or I could just find them on the Internet,' I said. 'Now that I know where they were and their dates of birth.'

'Even if you did, we would strongly urge you to come through us. We are used to this sort of thing. We can write an initial letter. It wouldn't mention your name in case the person who opened the letter knew nothing about the adoption, but from the way we worded it, if either of your birth parents were to read it, they would know it was about you. Very often we say we're trying to find relatives of a person born on such and such a date — and then give your date of birth.

'If your birth parents are no longer together, or are with other partners now, they may not have told their new partner about their past, about the adoption. So this is a very discreet and safe way of letting them know that you are looking for them. They can then respond to our letter accordingly.'

What she was saying made sense. I knew that. But time wasn't on my side. I could see "signing onto registers" taking time. I could see "writing discreet letters so as not to cause anyone any embarrassment" taking time.

I could see "me going on the Internet and checking names, addresses and dates" taking less time. And I wouldn't have to pay for the privilege. I could also see that Mary was very anxious that I wouldn't fuck this up. She had already made it clear that she would check with GP surgeries, which was great. But that seemed to be about the limit of any help she could offer at that moment. They were obviously better at things once the birth parents were found, and a meeting needed to be sorted out. I didn't want to upset her.

'I agree,' I said. 'I think that the letter idea is a great one.'

She smiled, stopped drumming her fingers on the table.

'I'm not that Internet savvy anyway,' I said. 'But I will go on those registers. They sound like a sensible first move.'

She nodded.

'It is the best way,' she said. 'And then if you come up with a result you can come back to me and I'll arrange to write a letter of approach.'

As I walked away from the offices after meeting with Mary Brookes my heart started pounding. Everything around me — the traffic; building work; shouting — it all grew louder. Deafening almost. The voices of passers-by rushed in and out of my consciousness. I started running. I gripped the plastic envelope which contained my hidden history. I realised I was humming in time with my steps. Still running, my breath getting quicker. I wanted to leap into the air. To bound along the pavement like a gazelle. I was filled with a lightness. An enormous smile spread across my face. My humming turned to singing. Out of the corner of my eye I could see concerned looks from other people. It made me laugh. I felt fantastic.

And tears streamed down my face, and fell to the concrete beneath my feet.

CHAPTER SIXTY

I ran as far as the train station. I had either made, or disturbed, plenty of people's day on the way. I leaned against the station wall to get my breath back. I still laughed and sobbed, but only from my mouth. The tears had dried up as I ran.

I made myself take deeper, slower breaths. Calmed my heart and pulse. I had bent some of the pages in the envelope where I had been gripping it so hard.

Three taxis waited outside the station. I took the first one.

I was still breathless inside the cab. My head throbbed from the exertion of running so far. But also from the exhilaration. I had felt free as I ran. Oblivious to stares and funny looks. I hadn't cared what people had thought as I'd skipped past them.

I now felt that I had everything I needed to move forward. Names and dates, places and jobs.

It felt like the time I had gone fishing with Dad and we both knew, even before we got to the lake, that we would catch something. That we would have a great day. It turned out to be our best day ever at the lake.

The Internet was a vast lake. But I knew which fish I was looking for, and I knew where they were. Or at least where they used to be.

I sat up straight in the back of the cab. Stared out at the world. Looked at it full on. Face to face. I pulled my shoulders back, tensed the muscles in my face and neck. My jaw felt firm. I taunted the dark part of my mind. Told it to "come on then — if you think you're hard enough". I started nodding. Building myself up inside. Putting on my invisible armour.

Then I noticed the taxi driver looking at me in his rear-view mirror. I smiled. And blushed. I looked out of the window again. This time I felt like the world was looking back at me and laughing.

As I walked up the path to the front door, I couldn't help feeling that if I didn't have my key, I could just punch the door open with my fist. If the handbag thief turned up today, boy would he be in for a shock.

I had my key.

Once inside I made myself a coffee and plonked myself in front of the computer. I put the clear envelope to one side and rested the sheets of paper on top of it. I took a pad and pen and put them on the other side.

As soon as I went on-line, the story about the missing girls was everywhere. Despite a massive search, neither girl had been found, or even sighted. I read every version of the story available. From the BBC to Yahoo and Reuters.

As I read I tried to look deeper into the story. Searched for clues that only I could find. Clues about Neil, or Doctor Jones, or Colin. As I watched the video footage of the area I looked for things I might recognise. Things I had seen in my dreams. I even looked for me. Looked for any mention of a mystery woman. One with scars on her head, front and back. One who was insane enough to hurt teenage girls. I took some solace in not finding anything.

Reading about the missing girls made my heart heavy for Michael and Rose. I opened the pictures folder on the computer and clicked through them. Rosie's fifth birthday, Michael's eleventh. I felt a sadness and a joy at the same time. I wanted them back. They should be at home. Should be with their mum and dad. It wasn't fair on them to be staying away.

I left the folder open on the computer and clicked back onto the Internet.

On Google Maps I found 18, Bay View Road, Cawsand in Cornwall. The village of Cawsand looked stunning. A lovely bay of clear water, blue and green. Craggy rocks and promontories. I could almost smell the freshness.

How could they have taken me away from that?

Footpaths trailed off through thick, green woods. I could imagine trudging along them, occasional glimpses of the sea through gaps in the trees. Sunlight warming my body on the beach, cool water tickling my toes. Perhaps I would have had a boat. Maybe a windsurfer. I'm sure I would have fished.

I switched back to my photos and found one of Mum and Dad. They had given me everything I wanted. But more than that, they had wanted me. The only consent form they had signed, was one saying that they consented to giving me all the love they could. I clicked on a picture of Dad, with his fishing rod. His face was wet, although the day looked bright. He smiled out at me, as he always did when he was fishing. I smiled back.

Back on Google Maps I printed out the page with Cawsand. The map version and the satellite image version. I found 18, Bay View Road, and highlighted it. I shuddered inside. Presumably I had lived at that house, if only for a few weeks. And even if I hadn't, my parents definitely had. Using the distance measurement in the corner of the map, I ran my finger from the house to the beach. I reckoned it was no more than 150 to 200 feet away. If I had grown up there I would have woken to the smell of the sea every morning. It would have been with me through the day. At night it would have infiltrated my dreams. In the summer I would have had to kick the sand from my toes before coming in the house. My hair would have been rough and straggly from the salt water. My body browned from days of swimming and playing on the beach.

A shadow came over me. I felt a chill. The sun disappeared behind a heavy cloud. My mother wasn't a safe pair of hands. My birth mother. She was unstable. This imagined childhood would never have happened. Instead I would have been in danger. Hiding from her. Trying not to say anything to tip her over the edge. Withdrawing into myself. Spending long hours in my bedroom. Gazing out of the window at the other children. Children going to the beach, going for walks along the dusty woodland paths. Coming back with salt in their hair, and sand in their toes.

She had loved me. She had loved me so much that she made the biggest sacrifice she could think of. She gave me another chance. Another chance at life. My first throw of the dice had come up bad. So she let me throw again. And this time I got a double six.

After looking at the area I came from I typed another search term into the search engine.

Amelie Lapton — librarian.

It came back with more than 750,000 results. But had replaced *Lapton* with *laptop*.

I tried all sorts of different combinations of names and words, places and jobs. My birth mother was hard to find. I tried looking for Amelie in France but realised I would have better luck finding that elusive needle in the haystack. Every time I thought of another approach, it ended in emptiness. Nothing of her.

I shifted the search to my father.

Richard Lapton — dentist.

Initially the search was as fruitless as that of my birth mother. However, within an hour I was pretty certain that I had located him.

My father, Richard Lapton.

Eventually my searches had come up with a Richard Lapton at a golf course near Cawsand. Headland Park Golf Course was close enough to Cawsand to make me feel shaky inside. He was listed under the "veterans" page. Lapton was not that common a name, so I did nothing to suppress the burgeoning confidence inside me.

I couldn't find any mention of my mother on the site. She didn't appear to play golf. She wasn't mentioned as his wife either, as some of the other member's wives were. A sickening feeling developed in the back of my throat. I had pinned my hopes on finding her. On talking to her, about her history, about her family. Were there any health problems? Were her relatives all in France?

I didn't want to think of her having died. I couldn't. I took hold of some of that confidence deep inside me and attached it to my birth mother. She would still be alive. I would find her. And I would find out what lay in store for me in the future.

I searched for images of Richard Lapton. Hundreds came up. I scanned them until my eyes hurt. I had no idea what I was looking for. Someone with great teeth I guessed.

I tried to tie down a current address for him, but couldn't. I didn't know what else to look for.

I had tried everything to find my mother too. I had imagined that they would both come up together. Find one, find the other. But that just wasn't happening. In the end I moved to the one search I had wanted to avoid. Death certificates.

Nothing came up for Amelie Lapton, but a nagging feeling hung over me as though I had missed something or hadn't looked closely enough, or for long enough.

I went back to the page where Richard Lapton had been listed for the golf club and printed off the contact details for the club.

The easiest thing would be to ring them. Find out Richard Lapton's details. If I explained who I was they would surely give me his address. I could even make something up if necessary. Say I was ringing from the police or the council or the hospital. I was sure it could work. But then what? Would I go down there? Down to Cawsand to find this man? *"Hi Dad, I'm the daughter you gave up for adoption thirty-seven years ago.*

How are you doing and how's Mum's mental state?".

I closed the Internet down and was left with Dad's smiling face still looking at me. I smiled and walked to the kitchen, put my empty coffee mug on the side and picked up the phone.

After speaking with Mum and Dad I felt even lighter than I had before. It really did feel like things were coming good, in spite of the psychiatric assessment looming up. Dad's comments and advice had always struck me as just the sort of things that dad's normally said. But I now realised there was a deep wisdom to them. He was one of the few people I still felt I could trust, even though he and Mum had kept the adoption from me.

He urged me to proceed with caution. It made sense to go through Mary Brookes and the letter approach, but time was against me. If anything happened at the assessment which meant I was likely to be detained, then I would have even more difficulty moving forward. He offered to drive me down to Cawsand.

'I have things I need to sort out here, Dad,' I said. 'I have to have a firm plan. I can't blow it. This is so important now, it has to be done right. You are right, we don't have the luxury of time on our side, but I still have to make sure I do it as well as possible. I need to find out as much as I can from him and my birth mother. I don't want to mess it all up by just turning up on the doorstep.'

Dad told me that the offer still stood, whenever I needed it.

After a hurriedly made, and eaten, lunch I went for a walk to think. I knew it was a risk (walking and thinking), but the car keys were still locked away in the car and I planned on going somewhere quiet. If I blacked out, my hope was that I wouldn't be able to do too much damage.

The afternoon air blew cold on my face. Sunlight, diminished by the clouds, tried its best to warm the earth. But it was fighting a losing battle. The sky showed a darkening colour of grey and blue smudged in together, as though some greater power was mixing things up for a storm. I tightened the belt around my coat.

The last time I had blacked out was at Mum and Dad's. Nothing had happened since. Even the argument with Neil hadn't brought anything on. The stress of the meeting with Mary Brookes ultimately made me laugh and sing. I could feel a new confidence about me.

So maybe I was safe. Safe to be around. Safe to have my children back home. Maybe I wasn't mentally unstable.

Of course I wouldn't know for sure until I made contact with my birth parents. Or until I had the psychiatric assessment. And therein lay the danger. I couldn't risk the assessment just in case I was committed somewhere. If I could just find out about my history, that would be the only way I would know for sure what my future might hold. Look back to reveal the future.

If my birth mother was living a relatively normal life, living with the madness, then I could too. Medical advances would surely mean that if she were diagnosed now, she would have been allowed to keep her child.

But I was only guessing. I had no way of knowing what happened to children whose parent was sectioned or diagnosed with a serious mental illness. I would kill before letting Michael and Rose be taken away from me. But who would I kill?

My mobile phone beeped at me. A message, from Neil. *Having to work late again. Probably be back by 8pm.*

Perhaps Neil was the answer. He was being worked too hard at the bank anyway. He could get a different job. Or maybe he could do some work from home. He could be there for the kids and to make sure I wasn't going off my nut and attacking them.

If I had only three weeks before the assessment, I wanted Michael and Rose to be at home. I needed them. I needed them there to tell them how much I loved them. To show them in all the ways I could that they were the most precious and important people in my life.

I flicked off the message from Neil, and dialled Abi's number.

By the time I got back home it was nearly 6:30pm. The dark skies had thrown the occasional raindrop towards me, but the clouds had managed to hold back the storm. Perhaps it would come later.

I rang Abi and told her that I wanted the kids at home.

'You've been so wonderful, Abs, as usual, but I've got stuff to talk to them about and I just miss them so much.'

Abi understood.

'I can ask Neil to pick them up on his way home from work,' I said.

'Is he not back yet?' she said.

'He'll be back about 8ish, so he could be at yours by about quarter to. Would that be OK?'

I hoped Michael and Rose wouldn't be too disappointed to be coming home. Hoped that they weren't having so much fun with Josie and Jess that they would never want to come back.

I rang Neil's mobile and then apologised for ringing him at work.

'Can you pick the kids up from Abi's at about 7:45pm?'

'As long as I've finished here by then,' he said. 'I thought they were staying there for a while?'

'I need them home, Neil. I'm feeling pretty good at the moment and I just want to see them, and talk to them.'

He didn't say anything.

'How's it going there?' I said.

'I've got loads to do still. But I'm working through it as quickly as possible.'

'Is there anyone else there?' I said. 'Or have you got to do it all on your own?'

'Just me,' he said. 'And the security guard. And he's not pulling his weight the way I would want him to.'

I smiled.

'See you later,' I said.

I hung up and put the phone back in its cradle.

Then I picked it up again.

I don't know what made me do it.

I don't think it was even a conscious thing.

I dialled Neil's direct work line.

I let it ring. Echoing in my ear. A click at the other end. The bank ansaphone clicked in. Maybe I hadn't given Neil long enough to get to the phone. I hung up and dialled again. Click. Ansaphone. Perhaps he was in the toilet. Give it a few minutes. Another try. Click. Ansaphone. Maybe he's on another call. Can't come to the phone. Maybe he doesn't answer the phones out of office hours. He doesn't want to be disturbed when he's working late. Doesn't have time to talk customers. One more try then.

He answers.

'Hello?' he said.

'Neil? Are you OK?'

I sound breathless, I know I do. I don't mean to.

'I'm afraid the bank is shut, madam.'

I realise that it doesn't sound like Neil. Not even a little.

'I'm sorry. I was after Neil Marsden. It's his wife.'

'I'm afraid everyone's gone home,' he said. 'I'm the security guard. There's only me here now.'

This doesn't make sense. I have only just spoken to Neil on his mobile. He must be in a different part of the building.

'I think he is still there,' I say. 'I believe he's working late.'

There is silence from the guard. And I instantly realise why.

'I mean, he might not be,' I say. ' I may have misunderstood when I spoke to him this morning. Perhaps it's tomorrow night.'

My face burned. I felt embarrassed.

'I came on at 5:30pm,' the guard said. 'and everyone was gone by ten to six. Everyone. I said goodbye to all of them.'

My breath caught in my throat. The phone in my hand suddenly felt like a grenade about to go off and needing to be dropped before the explosion came.

'Oh,' I said. 'Ah, actually I think I can hear him at the door now. Sorry to have troubled you.'

I put the grenade down and stepped away from it.

The house was silent. Even the breeze at the open window was hushed. No one was at the front door. Neil wasn't home. I was sure the security guard would have known that as well as I did.

Neil wasn't where he said he was.

He had just lied to me.

•

CHAPTER SIXTY-ONE

I didn't want to touch the grenade again. I reached for my mobile instead. Picked out the letters with my fingers.

Hi Neil, don't forget kids at 7:45. Get the security guard to help with your paperwork. Hope it all goes OK.

His reply came back within a minute.

Still chugging through it. Security guard no help at all. Maybe he's in the wrong line of work!

Another grenade. I dropped it into my handbag.

The missing girls shot into my head. I switched on the computer and found the News. *Missing girls still not found — Police very concerned for their safety — Parents urging them to get in touch — They won't be in trouble — Please just please get in touch.*

My heart ached. It was as though the skateboard attack had not just affected me, but had affected the whole world. The whole of my world. Since I had woken up from unconsciousness, everything in my world had been different. I wondered if this world was a parallel one. Had this world been happening while I was living my other world? My pre-unconscious world? Had I somehow fallen through a hole into this one? Knocked unconscious in my real world — woken up in this darker one?

In my other world, was Neil still my loving husband, who I trusted with my life? Was I still working at the school? Did I get the Deputy Head position?

If there were parallel worlds, running simultaneously, then there must surely be a way back into the one I inhabited before. I didn't have to live in this dark world. This world of lies and mistrust. I could go back. If only I could find the gap. The way through.

I typed *parallel worlds* into the search engine.

It took about ten minutes of reading to realise that I might have gone off on one. A reaction, no doubt, to finding out that Neil had lied to me.

Instead I clicked onto the bank's website. The one where he worked, and, naturally, the one where we had our bank accounts.

The site confirmed the bank's opening times. I already knew them anyway. I clicked the login button and signed in to my accounts.

We both had a separate account and a joint one. I noticed that the joint account was showing less money than I was expecting. I opened the transactions on the screen. There were dozens of withdrawals. Each one for £10. And there were multiple withdrawals on each day. But there were deposits too. Multiples of ten. Several days apart.

I frowned. I hadn't taken any money out.

Which meant that Neil had.

It wasn't possible to tell for sure, but every withdrawal looked like it came from the same place. They were all from the same bank's cash machines at least. Where was it? It wasn't his bank. So he wasn't using the one right outside where he worked. He was going to another one. Practically every day, several times a day. Taking out £10. Then every few days, putting money back into the account. But not the same amount. He was taking out more than he was putting in.

Unless it wasn't Neil. The handbag thief perhaps? But I had cancelled all my cards. Had I forgotten the one for the joint account? I couldn't remember. But my PIN number wasn't written down anywhere. They were all in my head. The thief couldn't have got hold of that. Not inside my head. Where the darkness and confusion lived.

I heard a noise coming from the kitchen. I snapped my head round, looked over my shoulder at the doorway. Nothing. But there was a noise. A tapping sound and a breath-like woosh, like someone exhaling a deep breath. I couldn't bring myself to look back at the computer monitor. At the same time I was rooted to the seat. If I could have sent someone else into the kitchen for me, I would have done.

'Hello?' I said.

My voice sounded too shaky.

'What?' I said.

Much firmer. Maybe even threatening.

I jerked out of the seat and stormed into the kitchen. Fists clenched and bared teeth.

'What the fuck,' I said.

But there was no one there. No one at the window. The window remained shut. No hand-prints or smears. No soil on the floor.

The boiler on the wall glowed its red light at me. The boiler had switched on. Clicking and wooshing. That was the noise I had heard.

I could see the headlines. *"Woman dies of fright as central heating switches on".*

I realised there was a growing anger inside me starting to boil, steam rising, bubbles popping on the surface. And I knew it would boil over soon. Just a soon as Neil walked through the front door.

But don't splash the kids. Boiling anger burns. Sticks to people like hot melted sugar. Scars and blisters. Mind the kids.

I turned the temperature down. Closed my eyes and stretched my neck. I rubbed my forearms. Breathed out through pursed lips. Got that temperature down. Only bring it to the boil when it's safe. When the only person who was going to get hurt from it would be Neil. Not the Neil that I loved. Not the Neil that loved me. But the Neil in this world. The one I ended up with when I fell through the hole. Let it all stick to him. Burning and scarring.

To take my mind off my simmering rage I decided to make sure the kids' bedrooms were ready for them. I wished I had thought about getting them presents. Just something little. A cuddly for Rose. Some killing game for Michael. Instead I wrote them a little note each and placed it on their pillows. Just telling them how special they were. How much I loved them.

I felt like leaving a different kind of note on Neil's pillow. But pushed the feeling back down into the simmering cauldron. Added it to the mix.

The mixture of excitement and rage was not a good one. I felt breathless and confused. Not sure where to go in the house. Not sure what to do. I was desperate to see the kids. To hold them to me, squeeze them tight. Make the most of every moment I had with them. But I was fearful of confronting Neil. I wasn't scared of him, of what he might do to me. I was fearful of what he had done. What had been going on without my knowledge.

God only knew how it might affect the kids. Me going insane and their father doing... well I just didn't know what he had been doing. I tried to make sense of the money going out of the joint account. Ran through all the reasons he might be doing it. It could be just to get cash to buy lunch. But that wouldn't make sense more than once a day. And why was he not using the cash point attached to where he worked? Why travel to another?

I tried to think of all the cash machines in town. Tried to remember which bank was associated with each one. I couldn't recall all of them. Why did he always apparently use the same one. Again and again, often ten or more times a day? So I pictured all the shops and businesses around the cash points. Maybe there was a brothel in town.

I couldn't see that.

Newsagents; fruiterers; butchers; restaurants; betting shops.

Betting shops.

That would make sense. He might have a gambling habit. There were at least two betting shops in the town, possibly more. If he had a problem with it, that would explain why he took money out from a different cash point, so his colleagues wouldn't see him.

It would also explain why he was taking out only £10 a time, if he was trying to restrict himself, but then coming back for more when he lost. That would also explain why not all the money was being paid back. How bad was it that he had to start using the joint account? He must have known I would see it eventually. Was it a call for help? Did he want to be caught?

But how could a gambling problem account for all the nights he'd been working late?

CHAPTER SIXTY-TWO

I thought back over all the nights Neil had told me he was working late and wondered how many of them had been genuine. I wanted to ring the security guard at the bank and ask him how often he'd seen Neil working after-hours.

I could cope with gambling. If he had a problem, I could help him. We could deal with it together.

Then the missing girls materialised in my mind. Still not found.

Was the money and his staying out late somehow connected to the missing girls? Neither of the girls looked like the ones in my dream, but surely there was a connection. My dreams must have been a premonition of some sort.

Neil and the kids arrived home just after 8pm. All were smiling. Rosie returned my hugs and threw herself into my arms. Michael sort of held my arm and allowed me to give him a kiss on the top of his head.

Neil kissed me on the cheek.

I found it difficult to make eye contact with him. I didn't want to boil over yet. Too much collateral damage. I was sure I could keep it at bay for the next hour, at least until the kids were in bed. I determined to concentrate all my attention on them.

'Who wants ice cream?' I said.

They both shot their hands up. Both shouted "me, me".

I sensed an awkward movement from Neil. But I still couldn't look at him. Maybe that was why he moved awkwardly, he could sense something from me. The steam rising from the top of my head, perhaps.

Michael and Rose bounded into the dining room. The chairs clattered as they pulled them out from the table and they at once started arguing about who was going to have the most ice cream, who was going to finish first, and who liked it the most.

Neil hung around the kitchen door.

'Have you eaten?' I said, my back to him.

'Not yet,' he said.

'I haven't done anything,' I said. 'But there are still a couple of things in the freezer if you want to do one of them.'

'OK,' he said. 'That's great. I'll do one of them then.'

His voice was hesitant. He sounded unsure. Like he'd missed something important somewhere, but didn't know what it was. I could imagine what was going through his mind. *Is it our anniversary? Is it her Birthday? Had I promised to take her out? Has she somehow discovered my gambling addiction? Does she suspect me of killing teenage girls and lying to her about working late?*

I wanted to scream at him right then and there. Wanted to turn and face him and scream. *Focus on the children, Christine.*

'I've missed you guys so much,' I called out. 'Have you been having a fantastic time at Abi's?'

They shouted and laughed back at me. Michael leapt out of his chair and charged around the dining table, making a noise like a racing car.

'I think you need to get a little bit more excited,' I said. 'Get some energy from somewhere.'

I heard another chair scrape and Rosie's voice joined Michael's. A higher pitched racing car.

Neil turned to face them. Relieved, no doubt, to have something else to concentrate on other than the obvious, but not understood, tension between us.

We both managed to spend most of our time talking and playing with Michael and Rose. Neil made his own tea, but when I went into the kitchen to get a coffee later I saw half the meal still on the plate.

I insisted on being the one to put the kids to bed. Rose smiled when she read my note. When I went into Michael the note was on his floor.

'I wrote you a note,' I said.

'I read it. Thank you. I put it on the floor.'

I picked it up and slipped it under his pillow. He shifted his head from side to side as though I had just put a writhing hedgehog under it.

'It's only a note,' I said.

'It crinkles when I move.'

I reached under the pillow again and pulled out the note. I folded it on his bedside cabinet and slid it between his clock and glass of water.

I didn't go straight downstairs. Instead I sat on our bed for a few minutes, gathering my thoughts and straightening my clothes. I wished we had a separate annexe to the house. I had a feeling I was going to find it difficult to stay in control and I didn't want to disturb Michael or Rose.

I crept downstairs when I felt ready. Neil was perched on the edge of the sofa. His hands were pressed palms together, the tips of his fingers resting on the end of his nose, as though in prayer. His eyes looked wide and his legs were shaking. He often shook his legs. I took it as a sign of restlessness, always wanting to be doing something. But tonight I could see it was nerves.

I walked slowly to the armchair and sat down, looking across diagonally at him. He looked over at me and tried to make his face do something. But it seemed paralysed. If he had been trying for a reassuring smile, he had failed. I took the lid off the cauldron inside me.

'So, how was work?' I said.

He blushed immediately. His eyes flickered as he tried to work out how much I knew. How much he should admit to up-front, and how much he could still avoid telling me. He hesitated. Tried to look me in the eye, but couldn't stop his eyes from veering off when he spoke.

'Oh, it was…you know…same old, same old,' he said.

The cauldron boiled over — quicker, even, than I had been expecting. My face burned and I gripped the arms of the chair. I thought of Michael and Rose upstairs and kept my voice to a hiss.

'Yes I do fucking know,' I said. 'I really fucking do.'

He parted his praying hands. And they slapped down onto his shaking legs. He opened his mouth but his deceiving brain hadn't yet decided what words he could use.

'I know you weren't at fucking work,' I said. 'I spoke to the security guard. You know? The one who was "helping" you with your work?'

He shifted about on the edge of the sofa. His neck had turned as red as his face.

I didn't think I could maintain the hiss for much longer. The rage was already screaming through my body. It was only a matter of time before it engaged my vocal cords too.

'And I know about the money. I know you've been taking it out, then putting some back, then taking it out again. Sometimes ten or more times a day. All from the same machine.'

I knew I was chancing it a bit with the last comment. I didn't know for sure it was the same machine. His lack of reaction told me the chance had been worth taking.

'And all this time you were telling me you had to work late. Night after night. Night after fucking night, Neil.'

His shoulders sagged. He closed his eyes. Then he shook his head and smiled.

Inside me, something exploded.

He opened his eyes as the first swing tore across his cheek. I could see the blood, drawn by my nails, popping up in spots from the open wounds. He slammed his palm to the cuts. Although I could see he was shocked, he managed to stand up. He wasn't smiling anymore.

I struck him again, this time on the other side of his face. Once again my nails drew blood. I knew I had to get as much of an attack in as I could, before he started attacking me. I was no match for his strength, I knew that, but I definitely had the initial element of surprise, and I knew I had the moral advantage. Plus I still had a bubbling cauldron of burning rage inside me.

I kicked out at him. Grabbed his ears and kicked at his legs. He tried to push me off, but I had such a firm grip of his ears it made him wince. He grabbed my hands and squeezed them. Desperate to make me let go of his ears. It worked. I shut my eyes and waited for the reprisal. He held my arms down at my side.

'Christine!' he shouted.

I opened my eyes. His looked into mine. Imploring me to stop.

I bared my teeth and lunged at his face. His head shot backwards, but not before I bit him just below the red-raw scratches on his cheek.

He turned away in pain and fell over the sofa onto his front. I screamed, and used my talons on his back, tried to rip the shirt from his body. He flailed his arms behind him, a desperate attempt to knock my hands away. He dragged himself up and, once again, got hold of my hands, held them tightly in his. This time he held himself further away from me. Looked down at my legs, checked to see what my next move was. For a brief moment everything stopped. As though the camera had clicked into ultra-slow motion. A bead of sweat flew from his face in an arc. I watched it float through the air. And in that brief moment, I realised that he wasn't fighting back. All he was doing, was trying to stop me from hurting him.

The realisation sent my mind spinning, but the moment was over.

I kicked his left knee, wrenched my hands from his, spat at him and slashed out at his face, catching the end of his nose with my nails.

He fell back again but my hand was caught in his shirt. It ripped as he fell. I scratched at his chest and stomach. As his shirt flew open the tops of his arms became visible. I went after them too.

Jagged lines of wounds and blood scored his body. Front and back, blood seeped from the open scratches. Even though the shirt still covered his back, blood had already patterned it from where I had dug through the shirt with my nails. And still he didn't fight back. Nor did he cover his face or any part of his body with his hands as I attacked. He just tried to hold my hands and wrists to stop me. Nothing more.

I think the cauldron boiled dry.

I think I stood back and looked at him.

I think I started to laugh.

CHAPTER SIXTY-THREE

The next morning I was woken by Rose running to the bathroom, flushing the toilet, then shuffling back to her bedroom.

At first I didn't remember the awful fight from the night before. But as I reached out, still half asleep, to touch Neil's back, the memories rushed into place.

Neil wasn't there. In fact, his side of the bed felt pretty cold. I forced my eyes open fully and blinked to get rid of the sleep. Daylight had already changed the room from dark and cold to light and cold. The curtains held the warmth back. I reached over to my clock and switched the alarm setting to "off". There was only another ten minutes to go before I was going to get up anyway.

I sat up in the bed and rubbed my eyes. I looked at Neil's side. His pillow still held the indentation of his head. There were some dark marks on it too. I pulled the duvet off his side and caught my breath. I put my hand to my mouth to stop the cry from coming out. Dark streaks lined the sheet. Deeply ingrained. Circles of dark, drying blood. Jagged lines of dark red, soaked into the sheet and, no doubt, the mattress below.

I coughed. Gagged even. So much blood. And I knew that I had done it all. With my nails and my teeth. I looked at my fingernails. Remnants of blood had dried underneath the tips. I didn't want to think about the possibility of Neil's skin being there too.

I climbed out of bed and took the duvet completely off. More blood on the underside of the duvet.

None on my side. Pure white next to dark red and brown. A peaceful night for me. A bloody one for Neil. Too much blood, I thought. More than there should have been from the injuries caused by my nails. What had happened after I came to bed? I couldn't remember coming to bed. Had I blacked out and attacked him some more? Was he dead?

I heard Rose coming out of her bedroom again. Skipping down the landing towards our room. I flicked the duvet out and laid it over the bloody sheet. It covered his pillow too. Rose burst through the door. She was singing.

I turned and smiled, held my arms open and she jumped into them.

'How was your night?' I said.

'OK, thank you. How was yours?'

I squeezed her and spun around, clutching her to me. She giggled.

'Where's Dad?' she said.

'Oh, he's had to go into work early,' I said. 'He's very busy at the moment.'

'Let's jump on the bed,' she said. 'Can I?'

'Maybe later, sweetheart. We've got to get ready for school now, and have brekky. You run off and have your wash while I get dressed.'

When she was gone, I checked to see what clothes Neil was wearing. His work suit was missing. He probably had gone into work early. I slid open the door of the en suite. Bloody tissues protruded from the bin. His flannel had streaks of red on it. I ran my thumb along the brush bit of his toothbrush. It felt dry. His razor blade the same.

I pulled on my dressing gown and ran downstairs. The sofa was tipped up. Chairs overturned. Pages from my crossword book lay scattered on the floor. Small, bloody streaks ran along the top of the sofa. Neil wasn't there.

I ran to the front door. His briefcase was gone too. I checked the kitchen. No dirty cereal bowl on the side. None in the dishwasher either.

Michael clumped about upstairs. I heard him whining. Rose

had woken him with her noise.

I rushed around the living-room picking up the torn pages, righting the furniture. I grabbed a tea-towel from the kitchen, held it under the cold tap and tried rubbing away the stain on the sofa. The redness came out of it, brighter than it had been before I rubbed it. It took quite a few minutes to make it look reasonable. I hoped Michael and Rose wouldn't notice.

I paused for a moment, tried to get my thoughts together. For the first time since waking up I became aware of the butterflies in my tummy, the pounding of my heart and the dull ache at the base of my skull. I couldn't seem to make my breathing anything more than shallow. I wondered if eating would help. What a stupid thought. But I could get the children's breakfast ready. Take my mind off what I had done.

But first I ran to the kitchen, threw the bloody tea-towel into the washing machine and picked up the phone. Neil's mobile went straight to voicemail. I looked over my shoulder to make sure Michael and Rose weren't there, then spoke quietly into the phone.

'Neil, it's me. Look, I'm sorry about last night. I don't know what happened there. I mean, I know I lost it. I know I attacked you. I'm so sorry. Please call me back if you get this. I was horrified when I woke up this morning. Please call me if you can.'

The red-rimmed kitchen clock showed almost 7:30am. Any moment Abi would be knocking on the door to take the kids to school. And she would be dying to know how the night had gone. I shouted upstairs.

'Michael, Rose. Come on you two. Breakfast is ready. Abi will be here soon.'

They clattered downstairs and I rushed them through breakfast. I had just sent them back upstairs to clean their teeth when the doorbell rang. I shouted to the kids to get a move on as I went to answer the door.

It was Abi. I noticed dark rings under her eyes.

'Hi,' she said. 'How was it?'

I managed a smile.

'Great,' I said. 'How are you? You look a little tired.'

She shrugged. She managed a smile too, but I could see it was forced.

'I'm OK. Bit of a disturbed night, that's all. Didn't sleep too well. And once I was awake...'

I felt my cheeks get hotter.

'Do you want me to take Michael and Rose back to mine after school?' she said, 'have them stay over?'

Hotter still. Neil must have gone round there in the night. He must have told them what I'd done. Shown them the wounds. He wanted the kids there, with him, away from me.

I hesitated.

'Chris?' Abi said.

But it would be better for the kids to be there. If Neil came home, we would obviously have a lot to talk about.

'Would that be OK?' I said.

She nodded.

'Of course. It's no problem at all.'

Rose bashed into my leg and hugged me. Michael ambled up behind her. I gave them both the biggest kiss I could. Hugged them both. Rose squeezed me back. Even Michael put his arms loosely around me.

'Stay with Jess and Jo again tonight?' I said. 'Lucky you.'

As they stepped out of the door Abi touched Rose's cheek and ruffled Michael's hair. The hairs on the back of my neck prickled. No forced smiles for them. Anyone walking past would have thought that they were her children, not mine. They all climbed into Abi's car. She waved goodbye to me. Michael and Rose were too busy with Josie and Jess.

As soon as they were gone, I tried Neil's mobile again. I didn't bother leaving another message. He would see that it was another missed call anyway so he would know how often I had rung.

Then I tried his work number. I got straight through.

'He phoned in sick a few minutes ago,' the girl said. 'Is everything OK?'

It must have sounded odd. Neil rings in sick, then five minutes later his wife rings in to speak to him.

'He is,' I said. 'Sick, I mean. I think he was going to the doctor, then I thought he might come into work. He must be on his way home already.'

As a liar I was anything but convincing.

I needed to find out where Neil was.

I rang Abi and Oliver's. Of course neither of them were there. Oli would have been at work and I had just seen Abi set off with my children to school. But I thought Neil might pick up. Might somehow know it was me ringing.

I thought about the amount of blood there had been on the sheet. I thought about how I had lashed out at my mum. Pushed her and Dad to the ground. I knew I was capable of hurting. I knew I had strength when I was blacked out.

And all that blood.

My heartbeat increased. A vein throbbed behind my right ear. I rushed to the back window and threw open the curtains. Half the lawn was covered in glistening dew, the other half in bright sunlight. I looked towards the shed. Its dark window, surrounded by cobwebs inside, showed me nothing. I slipped on a pair of shoes and made my way to the shed. My hand shook as I opened the door.

But he wasn't there.

So if I had killed him, I hadn't dumped him in the shed.

Although I had eaten nothing, something felt like it wanted to come up from my stomach. I swallowed hard.

I scratched the back of my head. The scar felt numb. I looked at my nails. The blood was still there. I needed to have a shower. I needed to think.

I dug my fingers into the soap. Gouged bits of it out. Then rubbed my fingernails against each palm. As the hot water soaked my body I checked myself for injuries from the night before. As I had thought, there were none. For some reason Neil hadn't fought back at all. Cowardice? Or guilt?

I had no idea what time he had come to bed after the fight. But he obviously had done. And I had no idea what had happened after that, whether I'd done something or whether he'd just woken up and left.

I tried to think about where he would go. Abi's and Oli's was the obvious choice. Oli and he were good friends. And Abi?

I put my head back under the shower, let the water run down my face.

If he was in cahoots with Colin or the doctor, he might go there. Or even to my mum and dad's. I could see him now, telling them what a shit I'd been. How I hurt him, and he'd done nothing to deserve it. Bastard.

I made a mental list of the people I needed to call after my shower. Probably after putting the bloody bedclothes in the wash.

With each phone call I made, I concentrated on how the person at the other end *sounded* rather than what they said.

It was easy to get hold of Colin Connell, and a nightmare getting hold of Doctor Jones. But I did it. To me, they both sounded suspicious. But not so much that I felt Neil was there with one of them. I took solace in the fact that Colin and the doctor weren't together too. If their conspiracy existed, they would now surely feel that it was falling apart and would probably gather together to try to sort things out. But they were apart. That was good.

Mum and Dad hadn't heard from Neil, or seen him, for ages. Not since the last time we'd gone over together. I didn't tell them that I had attacked him, but I did say we'd had an argument.

'If he rings,' I said, 'please can you ask him to call me.'

I forced myself to eat lunch. A cheese and tomato roll. I gagged on it. It tasted so dry. I must have had at least three glasses of water, but they didn't seem to help.

After lunch I started thinking about smashing one of the car windows so I could get to my keys. I knew it would be a risk driving, but I needed to try and find him. I decided to give it a little longer.

I went online to check the bank account. It didn't show any money being taken out today, although I suspected there was always a delay before it showed up. There were six extra transactions from the day before though. All £10, all from the same cashpoint. Neil had been at it again yesterday. Whatever *it* was.

I could barely breathe. I had to get out of the house. Had to find him. I ran up and down the streets near where we lived. Looked into bushes and behind bus shelters. I felt like a dog owner searching for their lost beloved animal. I had to stop myself from calling out his name every few seconds.

By late afternoon I had to give up and rest. The sky gloomed dark overhead and a chill swirled up. I sat down on a grassy bank in the local park to get my breath back. My head pounded and my eyes hurt every time I blinked. I must have been staring for hours.

I put my hand on my stomach, trying to calm my breathing and the feeling of nausea which had been my constant companion all day. I checked my phone for the millionth time. No calls, no texts, no voicemails.

I tried to put myself into Neil's mind. What would I do? I would walk around and think. I would spend the day away, out of contact, trying to make the other person feel guilty. Then, eventually, I would go home.

This thought energised me. I rang home on my mobile. No reply. The answer machine didn't switch on. I must have forgotten to switch it on when I'd rushed out earlier that afternoon. I stood up and started trotting home. I knew that he would either be there already, sitting, waiting for me, or I would be there when he got home. Sitting, waiting for him.

He wasn't there. So I sat. And I waited. I must have fallen asleep, because I was woken by the phone ringing in the kitchen. I shook myself awake and dashed to answer the phone. The microwave clock blinked 9:05pm at me.

'Hello? Neil?' I said.

When he spoke I could hear every word echoing. And an odd beeping sound, like a payphone, interrupted his speech. His voice was hoarse and low. I could hear tension in it. And possibly alcohol.

'Christine,' he said. 'It's me.'

It sounded like a growl, rather than a greeting.

'Neil, I'm sorry,' I said. 'Come home and we'll sort this all out. I'm so sorry.'

'Christine, listen to me. I can't come home.'

My heart sank. I was about to plead with him, to tell him that we could work through it. But his next words left me cold. And in an instant I knew that I had been right all along.

'Christine, I'm at the police station in town. I've been arrested.'

CHAPTER SIXTY-FOUR

I held the phone against my ear. A drummer took up residence in my chest and started pounding, as though making up for lost time. I couldn't speak. Even if I had been able to, I wouldn't have known what to say.

The phone clicked at the other end of the line. Too late I found my voice.

'Neil?' I said. 'Neil?'

His name tasted bitter on my tongue. I couldn't shut the drummer up, and now he had his foot against my lungs. Pushing them down, constricting them so that only a fraction of the breath I needed to live would flow into them.

I dropped the phone onto the work surface. It clattered to the edge and dropped onto the floor. I didn't try to catch it.

All I could think about was those poor girls. Missing, presumably dead, at the hands of Neil. I staggered to the kitchen sink, kicking the phone along the floor as I went, and threw up.

I knew what had happened to them. I had seen it all in my dreams. The terror in their eyes. The pain they had gone through. And I wondered now if the woman I had seen, writing at the table, was one of the mothers of these girls. Or if she was me, wretched and scared for not having spoken out. For not having done anything to stop my husband from killing.

I retched again. Turned the kitchen tap on and moved the washing-up bowl out of the sink. I should have moved it before being sick. I decided I would throw it away and just buy a new one.

I wiped my eyes and nose on my sleeve. My eyes were wet from the exertion of being sick, but I hadn't been crying. For the first time in a while, the stabbing pain came back into my leg. I kicked against the cupboard door underneath the sink, tried to take my mind off the pain. The pain from my leg and the pain from what Neil had done. I folded my arms on the edge of the sink and slumped my head onto them. Kicking the cupboard, fighting for breath and cursing the drummer in my chest.

It was too late to ring Mum and Dad. Too late to ring Abi. I wasn't sure that I wanted to speak to anyone anyway. I looked down at the phone on the kitchen floor. The battery sleeve had come off and another small piece of plastic lay next to it. It confirmed to me that it was the right decision to not call anyone.

It took me twenty minutes to get ready to go to the police station. Actually, it took me two minutes to get ready, but eighteen minutes to calm down.

The taxi was cold and smelled damp. I looked out of the window into the dark streets. I already knew that I didn't want to see Neil. I couldn't work out what was going on inside me regarding him. There was a feeling, I could only put it down to love, that seemed rooted to me. It was as though I was trying to pull it out, get rid of it, but it was dug in so deep that nothing I could do would shift it. But obviously I was pouring tons of other stuff onto it. Disgust, hate, vitriol. Everything related to the missing girls. I was frightened that if I saw him, it might bring up the deeply rooted feeling. The nice one. But what he had done was unforgivable. There could be no room for love.

'I see they've got someone.'

At first it sounded like a noise of the night. Just one of the many sounds floating around us that we subconsciously delete.

'I said, I see they've got someone.'

It was the driver. Looking back at me, over his shoulder.

'Sorry?' I said.

'For those girls. Apparently they've arrested someone.'

My stomach turned over. There surely couldn't be anything more to come up. I covered my eyes with my hand. Looked down at my lap.

'Have they?' I said.

'Yeah, some bloke off the Internet apparently. They knew him, the girls. Went to meet him. He was taking them on holiday apparently.

'One of the girls phoned home, to tell her mum not to worry. They'd seen all the hoo-hah in the papers and that. So one of them rang to say they were OK.'

I managed to answer.

'They're OK?'

'Yeah, who knows what might have happened if one of them hadn't phoned. But they've got the bloke.'

If the story of the arrest had been on the television and radio, everyone would have seen it. Everyone would have seen Neil. I thought about Mum and Dad. Thought about Abi and Oliver. My heart stopped as I thought about Michael and Rose.

'Did they show the man?' I said. 'The one who took them? Did they show him on T.V.?'

'He didn't take them, they went with him.'

I bit my lip.

'Was there a picture of him?'

'I don't know, love. I've been on shift since lunchtime, I've only got the radio. They mentioned his age, I think. Said he was fifty-eight or something. On the Internet he had told the girls he was eighteen. Bet they got a shock when they met him.'

Involuntarily my hand clamped to my mouth. Neil wasn't fifty-eight. Neither was Colin Connell. I pictured Doctor Jones. White hair, wrinkled face. He looked older than Colin

Connell. But how old? He could have been around fifty-eight, give or take a year or two.

I pulled my hand away from my mouth.

'They've only arrested one person?' I said.

'That's all there was, apparently. Just this bloke.'

I wanted to believe what the driver was telling me. But he drove a cab. How much of what he said could be construed as factual? What if he had got the age wrong? What if the man was younger than that? Neil's age?

'Do you know where they were found? Where they got him?'

'Up in the Lake District, apparently. The three of them turned up at a hotel near one of the lakes and that was when one of the girls phoned home. Apparently.'

I put a hold on all the hateful acid I had been pouring on that deep root inside me. Gave it some air.

But they don't arrest you for no reason. Neil must still have done something. He had sounded a little drunk. Perhaps it was just that. Drunk and disorderly. It wasn't completely out of the question. He used to play rugby.

But what about all the lies? The working late and the money from the joint account? Something wasn't right. If the police saw fit to arrest him, perhaps I should hold onto the acid a while longer. Even if it turned out he wasn't a killer.

'Are you alright, love?'

So maybe there wasn't a conspiracy between Neil, Colin Connell and the doctor. What a difference that would make.

'Love?'

Was he talking to me? I brought my eyes into focus.

The taxi had stopped outside the police station. The driver had turned in his seat and was looking between me and the fare reader.

'Sorry,' I said. 'How much?'

'Eight-fifty, love,' he said.

I gave him ten and told him to keep the change.

I climbed out of the cab and stood on the pavement. I expected the cab to drive off straight away. But it didn't. I looked back and could see the driver waving at me through the window. He held his radio mike in the other hand. He was obviously worried enough about me to make sure I made it into the police station.

Although I could see the main door to the police station, it took all my concentration to walk there and to maintain a reasonable line. If any police officer happened to be looking out at that moment I was sure I would have been breathalysed. I hadn't eaten properly for hours. And I had retched up whatever had been in my stomach. No wonder the world was spinning.

I was surprised at how dark the building looked. I would have expected all the lights to be on. To be able to see activity going on inside. I had assumed that police stations were buzzing 24 hours a day, but at nearly 10pm this one looked like it was closed for the night.

The main door was locked. An arrow directed me to push the button on an intercom to the side of the door. A man's voice answered my call. He sounded like he wanted to go home. I explained that my husband had been arrested and that I was there to see him. The door buzzed and I leaned into it. A click, and then it opened. As the door swung shut behind me, I heard the taxi cab finally drive away.

Inside the small reception area, three plastic chairs backed against a wall which was covered in posters and leaflets. Opposite the chairs was the reception desk itself. A thick sheet of glass partitioned those on my side, in the waiting area, from those on the other side, the police station proper. On my side, there was only me. On the other side, no one.

Another arrow pointed to a bell push on the desk. A small sign next to it suggested I ring for attention. I thought this probably wasn't necessary in my case as I had just rung to be let in the main door.

I paced up and down, glancing at the posters above the plastic chairs. Every one of them seemed to mention drugs, knives, guns and assault. For some reason Neil popped into my mind. On one of the posters someone had hand-written an abusive slogan. I wondered if the author might have been a weary police officer, rather than a drug-taking, knife-wielding, gun-runner who was on a break from assaulting people.

There was no clock that I could see, but it felt like minutes were ticking by. I wondered what was taking so long. Then I noticed a CCTV camera up high in one corner of the area. Were they leaving me here on purpose? Watching to see what I would do?

In a flash I remembered what I had done to Neil. All the blood on the sheet. Was I in trouble? Was his phone call simply a ruse to get me to come to the police station? My hands felt clammy. I pressed my guilty fingernails into my palms. I looked towards the main door and considered leaving. But they had already seen me on the CCTV. Obviously they had already seen Neil. I wondered how bad he looked. I walked over to the exit, put my hand on the handle.

'Mrs Marsden?'

I jerked my hand back from the door, as though a jolt of electricity had just passed from the handle into my hand. I spun around and saw a female police officer. She held open a door to the side of the reception desk. I was surprised I hadn't noticed it before.

I didn't remember giving my name on the intercom.

'Christine Marsden?' she said.

I nodded.

'Would you like to come through?'

CHAPTER SIXTY-FIVE

The police officer led me along a corridor with several closed doors either side. I shivered. There didn't seem to be any heat in the building at all. The corridor smelled of sweat.

'How did you know who I was?' I said.

The officer didn't look back.

'One of my colleagues,' she said. 'Said he thought he recognised you. Been to your address recently following an incident.'

I blushed. They had plenty to choose from. The crude graffiti on the side of our house; Me lashing out and collapsing into the arms of the police officer who was questioning me, and then refusing to be taken to hospital by the paramedics; The one where I fell asleep on the sofa and woke up thinking there was an intruder in the house. It could be any number of hysterical incidents.

'Oh,' I said.

I was right. They had been watching me on the CCTV. Watching me pace up and down. Watching me read the offensive hand-written slogan on one of their posters on the wall. They would no doubt think I had written it. Probably thought I was some sort of attention-seeking, loony.

At the end of the corridor she pushed open a door and held it for me.

'Please take a seat.'

I was surprised to see a room. I had expected the corridor to lead to another corridor, or a staircase. I guessed that one of the other doors I had passed along the way led to other parts of the building.

I had never been inside an interview room in a police station before. But I knew I was in one now.

I wondered if it was just a place for me to chat, or wait. Or whether I was about to be interviewed about something. Possible questions shot through my mind. *'Where was your husband on the night of the 25th? How often did he tell you he was working late? Did you know about his secret criminal activity? Mrs Marsden, why is your husband's body covered in bloody scratches and seeping wounds?'*

The police officer sat opposite me. She took a notepad from a desk drawer and a pen from her breast pocket.

'Your husband rang you?' she said.

I nodded.

'Did he tell you why we had arrested him?'

I shook my head.

For some reason my lips seemed clamped shut. As though to open them would be to condemn both me and Neil to whatever crime it was we were individually suspected of.

'He's been arrested on suspicion of an assault.'

My mind flicked back to all the posters on the wall in the reception area. Drugs; Knives; Guns; Assault. I supposed it had to be one of them. I would probably have preferred it to be drugs.

I risked condemnation and opened my mouth.

'Assault?'

'Do you know where your husband was this evening?'

Ought I to know? It might seem strange for me not to know. I wasn't sure what to say.

'I … wasn't sure,' I said.'

She gave me a look and frowned.

'I mean, I thought he might be at work, possibly. Or out somewhere.'

'Out somewhere?'

I knew I should have kept my mouth shut. I'd been doing pretty well up until then. The fact was, that since I had attacked him the night before, I had no idea where he had been.

'Where was he?' I asked.

I winced at the question. It had sounded confrontational, like a taunt. But I hadn't meant it to.

'He was arrested in the town. In the open ground behind the supermarket. Near the small industrial estate back there.'

I knew where it was. But what on earth had Neil been doing back there? Apart from assaulting someone.

'Who was assaulted?' I said.

'A young man,' she said. 'A member of the public saw the attack and called the police. Your husband was arrested at the scene, and the young man was taken to hospital.'

My heart skipped a beat.

'To hospital?' 'Is he badly hurt?'

'We don't have any details at this stage,' she said. 'We're waiting for an update some time soon.'

I pictured Neil behind the supermarket, pounding away at someone. He hadn't retaliated when I attacked him. Maybe this was payback for me, and some poor chap took the punishment on my behalf. I lowered my head and covered my eyes with my hand.

'Your husband has admitted the assault,' she said. 'He said the man deserved it. Deserved it for what he'd done.'

I looked up at her, but her eyes told me nothing. How could they? Only Neil could make sense of this.

'Can I see my husband?' I said.

She looked at her watch.

'You will have a chance to speak with him soon. Is there anything you can tell me that you think might relate to this assault?'

I shook my head. 'Nothing.'

She put the pen back in her pocket and picked up the notepad.

'Please wait here, Mrs Marsden.'

As the door closed behind her, I thought I heard a click, like a key turning in the lock.

Neil hadn't been arrested for taking two teenage girls away. He'd been arrested for assaulting a man. Relief flooded through me.

I pictured the man he'd attacked. Perhaps a money lender of some kind. Maybe he'd tried to call in Neil's gambling debts.

I tried to stop my racing mind. I needed to speak to Neil.

In the half an hour or so before the door opened again I counted all the books on two shelves, went through the timestables several times in my head and had just started counting the number of creases and bumps on one of the square polystyrene tiles that made up the ceiling.

Neil walked in first, a male police officer came after him.

My breath caught in my throat as soon as I saw Neil's face. He couldn't have looked worse if he had just walked away from a car crash. My stomach convulsed and I couldn't hold back a sob. *Your face.*

Neil sat down and nodded at me. I wiped the excess moisture from my eyes. The male police officer stood behind Neil.

'What happened?' I said.

'I'm sorry,' Neil said. 'I knew you wouldn't want me to. But I had to get him.'

'Get who?' I said, although I had an inkling I already knew.

Neil leaned forward across the desk. He lowered his voice, although not enough to keep what he said strictly between the two of us.

'The fucker that did it,' he said. 'The fucking bastard with the skateboard. I got him.'

I shook my head and reached out for Neil's hand, but the police officer held his hand up and shook his head. I pulled my hand back again. But not before I saw Neil's hand coming to meet mine. Bloody and bruised. Perhaps from the man he'd attacked. Perhaps from me.

'I'm so sorry, Neil,' I said. 'I'm so, so sorry.'

He shook his head. Smiled at me.

'I was lying to you,' he said. 'I didn't want you to know what I was really doing. Every night I was going to the same place you got mugged, looking for him, asking questions. I thought if I kept taking money out from the same cash machine as you did that night, he might attack me. Several times a night I would go back to the machine and make a big show of taking money out, just in the hope that the bastard would try it again.

'That's why we got those messages, Chris. On the wall outside, and scratched onto our wall in the living-room. He was warning me to stay away from him. To stop asking around. That's probably why the picture went missing too, so he knew what I looked like. He was in our house — you were right. It was him that came in.' Neil shook his head. A short laugh escaped from his throat. 'And then tonight, he finally took the bait. I know it was him. I know it was the same bloke. Skateboard, hoodie. He got the money right out of my hand. So I chased him. Caught up with him behind the supermarket. Something inside me just flipped. I think if someone hadn't walked by and shouted out... well who knows. I think they're going to arrest him too, after he comes out of hospital. He's not badly hurt. I didn't kill him. But they must do him for stealing my money, for coming into our house and for attacking you. They must be able to do the fucker for something.'

I could barely speak through my tears.

'But what about you?' I said. 'What's going to happen to you?'

Neil looked up at the police officer. The police officer shrugged his shoulders. Neil looked back at me.

'I don't know,' he said. 'I'm sorry, Chris. About this. I'm really sorry.'

'Well surely they must let you go. If he stole your money — that's mugging. All you did was chase him to get your money back. You weren't at fault at all.'

Neil looked down at the table.

'I went a bit too far,' he said. 'It wasn't deemed reasonable in the eyes of the law.'

'Look at you,' I said. My eyes flickered across the scratches on his face and neck. 'I'm so sorry.'

He raised his eyebrows and, almost imperceptibly, shook his head.

'I'm fine,' he said. 'He didn't do much damage. It looks worse than it is.'

If God existed, and if He decided there and then to give me the choice of being where I was, or being swallowed up by a gigantic hole, I would have gone with the hole. Neil had obviously allowed the police to believe that his injuries were from the man he assaulted rather than from his loving wife. Not only had he not fought back as I had attacked him, but now he had protected me from facing awkward questions from the police.

'How are you getting on with finding your parents?' he said. 'Any further down the line?'

I nodded.

'I'm getting there,' I said. 'But I could do with your help.'

He smiled.

'I'm a bit tied up at the moment,' he said. 'But when I'm free, I'll see what I can do.'

'What about work?' I said.

'I think I need a bit of a holiday,' he said. 'Besides, I've been working late a lot recently.'

CHAPTER SIXTY-SIX

Neil told me to go home to get some rest. He said we had a lot to do when he got back.

To be honest, I didn't want to leave him there at the police station.

If I had known what he had been doing, trying to find the guy who attacked me, I would have been angry with him. I would have told him to stop being so bloody childish and to get over it. Especially once I found out that the sole reason the attacker had come back to our house was to warn Neil off.

But a part of me ... quite a large part, was proud. Proud of what he had done. Proud of him as a husband and as a father to Michael and Rose. If I had been able to take a step back and think about things properly, I should probably have known that he was like that. From the first time we met, when he came to my rescue in a bar, he had always been protective. Not vengeful, but certainly protective.

This had all been too much for him. Revenge had to form a part of what had happened. He must have felt bad that he hadn't been there when I had been attacked. Hadn't been there to protect me. He hadn't been able to stop it. So the only way he could deal with it, was to go on the attack himself. Hunt the man down and protect me retrospectively.

Of course I felt proud.

And I felt like a witch. For what I had considered him capable of. Abduction, rape, murder. Conspiracy, disloyalty, unfaithfulness.

Even the police apparently only considered people capable of drug use, knife possession, gun-slinging and assault.

Either I was unusually and imaginatively suspicious, or the police were spectacularly naive and hopeful when it came to what human beings were capable of.

I had been at home for four hours, asleep on the sofa with the broken phone next to me, before I woke to the sound of a key in the front door. I ran to Neil and threw my arms around him. He winced, but didn't cry out. I stood back and undid his shirt buttons. He tried to stop me, but he was tired. I took his shirt off and pulled him gently into the living-room.

My lips trembled and I shook my head. Little movements, left then right. I didn't breathe in or out. I swallowed once and tried to smother the sob that seemed to be trying to escape my throat.

His body was covered in scratches. Dried blood, raw wounds, seeping gashes. On his chest, his arms, his back, his shoulders. It looked as though I hadn't missed a single bit of him during the onslaught.

I forced myself to look into his eyes. Mine misted over. I had to blink several times just to get the focus back. I lifted his hands to my mouth and kissed them.

'Neil ... I,'

He put his hand back to my mouth, stopping my words.

'We need to find your parents,' he said. 'But I really need to shower and sleep. It's been a long couple of days.'

I sat on the bed while he showered, listening to his involuntary grunts and noises, presumably as the soap and water touched those tender wounds on his body. He didn't know I was there, and I went back downstairs before he finished. I came back up half an hour later to find him asleep in the bed. I was pleased I had changed the sheets. I wondered whether I would need to change them again in the morning. His wounds would definitely take a while to heal.

I showered and joined him in bed. I listened to his snores, deep and penetrating. They made me feel safe. Made the world seem right again. He sounded contented. His heavy breathing rattled through me for what seemed like hours until

I eventually drifted off.

But the world wasn't right.

In my sleep I killed again.

In the morning we both slept in. Neil woke before me. I heard him in the shower. Less grunts and noises than the night before, but he was obviously still in pain. I pulled back the quilt and looked at his side of the sheet. A few stains from the wounds. Not as many as I was expecting, but more than I had hoped. I climbed out of bed, pulling the sheet off with me. I had a new sheet on before he came out of the en-suite.

He rang his office and told them he was sick.

Over breakfast he explained what had happened at the police station.

'It almost felt like they were on my side,' he said. 'Some of the time.'

He had been released on bail pending further investigations.

'They need to question the bloke in hospital,' he said. 'Get his side of the story. Which will no doubt be bollocks.'

I couldn't help staring at the marks on his face. I wanted to keep him here at home. Not let him go out anywhere. Not yet. I knew it was partly because I needed him with me. But it was also because I didn't want anyone else to see what I had done to him. I wanted to hide him until the scars and scratches had gone, and with them my guilt.

'I had the dream again,' I said. 'Last night. I killed again. Attacked, raped and killed. Then I dragged her body. Dragged it across the grass. Dragged it until the grass ran out. Until the earth ran out. Until there was nothing below us, then I let her body fall. Her and her dog, still wrapped around her wrist. The dog whined as it was pulled off the earth into nothingness.'

'Have you had a date through for this bloody assessment thing?' he said.

I shook my head.

'Then we still have time to get this sorted. I'd like to help … if you want me to?'

'My dad offered to drive me down to Cornwall, to find my parents. I'd prefer it if it was you.'

He smiled and took a large bite out of his toast.

'Do you know where we're going?' he said. 'Cornwall's quite a big place.'

'I have an idea. But it means a bit of subterfuge. Not sure it's strictly legal for someone who works in a respected bank.'

'Haven't you heard?' he said. 'I'm a dangerous criminal. I'm known to the "feds".'

'The "feds"?'

'I heard Michael say it.'

'Well that makes two of us known to them,' I said. 'You're the violent criminal and I'm the fucking lunatic. We should do well in Cornwall.'

I had searched on the Headland Park Golf Course website again, just to see if I could find any additional mention of Richard Lapton. I checked for photographs too. There were none. I also did another search for Amelie Lapton. Still nothing.

I had worked out that the journey by car from our house to the golf club would take about three hours. I rang Abi and asked if she was still OK with the kids.

'I'm fine, Chris,' she said. 'And the kids are having a lovely time. I think all four of them are treating it as a holiday.'

'This will all be over soon,' I said. 'Thank you so much for everything you've done. I don't know how I'd cope without you.'

I watched Neil making sandwiches for the journey, choosing what to wear, rushing about the place like a child. It made me wish I had gone with *him* to the Andes. He seemed energised by the thought of an adventure. On the journey I outlined my plan.

'I thought we could pretend to be friends of his,' I said. 'Looking for our old friend.'

Neil looked at me and smiled. Sneered really. 'And that's the plan?'

I smiled back at him.

'Chris, that's shit,' he said.

'It's all I could think of.'

'Well it's shit. We need to think of something better.'

I looked out of the car window for a while, nibbling my bottom lip and sulking. For some reason I had considered my plan not only brilliant, but also completely foolproof. I now felt like I had at school when I shot my hand up, convinced I knew the answer to a question from my English teacher, only to find that my answer was wrong.

I risked a peek at Neil. He still sported the smug grin he'd had when I first turned to look out of the window. I punched him on the leg. Gently, so as not to hurt him any more than I already had.

'It seemed like a good idea,' I said.

His smug grin became a full laugh. Which rippled over to my sulking lips, changing them too. First a smile, then a share in the laughter.

'I probably wouldn't make much of a detective, would I?' I said.

'Not much of one, Sherlock.'

Despite the derision with which my plan had been received, Neil wasn't able to come up with anything much better, although we finally settled on his idea. To be honest, I thought it sounded like my idea, just with different characters.

'We can say we're from the bank,' Neil said. 'I've got some of my business cards in the car, so it will carry some weight. We can say that a relative has died and we're trying to locate immediate family. We believe that Richard Lapton might be in line for something, as long as we can verify that he is who we think he is.'

I punched him on the leg again.

'Ha! I knew it was better than yours,' he said.

'You've just taken my idea and changed tiny little bits of it to make it sound like it's your idea.'

The smug grin stayed with him for longer than I had ever seen it before. As I looked at his face, I wished I could turn the clock back. Just long enough to file my nails down to nothing and to put tape over my mouth. Just long enough to look at myself in the mirror and give myself a damn good talking to. Long enough to come up with a better idea than his for finding Richard Lapton.

We pulled into the car park at Headland Park Golf Club just after 1pm. I was surprised how many cars were parked there. It was a windy day, drizzle filled the air. I wouldn't even have gone for a walk in it, let alone played a game. As we drove slowly past the cars I wondered if any of them belonged to Richard Lapton. My heart started pounding hard. I put one of my fingers to my mouth and chewed on an already jagged fingernail. Neil put his hand on my leg.

'Don't worry,' he said. 'I'm here too.'

We pulled into a spare parking space and stopped. Neil turned off the engine and looked over at me. I had one hand pushed hard against the dashboard, as though in readiness for a crash, and the other hand resting on my chest. Despite the power with which my heart was thumping away, I couldn't feel any beat through my chest. It was as though my heart had shrunk deeper within me. Hiding somewhere. Fearful and hiding.

Neil reached across to the glove box and pulled out a couple of business cards.

'They're both the same,' he said, passing one to me, 'but if I show my one first, you can just flash your one so they see the bank logo. Just stick your thumb over the name part.'

Had he done this before? Perhaps he really did have a secret life full of deception and subterfuge.

'Did you happen to see the name of the club secretary on that website?'

I shook my head.

'Should I have?' I said.

'I think the club secretary is the one in charge,' he said. 'Perhaps we should have rung first to try to get an appointment. We may have rushed at this a bit.'

'That's what I do,' I said. 'That's why you married me.'

He raised his eyebrows. This time I knew exactly what they meant.

'That's not why I married you,' he said.

I was bored with punching him on the leg, so I gave him a look instead.

'Come on,' I said. 'Let's just go.'

The first thing that struck me as we walked through the main doors of the golf club was the smell of beer. Beer and wood. And a fire. It was as though we had stepped back in time and found ourselves in an old country tavern. Black painted beams and internal leaded glass on every door added to the time travel experience. But this old fashioned world appeared strangely uninhabited by humans. Or any living thing. Either all the occupants of the cars outside had all been sucked into a black hole somewhere hidden on the premises, that we too were about to fall into, or they were out getting windswept and wet on the golf course. Given the choice, personally I would have chosen the black hole.

'I wonder where everyone is?' Neil said.

I was about to let him in on my theory, when a black painted wooden door opened to our left. A middle aged woman with black hair glided through the door. I wondered if her hair had been styled to match the decor. Both in colour and design. She looked surprised and a little alarmed to see us.

'Can I help you?' she said.

Neil stretched out his hand.

'My name is Neil Marsden,' he said. 'This is my colleague, Christine.'

I nodded at her and smiled.

'We're looking for the club secretary,' he said.

He handed her his business card, which she studied closely.

'I'm the club secretary,' she said. 'Marjorie Powell.'

Neil smiled at her.

'Thank you, Mrs Powell,' he said. 'We're trying to establish the location of a Mr Richard Lapton. The bank has been asked to verify him. It appears that someone who may be a relative of Mr Lapton, has sadly passed away leaving a not insubstantial amount of money in their bank account. We believe that Mr Lapton may have some entitlement.'

I was impressed. If it had been me who was the club secretary I would be spilling all I knew about Richard Lapton already. It made me realise how much you could get away with by using big words and loads of front.

Marjorie Powell took another look at Neil's card. I held mine in view, with my finger resting over Neil's name.

'And what brought you here?' she said. 'You've come a long way.'

'In the research we've managed to complete so far,' Neil said, 'we've traced quite a few Richard Laptons. You'd be surprised how many there are. But one of my colleagues came up with a Richard Lapton registered at this golf club — and that's why we're here.'

Marjorie handed the card back to Neil.

'My office is up here,' she said, moving back through the door she had just been coming out of. 'Would you like to come up?'

CHAPTER SIXTY-SEVEN

We followed Marjorie up the stairs to her office. Whilst she wasn't exactly honking for breath at the top, she did look like she didn't get much exercise. She certainly looked as though she had never picked up a golf club in her life. At least, not to play golf.

She sat behind a large desk and indicated that we take the seats in front of it.

'I must admit,' she said, 'to being taken aback when you said you were from a bank. You don't look like what I would expect people from a bank to look like.'

I was about to tell her that she didn't look like what I thought a golf club secretary should look like, but Neil got to her first.

'In sensitive cases, such as this, they prefer us to dress more informally. When you're going to someone's house, and you potentially have sad news to impart, it's felt that suits and ties are too austere. Too businesslike. We try to put people at their ease.'

Marjorie nodded, as though she was the one that had instigated this rule for the bank. I just sat back and basked in Neil's glory. He was masterful.

'In fact,' he said, 'if you have a picture of Richard Lapton, that would enable us to verify if he is the one we seek. That way, if he's not the right man, we wouldn't need any address details at all. We don't want to pry unnecessarily.'

Marjorie sat back in her seat. I could tell she was impressed too.

'You know, Mr Marsden, I think his photograph is in our members directory. We produce one every year. It has all members contact details, and for the past couple of years has included photographs. Not every member supplies us with one, but I have a feeling that Richard did this year.'

Neil looked at me and gave me his best professional smile.

'Well that would be terrific, Mrs Powell,' he said. 'Just what we need.'

I could only imagine how different this would be going right now if we had gone with my plan instead of Neil's. With me leading the conversation and taking charge of the operation, we would have been sunk even before being invited upstairs to Marjorie's office. I knew it would be inappropriate to punch Neil's leg.

It worried me that he was so good at spinning this web of deceit. It seemed to come as naturally to him as breathing. And he seemed to be enjoying it. There was no doubt in my mind that he was utterly wasted at the bank. When all this was over he should maybe get a job at MI5.

Marjorie flicked through a glossy A5 magazine. It took less than five seconds for her to find Richard Lapton.

'I thought so,' she said. 'Here's Richard.'

She held the magazine open and put it facing us on the table. Where Neil had been the one in charge up until now, I leaned forward with such vigour that I knocked against Marjorie's desk, making everything on it vibrate.

'I'm sorry,' I said. 'I couldn't see back there.'

Back there made it sound like I had been on the golf course itself, rather than just a foot away.

Under cover of the desk, Neil put his hand gently on my knee, just long enough to calm me down and to let me know that he was my strength if I needed it.

'What do you think?' he said, pulling the magazine closer to us.

The photograph was black and white. A head shot. Richard Lapton had thinning grey hair, but he wasn't bald. He looked tanned and happy. Wisps of hair had been lifted by the wind, the picture had obviously been taken out on the golf course. It looked as though too much sun over the years had evaporated much of the moisture from his skin, leaving wrinkles and lines carved into his features. I immediately looked at his teeth. They looked pretty good for someone of his age. I thought the photograph made him look arrogant.

'Look at those eyes,' Neil said.

It was so obviously a reflection of Rose's eyes that I had to look away for fear of giving the game away.

'Oh,' I said.

Neil looked up at Marjorie Powell. Her face expectant.

'I think this is our man,' he said. 'Could we take this?'

Marjorie nodded. I thought her eyes looked damp.

I found my voice.

'Is he a dentist?' I said.

Marjorie smiled.

'He used to be. He's retired now of course. He lives in St Germans.'

I struggled to contain the whirlwind that was buffeting inside me. I felt my body trembling. Neil noticed it too. He picked up the magazine and stood up.

'Marjorie, thank you so much for your help. On behalf of the bank I would like to thank you very much.'

He held out his hand and she shook it.

'I take it you don't want me to speak to Richard at the moment,' she said.

'We really need to speak to him first,' Neil said. 'It is quite a delicate matter.'

Marjorie nodded.

'I understand,' she said.

She walked us down to the main entrance and watched us climb into the car. Neil slammed the car door shut and spoke under his breath.

'Nearly there,' he said. 'Nearly there.'

It was becoming harder for me to keep control. Neil put the

magazine on my lap, reversed the car out of the space and drove slowly past the main entrance. He waved and smiled at Marjorie as we drove past. She smiled and waved back.

Fifty yards down the long entrance drive, I couldn't hold it in any longer. I thrust my head in my hands and wept. Huge sobs jerked my body. I knew Neil would be checking the rear view mirror to make sure Marjorie was out of sight. I assumed she was as Neil rested his hand at the base of my neck and caressed it.

'Oh, Neil,' I spluttered more than spoke, 'that was him, wasn't it? That was my dad.'

'Did you see Rose's eyes?' he said. 'I almost fell off my chair.'

Neil found a lay-by and pulled the car over. I cried for at least ten minutes. Neil's shirt was damp from my tears, so was the directory Marjorie had given us. I had never expected such emotion to well up inside me. The only reason I had wanted to find my birth parents, I thought, was to find out about any medical issues, mental health problems. To me, my Mum and Dad were my real parents and always would be. In fact, when I had thought about my birth parents I had thought of them as strangers. Not even friends. So my emotional outburst had been a shock. It made me wonder if perhaps I hadn't been entirely honest or clear with myself about how I felt.

'I'm sorry,' I said. 'I don't know where that came from. I hadn't expected to feel anything like that at all.'

'It's bound to be highly charged,' he said. 'He is your birth father after all.'

I opened the directory to his picture. I was sure I could see even more in it this time. Mostly Rose.

'That's your mouth,' Neil said.

'It's not,' I said.

'It so is.'

There was a mirror on the back of the sun visor. I adjusted it so I could see my mouth.

'It is a bit, I suppose.'

'And you've got his hair.'

Now the punch to the leg was appropriate.

'You were amazing in there,' I said. 'You're an expert liar.'

'An expert actor,' he said. 'I was playing a part. So were you. We did brilliantly. It couldn't have gone any better. Unless he had been there playing golf and she had dragged him in to see us.'

'This isn't the same address that was on the original adoption stuff,' I said. 'They must have moved.'

My use of the word "they" brought an instant silence to the car. It was the elephant in the room.

'I was going to ask,' Neil said. 'When we were in there. *Is there a Mrs Lapton?* But I wasn't sure how you would react, depending on her answer. We could always go back if you like, or ring her?'

'No,' I said. 'Let's just see, shall we. The fact that I couldn't find anything about her on the Internet, and the fact that it looks like she was the one who was ill, I'm not really holding out much hope anyway. But you never know.'

A calm came over me as Neil drove us through country lanes to the address printed in the golf-club directory. Glimpses of water were infrequent, partly because the hedgerows were so high, but also because we weren't really sure which direction the sea was in. I opened my window and breathed in. The smells of childhood flooded into the car. Fresh grass, clean earth, primrose and dandelion, cow-parsley and nettles. Livestock on the fields. And a hint of the sea.

I leaned back into my chair and closed my eyes. I saw Dad, with his fishing rod, Mum with her packet of biscuits. Summers spent climbing trees and going on imaginary adventures with my cuddlies along the carpet in the living room. Dad tried to teach me how to tie a fly, but since neither of us fished with a fly it turned into a chaos of giggles and laughter. Dad's face went so red from laughing I was scared he might keel over. But we're made of solid stuff, me and Dad. He didn't keel over. And I never learnt to tie a fly.

I hadn't done much better in the kitchen, with Mum. Flour dusting the air and my face. Sugar and butter beaten together, bits flying out of the bowl and onto the floor, and eggs poured, only a little bit at a time, but often way too much, to make fairy cakes. Mum always let me scrape the remainder out of the mixing bowl. Usually with a spoon, but sometimes with my fingers. And I was always the first one to try a cake when they came out of the oven. Even if I had made them for Dad's birthday, I would still try one before they cooled down.

'You should let them cool first,' Mum said.

'I do,' I said. 'They're cool enough for me.'

Walks in the woods, all three of us. Down by the water. Swimming in the lake.

I wanted to go back. I ached inside to go back to it all. I loved what I had now — Neil and the kids. But if only I could go back, just for a little while. There was something so different about childhood. Something wonderful and magical that just went from me as I got older. Why couldn't I hold onto it? Why had I allowed the world to take it from me? Suddenly I hated the world, real life. Hated the way it took our childhood away from us. I hated that we had to become something other than children, that we had to give up our childness — that was the price we had to pay for becoming an adult.

And once we'd paid the price, there wasn't ever any going back. Not really. We could act in childish ways, we could revisit childhood places. But we never got back the childhood itself.

My heart hurt. I squeezed my eyes tighter shut.

'Chris?'

I opened my eyes. Then squinted in the bright afternoon light.

'Chris?'

I put my hand to my mouth. He didn't need to say anything else. We were coming to a village. Not too big. It was the one we were looking for. St Germans. I opened my eyes wide now. Forgetting the bright light outside.

'Slow down,' I said.

'I am,' Neil said. 'I'm only doing twenty.'

'Slower,' I said. 'We want Pine Avenue.'

'I know, Chris. I'm looking out for it.'

I was going to say "well look harder" but managed to stop myself. I felt a tightness in my chest, like my stomach had expanded up into my lungs. I tried to roll my shoulders but my movements were too jerky to entertain rolling. My jerky eyes picked out Pine Avenue just as Neil raised his hand to point to it. He stopped the car at the side of the road.

'What do you want me to do?' he said.

I was astonished at how calm he sounded. I felt like I was sinking into an icy ocean with no life jacket, at night, and it had just started to rain. "Drowning" was too small a word to cover what I was going through at that moment.

A car drove past us and turned into Pine Avenue. I sunk down in my seat.

'Drive past,' I said. 'Just drive past the end of the road.'

Neil moved the car slowly forward. I peered up through the window as we inched past the end of the road. We were looking for house number 33. I must have looked at the wrong side of the street, because all the numbers I saw were even.

'Fuck it,' I said. 'Fuck it, let's just drive down there, Neil. The house will be on your side.'

Neil turned the car and headed back towards Pine Avenue.

'Are you sure?' he said.

'Damn right,' I said. 'Let's do it.'

CHAPTER SIXTY-EIGHT

Number 33 had a holly bush outside. Almost a holly tree. It was a tidy looking house. Painted white with neat borders and shrubs at the front. There was a garage, and no car parked in the drive. I could see lights on inside.

'Drive past,' I said to Neil. 'Not too slow, they might see us.'

Neil looked at me and drove on past the house.

'How far do you want me to go?' he said.

'Just up to the end, then turn round and come back again.'

On the return journey the house was on my side. I thought I saw shadows moving inside, but it might have been reflections on my window as the car moved forwards.

'Keep going,' I said again. 'To the end.'

At the end of the road Neil pulled over to the kerb.

'What now?' he said.

My thoughts were spinning away from me so fast I wasn't sure I could catch any of them. A boa constrictor had wound itself around my body and the air I desperately needed was only going one way — out.

I opened my door and pushed my head out. It would have looked like I was being sick to any onlooker weird enough to look. But instead I was gasping for air. Trying to suck it into me. I was aware of pushing at the invisible snake still wrapped around my torso. In the distance I heard Neil's voice. I signalled to him to just give me a minute. His voice fell silent.

When the snake finally slithered away, I turned to Neil. My face burned and my hand came away from it clammy.

'Sorry,' I said. 'I just needed some air.'

'Are you OK?'

'I'm fine. It's just ... you know.'

He nodded. Waited for me to speak.

'Now we're here,' I said. 'I don't really know what to do. I'm scared, Neil. I'm scared of what I might find. My mother might be dead. I might have the most horrendous mental illness waiting in my genes. Sleeper cells, primed and ready to activate as soon as they get the order to go.

'What if he doesn't want to know me? What if he's hostile? Or denies being my father? Or tells me to fuck off and never darken his door again? Of course I want to see him, and if my mother is still alive ... but the consequences could be enormous.'

'That's why we're here, Chris. The consequences either way are potentially enormous. You're already in the queue for a psychiatric assessment, which could happen any time now. Things are already not looking good. This has the potential to at least bring some clarity, some certainty. Even if there is no good news, at the very least you might find some truth.'

I knew he was right. There was nothing to fear here, except inaction. Failure to do anything would indeed be failure. To have come all this way only to turn back at the final hurdle would be madness — which of course was part of the reason I was there. But still something shook within me.

'Could you ring the doorbell?' I said. 'Ring the doorbell and run away?'

'Are you serious?'

'Then I can get a look at him when he comes to the door. Or maybe my mother.'

'Chris, that doesn't sound like a good idea, really. I'd be seen by someone. And these people, your father and possibly your mother, are getting on a bit. I don't think it's right to worry them like that.'

I stared out of the window but focused on nothing. I chewed on my fingernail again. Rubbed my itching eyebrow.

'Could you pretend to be someone?' I said. 'Like you did at the golf club. Just get him to the door, and pretend to be someone. A Jehovah or something?'

'Do I look like a Jehovah? Seriously? I wouldn't have the first idea what to say to him.'

'What about a salesman,' I said. 'You could pretend to be selling insurance or double-glazing. I'll hang around in the car and watch.'

'I can, Chris. But what good would that do? You already know what he looks like from the photo in the directory. You don't need to see him again. You need to meet him. Speak to him. I will come with you. We'll go together. We're in this together.'

Except that we weren't. Yes, Neil was with me. But he wasn't in it with me. I was the one with the mental illness cells, I was the one with the scars on my head and I was the one whose parent or parents were behind the door of number 33 Pine Avenue. Parents I had no knowledge of and who had no knowledge of me. Thirty six years with no contact either way was a lot to overcome.

'Come with me then,' I said. 'Stay with me and we'll go there now. We'll walk there.'

Neil parked the car up on the kerb as I tried to make my hair look decent in the sun-visor mirror. We climbed out of the car and Neil came round to join me on the pavement. He took my hand and squeezed it as we started off, step by step, down Pine Avenue.

I looked up at the trees for evidence that the chill brushing the back of my neck had been caused by a breeze. But the leaves were still. I felt the snake slip its body around mine again, and breathed as deeply as I could, before it became impossible to do so. The sound of our shoes on the pavement echoed around the empty space that seemed to currently exist inside my head. All the previous contents had vacated the area.

As Neil let go of my hand and took my arm instead, I

realised I was trembling. My whole body was shaking. As though I had been too long in the cold, and hypothermia was just setting in. I was relying entirely on Neil to keep our forward momentum going. My vision had blurred and my version of time had broken down. For the first time since becoming ill, I wanted a blackout. We may have walked for days, but all too soon the echoing footsteps died.

'We're here, Chris.'

We had stopped walking and Neil's voice was now the echo inside my head.

'You need to come back,' he said. 'Focus. Look at me, Chris. Make sure you're here.'

I turned my shivering head towards him and blinked my eyes several times. The colour had gone from his face and his frown ran deep. Because I was shaking so much, it made it look like Neil was too. I wished I could stop shaking so I could see whether he really was.

He held my shoulders and looked into my eyes. I thought for a moment he was going to shake me back and forth, like they do in the movies.

'Don't forget who you are,' he said. 'You're Christine Marsden. The best thing that ever happened to me. You're my wife, my lover and my best friend. You are the mum of Michael and Rose and you're everything to us.'

He leaned forward and kissed my forehead.

'And you're The Mighty Atom!'

The chill that had been touching the back of my neck turned to a warm breeze. The constricting snake was gone and the afternoon air flowed into me as it did to everyone else who breathed. My heart played its part by returning to its anatomically correct position, and functioning at something closer to its normal speed. And the vacant plot in my mind suddenly became filled again with all the paraphernalia and junk that had existed there before.

Before me I saw lists. Lists of questions I wanted to ask. All neatly written, all laid out in order of importance. At the top of the list, in large letters, was "WHY?". The last thing I wanted was for everything to sound like recriminations. I mentally moved the question to the bottom of the list and hoped it would stay there. And sounds came to me. Cars drifting past in the distance. Birds, closer by, calling to each other. And the rustle of leaves blowing. There was a breeze. And Neil, breathing slowly through his nose. Calming himself down subtly, in the hope that I wouldn't notice that he had needed to do it at all.

I nodded at him and breathed out a long sigh. He smiled at me and we turned together walking as one up the drive to the front door of number 33.

Neil stood back and let me ring the doorbell. Within fifteen seconds, which may have passed as fifteen years for all I knew, I was looking into the face of my father.

He looked first at Neil and smiled. His eyes drifted down to me and his smile widened. I smiled back. But something behind his eyes flickered. His head twitched as though a tiny pin prick had pointed him in the back of his neck. His smile shuddered slightly.

Neil looked at me. I stared at Richard Lapton.

He flicked his eyes up to Neil.

'Can I help you?' he said.

His voice sounded soft. A West-Country accent. But tinged with a hint of something else. Perhaps his education had taken place in London or the South East. He didn't sound posh, but there was definitely something added.

'Mr Lapton? Neil said.

'Yes?'

Neil looked at me again, forcing Richard Lapton's gaze to move with his. His old eyes looked into mine and the lines on his face quivered.

'My name's Christine,' I said.

Again something went off behind his pupils. This time a dozen pin pricks had stabbed him. A rash of colour ran up his neck. He seemed to topple backwards slightly and reached for the door frame to hold himself steady.

'Yes?' he said.

His voice sounded throaty. As fickle as his balance had been just a few moments earlier.

'Mr Lapton,' I said. 'I think it's possible that I might be your daughter.'

CHAPTER SIXTY-NINE

I'm not sure what kind of reaction I was expecting. Or even if I had thought far enough along to even consider a reaction. But having just heard that I might be his long lost daughter, Richard Lapton stared at me for a few moments with no flicker of anything, save for whatever it was that was happening behind his eyes. It could have been anything. Memories; recognition; regret; anger?

For me, time had slowed down. As though I had thrown a punch, and slow motion had kicked in before the response became visible. The world had suddenly become an unfamiliar place, with nature not performing in the way it normally did. Time, light and sound had all become altered. Jangled.

I felt as though we had all been dipped into this slow moving world. Like apples into toffee. Then some greater power must have noticed that there was a problem, because in an instant we were pulled out again.

A smile spread across his face. Not an *uncontrollable joy* type of smile, but one that seemed to say *I know you are — I was expecting you*. Whatever composure he lost with the slight topple and the red rash over his neck, he had now regained. Completely. He was taller than I was expecting. Not as frail as I had thought he would be. His eyes were clear and piercing. I managed a smile.

'You must come in,' he said.

He stood back from the door and waved us in with an outstretched arm. I immediately smelled a cat.

'Have you come far?' he said.

For a moment I was confused. This first meeting with my birth father seemed so anticlimactic to him that I began to wonder if we had made a mistake. I opened my mouth to speak, but no words came out. Just sounds, like stilted breaths pushed out by physical effort rather than as a result of routine bodily function.

He closed the front door behind us and walked us through to the living-room. The immaculate wooden floor echoed our footsteps back to us. Light walls, but not white. Two small paintings either side of a small window on one wall, a large flat-screen television on another. Furniture was tasteful but at a minimum. One armchair, one sofa. No sideboard, no ornaments. There were no photographs either. Richard Lapton was obviously someone who had a thing about cleanliness. I wondered if it was something to do with having been a dentist.

'Would you like a coffee?' he said.

Neil looked at me and I nodded.

'Yes please,' Neil said.

'I'll bring out milk and sugar and you can help yourselves,' he said. 'Please take a seat.'

We sat on the sofa and looked at each other.

'Nice place,' Neil said.

'A bit sparse,' I said. 'Perhaps he hasn't been here long.'

I couldn't see anything in the room that told me about Richard Lapton the person. No golfing paraphernalia, no memorabilia of any sort. Even the paintings on the wall were bland and of different styles.

There didn't seem to be a speck of dust anywhere. The contrast between there and home was stark. Even though it looked as though he lived alone, a flicker of hope burned inside that my mother might still be alive.

Within minutes he walked back into the living-room with a tray. The tray shook slightly as he put it down on a small coffee table next to the sofa. Three identical cups of black coffee; a bowl of brown sugar cubes; three teaspoons and a small jug of milk. As sparse as the room. He picked up one of the mugs, a teaspoon and two sugar cubes and sat down on the armchair.

'I can't believe it,' he said. 'I'm stunned. What a surprise.'

'My name is Christine Marsden,' I said, 'and this is Neil, my husband.'

Neil shifted forward in his seat and mumbled a "Hi".

'I only recently found out that I was adopted,' I said. 'And I believe that you are my real father. Do you think that's possible? It said in my adoption file that my father was Richard Lapton and my mother was Amelie Lapton.'

He didn't exactly flinch at the mention of my mother's name, but a ripple passed through him.

'You do look like her,' he said.

My heart fluttered a beat.

'It's uncanny really. I knew, as soon as I opened the door and saw you. I knew who you were. Christine. Still called Christine.'

'My adoptive parents didn't think it would be right to change it. They said it was a part of me.'

'Your mother loved that name.'

Loved?

'Is she …?'

'She died shortly after you were born,' he said. 'Very sad business.'

Did he mean her death, or the adoption? Or me and Neil sitting across from him now?

I swallowed hard and nodded. Kept my mouth clamped shut and swallowed again. I wanted to squeeze my eyes shut, but I knew to do so would start the tears rolling from them. I forced them to stay open.

Although I had expected bad news about my mother, I had, of course, been desperately hoping for good news. I had hoped to see them both, mother and father longing for the day I would turn up at their door.

'How did you know where to find me?' he said.

I had to clear my throat to speak. The words were caught somewhere, latched onto the sadness of my mother's death. I was angry with myself for feeling so churned up over someone I had never known, someone who was less than a stranger. Someone who had given me up.

I found my voice. Took control of my emotions.

'On the Internet,' I said. 'I found a mention of you on the Headland Park Golf Course website. It just sort of went from there really. And here we are.'

I didn't want to mention the deceit with Marjorie Powell. Not only did I not want to get her into trouble, but it didn't feel right to kick off this reunion by admitting to lies and falsehood.

'Aha! The good old golf club,' he said. 'And the Internet is an amazing thing isn't it. Everyone is available. No hiding.'

His eyes flicked up towards the ceiling then back down again.

'But you say you saw an adoption file,' he said 'Did that give you much information?'

'An address in Cawsand. It said that you were a dentist and that my mother was a librarian. Have you lived here long?'

'I moved here about eight years ago, after my second wife died. Apart from Ernie, my cat, I've been here on my own ever since. I suppose the golf club has been my salvation really. Stopped me from going under, you know.'

I couldn't imagine anything making him go under. He looked too strong for that. But losing two wives probably made you strong.

'They did tell us, at the time,' he said, 'that no one would ever see any files or information about the adoption. They told us that once you were gone, that would be it. No comeback, no contact — nothing.'

'They changed the law a few years ago,' I said. 'Giving both adopted children and birth parents the right to see documents relating to the adoption. So both can get in touch with each other.'

He shook his head. Still smiling.

'Well, I never knew that,' he said. 'A change in the law.'

Something moved behind him, behind the armchair. A ginger cat. Well groomed, but very thin. My father saw my eyes follow the cat. His smile disappeared and his eyes narrowed. He snapped around in his chair.

'ERNIE! Get out of here.' He took a swipe at the cat and it leapt away from him, disappearing into the kitchen.

'That damned cat,' he said. 'Always getting in the way.'

His smile returned and he looked at Neil.

'How long have you been married?' he said. 'Do you have children?'

Neil smiled at him, but looked back to me, forcing my father to look at me too. I suppose Neil thought that this was about me and my father and he obviously didn't want to take anything away from that.

'We've been married twelve years,' I said. 'We have two children. Michael, he's eleven, and Rose, she's eight.'

My father clapped his hands together.

'Delightful,' he said. 'How lovely.'

'Did you ever wonder about me?' I said.

The question shocked me. I had thought that the only reason I wanted to find my birth parents was to ascertain what was running through my genes. What kind of madness was lurking there. I had even forced the "why" question down to the bottom of my mental list. I had a feeling it was floating back up to the top.

His smile broadened.

'Often,' he said. 'Often thought about you and what your life had become. Difficult not to, you know. But you just try and move on, don't you. Just try to live your life. That's what I've had to do. There was no other choice really.'

I knew it was coming. It wasn't possible to keep it down. I

reached for Neil's hand and pulled it closer, squeezing hard. He squeezed back.

'Why was I put up for adoption?'

My father shook his head. His smile dimmed.

'Oh Christine. You were just a baby. I had just started a dental practice and was working all hours to make it work. Your mother wanted to work at the library, she liked books and I thought she was happy there. In a way, I think it was my fault. I was working so hard having set up the practice, working so hard to make sure we had a secure home. She hadn't had an easy childhood, you see. It was difficult for her. So a secure home was important to her. I didn't notice. I suppose I was so busy trying to make things right. But she was unhappy, I think. Perhaps it was because I wasn't around as much as we would have both liked. I asked her to join me at the practice. To help with paperwork and things, but I think she thought it would be too difficult for her, what with the language and everything.'

'The language?'

'She was French. She had only been in England for a year when we met. So she thought her English wasn't up to standard. In actual fact her English was pretty good. But that's why she wanted to stay at the library — she thought working with the books would help her to pick up more of the language.'

'So was she unhappy with me?' I said.

He shook his head. 'You weren't on the scene at that time. She had started to drink quite heavily while I was at work. She hid it from me. I had no idea it was going on. She seemed to go into herself, withdraw. Then she stopped working at the library, she'd pop in there from time to time for a couple of hours just to read, but really things were not good for her.'

He sipped his coffee and drew breath.

'I thought we were a happy family,' he said. 'I thought

everything was going really well. Yes, I was working too hard, but we both knew that that wouldn't last, just as soon as the practice became established.

'And then I came home one night and found the front door unlocked and open. I'd been working late again. She was lying on the kitchen floor. She had passed out. There was an empty wine bottle broken on the floor next to her. Emily was upstairs, crying. Anyone could have come in. Anyone.'

'Emily?' I said. 'Who was Emily?'

The smile appeared again.

'Emily is your sister.'

CHAPTER SEVENTY

A sharp pain shot through my unseen leg wound. A thumping started up in my head and my pounding heart slipped its moorings again.

Neil squeezed my hand tight, as though holding me through the emotion would keep me safe. He was the anchor I needed to keep me from floating skyward, unable to cope with any more of what life had to throw at me.

Like a rumbling avalanche, thoughts crashed down, only to be replaced, moments later, with a new crop. All tumbling on top of each other. Each one buried beneath the one following. My mental list of questions doubled in number. And I still hadn't had the full answer to one of my first — "why?".

'My sister?' I said.

It didn't sound as though the words had come from me. My mouth moved, my brain engaged long enough to get the two words out, but they sounded distant. As though spoken by someone else and echoed to us through this sparse room. I imagined us all sitting in a cave. Every sound amplified and thrown around the space by jagged formations and smooth rock-faces.

'You had an older sister,' my father said. 'Have an older sister, probably. Her name was Emily. She was still a baby, really. Not even a year I don't think. And your mother collapsed drunk on the floor with the front-door open. It was a shocking scene. Tragic.'

Again, more questions exploded into my head like popcorn. From what he had just said, it was clear that he didn't know where Emily was. Or even if she was alive.

The smile hadn't left his face. Not once throughout this imparting of information, and yet it had felt as though he was getting his own back. Getting back at me for arriving at his door and telling him I was his daughter.

'I had no idea,' I said. 'There was no mention of it in the file.'

His smile grew. He looked like his photograph in the golfer's directory. An uneasy feeling crept up my spine.

'After that, of course, it all came out. How much she had been drinking, how out of control she had been. And all the while I thought we had been working towards a shared dream.

'Within six months of that happening, Emily was adopted. Your mother couldn't look after her, you see. Of course I protested, even offered to give up the practice, but that would have meant no money coming in at all. We all just wanted the best for Emily, so adoption seemed like the only route. I didn't think I would ever get over it. It was one of the hardest things I ever had to bear.

'I didn't blame your mother, of course. But she blamed herself. She tried to pull herself together, tried to get straight, as it were, but it was always a struggle. You could see it in her eyes. I think there was something there, you see. Something running through her family, something fragile.'

Neil put his other hand on top of our already clasped hands. Shielding them. Keeping them safe.

'What do you mean?' I said. 'Something fragile?'

'I don't know. I think her mother was the sensitive type. I suspect her father was a bit of a rogue. That was why she came over here in the first place, to get away from them. I don't know the full ins and outs, she didn't really talk about it much. But I sensed she liked the security she felt with me. The feeling that everything would be alright, she'd be safe. Do you know what I mean?'

I nodded. Neil too.

'I really did everything I could. I worked less, came home during the day, tried to bring her back to normality. Then she got it in her mind that she was well enough to have another child. She was convinced that she would be able to cope. She convinced me too. That was when you came along. I really thought it was a turning point. I really thought that I would have a child to love and care for. To keep.

'But it wasn't to be. Even before you were born the authorities were making noises, looking back at what had happened before, looking into your mother's medical history. I think they had made their decision before they even came to see us. So once again our lives were ripped apart. You were taken from us.

'Well, I'll be honest, it almost finished me. It was almost too much for me to take. But I tried to hold strong — for your mother's sake really. Strong and supportive.

'But her drinking got worse after that. Her moods were appalling and she became quite physical. I would just take it, of course. I couldn't fight back, it wouldn't have been right. In the end I think life just got so unbearable that even the drink wasn't numbing it anymore.

'I encouraged her to seek out her family, to make redress between them all, but she was reluctant to do anything. We carried on with our daily lives. I pushed on with the practice, hoping that the extra money would bring some sort of stability into her life. She even went back to the library for a short while, but I could see it was no good for her.

'Then one morning I woke up and she wasn't there. In the bedroom I mean. It had become increasingly rare for her to wake up before me — because of the alcohol. But I thought she may have gone downstairs to prepare breakfast, she did every now and then.

'Every night she would leave her clothes on a chair by the bed, ready to wear in the morning. As soon as I saw her clothes still folded on that chair I knew that something was wrong. I felt her side of the bed and it was cold. I slipped out of bed and into my dressing gown.

'I found her on the stairs. She had tied one end of a rope to the top of the banister and the other end around her neck. I think she just climbed over the banister and hung herself. She had made no noise. And there was no note. The world had just got too much for her. And I could understand that. Losing my children was the most awful thing. It's something you never really get over, you know?'

I wiped the tears away from my eyes and dug into my pocket for a tissue. My nose was running and my body shook. Finding no tissue, I wiped my nose on my sleeve. Neil's arm came around my neck and shoulders, and he rested his head on mine. I sobbed quietly.

I was aware of my father standing up. The coffee mugs clinked as he picked them up and placed them on the tray. His footsteps echoed away to the kitchen.

'I'm so sorry, Chris,' Neil said, his voice barely above a whisper.

I shook my head.

'It's just so sad,' I said. 'So, so sad.'

A tap gushed in the kitchen, followed by the sound of a dishwasher being opened and the cups and spoons being placed in it.

The tears were dripping off my nose and cheeks and falling onto my trousers, making damp patterns of sadness.

My father's footsteps echoed back into the room.

'I'm sorry, Christine,' he said. 'I suppose this has all come as quite a shock to you.'

I sniffed and looked up at him. A benign smile on his tanned face. Looking down at me. He looked like he was sorry for me.

'It's OK,' I said. 'Was she ... I mean, had she ... been there long?'

'She was quite dead when I found her. The police suggested that she had got up in the middle of the night to do it. I had been working so hard that I slept through just about anything.

They said there was no way I could have prevented it. I suppose she had been determined, you see. Determined to make amends for what she thought she had done. She blamed herself for you and Emily. Blamed herself for the way things had turned out.'

'How were you?' I said. 'How did you cope?'

'The only way I knew how. I just threw myself into my work. It's what she would have wanted. It was our dream to make the practice work, to make a success of it. So that's what I did. I just got straight on with making it work. For her. For her memory.'

I realised I was burning hot. Not just my face, but my whole body felt like it was on fire. I sat back and fanned my face with my hand. Neil looked to my father.

'Is it possible to open a window?' he said. 'I think a bit of fresh air might help.'

My father nodded and walked to the small window between the bland paintings. He pushed it open, but not too far.

'Ernie has a habit of trying to get out of open windows,' he said. 'So I have to be quite careful.'

I stood and walked over to the window. My father stepped aside as I approached.

'Are you OK?' he said.

'I'm fine. I'll be OK in a minute. Just a bit of fresh air, that's all.'

The small window was slightly higher than head height, looking up to look out I could see grey clouds shunting slowly across a pale blue sky. I realised it had stopped raining. The world was moving on. Relentless and reliable. Never really changing. Individual stories developing all the time. Lives ending, lives beginning, lives struggling. But out of this little window, the world remained constant. Oblivious to my tears, not caring less, or more, about my sadness. I breathed in the air. Listened to the birds. Seagulls calling on the wind. Soaring on the breeze, searching for the next meal. I wondered how long seagulls lived. Did they die of old age? Why weren't our streets littered with the bodies of dead birds, just worn out of life, dying as they flew? What happened to all the dead birds? I turned from the window.

'What happened to her?' I said. 'Afterwards? Was she buried?'

'At the church in Cawsand. Her family didn't even come over. It was ever so sad.'

I nodded and swallowed back more tears.

'You said earlier that she got ... physical? What did you mean by that?'

'She wasn't herself,' he said. 'She would lash out, become more aggressive. She had an anger inside her.'

I couldn't bring myself to look at Neil. His scratched face and body were already etched into my mind.

'Did she ever hurt anyone?'

My father looked surprised by the question.

'Hurt anyone?' he said.

'Did she ever hurt anyone else?' I said.

He frowned. The lines already on his forehead deepening further.

'Part of the reason I wanted to find you,' I said. 'And my mother, if she was still alive, was because of what's happening in my life at the moment.'

I glanced at Neil. He gave me a tight smile.

'About three months ago,' I said. 'I was attacked. Mugged. Someone hit me over the head, and when I fell I hit my head on the pavement.'

I lifted the hair from my forehead. He winced at the scar.

'And since then I've been having blackouts and things. Voices and visions, nightmares. All horrible. And also I've been experiencing physical changes in myself. I've been more aggressive, more angry. And I've felt stronger too.'

My father sat back in his chair, folded one arm across his chest and rested the thumb of the other hand under his chin. He tapped his nose gently with his forefinger. He looked as though he was listening to a bedtime story. Eyes drifting off, imagining the scene I was painting for him. His ever present smile ever present.

'I have had swelling to my brain, due to the head injuries, but the doctors have become additionally concerned about some of the things that have been happening to me. I'm due to have a psychiatric assessment in a couple of weeks. To ascertain whether or not I have a mental illness.'

I swallowed and rubbed my eyebrow. My father continued tapping his nose, and eye-drifting.

'One of the questions the doctor asked me, was if there was any history of mental illness in my family. That was what started this whole thing off, finding my birth parents. That's why I only found out recently that I had been adopted. Because I asked the question of my ... adoptive parents. Obviously, they didn't know. So now I'm here. Asking the same question of you. Is there any history of mental illness in my family?'

My father flinched at the question. Stiffened. That gave me the answer. Not the answer I wanted, but the answer I had been bracing myself to expect. His head twitched slightly and his drifting eyes came crashing back to reality. His Adam's apple moved up and down as he swallowed and the redness returned to his neck.

'So there was something,' I said. 'Was it just her, or did it go further back in her family?'

A momentary confusion passed across his face, then his whole body seemed to relax.

'As I said,' he said. 'I think both her mother and father were unusual types. Who knows what went on back through the ages. I really didn't know much about them all. But there was obviously something not right in your mother. I hadn't wanted to tell you. You didn't really need to know. But seeing as things are happening to you to.'

I nodded. Tried to loosen my shoulders.

'I had expected it,' I said. 'It kind of makes sense. What about your family?'

'Mine? Oh, we're all fine. Apart from a tendency towards heart attacks. My father died of one, and an uncle. My brother has heart problems too. That's why I play golf. Keeps me going. Keeps my heart working, you know?'

'I wonder if it's possible to get medical records for my mother. And maybe her family?' I said.

My father shook his head.

'From all that time ago? I wouldn't have thought so. Do they keep records that long? I can't imagine they would. I wouldn't know where to start even. Perhaps the Internet?'

I hadn't really meant to ask the question out loud, my mind had just started tumbling thoughts again.

CHAPTER SEVENTY-ONE

We spent another hour with my father before he apologised and said he had an engagement that evening and needed to get ready. We exchanged phone numbers and agreed that we would meet up again very soon. I think he had been happy to see me.

As we drove away from his house I tried to work out what I was feeling. Too much. I ached for a past I never had, mourned for a mother I had never known and searched for something in my father. My stomach felt like a washing machine full of emotions, swirling one way then the other. Draining away then filling up again. Twisting and turning within me, becoming more and more tangled.

I focused on a black bird gliding over a wave of wind, wings outstretched, at one with nature. The world behind it, grey clouds scudding through the sky, continuing on as before. The same now as it was then.

I realised Neil hadn't said anything since we left my father's house.

'You're very quiet,' I said.

'So are you.'

I was allowed to be. I had just met my father for the first time that I could remember. I had just found out that my mother had killed herself after her children (including my sister) were taken away from her. And that mental illness coursed through her family like a river. Reason enough to be a bit pensive.

'I've got things to think about,' I said. 'What's your excuse?'

He smiled, but didn't take his eyes off the road ahead.

'Well?' I said. 'What's going on inside your head?'

Neil breathed in deeply. Thought for a moment.

'What did you think of him?' he said.

The question jarred me a little. It was too specific. What did I think of him? Rather than what did I think of it? I had been thinking of the whole thing. The meeting, his house, what we'd said to each other. Neil was obviously going somewhere with this.

'Of him?' I said.

'Of him,' he said.

'I thought he was lovely. Considering what a shock this must have been, I think he coped with it remarkably well. And his life has been so difficult. I can't imagine what losing me and my sister would have done to him. And then his wife ... my mother, committing suicide. It's awful. It's a wonder the poor man is able to keep going really.'

I shook my head of the sadness welling up inside.

'And his father having a heart attack,' I said. 'His brother ill too. So he has that hanging over him. Thank goodness he's been made stronger by all that's happened to him. He's had to make himself stronger. Can you imagine what could have happened if we'd turned up and his heart was weak?'

Neil still stared straight ahead.

'What did you think?' I said.

'I think he seemed nice,' Neil said.

'Seemed nice?'

'What do you want me to say, Chris? He's your father. You've just met him and he's your father.'

'What do you mean?'

'I mean that he probably came across different to me than he did to you. You were seeing him as your father, quite rightly. But to me, he was just a stranger.'

'He was a stranger to me too,' I said. 'How did he come across to you then?'

'It was probably the shock,' Neil said. 'You're right. It must have been a big shock to him. I don't know how I would react in a situation like that. It must have been so difficult.

Especially with me there too. He must have felt like he had to explain himself or maybe he felt ganged up on a bit. Maybe I should have stayed in the car.'

'Neil?'

At last he took his eyes off the road and glanced at me. He looked so serious. Eyebrows level, a slight crinkle in his brow, lips tight together.

'Tell me,' I said. 'Tell me what you thought.'

'I don't know,' he said. 'He sort of reminded me of an actor. Someone playing a role, rather than being real. I'm so pleased you've found him, Chris, but obviously I worry about you too. I don't want you being hurt. So maybe I was looking out for something that wasn't even there. Maybe I imagined it because I was feeling protective.'

'Imagined what?'

'Just things, really. He seemed so cool about us being there. Getting the coffees, sitting down and talking to us. It was as though he had rehearsed it over and over again. Almost cold, in fact. Talking about your mum, about your sister. Watching you breaking down in front of him, he just seemed to take it all in his stride. Seemed to let it all wash over him. Pass over him.'

'I didn't break down,' I said.

'You know what I mean. He didn't come to you. Didn't hug you. It was as though he wasn't really there. Physically he was, but emotionally I mean. Nothing there. That's how I saw it. I'm probably wrong. It's so hard, isn't it. Everyone's different, so I don't know what I should have expected. It was nice to see him though. How do you feel?'

Now I felt like I wanted to scream at him. How dare he say these things about my father? How dare he?

'I think you're wrong,' I said. 'I didn't see that at all. He was in shock. The man has to be careful of his heart, Neil. Think about the things he's gone through. He can't afford to let his emotions get the better of him. He must have learnt to control his emotions because of the heart thing. I think what you saw was just enormous self-control.'

I rubbed my eyebrow with the knuckle of my forefinger.

'And he probably doesn't want to get hurt again,' I said. 'Can you imagine? His daughters are taken from him, then years later one turns up again. He probably can't believe it. He's probably scared to give too much of himself straight away in case it all goes wrong again for him. He must be thinking that if he's too full on, it might put me off. It might scare me away and I might never come back.'

Although Neil was nodding as I spoke, I knew he was only doing it for me. Nothing I'd said had really changed what he felt. He wasn't patronising me, just trying to be understanding, maybe giving me and my father the benefit of the doubt.

'That's honestly what I think,' I said.

''I'm sure you're right,' he said. 'I think I was just being a bit too suspicious. I'm sorry.'

I looked back out of the window. The dark, soaring bird had gone, but the clouds still moved across the sky.

'Can we go to Cawsand?' I said. 'I want to find the church where my mother is buried.'

St Andrew's was the only church in Cawsand. It was larger than I had expected. Almost out of proportion to the tiny village. I couldn't imagine why they needed such a large church. The main road into the village was more like a lane. I was grateful that we didn't meet any cars coming the other way. Neil parked us right outside the church.

A rusty, decorative archway, rainbowed over the little gate that led to the steps leading up towards the church. Greenery was everywhere, as though it was trying to take over the church. The walls and steps, the building itself, all fighting against the flora surrounding it.

Behind the church the graveyard had all but lost the battle.

Brambles had engulfed many of the headstones. Lichen and bird muck covered much of the ones the brambles hadn't yet reached. Something caught in my stomach.

'This is so sad,' I said.

Neil pushed aside nettles with his feet, tried to read some of the headstones. Birds sang out from the surrounding branches, probably unused to being disturbed by anyone venturing there.

My mother's headstone was in a dreadful state. It was obvious that no one had visited it for many, many years. Neil held his arms around me as my tears fell. Nettle leaves shining wet below me. Deep inside my tummy was where I felt it. I could feel my heart still pumping. That wasn't broken, but I was. Right inside my gut. A huge hole had opened up within me, empty and vast. Neil tensed his arms and held tighter. I couldn't feel my legs below the knees. The sensation of nothingness swept over me. When my legs started to buckle, Neil must have thought I wanted to kneel down in front of her headstone. He gently lowered me to the ground.

But I didn't want to pray. I wanted to stand. To stand upright and be strong. To salute her for what she had gone through. I wanted to show her that I had strength too. That I was here thanks to her, not in spite of her. I willed the blood back into my legs. Forced the exhaustion out of my mind and capped the unbelievable sadness in my gut. I held Neil's arm and pulled myself to my feet.

'Come on,' I said. 'Let's get this cleaned up a bit.'

After cleaning my mother's headstone, and some of the surrounding growth, there was something else I had to do.

'Can we find the house?' I said.

'How could we come here and not look for it?' Neil said.

We walked only a few minutes from the church before we found Bay View road. Walking through the tiny streets of Cawsand gave me an incredible sense of deja-vu, even though

I had never been there before, apart from as a baby. I had been adopted almost at birth, so it wasn't probable for me to have any sense of the place. But something inside me said that I had been there before.

The house was plastered pale yellow on the outside. No front garden, and right on the road leading past it. But it looked like a road that was only travelled by pedestrians. No sign of cars anywhere.

'It's changed,' I said.

I blushed. The comment sounded pretentious.

'I mean, it must have changed — after all those years. I can't imagine it would have looked just like this back then.'

'It might have done,' Neil said.

I looked at the small windows facing the front of the house. Imagined myself looking out of them. But that never happened. I had been a baby. My mother would have looked out of them. Watching people walking by. Looking out for my father to come home from work. Was I getting a sense of her? Was part of me feeling what she would have felt? I wondered if she knew her daughter was here now. Looking in at the house, imagining her looking out.

I saw the staircase, tried to push it out of my mind. Her life ending there. Alone in the night, quietly ending it all, escaping the pain and the guilt. Finally beating the illness seeping through her mind.

I touched the yellow plaster. Pressed my hand against the house. Let the coolness of the stone pass onto my palm.

I had expected to feel something from the house. Like a tremor or some message from the past transferring into me. But I felt nothing but pain. Not from the house, but from within me. A yearning for something I could never have. Not in a "poor me" kind of way. More a "poor her". I wanted to be able to change what had happened to her. To somehow go back and make everything alright. To meet her on the stairs.

To tell her I loved her and that she was special. To beg her not to take the rope. To go back to her bed and wake up in the morning and live life.

But I understood.

In the end there was only one way to be rid of the madness within her. Only one certain way. And that was the way she took.

CHAPTER SEVENTY-TWO

One of the first decisions I made after meeting my birth father was to have Michael and Rose back properly. I reckoned that if I was going to hurt anyone, I would have done it by now. Obviously I had hurt Neil, but that was different. I hadn't blacked out then. To my shame I didn't even have that excuse. I had been fully aware during the whole thing.

It was lovely having them back again. Neil made sure that he was with me as much of the time as possible when I was with the children — just in case I went loopy on them. He went into work after they had left for school, and made sure that he was home as soon as possible after they got home. He used up a lot of his annual leave in half-days.

I saw Colin again. On my own this time. It turned out that the missing phrenology head, the scratches on his face and the bandaged wrist were all as a result of his cat — Mathilda. She had knocked over the head, which smashed on the floor, but she had stayed balanced on the small table she had knocked it from. Colin tried to lift her off the table so that she wouldn't cut herself on the broken bust, and she scratched him. He fell back and cut his wrist on one of the broken pieces. I met Mathilda. I still didn't like cats.

I had an appointment date through for my psychiatric assessment. It sent me into a frenzy of tidying up around the house. I had two weeks to go.

The dreams of the girls being killed and dragged into oblivion were a constant, though unwanted, companion. Whether awake or asleep they were always with me. Always there in my conscious and unconscious mind.

We talked more than we had done for a long time. Neil and

me. Talked about everything. All the things we had done together, all the things we would like to do in the future. At one level, it helped to keep me positive. To think about the places we would go and the lives we would live. But, of course, on another level it scared the shit out of me. I wasn't sure that my future held anything more than being secured in a hospital somewhere, medicated up to my eyeballs.

Dad was brilliant — the dad who took me fishing and helped explain the world to me.

'Chris,' he said. 'We will always be here for you. We'll make sure Michael and Rose aren't taken away. Neil is there for them, and we are too. Besides, you're not going to be locked up anywhere. You'll be fine.'

And when he said it, I believed it. Against my own thoughts and suspicions, I felt I could hold onto what my dad said, because he was my dad.

I told Mum, the one who baked cakes with me, about my birth mother. About her suicide.

'Oh how awful,' Mum said. 'I'm so sorry, darling.'

'He found her on the stairs,' I said. 'She had done it sometime in the night. Obviously just couldn't take it anymore. Neil and I went to her grave, . Tidied it up a bit. No one had been there for years.'

'Are you going to see him again soon?' Dad said. 'Your father?'

His words twisted inside me. I know he hadn't meant them to. He was just trying to be as understanding as possible. Trying to make it as easy as possible for me.

'You're my dad,' I said. 'You always have been and always will be. Nothing will ever change that. Richard Lapton is not much more than a stranger to me. He may be my birth father, but he won't ever be my dad.'

'I don't know what else to call him,' Dad said. 'Don't know the words to use.'

Neither did I. It was difficult for us all.

'Richard, I suppose,' I said.

'Are you going to see Richard again?' Dad said.

'I think so. There are so many questions that I feel I need answers to. I don't know about long-term, but certainly for the moment I think I need to see him as often as I can. What with the assessment coming up. I may not get the chance in the future.'

The next time I went to see my Richard, I went alone. I still couldn't risk driving. The train from Bristol to St Germans took just under three hours, including a change at Plymouth. A week had passed since our first encounter. In truth, I had wanted to go back down again the very next day, but we both needed a bit of time to soak up what had happened. I rang him instead, and he sounded happy to hear from me.

'I feel a bit funny about what to call you,' I said.

'Why don't you call me Richard.'

He met me at the station. Although the house was only a few minutes away, he had come by car.

'Shall I take you for a coffee?' he said.

We drove to the outskirts of St Germans and parked outside what looked to me like a large wooden cabin. There were quite a few cars in the car park and a campsite in a field adjoining the cabin.

'There are lots of places like this,' he said. 'Throughout Cornwall. Lovely food too.'

I hadn't realised how hungry I was. An "All day breakfast" was just what I needed. Richard had toast.

'I went to Cawsand,' I said. 'To the church. It's ever so overgrown there.'

'I haven't been down there for quite some time,' he said. 'I suppose it was too painful for me really. Brought back too many memories. Did you find …?'

I nodded.

'We cleared some of the undergrowth and brambles. Made it look a bit nicer. But the whole graveyard is seriously in need of some love and attention.'

I didn't mention going to the house. I didn't want to stir up any memories that he had buried deep within him.

He looked out of the cafe window. I wondered if he was looking in the direction of Cawsand.

'It was such a shock,' he said. 'You and Neil turning up like that. Took me completely by surprise. You know, you hope for things. Wonder if things will ever happen. And then when they don't, year after year, when you've waited for so long, you just resign yourself. Just accept that they never will happen. That your life just isn't going to be like that. And then there you were — on my doorstep. Just like that.'

I wanted to reach out and hold his hand. Break through the physical barrier that the years had built. Just a touch of our hands would heal us both, send the years flying away. His lips started trembling.

'Marjorie spoke to me, at the golf club,' he said. 'Told me that you and Neil had been to see her. She was under the impression that you both worked for a bank, that I had some money coming to me.'

He turned his gaze from the window and looked directly into my eyes. I blushed.

'I'm sorry,' I said. 'I didn't know how else to find you. It wasn't Marjorie's fault. Neil does work at the bank, but I just needed to get an address. I am sorry.'

His mouth tightened into a smile. His lips stopped trembling.

'It's all for the best though, isn't it,' he said. 'All's well that ends well.'

We sat in silence for a few minutes. Both staring out of the window, both caught up in our own thoughts. I wondered if any of those thoughts crossed over. Was he too thinking of my mother? Wondering what might have happened if she hadn't been afflicted? What if?

'How bad was she?' I said.

His head didn't move from the window. He blinked a couple of times, swallowed.

'Did you manage to find any medical records?' he said.

'No. You can't get that sort of thing Online. I spoke to the adoption adviser about it, but she said that it probably wouldn't be possible to find them even if they still existed. Most GP records are only kept for ten years after the death of a patient. It's longer for mental health issues, but not if the person dies.'

He stopped gazing out of the window and turned his attention fully to me.

'I don't really know what to say to you, Christine. I've told you what happened. First Emily taken away from us, then you. Obviously there was a reason for that. They don't just take children into adoption for the sake of it. They must have recognised the illness in her. Maybe she even recognised it herself, perhaps that was why she drank so much. It's hard to imagine anyone of sound mind taking their own life.'

'But what was she like with you? How was she around you?'

He put his finger to his nose, rested his thumb underneath his chin. Just like he had at his house the first time we'd met.

'I loved your mother very much. And she loved me. I never doubted that. In a way, that made it all the more difficult to bear. All her mood swings and strange behaviour. It seemed that for a long time I didn't really know where I was with her. All I could do was give her the best love and attention possible. And that's what I did. I just loved her.'

He smiled. And for a moment I saw what Neil had seen. An act. The briefest moment of performance. Then I blinked and it was gone.

'Was she getting help?' I said. 'Was she seeing anyone about it?'

'I think just her doctor,' he said. 'There wasn't much else could be done back then. A little place like Cawsand. Plymouth probably had mental health people there, but your mother never went to see any of them. I think she was in denial, you see. Didn't really think she was ill. Didn't think she had a problem. I encouraged her to get help. I offered to go with her to see whoever she needed to see. But she wouldn't hear of it. She was a strong woman. Very determined. Knew what she wanted.'

A warm feeling grew inside me. For the first time I was hearing the things I wanted to hear. About how like me she was. And how like her I was.

'Do you have any photographs of her?' I said.

He shook his head quickly.

'None, I'm afraid. I think she destroyed a lot of them herself. As though she couldn't bear to look at them. Because she blamed herself for what had happened with you and Emily. She didn't like to look at what she thought she had become. I managed to keep a few, of course, but I think they were all lost when I moved. You know how it is. Boxes of stuff from one attic to the next, never opened. I daresay there might even be one in the attic at home somewhere, but it's a nightmare up there. I can't even get up there myself now. Too old and shaky. Like I said to you before — things like pictures just bring back too many bad memories. It's hard.'

We left the cafe and walked to the car. At one point I thought he was going to take my arm, but I think he just stepped awkwardly on a pebble and nudged into me by mistake. We drove to his home. Ernie the cat sat in the living-room window looking out at us as we walked to the front door.

Richard fetched us both another coffee and we relaxed into the soft chairs in the sparse room.

'I've been given a date for my assessment,' I said. 'My

psychiatric assessment. It's in two weeks time. That was why I really wanted to try to find as much about my mother's history as possible. To see if it could shed any light on my current situation.'

Ernie hovered behind Richard's chair. I wondered if he might lash out at him again.

'It's such a shame they don't have the medical records,' he said. 'I'm sure they would have been so helpful.'

'I told you I get dreams,' I said. 'Dreams and visions. They're with me all the time really. Horrible nightmares. That's why I asked you if she ever hurt anyone else. Because in these dreams, I hurt people. Badly hurt them. Kill them, I think.'

'Could these not just be as a result of your head injuries?' he said. 'You said that your brain swelled?'

I nodded. 'I'm sure that some of the things I'm experiencing are as a result of that. I'm sure they are. My sense of smell has gone haywire for a start. But this seems different. It's like this is a part of me. Ingrained into me. That's why I think it comes from my mother. That's why it would have been so useful to find out about her family.'

We sipped our coffees. Behind Richard's chair Ernie arched his back.

'What was her maiden name?' I said.

He took another sip of coffee and stared over my head. Surely he didn't need to think about what his wife's name was? Or was he considering what I might do with the name if he gave it to me?

'The name was Pelland,' he said. 'But I don't want you getting hurt.'

'What do you mean?'

'I don't want you to be disappointed if you go looking for her family and don't come up with anything. They never really wanted to know much about her when she came over here. And they certainly haven't been in touch since she died. As you know, they didn't even have the decency to come to her funeral. I've only just got my daughter back, I don't want her getting hurt.'

I wanted to call him Dad. Or birth dad. Or something.

'I would only research it Online,' I said. 'I couldn't imagine going over to France looking for them. Besides, her parents would be dead by now, surely. Did she have any brothers or sisters?'

'None that I knew of. She rarely spoke of her family in France. I think she was pleased to be shot of them. Pleased to be starting over.'

I wondered how awful they must have been for her to want to move to another country and not stay in touch. How awful they must have been for not coming to her funeral. How awful they were for not caring about their grandchildren.

CHAPTER SEVENTY-THREE

Richard asked me if I wanted to stay the night at his house. I said no. For no other reason than I hadn't brought anything with me. I had always planned just to come down for the day. It felt a little odd staying over after only meeting him twice, even though he was my father.

'Maybe next time?' he said. 'It would be lovely to really get to know you.'

He gave me a lift to the station and waited with me until my train came. I think he was starting to feel more relaxed about the situation. I had been right. The whole thing was a massive shock to him. He obviously just needed a little time to get used to the idea of having a daughter again.

The Cornish landscape moved past the train with stunning beauty. I thought that it would be lovely to stay with him for a few days. I wondered if he had now started thinking about Emily. My older sister. I had already looked Online for an Emily Lapton but found nothing. Obviously her name would have changed to that of her adoptive parents. And if she had subsequently got married it would have changed again. Perhaps she wasn't even called Emily anymore either. I wondered if her parents had told her she was adopted. Whether she had grown up knowing. If she had been older when she was adopted, she would have known anyway. One day with her mother and father, the next day with new parents. How would that have affected her? Maybe it had been better not to know.

I decided to contact Mary Brookes again. I wanted to let her know I had met my father but also wanted to ask her about tracing my sister. I knew she would be disappointed that I had taken it upon myself to find my father without going through the "proper channels", but time was against me. With only two weeks until the assessment I had to move as quickly as possible.

I closed my eyes and let the gentle movement of the train pull me into sleep.

I saw the woman, writing at the table. The other woman who was the younger version of me. She snapped shut her writing book and looked up, her eyes wide. I moved towards her. She flinched away from me. I saw a sadness, something within her. Something her eyes couldn't hide. And a terror. Of something external. She was scared of me.

I woke up with a new idea in my head. A possible way to find out more about my mother's state of health.

But first I had to talk to Michael and Rose.

To them it was just about the most exciting thing they had ever heard. To find that they had a secret past. A hidden family that they knew nothing about. I didn't tell them about how my mother died, only that it was a long time ago. I expected them to feel sad, but they didn't. All they wanted to know was when they could meet Richard. They insisted that he should never be called Dad by me, or Granddad by them. Because Nanny and Granddad were their real grandparents. But they still wanted to know everything about him.

'I'm sure we'll all go down there one day,' I said. 'I'm not sure how much room he has at his house, but we could stay nearby. I'm sure he'd love that.' Although, as I said it, I realised that Richard hadn't asked about Michael and Rose at all. Or Neil. Perhaps he was still trying to get his head around that part of it.

Mary Brookes saw me a week later.

'You were very lucky,' she said. 'Finding your father without going through us could have been disastrous.'

'I have a sister,' I said. 'She's a couple of years older than me. She was adopted too. Before I was. Is there any way I could trace her?'

'Do you have anything other than her name?'

'Her date of birth, and roughly when she was adopted.'

'You could look on the adoption registers,' she said. 'If she's looking, there might be a match. You may have to update the names first, so that they include birth names.'

A tight ball scrunched in my stomach. I wished I had brought a bottle of water with me.

'Mary,' I said. 'I only have just over a week left before I have a psychiatric assessment. I haven't been able to find any records about my mother at all. She died such a long time ago. All the indications are that she was mentally ill. That was why she had to give us up. But I really need to find out exactly what was wrong with her. How it affected her day to day life.'

I rubbed my eyebrow. Mary nodded.

'I had this idea,' I said. 'A way of finding out a little bit more about her. About how she was when I was adopted, when she gave me up.'

From my handbag I took out the adoption file pages that Mary had given me before. I laid them out on the table. I pointed to a name on one of the pages.

'This person here,' I said. 'Janice Ward. She was the one who was in charge of all of this. Her name appears several times, and her signature. I think she was the one that wrote a lot of this stuff. She would have met my mother. Spoken to her. Perhaps more than anyone else, about all this. She would have seen what she was like.'

Mary knew where I was going with this. Even before I finished speaking she was shifting about in her chair, tapping her fingers on the table in front of us.

'Everything they would have done is confidential,' she said. 'And this person is probably long retired by now. She would have dealt with so many cases, there's no way she would be able to remember one particular case. And she certainly wouldn't be able to talk about it.'

'In a little over a week,' I said. 'I may be sectioned. Taken away from my children and husband.'

'Knowing what happened to your mother won't help,' Mary said. 'It won't change anything for you.'

'It will if I can find out exactly what was wrong with her. If I know what kind of mental illness she suffered with, it will help my case, I'm sure it will.'

Mary closed her eyes. Her shoulders sagged.

'I'll make a few enquiries,' she said. 'But I don't think we'll be able to do anything. I think you'd be better off trying to find your older sister. She may have found out more about her past than you have.'

I searched Online and by phone. Three days of effort found her.

Janice Ward.

There had been an address for her in my adoption file, but it was only the address of the office in Plymouth where she worked. I eventually found someone there who knew of her. She had apparently retired quite some time ago. They thought she was still local to the area.

Then on the evening of that day, four days before my assessment, Mary Brookes surprised me. She emailed me saying that she too had found Janice Ward, and had contacted her. She had explained my situation to her and Janice had agreed to talk to me. There was a phone number. My heart pounded and the adrenalin pushed up inside me. Neil and the kids were watching television. I grabbed the phone from the kitchen and took it upstairs with me. Shut the bedroom door and rang the number.

Janice Ward answered the phone. She sounded a bit like

Mum. Her voice was warm and gentle. Few words, but they all sounded like they mattered. Like they deserved your attention even if she was only talking about the weather.

'I was expecting your call,' she said. 'Mary Brookes told me that things were quite urgent.'

I was pleased she couldn't see me blush. The way she said urgent made it sound like life and death. I now wondered if this really qualified as urgent.

'It is to me,' I said. 'I have an assessment in a few days time, which may have a big impact on my future. It would affect not only me, but my children as well. And my husband.'

'Mary told me a little bit about your situation,' she said. 'To be honest, I think she was surprised that I remembered your case. We deal with so many. You try to remember them all, you feel like you should, but it's hard to remember sometimes — emotionally as well as mentally. But I do remember your case. At least I think I do, from what Mary told me.'

My body fizzed as she spoke. I curled and stretched my fingers. It was the same feeling I used to get from wearing woollen gloves and running around outside. Fizzy hands that I would clap together to dispel the tickling feeling, and warmth flowing over my body.

'I understand you've already made contact with your birth father,' she said. 'How has that been?'

'It's been lovely,' I said. 'He was quite shocked at first, which was only to be expected, but he's great now. I've been down there a couple of times to see him.'

'Where does he live?'

'In St Germans — not too far from Cawsand.'

'Mary said that your mother had died?'

'Shortly after I was adopted. She killed herself.'

Janice didn't immediately respond. I wondered if she had heard me. Wondered if mine really was the case she thought she remembered.

'I'm so sorry to hear that,' she said. 'Poor girl.'

Did she mean my mother or me?

'Mary didn't mention where you are living now, Christine. I'm in Plymouth — is that far from you.'

'I'm about three hours away,' I said. 'Between Bristol and Bath. Could we meet up?'

'I'm afraid I'm not particularly mobile anymore,' she said. 'It's quite difficult for me to travel. But I would be happy to see you if you could get down here?'

I was ready to catch the next train down there. I could probably be there by about 9pm.

'I can come down anytime,' I said. 'Tonight if you like.'

She coughed or laughed or something. I'm not sure if she thought I was being serious or not.

'Anytime in the next few days,' she said. 'I don't do much during the day.'

'Would tomorrow be too soon?'

'Tomorrow would be fine,' she said. 'What time can you get here?'

'I'll have a look and give you a call back. Is that OK?'

I spoke to Neil first. Checked if he was OK for me to disappear off down to Plymouth. He said he would take another half day and pick up Michael and Rose from school. Michael wanted to come with me to meet Janice. I said no.

I checked the train times and rang Janice back. We agreed that I would be at her house by about 10:30am.

My body still fizzed with excitement. I felt like I wanted to go out for a run, or tidy the house again. I did neither. Just paced around downstairs, walking from room to room. Sitting down then jumping up again just a few minutes later. I tried my crossword book but just couldn't concentrate. In the end, I had an early shower, spending ages soaking and washing and soaking again. I only got out when the water started to run cold. My fingers had crinkled, like they did when I used to have a bath when I was little. Mum used to say it was because I ate too many prunes. I didn't even know what prunes were.

Although I only had a few days before the psychiatric assessment, I felt as though things were coming together. Michael and Rose were back home; Neil and I were as close as we were when we'd first met; I had found my birth father; and now I was going to find out more about my birth mother.

Eventually the fizzing inside me subsided enough for me to go to bed with the expectation that I might actually get some sleep.

And I did.

Until I was woken by the ringing of the phone.

CHAPTER SEVENTY-FOUR

The phone was on Neil's side of the bed. He had answered it before I was fully awake. With one eye open, I checked the time. The numbers glowed red and fuzzy. It was 01:35 in the morning.

Neil switched on his bedside light. I squinted my eyes shut, put my hand over them to block out the light.

I could tell by his voice that he was fully awake now. And that sparked something inside me. I forced my eyes open, engaged my limbs and sat up. If the call was sufficiently important to snap Neil into a fully awake state, it had to be important. Neil turned to me and held out the phone.

'Christine, it's for you,' he said. 'It's Berriton hospital in Plymouth. Your father has had a heart attack.'

Even though I heard the word "Plymouth", the word that seemed larger was "father". So I immediately thought of Dad. I choked on the tears as I took the phone from Neil. Why had Dad had a heart attack? He was as fit as anything. It was only as I listened to the lady at the end of the phone that I realised it was Richard.

Of course it was Richard. He had a history of heart problems in his family. And immediately I knew it was my fault. It was me that had caused this. Turning up unannounced; finding him after all these years. All those questions I had asked him. Bringing up all the memories he had buried. I had dragged him through it all again.

'Christine?'

It was the nurse.

'I'm sorry,' I said. 'Is he ... OK?'

'He's very poorly at the moment. We've stabilised him and we're monitoring his condition, but he is in a pretty bad way.'

'I'll come down,' I said. 'I'm a few hours away, but I'll be there as soon as I can.'

'There isn't any point in rushing down here now,' she said. 'He wouldn't be able to see you yet anyway. If you want to come in the morning, that would be more sensible.'

Her words drifted through me. Not really catching as they went. I heard them without fully understanding each individual word. But I managed to grasp the gist.

'OK,' I said. 'I'll be there in the morning.'

Neil took the phone from me, put it back on his bedside cabinet.

If they didn't want me there until the morning, why had they rung me in the middle of the night? Was it just to mess with my mind? Getting their own back for having to look after my father at such an ungodly hour?

'Can I have my car keys?' I said.

'Christine.'

'I need to go down there. I need to be by his side. He doesn't have anyone else. It's because of me that he's there. I've caused this.'

Neil took my hand but I snatched it away again.

'You haven't caused this,' he said. 'If it had been the shock of seeing us, it would have happened that first day. He even invited you to stay over the last time you were there. It's not us that's caused the heart attack, Chris. It's certainly not you.'

My eyebrow itched. I wanted to punch the living daylights out of the duvet. Vent the feelings inside.

'And driving down in the middle of the night is a really bad idea,' he said. 'I wouldn't even want you driving anywhere during the day. But certainly not now. Not having been woken up with this news. It just wouldn't be safe.'

'Take me down there,' I said. 'We can go now.'

'Michael and Rose?' he said.

'Shit.'

'Chris, wait until the morning. I heard the nurse say that he wouldn't be able to see you now anyway. They probably need to be careful with him at the moment. If he's just suffered a heart attack it's probably not sensible to have visitors getting in the way.'

'I'm his daughter. I wouldn't get in the way. He would want me to be there.'

'Yes, but he wouldn't want you to be there as another patient. If you try to drive down there — who knows what might happen.'

I thought he was being unfair. I hadn't had a blackout for a while. In my view the risk was one worth taking. Neil took my hand again. He was a persistent bugger. Brave too.

'I can drive you down there in the morning,' he said. 'We'll get the kids off to school and ask Abi and Oliver to have them afterwards. I'll take the day off and drive you.'

I sighed. Blew out all the duvet punching feelings.

'I'll go,' I said. 'I'll get the train down there. You've already done loads. Michael and Rose don't need anymore disruption. I'll get the first train in the morning.'

He leaned over and kissed me. I expected him to lie down, turn over and go straight to sleep. But he looked into my eyes and smiled.

'Someone's testing us,' he said. 'Testing you. I bet they didn't think you'd be this tough.'

I didn't feel tough. I felt beaten. Not beaten in the "it's all over and I've lost" sense of the word. But in the physically beaten sense. As though I had been fighting since the day of the attack and I had been pummelled and beaten by onslaught after onslaught. I didn't feel sorry for myself. It wasn't that. I just felt physically battered. I wanted to float in a hot bath for a month. A bath of something with more substance than water. Something with the consistency of oil or cream. Something still liquid, but thick. Soft and surrounding. Warm and healing. For a month.

I hadn't realised I had closed my eyes.

'Are you OK?' Neil said.

I opened them again. He was smiling at me. Eyebrows raised.

Either I misread them, or his timing was shit.

'Are you still awake?' I said.

'I'm just going through the motions,' he said. 'Pretending I care.'

We hugged each other. I felt the ridges of his damaged cheek touching mine. His face was still warm and soft from sleep. I told him to turn his light off and get some shut-eye. As I lay back in the darkness, thinking about Richard, I tried to cobble together some sort of prayer that might somehow make him better. That might mend his damaged heart. The one that I had torn.

At 7:30 the following morning I stared out of the window as the train started its journey to Plymouth. I had Janice Ward's phone number with me to cancel our meeting. And I had a small suitcase in case I needed to stay down there to be near Richard. I had woken that morning thinking about Ernie, his cat. Not about Richard's heart attack, but about his bloody cat. Perhaps I really was mad.

I phoned Janice on my mobile and told her what had happened. I said I would call her as soon as I knew when I could come round, but it might not be for a while now. Maybe even after my assessment.

By 10:30am I was walking behind a nurse along a corridor to Richard's room in Berriton hospital.

'He may not be very responsive,' she said. 'He needs to rest.'

I tried to answer but the the words caught in my throat. I just nodded.

'Just come and get one of the nurses if you need anything. We'll just be along the corridor. Also he has a buzzer over his bed if you need to use it.'

I managed to croak out a 'thank you'.

I had expected serenity. I knew he was ill, but the fact that he was in hospital made me think of white sheets, an uncluttered area and a look of general improvement in the patient. My father's room displayed none of those things. Apart from the white sheets.

His face was grey. I could see why people said "ashen". His hair lay limp on his head. The white sheets were marked with stains, presumably from they'd first brought him into hospital. There was a nasty gash above his left eye, partly covered with gauze padding, but with enough of the wound showing through to make my stomach flutter. They hadn't told me about that injury. I guessed he must have fallen during the heart attack.

A drip beside the bed slowly allowed a measured amount of stuff into his body via a clear tube hanging from the back of his wrist. I rubbed the back of my wrist.

Wires protruded from under the bed sheets. They were connected to a monitor next to him. An oxygen mask hung over the bed, attached to a large metal oxygen tank behind the bed — as though he was preparing for several hours under the sea.

He looked much smaller than he had done previously.

I crept to his side. I didn't want to disturb him. Certainly didn't want to make him jump. I wanted to reach under the sheet for his hand. Let him know I was there — that he wasn't alone. But I held back. My cheek tickled and I wiped away a rogue tear. Urged myself to be strong for him.

I pulled a chair to the bed and sat down next to him. Watched his ashen face. Watched the tiniest movement of the sheets rising and falling as he breathed. A cold tremor swept across my back. As though someone had just opened a window. I worried that something might be about to happen to me.

Something I might not be able to control.

I stood up and moved, too quickly, to the door. I heard the chair clattering behind me. I had to get out of the hospital. I couldn't lose it. Not here. Not with Richard like he was.

I ran along the corridor, tried to remember the way out. My hair blew back as I ran. A gust of wind blowing into me as I moved forward. *Don't lose it, Christine. Don't blackout here.* The smell of the sea. My face wet with dew, wet with fog. *Keep running out of the hospital. Get to the reality of outside. Don't blackout here.* The sound of crashing. A deep thunderous roar. They are waves. Crashing waves. Thrashing against the rocks below. Screaming gulls carried on the wind. Everything buffeted. Pushed and pulled. There's the exit. Almost there. Slam into the doors. Push them open. Suck in the air. Pull it into my stomach and my lungs. Deep gulps of fresh air. Real air. *Pay attention, Christine.* Look. No fog; no waves; no wind.

I stopped running and flopped against a wooden bench outside the hospital. Smokers looked at me, then looked away as I made eye contact. I couldn't stay there, breathing in the smoke. I needed more fresh air. I stumbled off towards another bench further away. Sat down on it and breathed in, open mouthed. I didn't want to shut my eyes. I wanted to see the reality of my surroundings. Wanted to anchor myself firmly to where I was. My heart pumped so hard it felt like it was pushing my chest and shoulders up a few inches with every beat. Forcing the bones to give it room. Making way for the hard work it was being asked to do. For a flashing moment I wondered whether I had heart problems too, like my father.

I leaned my head back and breathed in slowly through my nose. Calmed everything down a little. Risked blinking. It was OK. I shut my eyes for a few seconds. That was OK too. Had I fought it off? Had I successfully won against the onset of blacking out? I could imagine what might have happened if I had stayed in Richard's room, with all the delicate wires and tubes monitoring him and delivering what he needed to stay alive. His room had been such an unreal situation. That was why I had needed to get out. Needed to find something real to hold onto.

I stayed on the bench for twenty minutes. Until I was sure I was through it.

I lowered my head as I walked towards the main doors of the hospital. I didn't know if it was a new bunch of smokers or still the same ones I had stormed through earlier, but I couldn't look at any of them.

I opened the door to Richard's room. Two nurses looked up at me. The chair I had knocked over in my rush to get out of the room had been moved back against the wall. My handbag placed on the seat. My father's head and upper body had been raised slightly. His eyes were open.

'Are you OK?' one of the nurses said.

'Fine,' I said. 'I just had to get some fresh air all of a sudden. I think I got a bit overwhelmed with it all. But I'm fine now.'

'How are you feeling, Richard?' the other nurse said.

He moved his head slightly.

'OK,' he said.

Hearing him speak took my breath away. He had looked so ill I hadn't imagined he would be able to talk. But his voice sounded so raspy and dry I silently urged him not to say any more for fear of permanent damage to his throat.

I moved closer. His lips were cracked. Splits of dried blood dotted along them. I could smell the open wound on his head and noticed that the gauze cover was gone. His face was still grey. His eyes distant and watery. They followed my movements.

'Christine?' he said.

'They rang me,' I said. 'I came down first thing. You get some rest. Don't worry about anything. I'm here.'

He nodded. Closed his eyes for a few seconds.

'Ernie,' he said.

'I can see to him,' I said. 'I'll make sure he's OK.'

'Keys,' he said. 'You'll need them.'

One of the nurses looked over at me.

'Don't worry, Richard,' she said. 'We've got your keys. We'll make sure we give them to Christine.'

'Stay there,' he said. 'Stay at the house. As long as you like.'

'I'm sure you'll be out of here in no time,' I said. 'I'll be able to stay there with you. Make sure you're OK. I can look after you and Ernie.'

It was now less than four days to my assessment. I needed to see Janice Ward, I still had another appointment with Colin and I wanted to be at home with my family. And I had only just managed to stave off another vision and blackout.

'Don't go, Christine,' he said. 'Stay here with me.'

'I'm here,' I said. 'I'm not going to go anywhere.'

CHAPTER SEVENTY-FIVE

I stayed at Richard's bedside for another hour or so. Talking to him quietly while he slept. I told him all about Michael and Rose. Told him how Neil and I had met. About how I'd hurt him recently and wished I hadn't. I told Richard that he had to get better. Had to come home soon. He had a daughter to think about now. I needed him. Ernie needed him.

Every now and again he opened his eyes and stared at the ceiling. Rasped a few noises from his dry mouth and closed his eyes again. His eyelids looked so pale I wondered if he could see through them. His tanned and weathered face now looked worn out. As though the life he had pushed away for so long had finally caught up with him.

Although the nurses told me I could come and go as I pleased, I was conscious of overstaying my welcome. I had no idea how much or how often Ernie needed feeding. I didn't know if he drank water or milk. But I had promised Richard that I would look after him, so that was the next thing on my list.

Being in Plymouth made me want to call Janice Ward and see her straight away. But I had to set my priorities. And of course Richard, at least for the moment, was my main priority.

I spoke to the doctor before leaving Richard, but he said it was too early to know what the future held. My father was stable. He seemed to be responding well to treatment. But it was likely to be a long journey. He was probably going to be in hospital at least for the next week. I asked them to ring me on my mobile if there was any change in him.

In the cab to his house I tried to work out a timetable of my own. I couldn't stay in St Germans for that long. But I didn't relish the thought of coming down and travelling back again in one day either. I considered whether I should take Ernie home with me. But if Richard made a fast recovery and came home, he would want him there for company. Perhaps a neighbour could look after the cat for a few days. Just popping in to feed it and let it out into the garden — or whatever it was you did with cats.

The house was stuffy. I immediately opened as many windows as I could. Breathed shallow little breaths to avoid taking in the stale air. Not breathing more fully until I could feel the fresh air circulating around downstairs. For the first time, I realised I had never been upstairs in his house. Not that there was any reason why I should have. But now I wanted to. I put my hand on the banister and slowly climbed the stairs. At the top I noticed a loft hatch directly above the landing. I thought of my mother. *I daresay there might be a photo of her up in the attic.*

The decor upstairs appeared to be no different to the style downstairs. Hardly any furniture. Clear wooden floorboards. Clean lines and no ornaments. The only difference was a single photograph in a frame. Ernie.

I counted three bedrooms. One had been laid out as a study and the other was obviously the spare room. Clean and sparse like everything else. I opened a few more windows and went back downstairs, walking underneath the loft hatch as I went.

Ernie made a point of coming up to me and rubbing himself against my legs. He had never even come close to me before, so I took this as a sign of hunger rather than affection. I found food for him and decided on water rather than milk. I also found his litter tray. I left that for later.

One of the keys on the bunch the nurse had given me opened a back door onto a small patio and garden area. I left it open for the cat to go out when he had finished eating. I wasn't even sure if he needed to go out, bearing in mind the litter tray, but it seemed like the right thing to do. I wouldn't want to be cooped up indoors all day long, even if I could use the toilets.

I rang Neil at work and told him how Richard was.

'They think he's going to be in for at least a week,' I said.

'So what are you going to do?'

'I don't know. I'll probably stay down here tonight. Maybe tomorrow as well, if that's OK. But I've got the assessment on Friday. I'll have to come back for that.'

'Can't you tell them to change it. They'll understand, I'm sure. Even if they shift it by a few days.'

'I'm not sure,' I said. 'I feel like it might go against me or something if I can't make it. Like a black mark against me.'

'I can ring them and explain,' Neil said. 'Of course they'll understand. They'll surely just rearrange it.'

'Let me see how I feel tomorrow,' I said. 'And I'll see how he is at the hospital. He might surprise us all and come out sooner. Even today he was sitting up and making conversation. Sort of.'

'Will you ring later to speak to the kids?'

'Of course.'

Ernie's collar tapped against the side of the water bowl as he drank. The metal clink echoed around the house. A secret feeling spun inside my tummy. I was alone in a house that wasn't mine. If I were a child I'd be nosing around the place. Opening cupboards, sliding out drawers, looking under beds. Just exploring the whole house. Going to places and doing things I would never dream of doing as an adult in someone else's home. But it's OK as a child. You can do that then. You can look in that cupboard. You can slide out the drawers. You can go in the attic.

The cat's collar had stopped clinking. I looked out of the window into the back garden. Ernie was stalking through a small bush. I couldn't see anything worth stalking, but obviously he was after something. My heart skipped a beat when I realised he could possibly jump over the wall surrounding the back garden. The sound of traffic rumbled from the other side and I remembered Richard saying that Ernie had a tendency to try and escape out of open windows. Escape to where? Just the back garden? Or onto the road as well?

I ran into the garden and tried to coax him back in, calling his name and clicking my tongue. When the coaxing failed I resorted to herding. Running towards him with my arms wide apart. Hissing at him. Using fear and aggression to get him to comply. Which eventually he did.

I searched through Richard's kitchen cupboards noticing what food he had in. I checked the fridge and freezer too. If he was going to be in hospital for a week, there were some things in the fridge that needed eating soon. It made sense for me to eat what was there and replace it when he was ready to come out. I made myself a coffee and grabbed a couple of slices of toast.

I should have probably put the television on, to stop me from thinking. But I didn't. I kicked my shoes off and put my feet up on the sofa. It wouldn't be right to take advantage. Wouldn't be right to go somewhere I shouldn't. Not up in the attic.

But what if he didn't come out of hospital? What if the worst happened? Then I would have to go up there. Have to search through his kept history. Have to hunt for a photograph of my mother. I was his next of kin. He had no one else — apart from Emily. I wondered if there might be a photograph of her. My older sister. Would she look like me? Did we both look like our mother? Our mad mother.

But Richard would come out. He would get better. I had told him to. Told him he had no choice. He had to come out. And that settled it. I wouldn't go into attic. Not without his permission. Not without permission given when he was well. Not under duress, with tubes and wires attached to him. But when he was clear thinking and happy. I would wait. I had gone this long without even knowing I had another mother, so a few weeks more, if that was what it took, would not do any harm. I itched my eyes. They felt sore and heavy. I hadn't slept properly since we had received the phone call from the hospital. I had been unable to sleep on the train down. And now I let them close. Just for a few minutes. Just to rest them. They were so tired. So itchy. Just a couple of minutes.

I woke up with a start and sat straight up. My mind raced as I tried to work out where I was. My heart thumped from the sudden exertion of waking up and from not knowing what was going on. It was so dark. So quiet. A shadow flitted across my face, brushing me with a breeze as it passed. I jolted and screamed. The shadow scattered away, claws metalling on the wooden floor. Ernie. A flood of memory rushed in and my pounding heart settled. I shivered. And I desperately needed the loo.

I stood up and peered into the darkness. I palmed the wall to find the light switch. Sleeping had not improved the quality of the coffee and toast taste in my mouth from earlier. I probably needed to clean my teeth as much as I needed the loo. I flicked on all the light switches I could find and made my way upstairs to the bathroom.

Even as I was dealing with my immediate personal hygiene issues, I was thinking about the attic. I thought I had won that argument earlier. I thought I had told myself that the right thing to do was to ignore it and wait until Richard returned, or became well enough to give his permission. I obviously thought wrong. Because now, apparently, I was thinking *what's the harm? It's only a rummage around in an attic. I had already hunted around his kitchen cupboards for food. What was the difference? It was just another room and another search.*

But you needed food to survive. You didn't need to search through someone's personal keepsakes for that. It was different.

But how personal were they? I was his daughter. She was my mother. I had as much right to see a picture of her as he had. More, in fact. I was related to her by blood. I had her damaged blood flowing through my veins. He didn't. He was only married to her. Just a certificate and some vows. Nothing as deep as blood.

But it was taking advantage. I wouldn't do it if he weren't in hospital. It wouldn't have even come into my head. How would I feel if someone came searching through my life when I wasn't there? Without my permission. How would I feel?

He might die. He might not come out at all. Then I would have to go through everything he had. Permission wouldn't even come into it.

I spat out the last of the toothpaste frothing around my mouth and walked downstairs, wiping my mouth on my sleeve. Ernie had squeezed himself under a small table in the corner of the living-room. I picked up my handbag from the floor and dug out my mobile. Dialled home.

Rose answered.

'Mum?' she said.

She sounded breathless. As though she had run to get the phone. I knew she hadn't by how quickly she had answered it. I wondered how long she had been sitting with it in her hand waiting for my call.

'How are you, Rosie Lee?' I said. 'You sound lovely.'

'I'm OK,' she said. 'How's Richard?'

'He's very poorly, darling. He may be in hospital for a week or so.'

She said nothing but I could still hear her restless breathing.

'But he's in the best place,' I said. 'They're looking after him very well.'

'He will get better, won't he?'

I swallowed. I wanted to tell her that he might not. That he might just die in hospital. I didn't want to keep things from her. The truth was never anything to be scared of.

'We all hope so,' I said. 'But heart attacks are very serious things. A lot of people don't survive them at all. It just shows how strong he is. And I'll be coming down here as much as I can to look after him.'

'Can we come down too?' she said.

'I'm sure he'd love to see you when he's feeling better. But too much excitement at the moment wouldn't be good for him. He spoke to me earlier. Asked about you and Michael.'

I was surprised at how easily this lie left me when I had been so intent just a few moments earlier on telling her the truth about how ill he was.

She huffed. She told me about her day, then told me that Michael was being annoying.

'That's what brothers are for,' I said.

I spoke to Michael too. He told me about a new game he wanted for his console, and could I look out for it down in Plymouth.

'I am a bit busy Michael,' I said. 'But if I come across it I'll see what I can do.'

Neil sounded tired. He had had just as little sleep the night before as I had.

'I'll probably be asleep a few minutes after the kids,' he said.

'Thank you,' I said. 'For everything.'

As long as I concentrated on other things, I wasn't bothered by the possibility of finding a photo of my mother in the attic.

I made myself a ham sandwich and a coffee and switched on the large television on the living-room wall. Before I sat down I rang the hospital.

'He's asleep at the moment. It's probably best that he gets plenty of rest tonight. Perhaps you could come in the morning?'

The smell of the ham reminded me of home. Making sandwiches for a day out, Michael and Rose hanging around looking for bits to nibble. It was just what I needed.

Without realising, I had zoned out from the telly. Feet up on the sofa, feeling like a naughty child again. Ready to explore and play in a house that wasn't mine. I flicked the television off and swung my feet to the floor. Ernie looked at me. I stuck two fingers up at him.

I think I had known all along that I would go up there. No matter what I said to myself, no matter what the rights and wrongs were, I had to at least look. I owed it to myself. I deserved to know.

I wanted to see my mother.

CHAPTER SEVENTY-SIX

I cricked my neck looking up at the loft hatch. I needed a pole or a stick. Something to push against the loft hatch which I hoped would then unlock and open down on hinges, like our one at home. I couldn't find anything at the top of the stairs.

I wasn't tall enough to reach the hatch, although I might have been able to balance on the top of the banisters and reach up. I didn't fancy that. Horrible images shot through my mind.

I dragged a chair out from the study bedroom and stood up on it. I was able to push against the hatch, but it didn't swing down. It just pushed up a few inches. It was one that needed to be pushed up into the loft, rather than one opening down. I needed something taller.

It took me twenty minutes to find a ladder. Stashed away in a corner of Richard's garage, behind an old plastic sheet, a large metal step ladder spattered with lumps of dried paint. The paint colour didn't match that of the house, so I wondered when it had last been used. I didn't want it to collapse under me. The metal felt cold as I carried the ladder upstairs.

As soon as I stepped onto the first rung the ladder shook. Or perhaps it was me.

Either way, it didn't feel very safe, particularly being so close to the edge of the staircase.

The loft hatch was not as heavy as I thought it would be. I pushed it up with both hands and slid it away from the opening into the attic. Slowly I moved my head into the darkness. My right shoulder nudged against a switch just inside the hatch. I flicked it down. A single light bulb hung from the rafters, lighting the entire space with bright light. The taste and smell of dust filled my nose and throat. A dryness hung in the air. My head and shoulders invaded Richard's private attic.

There was remarkably little to see. The entire floor area was boarded. It was almost another room. A dozen or so large boxes took up less than a quarter of the loft space. A few other items took up perhaps another quarter. A sparse loft to go with the rest of the house. The first things you stepped on in our loft at home were Christmas decorations. Pulled down at the end of November, chucked back up again at the beginning of January. Old clothes that didn't fit either Michael or Rose were bagged up and slung in a gap, until all the gaps were filled. No light, and the itchy, raspy fibres of insulation floating around the space waiting to attach themselves to your skin, or for you to breathe them into your throat and lungs.

My guess was that no one had been in the loft since the move. Everything looked as though it had been placed neatly down and just left there. Perhaps it had even been the removal men.

If I had felt childlike and excited by adventure before I opened the loft hatch, now I was positively fizzing. My stomach felt as though it was full of bubbles and my eyes had lost all their soreness from earlier. The boxes before me became presents. All for me. The only dilemma being which one to open first. And I could take as long as I liked. No one else was waiting to open theirs. I didn't have to share.

A fold-down metal loft ladder lay level with my left ear. I pulled the end of it and backed down the rickety step ladder, which was now shaking twice as much as when I had first climbed onto it. I moved it out of the way and stepped onto the sturdier loft ladder. My heart was spinning. My jaw ached as I suppressed excited laughter. I had to remind myself that Richard was desperately ill in hospital and that I was trespassing into his private life. My heart stopped spinning and a more business-like feeling came over me.

I walked over to the non-boxed stuff first.

The most obvious thing was an old bicycle. I had no idea how it had got up in the loft. Or why it was there. Not rusty, but definitely old. A black metal frame, with silver brake handles and pedals, as shiny as chrome. Despite the taste of dust in my mouth, there was none on the bike. It could have been put there yesterday. The brown saddle had been marked by the years and the tyres hung away from the rims. A pump rested between the upper and lower parts of the frame. A wicker basket attached by leather straps around the handlebars. It was a woman's bike. I gripped the handlebars and pulled on the brakes with my fingers. They squeaked as they moved. Had my mother used this bike? Was this how she got to the library? It seemed odd that Richard had kept the bicycle, but no photographs. It occurred to me that I hadn't seen any pictures of his second wife either. Perhaps he just wasn't one for memories.

A black box, tatty and worn, lay behind the bike. Not cardboard, but solid. Specifically made to hold something specific. It was heavier than I expected. I undid the catch and lifted the lid. An old gramophone record player. One with a silver trumpet speaker and green baize on the turntable. Cranked by a handle. The record needle as thick as my mum's knitting needles. I pushed the handle into the hole at the side and wound it up. The turntable creaked a bit, but still turned.

Two old table lamps to the side of the gramophone. Their bases wrapped in towelling. The creamy shades sporting brown stains; What looked like an old tent bag, with a tent inside, lay among a few rolls of spare carpet. As I hadn't noticed carpet anywhere in the house, I wondered if it had been left by the previous owners. Maybe the bike too, then. Maybe my mother hadn't ridden it to the library. Hadn't taken it down to the bay at Cawsand, her lunch clattering around in the wicker basket.

And suddenly I felt a great aching in my heart. What had she hoped for? That young woman. What had she hoped for her children? Family days on the beach? Gritty sand getting into their food as they played? Splashing about in the waves? Her girls. She would have thought about their future. Before the madness took her. Before she even became aware of what was inside her. She would have mapped out a life for her girls. How she would tell them about being good. Being virtuous. Always brush the sand and salt out of your hair at the end of each day. She would tell her girls about woman things, when they were old enough. She would put all her love into them. Give them everything of her.

And she did. Everything she didn't know she carried. Pumped from her body into theirs. Into mine. Into my sister's?

But how could giving us up have been the right thing to do? Knowing what she had passed on. Surely she should have kept hold of us. Kept us with her so she could protect us. Not pass us onto someone else, with our madness lying dormant, waiting for the time when it wakes up and ruins our lives.

But she had no choice. We were taken from her. She had no say in the matter. The decision was already made. For me it was made before I was even born. Before I breathed the air of this world my future had already been decided for me. Signed and documented by Janice Ward. While I was still being carried by my mother. Still in the protection of her body. And even there my future was being decided for me. The madness in her flowing into me. Just a speck inside her. And a speck when I came into the world. Everything about me already decided.

My tears splashed onto the wooden loft boards. I put my arm on the bike and leaned into it. Buried my head on my arm. I wanted to save her. Somehow go back and save her. Make her dreams come true. Let her have that life she longed for. Her and her girls, Emily and Christine. The three of us on the beach. Laughing and loving. Waiting for my father to come home from work. Telling him what we had done. How much we had played and loved.

Could we have stopped the madness from taking hold? Would Emily and I have filled her with so much love that there wouldn't be any room for the madness inside her? Would it have dissipated? Been smothered by the love? What if she had kept us? It might have saved her.

But what about the other girls? The girls in my mind. The dead girls. And the dog. Maybe they are me and Emily. Maybe that's what I'm seeing. Us being killed. Us being sent away from the mother and father that love us. Murdering our family and dropping us off the edge to be looked after by someone else. It's not real murder. It's not a real attack. It's us. Me and my sister. Forced to leave our family. Forced into the darkness of the unknown. But what about the dog? Maybe we had one.

I shook my head clear. Wiped the tears from my eyes and took deep, dusty breaths. Up in the rafters cobwebs trembled. Outside the wind blew across the roof.

A small, brown vinyl case lay on the floor. The only object that seemed to have a layer of dust on it. I opened the clasp and peered inside. Dozens of old records. The size of singles — 45rpm. Plus a booklet. Linguaphone — The entire French course. My heart went out to Richard. How hard he tried for my mother. Working so hard on his business, trying to learn her language. Desperate to give her the stability she had lacked from her own family. And for what? His children lost, then his wife.

I flicked through the language records. So old. So basic. Had my mother touched these? Had she played them for him? Helped him out if he struggled? Had she disagreed with any of the speakers? I clicked the lid shut.

The boxes loomed behind me. It was time to start on them.

Folders and papers. Yellow, green, pink and buff. Some faded. Some a little worn. Folders full of my father's business records. Patient records, old diaries, appointment sheets, financial information. Practically everything in the boxes was to do with business. The non-boxed items, the bike, the gramophone, the small pile of miscellany — that was the personal stuff. The boxes were business. My heart sank. I had hoped for more. Hoped for a trace of his life before. Her life. A thread, or jigsaw piece to add to the puzzle.

Dozens and dozens of folders. All marked up in date order. Only two boxes contained folders from before my mother died. The colours of the folders slightly more faded than in the other boxes. Fewer folders in the boxes too, more loose papers. Presumably less business at the beginning.

I wondered why Richard had said there might have been a picture of my mother up there. Or had he simply forgotten what was up there? It all seemed to be mostly business stuff. I pulled everything out of one of the two boxes, sat down on the dusty boards and piled the contents on the floor in front of me. I had time. I wasn't going anywhere. I would go through each document, every folder. I would search for Amelie.

I fingered my way through page after page. Mrs Davenport; Mr Richards; Penny Crowcher; James Beldin .... All patients of my father. Their addresses. Dates of birth. All personal information. What work Richard had done on their teeth. How much they paid for it. Some of these people would certainly be dead now. All would be older than me. A snapshot of a time past. The dental habits of strangers from more than a quarter of a century ago. A cold chill found my neck.

It took me twenty minutes to go through the first box. I put everything back in, just the way it had been. Then emptied the contents of the second box.

I could see the wooden edges of something sticking out from the pile of folders and papers, about half way down. My heart somersaulted but I ignored it. I started at the top of the pile.

Worked my way through the papers. The nearer I got to the wooden edged thing the more my stomach grew lighter. It seemed to lift me off the floor. Float me up to the roof. I forced air down into my stomach. Extended it using muscles and air to push it out. Two pages away now, and I knew it was a wooden frame. A photo frame. One page. I could see something through the last page. An image. My thumb and forefinger touched the corner of the last page. Pinched it tight and pulled it away from the photo frame.

My insides grew heavy. Everything pulled me down. The photo frame started shaking. My hand was already on it. Already gripping it. I couldn't stop the shaking. I spluttered. Coughed a weird sound out. I tried to gain control of my facial muscles. They were stretching through extraordinary smiles to tortured grimaces. Eyes wanting to clamp shut, mouth wanting to shout to the world. I lay back on the floor. A cloud of dust sprang up around my head. I held the photo frame, my arm extended, and focused in on my father. He looked the same. Younger, of course, but the same. I knew it was him. A happy look of confidence, even as a young man. I could see the power in his eyes. I recognised the church behind him. St Andrews church in Cawsand. The church where, just a few short years later, my mother — the woman on his arm — would be buried.

CHAPTER SEVENTY-SEVEN

I put the picture against my forehead and let the cold glass soothe me. My mother and father together, taking away some of my pain. I could smell the years on it. Its age. She was a young woman with a dream. With the hopes for children and a life. Family and love. I extended my arm again. Took in her beauty.

And I knew I had seen her before. Sitting at the table, writing. A look wide with fear on her face. Snapping her writing book shut. It was her. She was a younger me. A different me. She was my mother. I looked into her face. Into her eyes. I looked for a sign of the evil that was to take everything away from her. What was she telling me? What was she trying to say, even then? Her face had the innocence of a child about it. Unsure of what the real world might have in store, but full of hope.

I couldn't help looking behind her. Over her shoulder to the church. Not so green and overgrown as now, but still surrounded by thin trees. Did she know? Could she have known that she was just a few metres from her future? Her permanent resting place? Did she know how awful the journey was going to be to get there? Did she hope that one day her daughters would come and find her there? Would clear away the years and give her the love she had wanted to give them?

I don't know how long I lay there in the dust, gazing at my parents, taking in their youth. I think I could have slept there, let the photo rest on my tummy and just close my eyes. Sleep with them until the morning. But I didn't. I sat back up, put the photo frame to one side and reached over to the rest of the folders and papers in the pile. Now that I had already found my prize, I flicked through the loose papers and contents of the remaining folders much quicker than I had previously. So quickly, in fact, that in the last folder I checked, I almost missed it.

The folder was pale yellow. Apart from the date, it was identical to all the other folders in the boxes. Just another collection of business papers from that year. My fingers flicked rapidly through the papers, even passed over two or more at a time, my mind now taken up with the image of my young mother and father and therefore barely paying attention to anything else. And so I almost missed it. In fact, I did miss it with my mind. It was only the difference felt by my fingers that registered deep within me. They had passed over something different to just paper. Touched something firmer and thicker. Something buried within the business papers. Hidden within them. My fingers reversed their action and moved back to whatever it was they had touched. They waited there for my conscious mind to catch up.

If I had thought the photo frame had been my prize, I had now died and gone to heaven. My free hand shot straight to my mouth, clamped over it. As I breathed in through my nose a lightness came over my mind. I thought I might pass out from the lightness. A gentle vibration travelled from my fingertips, up my arm and from there, all around my body.

Her image blasted into my mind. Slammed into me.

She was sitting at that table, concentrating, working hard. Putting all her efforts into writing. Her face was tight, her brow furrowed. She hunched over the table, her pen gripped so tight in her hand it looked as though it would be clenched in that position for ever. She was in the kitchen. Looking over her shoulder towards the front door, then back to her writing. Then back to the door again.

I knew the look of someone writing a diary. Recalling what had happened to you, smiling as you remember, then scowling as you remember something else. She hadn't been writing a diary. Her demeanour was all wrong. She looked more like she had been writing a letter. Telling someone about something. Writing in earnest about something important to her.

Then her head snaps round to the door. She slams her writing book shut, rests her arms on top of it. That look of fear again, her eyes wide but reflecting nothing.

And I know that I have found her book.

Rather than pull it straight out from the folder I peel back the papers on either side of it and look down at the cover. Faded, coloured, vertical stripes. It reminded me of parties and paper plates. The book was slightly smaller than A4 size and about a centimetre thick. It was like a child's exercise book. It was the one from the dream.

As I slid it out from the folder my hand grew warm. It felt as though the heat came directly into me from my mother's book. I held it in my hand for a few moments, gazing at it. Then I put it to one side. If there were any more shocks to be found in the folder I would rather get them all out of the way at the same time, rather than coming across new things piecemeal.

But there was nothing else for me in the folder.

I picked up the exercise book and ran my fingers over it. I held it under my nose, searching for the scent of my mother. A cloud settled in my stomach, ready to carry me away, or to fill me with rain. I was scared to open the book. What if there was nothing there? Just blank lines and pages? What if there was too much there? The full horror of her madness? I was sure that whatever happened when I looked inside, it could only be an anticlimax. How could it be anything else? My expectations were already too high. I already hoped to read about how much she loved me, about how heartbroken she was to let me go, about how her life just crumbled after I was gone. I already expected to read about a fairy tale love between her and my father. About the beautiful days on the beach, how he rescued her from her family and tortured life, like Neil rescued me from the drunks in the pub when we first met.

And if none of that was there — what then?

I opened the cover.

A small black and white photograph of my father was stuck on the inside of the cover, below that was a black and white one of my mother. He wore a suit and carried a briefcase. Either just finished or just about to start a day of work. My mother smiled out from her photograph. Her hair long and loose. She wore dark trousers and a lighter jacket. It was difficult to tell the colour. Her right arm and hand rested over the handlebars of a bicycle. Black frame, silver pedals and a wicker basket on the front. I looked over at it leaning against the loft wall.

The first page, opposite the cover, had her name, written by her, and the date the book was started. I ran my finger over her name, traced the letters as she had written them, wrote her name with her. I turned the page. The two page spread before me was full of writing. Every line covered. It was as though she'd thought she might not ever get another exercise book, so she had to use every available space. I wondered why she had wasted so much space on the first page by just writing her name and the date.

It wasn't messy, just busy. Even words written up the side of the page. I wondered if this was the product of a tortured mind. She was OK writing her name and the date, but horrendously out of control with everything else. I studied the pages closely, touched the full stops and commas. Looked for recognisable names. Place names, person names, thing names. I turned the next few pages. All the same. All jam-packed with words, every space used, and virtually all impossible for me to understand. She had written in her native language — French.

Of course I understood some words. But French was not really my thing. I had been better at German, reasonable at Spanish, but not really French. It seemed bizarre to me that I had been so bad at it, now that I knew I had some French blood running through my veins.

I turned back to the first page and struggled through it the best I could. But I wasn't getting a sense of anything. I couldn't even make out one in ten words. I flicked the pages over one by one. I needed Cathy from the school. She was fluent in French, taught it brilliantly. I needed her there with me right then, sitting in the dust next to me, reading my mother's words out loud, taking me back to the kitchen where she wrote them, enabling me to sit next to my mother all those years ago.

Turning more pages. More tortured writing. Heavy crossing out on some words so that it was impossible to read what had been there. The ink changing colour as she changed her pen. Blue to black, then back to blue. Red for a few pages, then green, then blue again.

I turned the page and my heart stopped.

A terrible chill instantly covered my entire body. I retched but nothing came up. I tried to draw in breath but couldn't, my lungs weren't working.

The exercise book fell to the floor and I scrabbled backwards away from it, kicking my legs out to propel myself. A sharp pain dug into the palm of my right hand, a splinter had embedded itself, blood creeping round the edges. I heard a noise, a clattering, something downstairs. And up in the attic too. Something loud, coming for me. I didn't know where to run. I had to get away from up here, but I couldn't go down there. More pain in my hand, another splinter. Blood now dripping onto the dusty wooden floor of the loft. Still moving backwards, away from the book, away from what I had seen. Almost at the loft hatch, but I can't go down there. I called out. Shouted loud. I called out a name.

'Neil!'

CHAPTER SEVENTY-EIGHT

Two things happened after I called out Neil's name.

The first was that a splinter needled through my trousers into my backside. The second was that I hit my head on a crossbeam.

Both of those things caused me to stop my panicked retreat from my mother's exercise book. They also made me curse Neil.

I rubbed my head with my left hand, then squeezed the splinters out of my right hand. The one in my backside turned out not to be a splinter at all. Instead I had backed onto the point of a bent nail that was sticking out of a floorboard.

The noise I had heard downstairs was actually the rattle of the metal loft ladder as I moved across the loft floor. The noise in the loft had been the sound of my mother's bicycle scraping against the bare loft wall as it slid to the ground. I must have unbalanced it when I touched it. Unbalanced seemed to be a theme.

I made my way back to the book lying on the floor. It was still open at the pages that had caused my panic. They still caused my heart to tremble now.

On each page, a newspaper cutting, both from different dates. I couldn't tell if they were from a local newspaper or a national daily. The headline on the first read "Missing". The headline on the second from nine days later read "Missing Girl — Body Found".

I turned the page. Two more newspaper cuttings, less than a month after the first two: "Another Girl Missing"; and "Second Tragedy As Girl's Body Washed Up".

The tears poured from my eyes, I had to wipe them away to read the articles. These were the girls from my dreams. Both of them. No doubt at all.

According to the articles, each girl had died while walking on Rame Head near Cawsand, notorious locally for sudden changes in the weather. It was thought that on each occasion the girls had been caught out by the incoming mist and strong winds and had fallen to their deaths onto the rocks several hundred feet below. Their bodies hadn't been found for over a week. One of them fell still holding her dog's lead. The dog was still missing. Both papers were dated almost twelve months before I was born.

But surely this wasn't the truth. It hadn't been an accident, had it? Hadn't I killed both of these girls? Hadn't it been me, with my mother's madness running through me, guiding my hands, making me do what I hadn't wanted to do? Just as it had made her do it all those years earlier.

No wonder the writing in her book was tortured. No wonder she had written so much, trying to rid herself of what she was. What she had become. I put my hand to my stomach and tried to breathe as deeply as I could. It churned like never before, rolling waves of nausea as it tumbled over and over. I grabbed the photograph of my mother and father, raised it above my head, ready to bring it crashing down to the floor. My mother, the murderer. The killer of young girls. The person I had felt sorry for just a few minutes earlier, taking the lives of two innocent girls.

That was when the full horror hit me. It was reparation. Her girls had been taken from her. An eye for an eye. She was only doing what was right. She was only doing what any mother would do. What I would do if Michael and Rose were taken from me. Retribution was an honourable thing. Putting the balance right again. Making the world fair. How can it have been wrong? The noxious toxin of the insanity made her do it. It skewed her world so that everything that was wrong was made right. Evil deeds became glorious acts. Showing how much she loved her girls. What she would do for her innocent girls. How can that be wrong?

But I hadn't been born yet. I hadn't been taken from her yet.

So why had she done it?

The realisation of what I could become hit me. First hand I could see how the madness might take me and change me, even more than it already had. If Michael and Rose weren't taken from me, I would surely be taken from them. There was no doubt that I would be sectioned. If not in a few days time, then certainly in the future. Unless medicine had advanced so much since then that my worsening condition could be treatable. But how long for? At what point would it take me over completely?

The girls' injuries were all consistent with falling onto rocks. It wasn't unusual for the bodies to take a week or more to come ashore. The tides around Rame Head were as uncontrollable as the weather. Pushing flotsam into the mess of rocks at the base and slowly working it around to the beaches of Cawsand and Kingsand, or around the west to Porwellham Bay.

The girls didn't know each other, they weren't friends, didn't go to the same school. There didn't seem to be anything to link them. One girl had obviously been walking her dog. But the other, her parents couldn't understand why she had even gone up on Rame Head. They didn't have a dog. They would walk up there as a family occasionally, but there was no reason for her to go up on her own.

I thought about the library. Would they have both been members of it? Was that how my mother knew them. One of the girl's names looked familiar. Barbara Stannard. The other girl Laura Evans didn't ring any bells. I had no idea why Barbara did.

I put everything back in the box. Apart from the photograph and the exercise book. I tried to make everything look just as it had. Although I was going to tell Richard that I had found these things, for some reason I felt like had to cover my tracks in the loft. I arranged the boxes how I thought they had been and went back over to the bicycle. I stood it up and touched the handlebars again. Then I swung my leg over the centre frame. I sat on the saddle and supported myself against the loft wall. My feet found the silver pedals and my thumb found a chrome bell on the handlebars. I flicked it. The sound echoed around the loft space. Had my mother been the last person to make that sound?

I climbed off the bike and laid it back against the wall, then I grabbed the photograph and the book and struggled down the loft ladder. I washed the blood and dust out of my splinter cuts before risking the shaky step ladder to close the loft hatch back up again.

I was amazed at how late it was. I must have been in the loft for over two hours. It was gone 11pm. I texted Neil to see if he was still awake. My phone rang a few seconds later.

'Is everything OK?' he said.

'Everything is fine,' I said. 'Apart from a couple of splinters and a bang on the head.'

'What happened?'

'I was up in Richard's loft. It was a bit naughty of me really. But he had said there might be a photo of my mother up there, do you remember? Well, I found one.'

'That's fantastic,' he said. 'What was she like?'

'She does look a bit like me. He was right. Or I look like her. But I found something else too.' My voice choked a little as I tried to keep it together. I tried to detach myself from what I was saying, tried to imagine I was just reading it, from a book or something. Neil waited for me to speak. 'I found a book. A journal, I suppose. Written by her. It's all in French, but there are some newspaper cuttings in there. They are about the girls. The girls in my dreams. I recognised them both from their pictures in the newspaper. They both died, years ago, they went missing and were found dead, washed up on the beach near where they lived.'

'Christine,' Neil said.

'It was them, Neil. I know them so well by now, I see them every day. It was them. But the newspaper said it was an accident. They both fell from the cliffs near Cawsand, near where my mother and father lived. And I know it wasn't an accident. I know that she did it, that she killed them. And I think the madness was telling her that it was alright. After my sister was taken from her, it was alright to kill two other innocent girls to somehow make up for it. It was definitely them, Neil — they even mentioned the dog.'

'So what are you going to do now?' he said.

'I don't know. I was thinking I might take the journal to show Richard.'

'Is that wise? If he's just recovering from a heart attack, showing him that could be the worst thing to do. He obviously doesn't know about it. Does he?'

'Of course he doesn't.'

My tummy trembled. I hadn't considered that. Was it possible that he did know what she had done? Might he have protected her?

'It was reported as a tragic accident,' I said. 'There would be no reason for him to think anything different. I'm sure he didn't know.'

'So maybe it was an accident, Chris. Maybe she didn't kill them. Dreams are unreliable at the best of times. If the paper said it was an accident, and everyone else thought that too, the police, the families, then maybe that's really what it was.'

I blushed. My face burned.

'My dreams,' I said, 'these ones ... they are real. And not just in dreams. I see them during the day too, like they are a part of my mind. They're there all the time. I replay it over and over in my head, I live it, smell it and hear it. It has to be real. Where else would they come from? How could I have made it all up? And I know it's those girls. I recognised them. Even one of the names seemed familiar. I'm sure I've seen her name somewhere before.'

'Can you make out any of the journal? The bits in French?'

'Not really. I was going to ask Richard if he could read it, but perhaps that's not such a good idea now. The other thought I had was Cathy at school. She's fluent in French. I'm sure she'd have a look at it for me.'

'When are you going to come back?' he said.

'I think I'll see how he is in the morning and decide then. If he's really bad or if he's about to come out then I might stay down here. But otherwise I'll maybe come back.'

'What about Janice Ward?' he said.

'I'll just have to try to fit that in when I can. I'll call you in the morning. Are you going to be OK?'

'I'm fine,' he said. 'We just miss you. Take care of yourself, won't you. Don't go getting any more splinters.'

'You know I love you, don't you?'

'I know that you're mad,' he said.

'Bastard.'

In the morning my hand ached. I couldn't believe just a couple of splinters could be so bloody uncomfortable. I ate breakfast and showered and then fed Ernie. I decided not to let him out, but I did manage to sort out his litter tray. I was almost sick doing it, but I cast my mind back to changing the kids' nappies when they were babies. It was a walk in the park after that.

As I got ready to go to the hospital there was a ring on the doorbell. A lady with white hair and expensive jewellery stood on the doorstep. I noticed she wore blue slippers on her feet. They looked a few sizes too large for her.

'My name is Thelma,' she said. 'From next door. Is everything OK? We saw the ambulance the other night, and there was no reply when we rang. Is Richard alright?'

I invited her in and explained what had happened.

'He's always struck me as such a healthy man,' she said. 'With all that golf he plays. Are you ... a friend?'

'Yes,' I said. 'I just came down for a day or so, to make sure the cat was fed and to make sure Richard was OK?'

'Well if we can help?' she said. 'We normally come in and feed Ernie when he's away at a golf event. We have keys.'

'Would you mind?' I said. 'That would be so helpful. I may have to go back home for a few days anyway.'

Thelma gave me her phone number and insisted that I ring to ask for help.

'He's such a lovely man,' she said. 'You never get to choose your neighbours, do you? So we're very fortunate to have him.'

I was at the hospital by 9am. I had the photograph and the journal in my overnight case, but I wasn't going to show them to Richard.

He had made some progress in his recovery but was sleeping.

'These first few signs are encouraging,' the doctor said. 'But he's not out of the woods yet.'

'I may have to go back up to Bristol,' I said. 'And I might not be able to come back down for a few days. Will you contact me if there's any change?'

Despite apparently making progress he looked worse to me. Grey stubble made his face messy. He looked a bit grubby. I sat with him for an hour while he slept. For much of the time I talked to him, not sure if he could hear me or not — it didn't matter.

I didn't mention what I had found in the loft. I didn't mention the loft at all. But I told him that I loved him and that

I was proud of him for what he had done for my mother. How he had been there for her and tried to help her through her illness. I told him how much I admired him for his strength of character and how I knew he was going to get better.

In my heart I prayed that he hadn't known what she had done, that he was as innocent as those girls.

CHAPTER SEVENTY-NINE

I took a cab from the hospital directly to the train station. Richard didn't need me at the moment, and I had a lot I wanted to sort out. My psychiatric assessment was due the next day and I needed to find out what my mother had written in her journal.

I scoured the pages on the train and tried to work out more than I had done the previous night in the loft. But my French hadn't improved overnight. I found myself looking at the other passengers, trying to decide whether or not they could speak French by how they looked. If Cathy couldn't help me, if she was too busy, my plan B was to go Online to translate it. But my experience with those services in the past had been chaotic at best. Cathy would be my ideal.

I rang Janice Ward and explained that I may not now be able to see her until the following week — several days after my psychiatric assessment. Obviously this was a cause of concern for me. If I ended up being sectioned I would have missed the opportunity to find out more about my mother at the time of the adoption. I could ask Neil to drive me down and back in a day, or I could get the train, but it was quite a trek. It might have to wait. I rang Thelma, Richard's next door neighbour, and asked if she would look after Ernie for a few days. She was delighted, of course, and asked me to pass on her best wishes to Richard. I wondered if her large blue slippers had belonged to a Mister Thelma.

I rang Colin to say that I might struggle to make my appointment the next day — the same day as my assessment. I just couldn't see that happening.

'I'm sorry, Colin,' I said. 'But it might be better just to forget it.'

'I want you to come straight after your assessment,' he said. 'If your assessment is at 9am you can probably be at mine by about 11am.'

Was he being deliberately stupid, or just trying to make me feel better?

'I might not be able to,' I said. 'If I'm sectioned ...'

'Christine,' he said. 'I'll see you at 11. I've been discussing your situation with a colleague of mine and if what he suggests is correct it may change things significantly. I need to run through a few more things with you in person, but we can do that after you get back from the hospital.'

'But that's my point,' I said. 'I might not come back.'

'I'll see you at 11,' he said. 'Call me if you're running late. I can see you earlier too. Just come as soon as you've finished. Neil can come too if you like.'

'OK,' I said.

There didn't seem any point continuing my protests and "what ifs?".

Finally I rang Neil to let him know I was on my way home.

'I'll meet you at the station,' he said. 'What time do you get in?'

'Neil, your work. Don't worry. I'll just get a cab. I've only got my overnight bag anyway.'

'What time?'

'It's due in at 1:48pm,' I said.

'I'll see you there.'

It was good to get home again. Although I had only been gone a couple of days, it felt like an enormous amount had happened. I showed Neil the photograph and the journal.

'She does look like you,' he said.

I opened the journal and pointed to the small photograph of my mother — the one with the bicycle.

'That bike was in the loft,' I said. 'I sat on it. Rang the bell. It was hers.'

Neil looked at me sideways.

'It seemed like the natural thing to do,' I said. 'It's only odd out of context.'

He looked back down at the pages.

'See how every bit of space is covered,' I said. 'She's even written up the sides of the pages.'

I turned to the first of the newspaper cuttings. Neil took the journal in both hands and scanned the articles.

'It's definitely them,' I said. 'I know it is.'

He nodded as he read.

'It's unbelievable,' he said. 'So sad. Two girls, the accidents so close together, less than a month between them. And how awful that the bodies didn't turn up for over a week. Can you imagine how those parents must have felt?'

'But now I'm lost,' I said. 'After what you said, about it maybe just being an accident like the paper said. It's made me think all sorts of things. Am I really mad after all? Was she really mad at all? Have I just imagined the whole thing? Even now, as we're talking, I can see them in my mind. I can recall what happened to them. To me it is real. But the papers and the police all say something different.'

'Maybe it's all connected to the bash on the head,' he said. 'It was a pretty severe thing. Maybe the girls just look like the ones in your dreams. A lot of teenagers look the same, no matter what the era. Your brain swelled, the doctors told you that. That must have some sort of effect. Perhaps these nightmares are simply as a result of that, and nothing else.'

'But she was mad,' I said. 'Richard said as much. The torrent of words in here say as much. And the fact that my sister and I were taken away from her says it too.'

'She may have been ill,' he said, 'but that doesn't mean she killed those girls.'

'She killed herself,' I said. 'I think she killed the girls too.'

Cathy came round after school and took the journal away

with her. She promised she would have it all done as quickly as possible.

'Are you sure you don't mind?' I said.

'It'll be great for me to something other than schoolwork,' she said. 'And it's lovely to see you again, we all miss you at school. I might even have this done by tomorrow.'

When Michael and Rose got home from school we all decided to grab a fish and chip takeaway for tea. I was too shattered to cook, and Neil's microwave meal talents didn't stretch much further than a single person.

After we'd eaten I made Michael and Rose sit either side of me on the sofa in front of the television. I put an arm around both of them and held them tight. Poor kids. They both squirmed after just a few seconds, Rose more than Michael. But they put up with it for longer than I could have expected. Ten minutes squashed with their mum was just about bearable. They knew I had an "appointment" coming up the next day, although they didn't know the potential consequences of the results. I wondered if that was why they let me squish them.

They were both saved by the bell. Neil answered the phone. He called to me from the kitchen.

'Christine?'

It was Colin.

'I just wanted to let you know that I am available any time tomorrow morning. Early if it helps. And it needn't be for the full hour necessarily. Just half an hour. I just have a few questions that I need to ask you and something I want to try out. So any time before or after your assessment.'

I felt a twinge inside. I was surprised that he had rung me at home, and at this time of night.

'I'll do the best I can,' I said. 'If I can't make it, maybe I'll send Neil along anyway.'

By the time I got back to the sofa, Michael and Rose had

disappeared upstairs. I didn't blame them.

No sooner had I sat down when the phone rang again.

'I'll get it,' I said. 'It's probably Colin saying he can't see me after all.'

It was my father — Richard.

'It's so good to hear from you,' I said. 'How are you?'

His voice was faint, and still raspy. But there seemed more energy behind it than when I had seen him at the hospital the day before.

'I'm feeling much better,' he said. 'Stronger by the hour. I wanted to thank you for coming to see me yesterday. And also today.'

'I thought you were asleep?' I said.

'The nurses said that you'd come. Said you stayed with me, talking to me for an hour or so.'

'I'm so glad you're on the mend,' I said. 'Do you know when you'll be out, or is it a bit soon for that?'

'Not just yet, they said. They need to keep an eye on me for a few days first I think. Perhaps after the weekend.'

I thought about my assessment and hoped I would still be around to make the trip down to see him.

'I'll come down,' I said. 'I'll make sure I'm there when you get home. I stayed over last night, fed Ernie and stuff. I only came back up here because I have my assessment tomorrow. If it all goes OK I could even come back down tomorrow. I could be there by late afternoon, to see you.'

'I hope he wasn't any trouble to you,' he said. 'Bloody cat can be a nuisance sometimes.'

'It was nice to have company,' I said. 'Thelma from next door is looking out for him at the moment.'

'She's a bloody nuisance too,' he said.

'I hope you don't mind,' I said, 'but I went up in the loft. You said there might be a picture of Amelie up there. I hope you don't mind.'

He didn't say anything. I couldn't even hear his rattling breath.

'Richard? I'm sorry, perhaps I shouldn't have done. But I did find a picture. You were right. It's one of you and her.'

He coughed and I heard a nurse's voice in the background.

'Richard?'

'I'm OK, he said. So you found one. I thought there might be one left.'

'And I found a book. Like a journal. It had a photo of you in the front — and of her. She's written it in French. I've given it to a friend of mine to translate. I brought it with me to the hospital this morning to show you, but because you were asleep…'

More coughing. More nurse voices.

'Where did you find it? he said.

His voice had changed and I knew I shouldn't have mentioned the journal. It had obviously caused him discomfort. It was too soon after his heart attack to bring up the past.

'It was in among some old papers — dental records I think,' I said. 'I'll show you when I come back down. We can go through it together if you like. Maybe when you're feeling better, when you're out of hospital. Besides, it needs translating first, so I probably won't get it back until tomorrow at the earliest.'

I heard him say something but couldn't make out what it was. A female voice came on the phone. The nurse.

'I'm sorry,' she said, 'but I think he needs to stop talking now. He's coughing quite a bit and we need to settle him down.'

'OK,' I said.

'He's definitely on the mend though,' she said. 'He might even be out of bed tomorrow, walking around a bit. We'll call you and let you know.'

CHAPTER EIGHTY

I wouldn't even describe it as waking up. To do that, you have to be asleep in the first place, and I was pretty sure I hadn't been there. I suppose you could call it a reluctant acceptance that the morning had arrived.

My psychiatric assessment was due to start at 9am. I had spent the night going over so many different scenarios. What I would say; how I would answer certain questions (not that I knew for sure what any of the questions would be); how I would try to seem normal, happy and with it; and how I would punch the psychiatrist and dive through a window to make my escape if I had to.

I hadn't been asked to pack any sort of suitcase, which I took to be a good sign. Unless, of course, you had no choice about the clothes you wore once you were sectioned. Every patient the same, sloping around the place in hospital gowns, a distant look in their eyes.

I made such a fuss over Michael and Rose before they went to school, I think it was a relief for them when Abi arrived. Neil took a day off work to drive me to the hospital — and then, hopefully, bring me back home again.

'What if I can't come home?' I said. 'What if this is it? If this is the last time I'm allowed to be free?'

'You have to come home,' Neil said. 'I can't live on microwave meals and tap-water for the rest of my life.'

I had to ask Neil to pull the car over three times on the way to the hospital. Either I had eaten something dodgy, or I was shit scared.

'I'm shit scared,' I said.

Neil reached over and squeezed my hand.

'Me too,' he said. 'But whatever happens we'll find a way

round it — we always do.'

I managed a weak smile, but I wasn't sure that we could ever find a way round this. Being ill was one thing. Being sectioned and medicated forever was quite another.

We sat down in a waiting area. It felt like the imprisonment had already begun. No other patients and no hospital staff. Just us. A light flickered overhead in the ceiling, making a ticking noise every time it went off and on. It was as though it too was troubled and couldn't get things quite right. I put my hand to my forehead to block out the flashing. It didn't help.

'For fuck sake,' I said.

Neil squeezed my hand again.

'I'll ask if I can come in with you,' he said. 'It'll mean there are two of us when it comes to making the escape.'

A young nurse walked along the corridor towards us. She didn't look much older than Michael.

'Mrs Marsden?'

I nodded.

'Would you like to follow me?'

'OK,' I said. 'Is my husband allowed to come with me?'

She looked at Neil. He smiled at her and raised his eyebrows.

'Of course,' she said.

We followed her along the corridor to a wooden door. The name on the door said Mr Saez.

Mr Saez turned out to be a Doctor Arnold. And Doctor Arnold was a she. The room was not unlike Doctor Jones' surgery at the health centre. Neil and I sat next to each other, Doctor Arnold sat opposite us, behind a desk. I reckoned she was a couple of years younger than me. Pretty, with hazel hair. She smiled at Neil. I wished we had Mr Saez instead.

'Christine,' she said. Her voice was pretty too. 'Have you been keeping a diary?'

I looked at Neil.

'A diary?' I said.

'Did your doctor ask you to keep a diary running up to this assessment? To list down any feelings or episodes you might have had?'

'He didn't mention it,' I said.

I could feel Neil looking at me, Doctor Arnold too. I blushed. Had I messed up already?

'That's OK,' she said. 'It's just that some do.'

I was disappointed to have got off to such a bad start. I couldn't remember Doctor Jones asking me to keep a diary, but he may have done.

'Can you tell me a little about why you're here today?' she said. 'What brought you to need this appointment?'

She looked at Neil and smiled. I wondered whether punching her on the nose would indicate insanity or not.

I told her everything I could. Neil sat and listened. He paid attention to me, not to Doctor Arnold. That made everything a little easier. She asked me to answer some written questions; asked me to tell her the date; to remember an address; to draw a clock. Asked me about my family history. I didn't tell her much. Couldn't tell her much. Not until *after* I had seen Janice. I told her *that* in the hope that she would let me go. That she wouldn't immediately tell me to take off my clothes and slide into a hospital gown and go and wander around with the other inmates.

She took a blood sample and said that it might be useful to have a urine sample too. She read my MRI scan report and asked me more of the same sort of questions. Could I remember a recent news item? What was my home address? What were the names of my children? Exactly how strong was my sense of smell? How often did I hear voices?

'Would you say that you have felt depressed in the last few months?' she said.

I didn't really know how to answer that. How would anyone feel after being attacked; then having visions; voices and nightmares come over them on a regular basis. Then stalked by the attacker; have their husband arrested; find out they are adopted and that their birth mother killed herself and was, in all likelihood, insane.

'A bit,' I said. 'I've had quite a lot going on.'

'Have you considered suicide?' she said. 'And if so, how many times?'

'At the beginning I was pretty low,' I said.

'So is that a yes?'

'Yes, I suppose so. Maybe once or twice.'

I heard Neil take a sharp little breath. I hadn't told him about how I had felt.

'But I don't feel like that now,' I said. 'Definitely not.'

'And what about other people?' she said. 'Have you felt like harming others?'

The heat rose up from my neck, no doubt carrying a red blush with it. I shut my eyes for a moment. Replayed the flailing arms and fingernails and Neil's bloody bed-sheet. Replayed lashing out at my mum and dad as I blacked out and ran off into the woods. Replayed wanting to throw Michael and Rose against the wall of the living-room at home. Wanting to kill the woman in the back of my car. The woman that never really was there. The woman I now knew to be my birth mother. I guessed that this was the bit where she would press a buzzer and heavy men in black clothing would come in and handcuff me before dragging me away to my padded cell. I opened my eyes and prepared to confess.

'She wouldn't hurt a fly,' Neil said. 'She's the most gentle person I know. She doesn't have it in her to hurt anyone. So I can answer that one for you.'

He looked at me and nodded. His eyes were wet.

'Christine?' she said.

Neil nodded again. Pushed me with his eyes.

'No,' I said. 'I wouldn't ever want to hurt anyone.'

The whole thing took a little over an hour. Neil sat with me throughout. In the end I didn't need to give a sample of my urine. A small relief.

The worst time was when she walked out of the room with all my notes.

'Please make yourself comfortable,' she said. 'I won't be long.'

Under the circumstances it wasn't very easy to make myself comfortable at all. In fact I was in danger of giving a urine sample whether she wanted one or not.

'Don't worry,' Neil said. 'We'll deal with whatever she comes back with.'

By the time the door creaked open again I was trembling. She sat back down, looked at my notes again, then looked at me.

'In our view,' she said, 'the things you are experiencing are probably as a result of the head trauma you received. There are some slight anomalies, which is why we need to wait for the results of the blood test as well, but generally you are in pretty good health. I think your brain has taken longer to heal than it perhaps might have done, but as long as that goes back to normal everything should be OK. We'll get the results from the blood test in a day or so. We can pass them onto your GP or we can contact you by letter.'

I tried to process what she was telling me. I was struggling to breathe out. OK at sucking air in, but crap at getting rid of it again. I was filling up with air. Was this hyper-ventilating — or the opposite?

'OK,' I said. 'By GP would be fine.'

She smiled.

I floated back to the car. I'm sure if Neil hadn't held onto me I would have drifted away into the clouds. We drove directly to Colin's house.

'Come in,' he said. 'How are you feeling?'

'Euphoric,' I said. 'I think.'

We walked through the hallway to his study. He didn't offer us a drink or anything to eat. He sat down in front of me and tapped his fingers on the coffee table.

'How long have you got?' he said.

'Let's go for the hour,' I said. 'But if I get a call from the hospital in Plymouth I might have to leave sooner.'

'Tell me about the dreams and visions you've had since your accident.'

My shoulders sagged and a sigh escaped my mouth.

'I know we've been through it before,' he said. 'But just go over it for me again, please.'

I recounted all the dreams I had had. The girls, the dog, the vision on the stairs, the woman writing at the table. I went over them all. Each one individually from when they had first begun. As I was talking Colin picked up his notebook and pen and wrote something. Occasionally he would nod, then smile like an excited child, then become solemn and write something else. If I paused to think, he said nothing, just looked at me, encouraging me to continue. When I finished he looked down at what he had written for at least a minute before speaking.

'Is there anything that strikes you about all these?' he said.

I wasn't in the mood for mysteries. He was supposed to be the one with the answers, not me.

'They're all shit?' I said.

He looked up at me and smiled.

'Do you mind if I feel your head?' he said.

I looked over at Neil.

'Are you serious?' I said. 'I thought you said all that was pseudo-science?'

'It is,' he said. 'The thing about all your dreams and visions is that they never change. They are always the same. If there is any difference in them, it's only to add more detail. They become clearer.'

I couldn't think of anything to say.

'This is not the case with typical post-traumatic-stress sufferers. Normally their dreams are similar, about the same sort of thing, but often with different outcomes each time, or with unusual additions. Yours are not like that.'

I nodded. Colin stood up and walked towards me. I backed into the chair.

'It is pseudo-science,' he said. 'But I'd like to try an experiment. Just to see if it backs up current thinking. Do you mind?'

He walked behind my chair. I turned my head to watch him.

'Just look forward,' he said. 'Keep your head straight.'

His fingers pressed against the sides of my head. Gently pushing into the skin. My neck tingled as his fingers moved over and behind my ears. I think I blushed. I hoped Neil hadn't noticed it. Colin's hands moved forward, fingers massaging against my forehead. I closed my eyes.

'The frontal lobe,' he said. 'It's very often where the character comes from. Damage to this area can change a person's personality quite drastically. In phrenology this area was thought to represent perception, understanding and memory. One of my colleagues is involved in cellular memory. He's the one I've been talking to about your situation.'

His fingers skated around the raised scar on my forehead. They felt warm against my scalp. I wondered if he had ever touched his wife's head in this way. Then he pulled his hands away and walked back to his seat. I just managed to get my eyes open before he turned to face me again. I stretched my neck and shoulders.

'Sorry about that,' he said.

'That's OK. Did it work?'

'I don't think you're suffering from post-traumatic-stress at all,' he said. 'I don't think that's ever been the case.'

Wasn't that what I had told him right at the start?

'Right,' I said. 'I didn't think it was.'

He nodded and smiled.

'Of course you didn't,' he said. 'You know how you inherit certain characteristics from your parents? Like the same eyes, or the same nose. Sometimes the same personality, those sorts of things?'

'Of course,' I said. 'My mother's madness …?'

'Possibly,' he said. 'But inheriting her madness wouldn't necessarily bring on these dreams. Madness, per se, wouldn't cause these hyper-specific episodes.'

'OK?' I said.

'But inherited memory would. And that's what I think you've got from your mother. Part of her memory.'

CHAPTER EIGHTY-ONE

Colin explained the science behind the thinking. I listened, but didn't really take much of it in. As soon as he had mentioned inherited memory something went off within me. Like a cannon that goes off when boats cross the finishing line in an Atlantic race, my internal cannon had signalled that I too had crossed the finishing line. It was as though everything had slotted into place. I knew he was right. That was what I had inside my head. They were memories. Not premonitions, not simply nightmares, although nightmarish they were, but solid, distant memories. And they were a part of me. Just like any other memory.

'And who knows what triggers these things?' Colin said. 'In your case, it was most likely the head trauma, but it may not have been. It could equally have been a new smell that brought all this back for you. Because that's really what it is — it's bringing back your memory.'

I zoned out again and brought up the visions and dreams I had been trying to suppress. I played them through as memories, thought of them as memories for the first time. I gave them permission to be there, in my mind.

But something didn't quite square. I could accept the visual memories, but what about the voice I had heard? What about the vision of the girl on the stairs at home? What about the physical changes I had felt?

I tried to ask these questions of Colin, but my throat had dried and my words died before they even made it out of my mouth. I mimicked having a drink with my hand. Colin stopped talking and stood up.

'Water?' he said.

I nodded.

'Neil?' he said.

Neil nodded too.

I swirled it around my mouth before swallowing, feeling it flow down my throat. Lubricating and cool.

'What about the girl I saw on the stairs?' I said. 'The physical changes, and the voice in my head? What about the fact that I wanted to hurt Michael and Rose? That's not part of inherited memory.'

He dipped his head to one side. Tapped his pen on the top of his notebook.

'The field of cellular memory isn't just concerned with the brain,' he said. 'It suggests that all cells have the capacity to remember things. Things like function and how they are supposed to be when they are well. Like factory settings in a way. It may be possible that some other characteristics have come across too.'

'Is this genuine?' I said. 'I mean, why isn't everyone like this?'

'It's possible that they are,' he said. 'But they may just not be attuned to their bodies in the way you are. It's not a new science, but it is controversial.'

I closed my eyes and massaged the bridge of my nose. Allowed my thumb to rub along my eyebrow.

'So I may still have her mental illness,' I said, 'as well as the worst parts of her memory.'

'It's possible.' Colin said.

Neil and I talked very little on the way home. There was too much for us to take in.

'I need to go back down to Plymouth,' I said.

'Today?' he said.

'In the morning,' I said. 'I need to. I need to see Janice Ward before the results of the blood test come back. I have to find out more about my mother. And I'll see Richard too. Make sure he's OK. I'll spend the night down there and come back on Sunday.'

'I'll drive you,' he said.

I touched his leg.

'I'll get the train. I'd prefer that. It'll give me time to think about things. And Michael and Rose will still have you around.'

When we got home I rang Janice.

'Of course I can see you tomorrow,' she said. But not until 3:30pm. Will that be OK?'

'That's fine,' I said. 'I'll get the early train down anyway and visit the hospital.'

The next morning I decided to go first to Richard's house in St Germans.

Ernie scowled at me as I walked through the living-room. It was as though he knew I had breached Richard's trust by going into the loft the last time I was there. I told him to piss off. A knock at the front door stopped me halfway through taking my coat off.

'Hello again.' It was Thelma. 'Back so soon?'

'Yes,' I said. 'Just a few things I needed to sort out. And Richard's on the mend already.'

'Oh, that's fantastic news,' she said. 'When will he be out?'

'I'm not sure yet. I hope to see him later. I'll find out then. Thank you so much for looking after Ernie.'

She smiled as though she'd been looking after a grandchild or something.

'He's such a poppet,' she said. 'Just like Richard.'

I smiled at her. It seemed to work.

'What's the best way to get to Rame Head?' I said.

'Rame Head?' she turned and looked up at the sky. 'It might be a bit bracey up there at the moment.'

The wind was brisk, but the day was mostly bright. I wasn't sure what she was basing her forecast on.

'I just fancy a wander,' I said. 'I'll only be up there a short while.'

'There's a church in Cawsand,' she said. 'A large one as you drive into the village. A footpath leads up past the church, up the hill through some woods and out onto Rame Head. But the weather is very changeable up there. Very windy too. Make sure you keep to the paths. Don't go too near the edge.'

I covered my smile with my hand. It sounded like a warning out of a horror movie.

'Thank you,' I said. 'I'll make sure I'm careful.'

I already knew the church in Cawsand. I spent a few minutes at my mother's headstone then found the wide path running along the southern side of the church. It started out as a stony lane leading to three cottages overlooking the bay. After passing the cottages the lane quickly became a narrow footpath. A mixture of sand and pine needles on a dry, mud base. It was just like the seaside of my imagination. The gentle waves brushed against the shore in the bay below as the footpath steadily increased in an upward slant. Already my breath was coming faster. I undid the buttons on my coat, let the wind fill it with cool air.

After ten minutes the woodland path gave way to open land. The gentle waves from the bay behind me had been replaced by a crashing roar from somewhere up ahead. The pine needles and sand were gone. Now darker pebbles and heavy earth lay beneath my feet. A blast of wind almost knocked me off balance. My fingers grew cold and I fumbled to do up the buttons on my coat. I passed a gorse bush.

I pushed on, further up the hill. The sea to my left looked cold and dark. The bright sky of the day had become sullen. It seemed to reflect the mood of the sea. Gorse bushes now all around me. The pretty yellow flowers in stark contrast to the dark-green spikes.

A gull screamed at me as it flew over my head. I ducked down, even though it was way above me. I looked back along the path and tried to set my bearings. Perhaps Thelma hadn't been melodramatic after all.

Another ten minutes hard walking and the ground levelled out. Apart from gorse, Rame Head was desolate. I could imagine it being stunning in Summer, but at that moment it looked hellish. The dark sea spat out large white flumes as wave after wave smashed against the jagged rocks just off the head. The roar sounded like some prehistoric leviathan patrolling the foot of the cliffs, threatening all who dared to come near, either by land or sea.

Something made me stop. I spun around and thought I just caught a glimpse of a figure. No more than fifty metres away, ducking behind a gorse bush. The sea, now on my right, pushed up more spray. Water droplets smacked into my face as I started walking back down the path. Thirty metres to the gorse bush now, and another seagull screamed overhead. My ears stung from the vicious wind and spray. The leviathan still prowled at the bottom of the sheer cliffs. The sea spray became heavier, more like mist. More like fog. Ten metres from the gorse. Something dark within it? I couldn't be sure. Too misty. I can't see the path now. The weather has taken it, the wind has confused me, buffeted me off course. A sweet smell. Sweet and sickly. A girl is walking up the path towards me. She's smiling at me through the mist. Waving at me and breaking into a trot. I have to warn her about the dark something in the gorse bush. But she can't hear me shout. I can't hear me shout. A stabbing pain in my leg. She's getting nearer now. Her dog is running ahead of her. She pulls back on its lead. It's Barbara. Barbara Stannard. She's still smiling.

I realise there's something cold on my cheek. Damp and cold. It feels like my hand. When I open my eyes I know immediately where I am. Tangled brambles, rough undergrowth and the smell of damp earth. I am leaning against my mother's headstone in the graveyard of St Andrew's. The hand supporting my head lies along the top ridge of the headstone. I am sitting on the ground. My mother lies in the ground directly beneath me.

A pulse pumps through my ear. Slow and firm. My breathing is steady and my head feels clear. I check my fingernails for blood.

The sky was darker. I rummaged in my coat pocket for my mobile so that I could check the time. But I couldn't find it. I searched the undergrowth around me, but it wasn't there. I must have lost it up on Rame Head. It would have to stay lost. Then I noticed the clock face on the church. It was 2:45pm. I had probably been out for about 45 minutes. Less than previous blackouts. My shoulders ached and I stretched my neck back. When I stood up, I realised I had scratched my left leg on brambles. A few thorns had gone through the trousers and into my shin. I pulled them out and rubbed it with both hands. I brushed off the leaves and mud that had found their way to my coat and trousers and left the churchyard. Cawsand's little beach was empty. I stood in the sand and looked out into the bay. No angry leviathan poked it's seething head around the rocks. No violent weather approached across the water towards me. Gentle waves and a cool breeze. Even the seagulls sounded more friendly.

I found a phone-box and called a taxi to take me to Janice Ward's.

CHAPTER EIGHTY-TWO

Janice Ward came to the door with two walking sticks, one in each hand. Everything about her looked rotund. She was smaller than me, perhaps only five foot and a smidgen. She had white hair and round, blue-rimmed glasses.

'Come in,' she said. 'It's lovely to see you again.'

Her comment threw me.

'You were only a baby the last time.'

'Of course,' I said. 'I hadn't thought about that.'

Her house smelled old. Smelled of rugs and electric fires, of teapots and woollen cardigans. But I didn't feel the need to open any windows.

'I'll get us some tea,' she said.

Although similar in size to my father's house in St Germans, the interior was the complete opposite. Janice had collectibles everywhere. Thimbles lined up along the mantelpiece, brassware hung on one wall, porcelain figures filled a glass fronted cabinet, egg cups covered a small table. There were nik-naks all over the place. The carpet in the living-room had seen better days, small ridges ran along it in lines where the threads of carpet had become detached and pulled away; faded colours; dark stains, then lighter patches, presumably where she had tried to remove some of the dark stains. But the room didn't feel dirty. I had none of that clammy feeling on my palms that I sometimes got when I visited the homes of some of the children at school.

'Make yourself at home,' she said from the kitchen. 'Sit yourself down.'

She wheeled in a trolley with two cups of tea sloshing around on the top. I stood up to take them from her.

'I've managed to keep some of it in the cup,' she said. 'It's this bumpy floor.'

She smiled. Her grey teeth wonky in her mouth, but more like a dear old lady rather than a wicked old witch.

'It's so kind of you to see me,' I said. 'I know this isn't normally the done thing.'

'Oh I'm too old to worry about "the done thing",' she said. 'Sometimes people are more important than rules.'

She sat down next to me on the sofa.

'Besides,' she said. 'I don't know how much I can tell you after all these years.'

'Anything would be a help,' I said. 'I've already found out some things.'

She patted my leg and shuffled herself further back into the sofa. She leaned her sticks against the arm.

'You tell me what you know,' she said. 'I'd love to hear it.'

'I only found out recently that I was adopted,' I said.

I told her everything my mum and dad had told me about the adoption. She nodded when I mentioned that they had been told not to say anything to me about it. I told her how I had reacted at first.

'Then I had the meeting with Mary Brookes,' I said. 'She showed me my adoption file.'

Janice smiled as she listened, sipping occasionally from her cup of tea.

'And I used the Internet to find my birth father. It was quite easy, really. He lives in St Germans now. I've been to Cawsand, seen my mother's grave. I went up on Rame Head before coming to see you.'

I didn't tell her about the blacking out and waking up leaning against my mother's headstone.

'Tell me about your birth father,' she said.

I shook my head. 'He's a lovely man. It was a bit of a shock to him, at first, me turning up. Of course it would be. But he came round very quickly to it. Told me little bits about my mother. Told me about how she died. And I found out that I had an older sister. That was a shock too.'

A slurping sound came from her mouth as she took another sip.

'But, as you know, he's in hospital now. He had a heart attack. They say he's on the mend. He might even have been up and about today. I'm going to visit him after you and I have finished.'

Her teacup rattled against the saucer as she put it back down on the trolley. She dabbed her lips with a small handkerchief she retrieved from up her sleeve. She moved her sticks and shifted around to face me. I smiled at her, hoping I had told her everything.

'I remember your mother,' she said. 'She was a beautiful young woman. Long black hair and lovely eyes. You could see that she was French. She just had that look about her. She had beautiful skin.'

Janice rubbed her cheek as she spoke, rippling the soft age-lines beneath her eyes.

'Every adoption case has a sadness about it,' she said. 'And a happiness too, if the child goes to a caring and loving home. You can never be a hundred percent sure when you place a child, but your new parents seemed like lovely people.'

My stomach somersaulted.

'I couldn't have asked for a better mum and dad,' I said. 'I had a wonderful childhood. And they love my children so much.'

Janice closed her eyes for a moment and breathed in deeply.

'I helped place your sister too,' she said.

My hand shot to my mouth. My somersaulting stomach constricted.

'Although, I don't know who she went to. I never came into contact with her adoptive parents. But I helped your mother with the process.'

'I had no idea,' I said.

'She was a delightful child. Older than you were at the time of your adoption. A very gentle nature. No trouble at all.'

Tears were already rolling down my cheeks.

'Did you ... choose my parents?'

'They chose you, dear,' Janice said. 'Of course we met. They had to go through so many hoops to get you. Every couple who adopted had to. All sorts of checks were made, and even then they had to wait six months before it was all official.'

'Do you know who dealt with my sister's adoption? I mean who ... passed her on?'

'She was placed by my boss at the time, Phillip Townsend.'

'You're not still in touch with him by any chance?'

She rubbed her cheek again.

'Phillip died about ten years ago I believe. I'm sorry.'

We both sat quietly for thirty seconds or more.

'She was very brave, your mother,' Janice said. 'What she did showed remarkable courage. She was heartbroken, but felt it was the right thing to do.'

I was surprised when Janice leaned over and took hold of my hand. I struggled to keep her gaze.

'You want to know the truth, don't you?' she said. 'You want to know the circumstances?'

I nodded.

'Of course,' I said. 'That's why I'm here.'

She pulled my hand towards her and cupped her other hand over it.

'After Emily was adopted I think your mother didn't want to have anymore children.'

Now I knew why she had taken hold of my hand.

'She loved children,' Janice said. 'But I think she felt it wouldn't be fair to have another child. To bring a child into her world. She would have feared for its safety. For your safety.'

I swallowed hard. Tried to relax.

'Right from the start she came to us,' she said. 'It wasn't the other way round. Often in cases like this we take the child into care. The parent has no choice. But because there was never any evidence of wrongdoing or harm, we wouldn't have ever become involved unless your mother hadn't come to us.'

I wiped the tears away as best I could, but I was fighting a losing battle.

'That was with Emily,' she said. 'But it was also the same with you. She came to us. She specifically asked for me. Asked if I would deal with her again. Deal with you. Normally we can't grant requests like that, but the workload was such that I was the only one available. It suited me because I liked your mother, but it was heartbreaking at the same time. Giving up another little child must have been the hardest thing. Especially through no fault of her own. If she could have found a way to keep you, she would. But she was convinced you were in danger.'

'She would have kept me?' I said.

'She would have kept you both, if she could. She did consider going back to France at one point.'

'But she couldn't because of her parents?' I said.

'That's right. And she really had no one else to turn to. Certainly in this country she knew very few people. It was a tremendously difficult time for her.'

'How bad was she?' I said. 'How bad was her condition at that point?'

Janice looked as though she hadn't understood the question.

'What do you mean?' she said.

'My mother's mental illness,' I said. 'How bad was it?'

She blinked and frowned.

'What mental illness?' she said.

I shook my head.

'Your mother was one hundred percent fit and healthy. She

didn't have any health issues. And she certainly had no mental illness.'

My eyes blanked over, Janice went out of focus. I squeezed them shut then opened them again.

'I thought she was ill,' I said. 'That's why she had to have us adopted. You said she was scared for our safety. Scared of what she might do to us.'

Janice shook her head.

'No, Christine. That's not right. Your mother loved you. She never would have hurt you.'

'But her family in France. Weren't they mentally ill. Wasn't that why she didn't take us over there?'

'Her parents had both died,' she said. 'In a house fire. They weren't ill at all. We looked into the medical background of both your mother and your father. There was no mental illness anywhere as far as we know.'

But if both her parents were dead, why had Richard told me that they had refused to come to her funeral? Unless he didn't know they had died.

'She wasn't ill at all?'

'Neither of them were.'

I didn't understand what was happening. I wondered if Janice had got the wrong person after all. Perhaps she wasn't remembering my case, perhaps it was another. None of this made any sense.

'But why was she scared for our safety then?' I said. 'Why did she give us up?'

Janice pursed her lips and patted the back of my hand. She hesitated for a moment, then found the momentum to speak.

'It was your father,' she said. 'Amelie was scared of what your father might do.'

If she had slapped me across the face it wouldn't have stung more.

'My father?'

The one I had just found, the one who I was about to visit in hospital. The kind and lovely neighbour that Thelma was lucky to have. The man who loved me.

'I'm so sorry, Christine,' she said. 'Your mother told us about your father. Told us what he was like. Apparently he was violent towards her. He was aggressive. Drank heavily. She said he was very controlling. But she couldn't leave him. She had nowhere else to go. He frightened her. He never hit you or your sister, but your mother was scared for your safety. She told us that he used to pay too much attention to some of the young girls in the village. She said he would sometimes bring patient records home at night and they were invariably the records of teenage girls. She said she had her suspicions about something terrible that he had done, but she had no proof. She wouldn't say any more than that. We could only comply with her wishes. We had no additional powers beyond that.'

'But if she didn't want any more children after Emily ...?' I said.

'It was your father,' Janice said. 'Your poor mother said that he had forced himself on her.'

'He raped her?'

'Your mother didn't use that word. Back then, some men still thought they had certain rights within marriage. I think she was too scared to use the word "rape".'

My stomach convulsed. A sound left my throat and spluttered into the room. Janice let go of my hand.

'I'm sorry,' she said.

I shook my head.

'It's OK.'

I was the product of a rape. An attack by my father on my mother. No love, just evil desire.

Janice must have read my mind.

'She loved you, Christine,' she said. 'She loved you so much. I knew your mother. I was with her at the two most emotional moments in her life. There is nothing to compare with giving up your children. I have told you nothing but the truth today. I've kept nothing from you. She loved you.'

I couldn't talk through the tears. I just nodded and patted her hand. I thought of my mother's headstone, thought of Rame Head and thought of Barbara Stannard and Laura Evans. And in an instant I knew where I had seen Barbara Stannard's name. It was in my father's loft, one of the patient sheets in the boxes. And I bet Laura Evans was there too. That was the link between them. That was why they died. It wasn't my mother at all. It was Richard.

CHAPTER EIGHTY-THREE

As I sat on Janice's sofa trying to hold myself together, everything fell into place. Just the right pieces filling the gaps in my mind. The dreams, the visions, the nightmares were all my father's. It was his memory I had. My mother did the only thing she could to protect us from him, she gave us a new chance. A chance to start over with a family where both parents were loving. Where there was no danger.

Janice put her arm over my back and shoulders as I hunched over on her sofa, crying. I thought I would never stop.

I knew that Richard had killed Barbara Stannard and Laura Evans. And my mother obviously knew it too. Was that why she killed herself? Because of what she suspected him of? Or had he killed her too? Of course he had. Whether he physically tied the rope around her neck or not, he was the one that killed her.

I stopped crying and a burning heat flowed through my body. My breathing grew deeper and I filled my lungs with air. I had to see him. I had to go to the hospital and thrust my rage at him. I needed him to feel the pain of my anger. Old man or not, ill or not, he deserved to know how it felt to suffer.

'I'm so sorry, Janice,' I said. 'It's just so much to take in.'

'Don't worry, dear,' she said. 'I understand.'

'Thank you for all your help,' I said. 'I'm so grateful.'

I left Janice's house and walked into the cold evening air. My eyes stung as I walked against the breeze. The rage continued burning inside me. I still wanted to see Richard. To hurt him like he had hurt others. But what would it achieve? It would make me as bad as him. Like father, like daughter. I didn't want that. That wasn't me. I could leave Plymouth now. Catch a train and be back home by 9pm. Leave it all behind. Pretend it never happened.

But I couldn't do that either. It was a part of me. It always would be. A memory passed on to me by my father. I had to at least know why. Why he had done what he did. I wanted to hear him admit it. To confirm everything I thought to be true. I couldn't live a normal life without knowing. If he didn't kill them, if it was just something my mind had made up, if it turned out to be my own madness, I needed to know. And the only way I would know for sure was by talking to Richard. By asking him the questions.

I delved into my handbag to find my phone, before remembering I had lost it somewhere on Rame Head. I decided to turn up at the hospital and hope he was awake and well enough to talk to me. Or well enough at least to listen. It was almost 6pm.

I paid the taxi and strode with purpose into the hospital. My footsteps echoed along the corridor towards my father's room. To me they sounded determined. Like a vigorous march, not to be put off until the destination was reached.

I walked past the nurses station. It was empty. A moments hesitation, then I pushed open my father's door.

An elderly woman lay in the bed before me. Hooked up to tubes and wires, just as my father had been. I recognised one of the two nurses attending to her. She looked over at me. I blushed, realising I had opened the wrong door, but the nurse said something to her colleague and rushed over to me. She ushered me outside into the corridor.

'Mrs Marsden,' she said. 'We tried ringing you.'

The anger I had been feeling vanished. And I realised that I hadn't got the wrong room. Only that my father was no longer there.

'I've lost my mobile,' I said. 'What's happened? Where's my father?'

'He's gone,' she said. 'He discharged himself.'

'Discharged himself?'

'After you spoke to him on the phone he seemed to change. He became irritable and distracted. But he found a new energy from somewhere. I don't know what you had said to him, but he insisted that he was feeling fine and he wanted to leave.'

'He didn't sound fine,' I said.

'In our opinion, he wasn't,' she said. 'But he just up and left. The doctor insisted that he stay here. But we had an emergency come in and while we were all busy, he left. As I say, we tried ringing you. We rang your home phone too, left a message to say that he had gone. We don't have any other numbers for him. No other relatives.'

'Did he say where he was going?' I said. 'Before he left?'

The nurse shook her head.

'Home, I think. But we don't know for sure. We can't keep people here against their will. If they want to leave, they can.'

'How long ago did he go?'

'A few hours ago. The emergency came in at about 3pm. We went to check on him at quarter to four, and he was gone. He had been walking about a fair bit before then, but he definitely wasn't well enough to go home yet.'

'Thank you,' I said. 'For looking after him. And for trying to get hold of me. He's probably just gone home. I'll go there.'

'There's some stuff you need to take for him. There are several ECG reports for his doctor and a breakdown of all the superficial injuries he sustained during the heart attack. If you could just give them to him or to his GP. If he is at home, it would definitely be in his interest to come back to hospital. He really does need to be here so that we can monitor him during his recovery. He would be better off back here.'

She walked me to the nurses station and handed me a brown envelope. At the hospital entrance I jumped in a taxi and gave my father's address.

The evening was starting to draw in. Rush-hour traffic was in full swing and the dark clouds above seemed to be moving quicker than the cars. I opened the brown envelope from the hospital. Several printouts, presumably the ECG's, a letter written for his GP outlining the heart attack and the medication he had received. It finished by stating that he had discharged himself early, against the advice of the doctor.

Another sheet of paper highlighted the other injuries the nurse had mentioned. A few scratches and bruises; the nasty cut over his eye; and something else that chilled me. "Deep scarring and damage to upper left thigh. Probably an old injury, no current signs of trauma."

The taxi pulled up outside my father's house. I paid the driver and watched him drive away. A street lamp flickered nearby. It reminded me of the flickering light at the hospital while Neil and I had waited for my psychiatric assessment. Not quite on, not quite off.

The house looked dark. A small light glowed in the living-room, but nowhere else. I couldn't see any sign of movement. I wondered whether he might have gone somewhere else, perhaps next door with Thelma. I wished I had asked the taxi driver if anyone else had been dropped off there that afternoon.

I put the brown envelope in my handbag and took the house keys out. How had my father got in if I had his keys? I glanced over the tiny front garden in case he was collapsed on the ground somewhere. There was no one there.

I put the key in the lock as gently as I could and turned it. The other keys on the bunch rattled against the front door. I put my hand around them to stop the noise.

I closed the door behind me and stood still, waiting for my eyes to adjust to the gloom. I spoke quietly, not wanting to startle him.

'Richard?' I said.

Nothing. I took a couple of steps further into the house.
'Richard?'

A smell hit me. Metallic. A dull smell. It reminded me of blood. My heart went into a trot. I took another few steps, trying to scan the dim living-room at the same time.

'Richard?' I said again.

The smell grew stronger. Blood and something else too. Urine?

Something bad had happened to Richard. I moved quickly to the wall and found the light switch.

As the room lit up I immediately saw the blood streaked across the wooden floor. The clean white wall had been spattered red.

Ernie's lifeless body lay at the foot of the wall. I held my hand to my mouth and kept the retching down. He looked like he had been hit by a car. But I knew the damage had been caused by a human. Kicked in the head, slid across the floor and his skull stamped on. The shape of a shoe was clear. Bloody footprints led towards the kitchen. I followed them.

CHAPTER EIGHTY-FOUR

I reached around the wall and flicked on the kitchen light. There was no one there. After seeing Ernie I had made the decision not to call out Richard's name anymore. I wasn't sure what was going on, but it didn't feel right.

The blood led to one of the kitchen drawers. My heart went from a trot to a canter. It was the cutlery drawer.

I knew now what had given him the extra energy after my phone call. I had told him about the journal. That it was written in French and that I was getting it translated. He would have known what that could mean. It would all come out. The way he treated my mother. The way he was around young girls. She must have confronted him with these things. He would have known that she suspected him. I wondered if she questioned him about the missing girls. If she had asked him about the wound on his leg. She must have done. Janice said she was a brave woman.

I looked around me. Glanced into the living-room again, just to make sure there was no one behind me. I trod slowly across the kitchen floor to the open drawer. I pulled out the largest knife there. A small vegetable parer. No more than four inches in length. I checked the back door, but that was locked. Completely against what I had decided just a few moments earlier I hummed his name again.

'Richard?'

A creak. It came from upstairs. Canter to gallop. I gripped the knife and walked to the bottom of the stairs. If he could hear me, why wasn't he answering? I couldn't come up with a reassuring answer. I flicked the kitchen light off again. A dim light shone from upstairs. Right at the top of the stairs. From the loft.

I stopped myself from calling out again. Stepping up the stairs one at a time, I was grateful that none of them creaked. My eyes remained fixed on the loft opening. The metal ladder was down. I wondered if Richard had gone up there to destroy evidence, to get rid of all his patient records.

I reached the top of the stairs and stood, motionless, for a minute or so. The house was so quiet that all I could hear was the blood pulsing through my ear. Although my heart was pumping at breakneck speed, it made no noise. Nothing to disturb the silence. I held the tiny knife in front of me and stepped over to the ladder. In the low light from above I made out a dark stain on the bottom step. Blood?

I took hold of the ladder and stood up on the first step. It rattled. The noise seemed deafening, as though I would hear nothing over the top of such a clatter. I shot a look behind me. Only darkness and shadows. I moved slowly up the ladder. As I reached the upper steps I realised I was hunching my body, making myself smaller, delaying the moment when my head would be vulnerable, poking through the loft opening.

I decided that fast was going to be better than slow. Whatever was waiting for me, it wouldn't do any good to hesitate. Get straight in there and face it. He had killed those innocent girls. He had killed my mother. He was a frail old man just recovering from a heart attack. I had nothing to fear from him. He deserved to feel my rage.

I put both feet on the next step, gripped the vegetable knife and pushed myself up.

The loft was a mess. Everything had been thrown around. Huge holes and dents in the boxes, presumably from kicks and punches. Slash marks too. I flicked my head around as quickly as I could, taking in everything before me. I couldn't see my father. He may be hiding behind the mess of boxes, but I didn't think so.

My mother's bicycle was bent out of shape. The gramophone

box broken in two. Records smashed on the floor. Dust hanging in the air, having been disturbed by the whirlwind of destruction.

My rage intensified. I moved my right foot up to climb into the loft and put my hands either side of the hatch for support.

From below a steel hand gripped my left ankle. My heart stopped.

I looked down and saw him there, looking up at me. His eyes still as dark as when he had been in the hospital, but his face had gained colour. Even in the dim light from the loft I could see his red cheeks. I kicked my left leg but his grip squeezed tighter. I didn't bother with whispering now. I was happy with full on vocals.

'What are you doing?' I screamed.

He smiled.

'Richard?'

He pulled hard on my leg. I scrabbled around, trying to keep my balance. The metal ladder rattled and shook and I tried to grab hold of the top step.

But I couldn't hold on. I felt myself slipping. Instinctively I put my arm up to my face as I smacked against the wooden edge of the loft opening. My teeth dug into my arm and I squeezed my eyes shut. Up to that point I had managed to keep hold of the tiny knife, but now I heard it clink against the ladder steps as it fell.

I fell too. Cutting my arms and face on the metal steps, scraping my legs as he pulled me down. Then a slash against the back of my leg. A warm, burning sensation. He must have cut me with a knife. It felt much more dangerous than my vegetable parer.

He still held my ankle as I hit the floor face-down. The breath was knocked out of me and I choked. I managed to turn to face him but it was difficult to see in the dim light from the loft.

A flash of silver as he slashed his knife towards me. I could see it was large. I tried to suck air into my lungs, but the pain in my stomach prevented it. I felt like I was drowning. I fought to spit some words out.

'Why did you do it?' I said. 'Why did you kill them?'

For a moment he stopped, as though I had punched him. He let go of my ankle. But he recovered quickly and slashed at me again. At last I pulled some air into my chest. I kicked out with both legs, tried to keep him away from me. I shuffled backwards towards the top of the stairs. He leaned against the loft ladder and caught his breath.

'You bastard,' I said. 'You evil fucking bastard.'

This got him moving again. But now I was climbing to my feet. As he launched against me I got my hands up to his wrists. Held them as tight as I could, tried to push him away. I could smell his hospital breath in my face. Feel the heat of it. I kicked one of his shins and he went down. I grabbed his knife hand and twisted his wrist.

He kicked my leg away and I fell towards the knife. I turned my head away but the blade caught the side of my face, cutting my cheek. His elbow slammed against the side of my head, rolling me away from him and onto my back. Despite the pain I struggled to my feet, but I was completely disorientated. My ears buzzed from the impact and I couldn't focus my eyes at all. Richard had become a dark shape. It came towards me. Another flash of silver and I put my hands up. I screamed as loud and as long as I could. Gave it everything, put the last of my strength into it.

Something ploughed into the other side of my head. A blinding light flashed through my eyes, as intense as the pain that came with it. The world gave way beneath me and all light was gone.

'Christine?'

They are too far away for me to hear clearly.

'Christine?'

A hand holding mine. The rustle of jackets. A crackle on a radio.

'Chris?'

Neil?

I try to open my eyes, but only one works. And that hurts like hell.

'Don't move,' another voice. 'Just stay where you are for the moment.'

I remember Richard, and start. But a hand restrains me.

'Chris, it's me.'

It is Neil.

'It's all OK. We're here. Everything is OK.'

I manage to force the other eye open. Two paramedics, Neil and someone else. Thelma.

I turn my head to the side. Richard lies on the floor a few feet from me. His eyes wide open. His face stretched in pain. There is no life in him.

'They think he had another heart attack,' Neil said. 'He would have killed you.'

How was Neil there? Surely he hadn't heard my scream?

'How?' I said.

Neil smiled.

'Cathy did the translation,' he said. 'She said you needed to see it urgently. I couldn't get hold of you on your mobile. I read the translation. I saw what he had done. How dangerous he was. And then there was a message to say that he had discharged himself from hospital. I knew that you had told him you found the journal. And I knew straight away that he would want to stop you from telling anyone. I tried and tried to get hold of you, but your mobile just went straight to answer-phone.'

The paramedic put a hand on my forehead.

'I decided to drive down here,' Neil said. 'I was outside when

I heard you scream. I slammed on the door but no one came. Then the lady from next door came out. I told her I had heard you scream and she got her key. As soon as we came in we saw the cat. We heard a noise upstairs and I ran up. He was already dead. Just lying there, just where he is now.'

The paramedic moved his hand away and I shook my head.

'He killed them,' I said. 'He killed those two girls.'

'I know,' Neil said. 'The police will be here any moment.'

I raised my eyes to the loft hatch.

'Up there,' I said. 'The records of the girls that died. They were both patients of his.'

Neil nodded.

'It's all in the journal,' he said. 'She suspected him of trying to use drugs from the dental surgery to numb them. To try to put them to sleep. Your mother wrote about it all. She thinks he tried it out on her first, then when she passed out he pretended she had got drunk. She was so scared of him.'

I shut my eyes and tried to breathe as normally as I could. My ribs hurt along with every other part of me.

'Michael and Rose?' I said.

'With your mum and dad,' Neil said.

I smiled.

'I'm not mad,' I said. 'Everything is OK. I'm not mad.'

Neil squeezed my hand.

'Didn't I always tell you that?' he said.

I opened my eyes and looked up at his face.

He raised his eyebrows.

CHAPTER EIGHTY-FIVE

A week after Richard's fatal heart attack, I watched his coffin sink down into the flames at the crematorium in Plymouth.

I cried. The rage inside of me swirled with the thoughts of what could have been, and then clashed with the knowledge of what was, and I cried.

Neil had offered to come with me, of course, but I said no. I wanted to be there on my own.

As I left the crematorium I thought I spotted Janice Ward leaving in a taxi, but I could have been mistaken.

It took another three weeks for the swelling inside my head to go down. Three weeks for the dreams to lessen, three weeks for the visions and smells to diminish and three weeks for the pain in my upper leg to subside.

During the three weeks I worked out dates and events and realised that Richard had killed both missing girls shortly before my real mother had become pregnant with me. Before he had raped her. My real sister, wherever she was, would still have been a baby at the time.

It was true that Richard had been a monster, and I was pretty sure that was why the feelings I had experienced had been so strong.

Of course it crossed my mind that he killed my mother. Perhaps she had threatened to leave him. I would never know.

But I knew I had seen her, perhaps only as Richard had seen her, through his memories, but at least I had seen her. And that was enough.

Neil and I were sat the other side of Colin Connell's coffee table, books either side of us, and Colin, smiling, opposite.

'So your final visit, Christine,' he said. 'How are you feeling?'

I reached over for Neil's hand and he took mine.

'I'm feeling good,' I said. 'It's all just a bad memory.'

I didn't smile as I said it.

Colin wasn't sure if I had just made a joke or not.

I helped him out and smiled.

'As the swelling has gone down it's like the memory bit inside my head is closing up again,' I said. 'It opened up and I became aware of the memories I'd inherited from Richard — now it's closing again.'

'And the physical sensations?' Colin said.

'Pretty much gone,' I said. 'Obviously all these things are a part of me, deep inside somewhere, but as long as I don't get mugged on a regular basis I should be OK.'

Again he wasn't sure if I was joking.

'You know where I am if you need me in the future,' Colin said. 'I'd be more than happy to continue seeing you, both of you, if you think it might help.'

I shook my head. 'I'm OK, Colin. Thank you. I've got my head around it all now, pretty much. I understand what happened, I've made sense of the things I saw and did. The blackouts were as a result of the head injury, the things I did during the blackouts were as a result of Richard. The whole mess got whizzed up in a blender in my mind and body and — "hey presto" — out popped Christine the nutter.'

I let go of Neil's hand and did a weird kind of jazz-hands type movement.

Neil and Colin looked at each other.

'And how are you, Neil?' Colin said.

Neil shook his head and raised his eyebrows.

'I'm good,' he said, and looked over at me.

'He's promised not to lie to golf secretaries, and not to hang around street corners hoping to beat up muggers,' I said. 'And I'm going to make him promise not to work so late anymore.

And to never do another barbecue.'

Something tapped the window behind us and made me jump.

'It was a leaf,' Colin said. 'The weather's on the turn again.'

I gave Colin a hug as we left, so did Neil. In fact I was pretty sure Neil wiped his eyes, but he turned his head away when I looked.

Colin was right, the weather was on the turn.

As Neil and I walked arm in arm along the garden path to the gate, the wind picked up again. Stuff on the air buffeted my face and lifted my hair.

And I caught the smell of something.

Involuntarily I squeezed Neil's arm with mine. My footsteps faltered.

The smell grew stronger.

Neil looked at me.

'Christine?' he said. 'Chris? What is it?'

He looked into my face. His brow was furrowed, his eyes had narrowed and he looked the very picture of concern.

'I can smell something,' I said

'Chris, you're crying? What is it?'

The wind lulled and the smell stayed with me. A beautiful smell, full of love and childhood and happy memories of dead-heading in the garden.

'I can smell roses,' I said.

The End
Thank you for reading

I sincerely hope you have enjoyed your reading experience. If you have, please consider giving this book a favourable review.
If not, please do get in touch and let me know. My personal email is
tom@thomaswymark.com
Please check out my other works and join my New Releases mailing list at
www.thomaswymark.com
Thank You

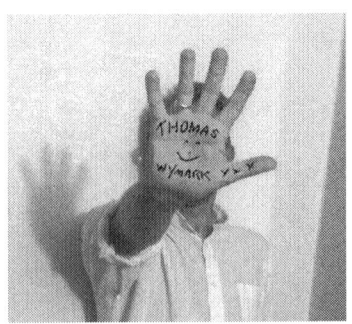

By Thomas Wymark

INHERITANCE

Deep in her mind Christine Marsden is witnessing the murder of young girls.
And now she has urges to hurt her own children.
After a head injury leaves her having nightmares and visions, Christine is convinced something inside her brain has broken and she is slowly sinking into insanity.
Terrified of what she might be capable of she fears that in losing her mind she will also lose her husband and children.
Christine embarks on a desperate fight to try and halt the fracture of her mind before it's too late, and in doing so discovers the hidden truth behind the dark horrors she is experiencing.

SUDDEN EXIT

It's a fairly normal day for Michael Leon - until a stranger plummets from the sky and comes to a sticky end on the guinea-pig hutch in the back garden.
After the authorities haul away the remains of the body, Michael finds something that could change his family's lives forever.
So he makes a choice.

But when his family is threatened and his options turn from bad to worse, Michael regrets his choices.
But by then it's too late.

YOU CAN'T GET THEM BACK

Stuart Burton is on his way to the hospital. His wife is about to give birth to their second child. He can't be late.
But there is an accident and Stuart ends up in a coma.
When he wakes up, everything in his world has changed.
The police are questioning him about three murders he knows nothing about.
And no one is talking about his wife.
Stuart embarks on a tense and emotional journey to find out the truth about the accident and to get back everything he's lost.
But you can't get them back …

DIG DEEPER

An earthquake hits a small Italian town in the middle of the night. The next morning Amy Smith, a British journalist, is missing.
Sal Smith gets ready to fly out to find his wife, only to get the call that her body has been found in the rubble. So now his concern is to bring her back home for burial.
But in Italy he finds that the story she was following grabs his attention.
And then a text message suggests that maybe Amy wasn't killed in the earthquake at all.

BEFORE OTHERS DIE

Sal Smith is asked by a friend to look into the death of his

brother-in-law. The police say it was a burglary gone wrong.
The man's sister says it wasn't
Sal quickly uncovers a disturbing truth … that more people will be killed.
With the clock ticking, Sal has to get to the bottom of a horrifying secret so deeply buried that others will kill to keep it that way.
And he needs to find out what really happened to the murdered man - and why - before other die.

NO MORE SUNSHINE
(A Short Story)

There is only so much a person can take!
Terry has reached breaking point. Work, wife and life are bearing down.
Then he comes up with a plan …

Printed in Poland
by Amazon Fulfillment
Poland Sp. z o.o., Wrocław